PROVOKE
THE DEVIL

Photographic acknowledgements:
Front cover upper: Paris, Parade auf der Champs Élysée, 1940, author unknown, source: Deutsch-es Bunderesarchiv, Bild 146-1994-036-09A/CC-BY-SA, licensed under the Creative Commons Attribution-Share Alike 3.0 Germany.
Front cover lower: The ruins after the bombing of Guernica on 26 April 1937, author unknown, source: Deutsches Bunderesarchiv, Bild 183-H25224/Desconocido/CC-BY-SA, licensed under the Creative Commons Attribution-Share Alike 3.0 Germany.
Part One title page: Traffic jam downtown Los Angeles at 7th Street & Broadway, ca. 1920s, courtesy of the Security Pacific National Bank Collection of the Los Angeles Public Library.
Part Two title page: Hitler at Nazi Party rally, Nuremberg, Germany ca. 1928, author unknown, source: U.S. National Archives Collection of Foreign Records Seized, Heinrich Hoffmann collec-tion, permission authorized under United States public domain designation.
Part Three title page: Soldiers Fighting During the Siege of the Alcázar in Toledo, Spain 1936, author unknown, source: jwEXKWybSQ_Icg at Google Cultural Institute, permission authorized under United States public domain designation.
Part Four title page: Hitler in Paris, 23 June 1940, Heinrich Hoffmann Collection, author un-known, source: U.S. National Archives and Records Administration, permission authorized under United States public domain designation.

"Provoke The Devil," Douglas Clark. ISBN 978-1-62137-839-6 (softcov-er); 978-1-62137-840-2 (hardcover); 978-1-62137-841-9 (eBook).

BY DOUGLAS CLARK

To Josie

PROVOKE THE DEVIL

A NOVEL

DOUGLAS CLARK

"The belief in a supernatural source of evil is not necessary; men alone are quite capable of every wickedness."

-Joseph Conrad: From *Under Western Eyes*

PART ONE

LOS ANGELES, CALIFORNIA

CHAPTER 1

Marc Fraser was enjoying a Scotch at the Writers Club on Sunset Boulevard in Hollywood near Highland Avenue. The ivy-covered building was the social club of the Screen Writer's Guild. Fraser was not a screen writer but was friendly with many of its members through his father's connection to the film industry as an executive with Metro Goldwyn Meyer. Here the liquor was first-rate, smuggled *real stuff*, not some disgusting alcohol-based concoction made illicitly.

Prohibition was into its ninth year. The monumentally ill-conceived exercise attempting to regulate American morals by narrow-minded pressure groups had not only failed but had given rise to unintended social problems of vast proportions. Beyond providing the funding basis for the creation of organized criminal enterprises throughout the country, illegal liquor now fueled wholesale corruption of otherwise law abiding society. People that drank had every intention of continuing to drink, especially since it was not illegal to drink under the law, only to sell alcoholic beverages. Corruption took the form of public servants, most significantly law enforcement, facilitating the satisfying of the public's thirst by collusion with criminal elements. Simply too much money was involved. There could be no party-decade of the 1920's without booze.

Fraser was a newspaper reporter for the Hearst-owned Los Angeles Examiner. His current drinking companion was working on a screenplay involving bootlegging of a criminal gang, corrupt cops, and a crusading hero. The stuff of real life. Covering Los Angeles crime, Fraser was himself investigating police corruption. He was acting as his friend's technical consultant.

Fraser's current journalistic investigation involved an ugly extension of this climate of official Los Angeles corruption. Murder and the cover-up of a murder. The murder of a prostitute most probably by a Los Angeles Police lieutenant. Fraser had already been warned off. Not his style to back away from a story though. What if this real-life murder story could be incorporated into his friend's screenplay?

"I like the idea, Marc, but the prostitute angle, I don't know. Harder sell to a studio. Violence is ok, but sex is always touchy. Got to keep the sex as implied. Maybe if she was a girlfriend, not a hooker?"

"But your story is about the corruption caused by Prohibition and bootlegging. If she's a girlfriend then you lose that connection. That connection is the protection racket of organized crime's bordellos, gambling, and extortion enterprises funded by bootlegging profits," Fraser said. "That's where they reinvest those profits."

"I know. I'll wrestle with the idea some more," his friend said. "Let me ask you something. With so many of the cops turned bad are you in any danger doing stories like this?"

Fraser knew the answer. Of course he was but he didn't want to worry his friend. "Perhaps. But cops are still afraid of the press. Especially a paper like the Examiner. Hearst has too much clout. Still, I'm careful."

It was a dark overcast evening in early December. The first winter rain had abated to a drizzle. Fraser was glad he would not have to drive far. He lived a couple of miles to the north near the Cahuenga Pass as the elevation increased through the mountains. He had a piece to work on that would appear in the newspaper the day after tomorrow. It was a bombshell so he was anxious to flesh it out tonight so he could polish it by the two o'clock press deadline tomorrow. And of course he still had to sell it to his editor.

Fraser left the Writers Club and walked toward his car parked in front on Sunset Boulevard. Two men exited a car parked behind his as he approached. Both were dressed in dark suits. As Fraser was about to pass their car, one man came around the front. The other fell in behind him.

"Stop right there, Fraser," the man said holding a revolver and barring Fraser's way. "You'll be coming with us. We can do this easy or the hard way. Suit yourself. Now put these on your wrists."

The guy with the gun extracted handcuffs from his coat pocket.

Fraser turned to look at the man behind him. He was holding a slim-bladed knife. A grin on his face.

"Are you guys cops?" What am I being arrested for?"

"Didn't say you were being arrested. Just coming with us. Now put the cuffs on."

Fraser was not about to go off with these goons whether cops or not. That could only end badly. Out here in the open he still had a chance. He had to assume the guy with the gun preferred not to shoot him. Probably didn't want to kill him much less draw possible witnesses. But the guy with the knife could mean all sorts of ugly possibilities.

According to his boxing mentor from high school, success in street fighting meant surprise and landing the first blow. A calculated risk that might get him shot weighed against the uncertainty of being abducted for some sort of nasty physical abuse? An instantly clear choice.

Fraser reached out to take the handcuffs with his left hand. The guy was holding the revolver in his right hand so Fraser's hand crossed in front. With a sudden motion, Fraser threw his left hand against the guy's wrist holding the revolver, deflecting the weapon to the side. This was immediately followed with a straight blow to the man's nose with his right fist.

The tactic was effective catching the gunman by surprise. Fraser could hear the nose cartilage break with the blow. The old ex-boxer movie studio janitor, Guido Leopardi's favorite axiom stated, *go for the nose*. A good blow there took the fight out of your opponent.

The gunman went down with blood spewing from his shattered nose. But the guy with the knife was quick to grab Fraser from behind with an arm around his throat. With a shooting pain in his right side Fraser knew he had been stabbed. Reacting, he came around with his elbow catching the second assailant on the side of the head. It was enough to cause the guy to release his hold.

Little fazed by the blow, the assailant still held the knife. His accomplice sat on the ground holding his nose. Blood streamed through his fingers while attempting to recover the dropped revolver with his other hand. This was not over yet.

As Fraser turned to kick the revolver into the gutter awash with a rapid flow of rain water, the guy with the knife lunged at him catching the long stiletto-like knife blade in Fraser's overcoat but not connecting with flesh this time. For a moment the knife caught in the overcoat affording Fraser the opportunity to land a blow to this guy's nose as well.

Still holding the knife, the man staggered backward stunned by the blow. Enough of a lapse for Fraser to move in with a barrage of jabs to the man's face. The blows went undefended until he went down dropping the knife. The guy seemed barely conscious.

Fraser quickly picked up the knife. Searching the knife assailant, he found a revolver in a shoulder holster. He had to be quick about this realizing he was wounded. How bad he didn't know. The adrenalin keeping him functioning would eventually turn into shock.

He also found the knife-guy's badge and identification. Detective LAPD.

Holding the revolver, Fraser turned to the first assailant, "Throw me your badge and ID."

The cop fumbled in his pockets eventually tossing over his badge and wallet.

"Where were you going to take me?" Fraser said.

"Fuck you. You know this'll go badly for you when we catch up with you again. You can't run from the LAPD." The blood running into his mouth from his nose sprayed with the words.

Fraser needed to end this and get away. Get medical attention. If the wound was bleeding internally he didn't have much time.

"I assume your friend also has a set of handcuffs?"

The detective made no response.

"Get his cuffs. Handcuff him to the bumper. Handcuff yourself to his other wrist."

The detective glared at Fraser not moving.

"Do it now! Otherwise I shoot your friend in the leg, then you next. It'll bring witnesses. You'll have to explain how a newspaper reporter got stabbed by a couple of LAPD detectives then got shot by their own gun. I image whoever sent you would not welcome that attention. So get to it."

A minute later the detectives were secure. Two sorry looking rain-soaked thugs. Blood running down both their faces soaking their shirts. No badges, their guns thrown in the flooded gutter.

Fraser got behind the wheel of his Packard roadster coupe. He first folded his overcoat on the seat to protect the leather seat from the spreading blood now soaking his shirt and trousers. There was a hospital only a few miles to the east, Hollywood Presbyterian at Sunset and Vermont. Already feeling light headed, he hoped he could hold on long enough.

The last thing he recalled was discarding the badges and police ID's out the car window.

Fraser woke the next morning to the bright lights of the hospital recovery room. Still groggy from the anesthesia, the attending physician told him he would fully recover. Bad stab wound but fortunately no major organ damage. Just a nick to his liver. The internal bleeding had been manageable once under surgery.

From the post-op he was wheeled into a pleasant room with light pouring through the window. His father and stepmother were waiting for him.

After the usual tearful exchanges with his stepmother, his father said, "This wasn't a mugging was it? Do you know what happened, Marc?"

He wasn't going to lie to his father but neither was he going to add the worry that the attackers were from the LAPD. Even he wasn't sure how he was going to deal with that. Obviously the entire LAPD was not corrupt, much less violently preying on civilians. But who could be trusted?

"The doctor says you'll be here for a couple of days," his father said. "When they release you how about staying with Margo and me until you're back on your feet?" He wanted to say more. Wished his son were doing something other than investigative journalism. Something like this was bound to happen. His son must be making dangerous enemies. Best not to raise that argument now.

"Ok, Dad. I'll consider that."

"Unfortunately we have to leave now. There's an LAPD detective captain waiting to talk to you about this assault. Randal Schmidt is also waiting, demanding to see you. The police captain told him he'll have to wait his turn."

His stepmother kissed his forehead. "Your Dad is going to the office but I'm staying. I'll be back in to be with you once these other people have gone, Dear."

"Thanks, Margo. Go ahead and tell the police officer I'll see him. Tell Randal to keep his shirt on. Tell him I'm going to be ok."

The detective entered Fraser's room. A bookish, stout man probably early fifties, balding, with wire rimmed glasses. Cheap suit with a terrible tie, holding a hat that could use a cleaning.

"I'm Detective Captain Frank Carmody, LAPD. I understand that you're going to recover, Mr. Fraser. Glad to hear that. Care to tell me what happened?"

Carmody sat down in a chair.

"As a matter of fact I don't, Captain. Not without an attorney present."

Carmody just nodded. "You're not under any suspicion, Mr. Fraser. You're a victim of a brutal assault. Lucky not to have been killed."

"Come on, Captain, quit dancing about. Why is a captain investing an assault? You know damn well why I'm not talking to you. I'm a reporter."

Carmody pursed his lips and looked down at the floor. "Perhaps. But I suppose it's because the two Cretans we found handcuffed to their car bumper were LAPD detectives. Badges gone. Service revolvers left in the gutter. Both a bloody mess. Both with broken noses. Found by someone leaving the Writers Club. A place I understand you frequent. All this within an hour of you showing up here just a few miles from that scene with a stab wound."

"Don't see the connection to me, Captain. I don't know anything about that. Just a coincidence. Two different assaults. And why would cops resort to stabbing someone?"

"Because they're dirty, Mr. Fraser. But you know that already. So I'll confirm something for you but it's off the record, at least for now. The two cops are a couple of detectives from a South Central precinct. Not my guys. Names are Dombrowski and Felgenhauer. Dombrowski is known to carry a switchblade. I would guess he was the one that stabbed you. Never found that switchblade. But no matter. I understand your position. Why link yourself to what is being documented as an assault on these officers? By the way, they haven't named you. Too much explaining. Gave some cock and bullshit story about a gang of black armed guys that held them up. In upscale Hollywood of all places."

Fraser said nothing.

"Ok, what I'm saying is we're on the same side. I'm dealing with the same problem you're trying to expose. I work out of headquarters division. Major crimes investigation. I report directly to Deputy Chief Monahan. He's a good cop. All the LAPD isn't rotten."

"Just enough though to make it impossible to clean up the corruption. Especially since even some LAPD brass are dirty," Fraser said. "And then of course you have the City Hall gang. Talk about a den of thieves."

"Let's talk further after you've recovered, Mr. Fraser. Before that, do me a favor. Look up this assistant district attorney. You'll like her. A young fire-eating crusader like you. Name is Abigail Blumenthal. Here's her card. The three of us might have something in common."

Carmody stood up. "Take care of yourself, Mr. Fraser. We'll be seeing each other again. Still wondering though how an educated handsome young lad like you learned to handle himself enough to be able to kick the shit out of the likes of those assholes?"

CHAPTER 2

Marc Fraser arrived at Los Angeles' La Grande Train Station just east of downtown after the four day trip from Manhattan. He had made the exhausting cross-country trip several times since his father had made the bold move to Southern California two years before after the death of Marc's mother. While a New Yorker, Marc Fraser liked Los Angeles. For both good and bad comparisons, it was not New York. On the negative side was the sprawl. Everywhere had to be accessed by automobile. No subways. Buses made no sense if any distance was involved with all the stops and transfers. You couldn't walk to anywhere. Vast fields of towering ugly wooden oil well derricks were a pervasive sight throughout the entire Los Angeles basin. The City was still comparatively young and still trying to establish its cultural identity. Rapid growth was checked only by the nagging shortage of water.

But the year-round good weather trumped all the drawbacks. And because of the weather its signature high-profile industry was motion picture production. You could shoot movies on location all year round. Land was cheap to build film sets. Desert landscapes for the burgeoning western genre films were reachable in a couple of hours. Endless beaches. Motion pictures put Los Angeles on the international map. And it was the film industry that brought Marc Fraser's father to Southern California.

After the death of his wife, Douglas Fraser, a lawyer specializing in international law, was wooed away from J.P. Morgan Bank by the movie theater magnate Marcus Loew. In 1924, Loew bought Metro Pictures, Goldwyn Pictures, and Louis B. Meyer Pictures to provide his own supply of movies to the Loew's Theater chain. Loew's was headquartered in New York while these production operations were in Southern California. Needing someone to run these combined Hollywood studio operations, Loew made the successful producer Louis Mayer vice-president. The new studio enterprise soon adopted the abbreviated acronym MGM.

Douglas Fraser became chief counsel for MGM with the delicate task of reporting both to the strong-willed Louis Mayer and corporate's number-two man, Nicholas Schenck in New York. Mayer and Schenck never got along. Ultimately both came to depend on Fraser for his business acumen, never skewed by a hidden agenda or bias to either boss. Fraser became the mutually trusted go-between.

Marc Fraser had just graduated from Columbia University in Manhattan with a degree in journalism. It was his father's alma mater but the son had no interest in pursuing a career in law. His older sister was a practicing physician, married to a physician. Marc had literary aspirations. Since he came from modest wealth that cushion afforded a degree of choice to pursue a less certain profession.

After graduating from the New Hampshire preparatory school Phillips Exeter Academy he was able to enroll at the Sorbonne in Paris. His mother was French so he spoke French fluently and travelled there every year. He loved Paris more than New York.

What really attracted him to Paris was the literary scene of the mid-1920s. He knew of Gertrude Stein's famous salon on the rue de Fleurus on the Left Bank. It was a social haunt of many great writers, including American literary figures like Sinclair

Lewis and Sherwood Anderson. Acclaimed painters including Pablo Picasso and Henri Matisse frequented her home making for a stimulating aggregation of art in all its forms. Paris seemed the center of Western intellectual creativity with the unique rhythms of the City of Light as the background.

Fraser was not exactly a casual student, just vague as to precise direction. He took keenly to history and philosophy. Excelled in languages. The written word drew him. A career in writing had not clearly formed until a fateful encounter with one of the habitués of Stein's salon. A young writer though not yet famous. Only five years older, the big American was already a working foreign correspondent and World War One veteran. He wanted to write fiction based upon his experiences. His name was Ernest Hemingway.

They met at the Paris Left Bank English bookstore, Shakespeare & Company, close to Fraser's apartment just west of the Sorbonne. Fraser was enthralled with Hemingway's war adventures as an ambulance driver in Italy. Hemingway was impressed with Fraser's fluency in French and familiarity with Paris. They struck up an instant friendship. For Fraser, his career direction became clear. Take up journalism like Hemmingway. Create a foundation of experiences, perhaps adventures, from which to write friction.

Fraser's mother was a Parisian. His father met her in 1899 in Paris. The senior Fraser was a lawyer working for J.P. Morgan Bank in New York on a business trip to the Rothschild Bank in Paris. Jacqueline Laurent attended the rounds of meetings, acting as interpreter for Douglas Fraser. However, she was more than just staff at the bank. She was the granddaughter of James Mayer de Rothschild, founder of the French branch of the Rothschild banking family. Apart from being rather independent and distressing her parents with little interest in pursuing marriage, Jacqueline was well educated with degrees from the Sorbonne in literature and language. She was also modestly wealthy.

After concluding his business Douglas Fraser stayed an extra week in Paris. He was smitten with Jacqueline Laurent, spending each day that week courting her. Two transatlantic trips and six months later they married in Paris at an elaborate wedding at the Ritz Hotel.

The untimely death of Marc Fraser's mother only months after her diagnosis of pancreatic cancer devastated the family. For Marc Fraser there was no question about remaining in Paris. He must return to the United States to be closer to his father. Leaving his beloved Paris, he at least now had a career direction. An exciting pursuit perfectly aligned to his desires. Upon returning to New York he enrolled at Columbia University majoring in journalism.

Following soon after his mother's death, his father was offered a senior position with the newly formed Loews' subsidiary film studio in Southern California. Both Marc and his sister encouraged their father to take the plunge. Obviously remaining in his Manhattan apartment without Jacqueline would be difficult. Apart from that, they knew their father was tiring of the bank, doing the same types of international financing deals year after year. Why not get away to a new environment? Some place interesting? If it didn't work out then take a position with an international law firm.

Marc Fraser roomed with his married sister in New York while attending Columbia. Each of the last two summers he spent working in the publicity department at MGM in Culver City in Greater Los Angeles. Upon graduation he decided to join his father in Southern California at MGM with a full-time position in the publicity department. Certainly temporary. Publicity in the film industry wasn't close to journalism but he liked the quirky, artsy actors, technicians, screenwriters, and set designers. What better way to engage himself while casting about for a real journalism job?

There was also another perk to the job. Not only the sun and beaches of the Southland with scantily clad women, but the studio itself was populated with endless numbers of beautiful women from aspiring actresses to extras to staff. For a good looking young man of twenty-two with good prospects, and an insider within the film industry, there was no shortage of sexual opportunities.

Accordingly, this was Fraser's third date with an aspiring actress under contract with MGM named Joanna Gresky. Not only a real beauty, she was lively, outgoing, and particularly energetic in bed.

Over dinner Gresky said coyly to Fraser, "Do you know Marion Davies?"

"Everyone knows her. She's starring in that movie you're in, *Lights of Old Broadway*. The newspaper tycoon Hearst is financing it. My father told me about the deal Hearst did with MGM last year to make his movies rather than just have MGM distribute them. Even though he's got his own studio Cosmopolitan Productions based in New York. Everyone says he started Cosmopolitan so he could put his girlfriend Davies in starring roles. The old lecher. He's old enough to be her father."

William Randolph Hearst started Cosmopolitan Productions in 1918 at the same time he started what would become a lifelong relationship with Marion Davies. Hearst was thirty-four years older than Davies. While common knowledge, their liaison was not mentioned in the newspapers consistent with journalistic practice at the time. Such private matters only became fair news copy if it became part of some legal proceeding.

"That's not fair. Marion's a great actress without Mr. Hearst's backing. She's really funny and pretty. Anyway, she's become a friend. I love her. Doesn't put on airs even though she lives like a princess. Mr. Hearst is a great guy too. I've been to a couple of their parties. Big house in Beverly Hills on Lexington. Been out on his big yacht too. Hey, I even met Charlie Chaplin at the last party."

"His yacht? You mean the *Oneida*?"

"Well I don't know its name. How would you know it?"

"Joanna, don't you remember the headlines a couple of years ago with the death of that film producer, Thomas Ince?"

Joanna looked sheepishly at Fraser, "Vaguely." She actually didn't while still living in her native Buffalo, New York at the time.

"Joanna, it was in all the papers. This guy died after partying on Hearst's yacht. Big scandal. Question was whether he was murdered or died of natural causes. All sorts of wild speculations. Hearst, Davies, and even Chapin were all mentioned."

Fraser was now intrigued. Not about Davies but Hearst. His girlfriend was friends with Marion Davies. The mistress of William Randolph Hearst the biggest newspaper publisher in the country. What an opportunity for an aspiring journalist looking for his first real job.

"Running with the big dogs huh, Joanna? Can Hearst get you bigger roles?"

"Maybe. Who knows? Anyway I don't talk about being Marion's friend to many people. They wouldn't understand. Probably not believe me. I'm one of the very few at the parties that isn't a celebrity or a big shot. So, would you like to come with me next time I'm invited?"

Fraser hid his enthusiasm at the opportunity to maybe meet Hearst. If you had an eye on a career in journalism then you knew of William Randolph Hearst. By 1925 the Hearst publishing empire was the largest in the country consisting of twenty-eight newspapers, Hearst Metrotone News producing silent newsreels, and the International News Service, INS a U.S.-based news agency wire service.

The story of Hearst's journalistic origins was legend. At age twenty-three he took over as publisher of the San Francisco Examiner in 1887. Hearst's wealthy father had acquired the newspaper as payment for a gambling debt giving it to his directionless son. The younger Hearst found his calling parlaying the San Francisco Examiner into the flagship newspaper of a vast publishing enterprise.

"Yeah. Sounds like it might be fun."

Gresky smiled. This time she could take her own handsome man rather than fending-off the drunken advances of old rich guys.

"How about tomorrow then?"

"Ok. Sure that will be ok with Marion?"

"I already told her about you."

Joanna Gresky spent the night at Fraser's apartment in the Los Feliz district east of Hollywood with the foothills of Griffith Park just to the north. The party in Beverly Hills was to start in the afternoon around the pool. They slept in late. It was July, already hot by midday. Gresky scrambled some eggs for breakfast while provocatively wearing only Fraser's shirt. Too alluring. The eggs went cold as they returned to bed to make love again. An electric fan brought some relief to their sweating exertions.

They showered and dressed for the party. Fraser wore a short-sleeved shirt with tailored summer-weight slacks and two-toned wingtip shoes. Gresky was going into the pool so she wore a swimsuit underneath a strapless dress, taking a small bag with some underwear and a sweater. They looked quite the attractive couple.

The party was well underway when they arrived. Fraser could see what Gresky meant by Davies' guest list by looking at the automobiles parked in the long circular drive. Cadillacs, Auburns, Mercedes, Duesenbergs. No Fords here. Fraser did not feel out of place with his flashy red Packard roadster, a graduation present from his father.

A maid escorted them through the elegantly decorated house to the expansive portico in the back extending to the large swimming pool. The rear of the property was secluded by a tree-rimmed garden. Around the swimming pool was a wide deck populated with lounge chairs and umbrellas. White liveried waiters served iced drinks to what must have been fifty people.

Sighting Marion Davies, Gresky tugged Fraser along by the arm.

After kissing Marion on the cheek, "Marion, meet Marc Fraser."

Fraser extended his hand. Davies grasped it but quickly moved to give him a quick kiss on his cheek."

"No formality here, Marc. Especially for handsome men. You're a New Yorker according to Joanna. I'm from Brooklyn. And you?"

"Manhattan. Just finished my degree from Columbia. Journalism."

"Journalism? Then W.R. will definitely want to talk with you. He'll be here soon. Joanna says you're working at the studio."

"Yes. The publicity department, at least for now. My dad is the chief financial executive at MGM."

"Yes, I've met him. W.R. knows him too. He and your father worked on a lot of contract stuff together. W.R. says Douglas Fraser is a good guy not a tightwad like Louis Mayer," Davies said impishly putting her hand to her mouth. "Oh my. Don't repeat that. Here, let me introduce you around to everyone."

Fraser hoped that Davies might mention his journalism degree not just his publicity job to Hearst.

The assemblage of guests was impressive. The pretty people were mostly from the movie business. The not so pretty represented wealth and power of Los Angeles.

"I was hoping to meet Charlie Chaplin. Is he coming?" Fraser said in a whisper to Gresky.

"Hush. Don't bring up his name. Rumors are running wild about him and Marion. Right know he's out of favor with Mr. Hearst."

"Is it true?"

"I don't know. Haven't known Marion that long. But Chaplin's a really handsome guy with a bad reputation when it comes to women. So who knows?"

Fraser knew enough about Hollywood from stories his father told. A constant effort went into covering for the peccadillos of their stars to avoid public scandal. Public outcry from religious groups over perceived immorality in Hollywood movies had been growing throughout the silent film era. Now that *talking pictures* clearly represented the future, spoken words would add another dimension for controversy. Cities and states had established censorship boards. The industry formed the Motion Picture Producers & Distributors Association several years previous to institute their own self-censorship to ward off feared federal regulations.

On a practical note, the star system created on-screen personalities that the viewing public came to expect from the actors' real lives. America's sweetheart shouldn't be sleeping around. The dashing leading man shouldn't be a drug addict. Neither gender should be engaged in sexual relations with others of the same gender. Sodomy laws existed in every state. So studios went to extraordinary lengths to keep their wayward charges out of the gossip columns.

Fraser glimpsed a sampling of the real lives of film stars that day at Davies' house. Here they could be themselves among their own.

"Pola, let me introduce Joanna's new beau, Marc Fraser," Davies said.

The beautiful Polish-born European actress Pola Negri was reclining on a lounger in a bathing suit. Pulling down her dark glasses she said, "Ah, another handsome young man. Rudy, you have some competition here, Dear."

Fraser's glance followed Negri's turn to her left. Standing at a drink cart pouring Champagne from an ice bucket was Rudolph Valentino. Signature slicked-back hair, dark complexion, a colorful shirt with a bright scarf. Heartthrob of women. If you went to the movies, you knew Valentino. Fraser smiled remembering the piercing eyes conveying an ill-defined latent sexuality from his movie *The Sheik*. In an industry full of handsome men, Valentino still stood out.

Valentino walked over and Negri said, "Rudy, this is Marc Fraser."

Valentino said in Italian, "*Piacere di conoscerti.*"

Perhaps to assert his stature among these giants of film, Fraser responded in French, "*Un véritable honneur, monsieur.*"

"Are you European also?" Negri said in broken accented French. "I know a little French and some German. Rudy is teaching me Italian. But French is so beautiful. Joanna, where did you find this delicious man?"

Fraser said, "My mother was French. We often spoke French at home. I went to school in Paris for a couple of years."

Valentino smiled and shook Fraser's hand.

Davies saw a newly arrived guest and said to Gresky, "Joanna, you know everyone. Introduce Marc around while I say hello to John and Greta. Get yourselves some drinks."

Fraser recognized them instantly. John was John Gilbert another glamorous leading man. Greta was Greta Garbo the recent Swedish import by MGM. They were jointly starring in Garbo's second U.S. movie that Fraser was working on in the publicity department. Even he knew of their rumored romance.

While Fraser poured them Champagne, Gresky said, "Pola and Valentino are lovers. At least that's what they look like."

"What's that mean?"

"I mean that Valentino was married twice before. I'm told both women were lesbians. Rumor has it they may have been *lavender weddings*. You know, just to hide they are homosexual."

"So you're suggesting Ms. Negri might be a lesbian?"

"God no. Before Valentino she had an affair with Chaplin. And Chaplin certainly isn't a homosexual."

"So you're implying Rudolph Valentino might be homosexual? Sounds like a bunch of wild speculation. Are all you actors a little nuts?"

Gresky punched him playfully in the shoulder. "Ok mister smart guy. See those two good looking men on the other side of the pool? Know who they are?"

"The one guy looks familiar but I can't place the name."

"William Haines. Bigtime leading man. The other guy that kind of looks like him is Jimmie Shields. Shields used to be

Haines stand in. Now they're lovers. It would destroy Haines career if that ever became public."

"Well it doesn't bother me either. Whatever people do with each other is only their business. It's just the bible-thumping public that has a problem with homosexuality. For that matter, there're not too keen on conventional heterosexual screwing.

"That's the whole problem we wrestle with in the publicity department. We try to mold you actors and actresses into images shaped on-screen then work hard to cover up all the things you people do to fuck it up."

Gresky grinned. She was partly showing off her insider knowledge. The whole place reeked of extremes of arrogance and insecurity. Of the other guests, there were only two married couples. Among the others it was not clear if these were relationships, or even who was with whom under what circumstances. This was not Averagetown, USA, this was Hollywood. It was not pervasively a den of iniquity but it clearly didn't function under the same social conventions of their audiences.

A short time later the great man himself entered, William Randolph Hearst. Fraser knew Hearst was much older than Davies but he was still taken back upon seeing them together. A man well over six feet in his sixties, heavy in the waist, kissing the diminutive beautiful actress still in her twenties.

Making the rounds with Davies to greet all of the guests, Hearst eventually came around to Fraser and Gresky.

"Hello, Joanna. You're looking especially lovely," Hearst said and kissed Gresky on the cheek then turned to Fraser extending his hand.

"This is Marc Fraser, W.R.," Davies said. "He's Douglas Fraser's son. Works in publicity. Just got his degree in journalism."

"Is that so? Where did you go to school?" Hearst said.

"Columbia University, sir."

"Ah. Heard it's a first rate college for journalism even though it was endowed by my old competitor Joseph Pulitzer. Won't hold that against you. So are you interested in publicizing films or real journalism?"

"Not publicity work that's for sure. I'm casting about for a newspaper job. The MGM job is just temporary until I find a good opportunity."

"Are you from Southern California?"

"No, Sir, I grew up in New York City. Spent my last two summers out here after my father took the position at MGM. I do like the weather."

"All of us New Yorkers like the weather here. But it doesn't have the ambience of New York. New York's the center of most everything. Los Angeles is only the center of motion pictures and great weather. Personally I favor San Francisco. After I greet some other guests let's talk some more, young man."

Gresky said, "Looks like you made an impression on W.R." There was maybe a hint of envy in her voice Fraser attributed to his upstaging of her special stature within this coterie of the filmmaking elite.

With drink in hand, Hearst eventually motioned Fraser to join him at a table under the balcony affording the best shade. Hearst shed his suit jacket and rolled up the sleeves on his dress shirt, loosening his tie. The heat of the afternoon was causing him to perspire. Davies was flitting among her guests so it was just the two of them.

"What makes you want to get into journalism, Mr. Fraser?"

"Besides liking to write and I think I write pretty well, it strikes me as something where I can make a difference. I hold the view that news reporting is the only way to force honest government. The first amendment is the most important part of the Constitution. It allows the press to shine a light into the dark smoke-filled back rooms of power."

"Well now, that's quite a grand pronouncement. The first amendment can be seen as a curse that allows all manner of offensive speech."

"That's its intent. If it's to be open to all speech then you have to accept what you might find objectionable. The alternative is for some group to act as a censor. I don't know of any group that I trust to censor what I want to read. Certainly not the government. That's a recipe for dictatorial power."

"That's laudable. However the newspaper business is just like any other business. It needs to be profitable. The news needs to be presented in a marketable fashion. It needs to sell. The product needs to be better than your competitor. At times it may even satisfy your lofty view while still being profitable. Like all of us you'll have to find that balance. How you'll pursue your own sense of ethics while delivering marketable copy. That balance is somewhere between hack and crusader."

"Yes, sir. I understand the reality is not that clearly defined. After all, I work in a movie studio's publicity department where truth is not the governing objective. Even outright fabrication. But it doesn't pretend to be news. It's just marketing.

"But news doesn't have to be dull. There's no fiction as good as reality. It's a matter of finding interesting material. Real dirt sells best of all."

Shameless pandering. Hearst publications were notorious for headlining scandal.

Hearst chuckled, "Couldn't have said it better myself. *Real dirt sells.* I like that."

Hearst leaned over the table on both elbows. "Do you think you have the sand, Mr. Fraser? What it takes to ferret out the dirt? The dirt that sells?"

"I think so. I'd like the opportunity. It's about being clever and hardworking. It's about getting inside how things work and discovering how people leverage things illegally."

"And what people might those be?"

"Politicians, cops, businessmen, gangsters. It's about money. One journalism professor said to always follow the money when pursuing a story. Everything ultimately is about money."

"I don't know if you're all talk or a prospective first-rate investigative reporter. But you've impressed me enough to find out. Want a job as a reporter right here in Los Angeles?"

Fraser could hardly believe his good fortune. Smiling broadly he said, "Absolutely, Mr. Hearst. That's very generous, sir. I won't let you down."

"It's not me you have to impress, it's your new boss. Take this to the Examiner's managing editor, Randal Schmidt. Good newspaper man but a tough editor. He won't appreciate my meddling but he'll be fair. You can learn from him but you'll have to perform. Give him this card. The Examiner's offices are on Broadway at the corner of Eleventh."

Hearst wrote a note with a fountain pen on the back of a business card, handing it to Fraser.

Randal, This is Marc Fraser. Put him to work as a reporter covering crime and corruption. Tell me how he works out. WRH

CHAPTER 3

By 1928 Marc Fraser had been with the Los Angeles Examiner for two years. Things had worked out very well. The beginning however was anything but promising.

That first Monday after the Davies' party Fraser was ushered into managing editor Randal Schmidt's office by a secretary. The place looked like a bomb had gone off. Papers covered the desk in seemingly disarray. Some had spilled onto the floor. An ashtray was overflowing with cigarette butts. The air was dense with cigarette smoke. Decidedly unpleasant since Fraser didn't smoke.

Standing behind the desk was a short balding middle-aged man with shirtsleeves rolled up, tie pulled loose, and a cigarette dangling from his lips dropping ashes on the papers.

"And who are you?"

"My name is Marc Fraser, Mr. Schmidt. Mr. Hearst sent me?"

"The Chief sent you? What the hell for?"

Fraser handed Schmidt Hearst's business card which Schmidt took with nicotine stained fingers.

"Shit. What the fuck's this about? You a reporter?"

"Not exactly, sir. But I'll be a damn good one if you'll give me the chance."

"Jesus H. Christ. You mean you have no experience?"

"Just a degree in journalism from Columbia, sir."

"Just a college degree? So now you think you know what's what in the newspaper business? If that doesn't fuck all. Not tough enough that I have to battle the Los Angeles Times every day and watch every penny to stay on budget, but the Chief saddles me with a green reporter. Wants you to cover crime and corruption like you would have any idea where to begin."

"I'm a quick study, Mr. Schmidt."

"You'd better be, Fraser. I'll give you a chance because the Chief says so. So here's the deal. You'll spend the next couple of weeks shadowing one of our experienced reporters. Learn the protocols. Learn how things are done here. But I can't afford the time for you to develop skills that should take years. You either hit the ground running and give me good copy soon or I tell the Chief it just didn't work out."

Fraser turned out to be a natural at ferreting out a good story. Creative, clever, hardworking, and single minded in the pursuit of a story. Sometimes devious, always persuasive. He was able to frequently get deeper into events giving his stories a depth beyond just the typical reporting of the known facts. For his initial bluster, Randal Schmidt was an astute newspaper editor. He knew how he wanted stories framed. Knew what sold newspapers. Fraser was soon delivering copy with creative background work and a particularly hard-hitting writing style. As an added bonus, Fraser was his own photographer giving his stories visual play and costing the paper nothing extra.

The photography angle was an extension of Fraser's hobby. He did not carry the bulky large format cameras common to news photographers of the time with their large flash attachments. As a birthday gift the prior year, Fraser received the German company Leica's first successful 35mm camera just introduced in 1925. This new camera was small enough to carry in a coat pocket.

During his previous summer's work at MGM, Fraser was introduced to the basics of photography. Beyond the technical aspects, a noted cinematographer gave him an appreciation for the artistic quality of photographs, particularly the use of lighting. Fraser learned techniques of exposure to create artistic effects that did not require artificial lighting. Photography was all about the use of light. The knowledge came in handy taking reportage photos without the benefit of flash lighting.

Fraser experimented, also developing his own film. That was essential since a favorite subject was women in nude poses. While actually about art, it was also effective in maneuvering women into bed. As a reporter it allowed for his small camera to always remain accessible.

After a year covering crime Schmidt redirected Fraser toward more complicated investigative stories pursuing corruption in the California Southland. Fraser proved particularly creative in giving the reader a sense for the victims and perpetrators as people not just statistics. His stories were often coupled with lurid photos of violent crime scenes. These were made possible through cultivating relationships with key police officers. The same police provided him insider information. A fair amount of hard to get good liquor became profitable barter. Police would look for opportunities to pass along undisclosed confidential material.

Schmidt recognized Fraser's talents as particularly suited to pursing larger stories of pervasive corruption in the City of Angels. Fraser had become cozy with a broad spectrum of the city's underbelly.

The Examiner was increasingly targeting reporting on corruption. The second term mayor, George Cryer ran on an anti-corruption platform. Prevailing feelings however suggested that the City's politics were actually controlled by political boss Kent Kane Parrot along with a collection of bootleggers and criminals including vice kingpin Charles Crawford. Crawford's reach was so well entrenched that his crime syndicate was known as the City Hall Gang. Mayor Cryer was simply a figurehead.

The 1920s saw explosive population growth in Los Angeles accompanied by expansive building projects. The publisher of the Examiner's rival newspaper the Los Angeles Times, Harry

Chandler, was financially and publically involved with many such large scale development projects. As such, the Times was less aggressive in pursuing official corruption not knowing what unwelcome association might come to light. Hearst had no such business interests in Los Angeles. Randal Schmidt therefore intended to exploit the opportunity to take the aggressive lead in pursuing Los Angeles corruption.

Fraser had more than proven his worth. Schmidt had authorized an expense account higher than any of his other reporters. Fraser's largess in buying illegal liquor and passing out money for information was a solid investment. This latest attack on Fraser by the two detectives was testimony to his effectiveness.

"Jesus Christ, Fraser, I thought you knew to be more careful," Schmidt said when he was finally allowed to see Fraser in his hospital room. "Who was the guy that just left?"

"Detective Captain Carmody LAPD."

Schmidt was about to light a cigarette.

"Randal, you can't smoke in here."

Schmidt returned the cigarettes to his pocket. "A captain? What the fuck happened anyway? The doctor says you were knifed."

"Yep. Two guys confronted me outside the Writers Club. Turns out they were cops?"

"You know them?"

"No. But Carmody told me their names. Anyway they wanted to take me for a ride. I wasn't about to go with them so I put up a fight."

"What happened?"

"Caught 'em off guard. Enough to get away. Not cleanly as you can see. One of the guys knifed me. But I banged them up pretty good. Broke their noses. Left them handcuffed to their car."

"Who were they?"

"According to Carmody they were known dirty cops."

"So what did you tell this police captain?"

"Nothing. They didn't identify me so I decided not to acknowledge the assault. But I know it's about that prostitute's murder. The one murdered by that LAPD lieutenant."

"Yeah, but you can't prove that. The guy's untouchable."

"Eventually I will, Randal. Someone will talk. Just have to find that someone that has it in for this police lieutenant."

"You're like a dog with a bone, Fraser, but I'm glad you're still amongst us. When you're back on your feet I've got a new assignment for you. The harbor. Nothing new about crime on the docks, but with LA's growth it's gone way beyond dockside theft. It's a cesspool of corruption at every level. Bribes, kick-backs, rigged contracts, who knows what. Must reach into city hall and the county government. All manner of assholes to make good news copy. Just your cup of tea."

By News Year's Day, 1929 Fraser was out of the hospital. His injury had been serious. Only after another two weeks was he able to take up his new assignment to start probing the graft at the adjoining Ports of Los Angeles and Long Beach. The murderous cop was not however going to be forgotten. The cop was corrupt so there would be continued opportunity to entrap him. All it took was some confederate willing to give him up for some personal gain, a grudge, or to bargain for a lesser sentence.

1929 started as a year of great expectation for the country. A new president was about to be sworn into office. The economy was booming. The great Babe Ruth continued his decade-long home run bombardment to the thrill of even non-fans of baseball. Motion pictures made the leap into *talkies.*

For Marc Fraser the attack that put him into the hospital was not going to scare him off. It did however make nailing the murderous LAPD lieutenant a personal matter. The first order of business was to find a new line of investigation. All he had was a lot of indirect peripheral interviews, fairly well established facts, but no evidence. Before he could consider checking out this woman prosecutor Carmody had suggested, he would need a better plan. And speaking of checking out, he had to vet this

Captain Carmody as well. Was he the type of cop he claimed to be?

Carmody did check out. Also his boss the deputy chief. It wasn't that the corrupt cops were unknown, just that they could not be reached because the corruption went too high up. Way higher than this lieutenant rumored to have murdered the prostitute. The lieutenant was part of cadre of officers deeply entrenched with criminal gangs engaged in bootlegging, racketeering, and vice. The police were on the payroll, sometimes even directly participating. Availing themselves of booze and prostitutes was just another perk.

Through his investigation, Fraser had pieced together what probably happened. The coroner said she was beaten to death. No weapon, just fists. Having passed some money to an attendant, Fraser viewed the corpse on the autopsy table. The young woman had once been pretty. Now she was unrecognizable.

The dead victim was found in the alley behind the Pacific Club in a trash bin. She was naked with no clothing found near the body.

Fraser had been simply lucky. It was early evening on the night the woman was murdered when the call came into the Hollywood precinct. Fraser was interviewing a couple of detectives there about an unrelated murder case. Arriving on the crime scene, Fraser not only got photographs of the victim but accompanied the detectives inside the Pacific Club to interview witnesses. The investigating detectives knew the score with the Pacific Club. However, now stuck with Fraser's presence they had to go through perfunctory motions of interviewing everyone.

Obviously the victim had been killed inside the brothel. It was soon established she was a resident prostitute although the patrons and staff referred to her as a *hostess*. The establishment made no attempt to hide the fact they sold liquor and little attempt to deny that girls were available for sex. Those interviewed claimed no knowledge of what happened to the poor girl. However, bits of information were still picked up. Beyond expressions of horror, Fraser was able to observe fear and even anger among several of the other working girls. He also had their names and addresses as they gave them to the detectives.

That was where Fraser started. He carefully interviewed the women from the Pacific Club, careful to talk to them away from their apartments, typically shared with another prostitute. Although terrified, two of the girls gave him enough information to pursue new lines of investigation. That eventually led to his stabbing outside the Writers Club.

Now he was back in the hunt with a vengeance. While he probed into graft at the ports he would continue to work on bringing down this murdering cop and those protecting him. And of course Detectives Dombrowski and Felgenhauer.

After as few months of research work Fraser determined that all of the various manifestations of corruption were interconnected. It was not necessarily centrally controlled however all the players were in some way connected, all collectively benefited. Organized crime was active in Los Angeles as in all the major U.S. cities. Their revenues came principally from bootlegging. So did illicit LAPD revenue from their provisional partnership with organized crime to protect wholesale bootlegging while also protecting the retail speakeasies. But official graft of city and county public officials spread beyond illegal liquor. Bribes, kickbacks, inflated contracts, shell contracts, bid-rigging, and all manner of creative illicit mechanisms permeated public enterprises. Los Angeles' explosive growth fueled opportunists of every stripe.

The Pacific Club was owned by vice kingpin Charles Crawford. Not directly of course, but through a dummy partnership of a cousin and his wife. Most brothels were tipped off when a raid was imminent, but not the Pacific Club. No reason to since it was so tight with the LAPD that it was never raided. It was an expensive brothel and speakeasy serving the best booze and the prettiest broads. This was above the pay grade of the ordinary LAPD flatfoot.

One would think that with a metropolitan police department headed by James Davis, nicknamed 'Two-Gun Davis' for his reputation as an advocate of brute force policing and a former head of the vice squad, that he would crack down on official corruption. However, his idea of reform was to turn the LAPD into a blunt instrument to enforce public order. Attack violent criminal elements. White collar crime was largely ignored.

The result only fostered increased LAPD entanglement in public corruption. While not rumored to be on the take himself, Davis' administration was disinclined to pursue the unpleasant task of rooting out criminal behavior within its ranks. As long as criminal elements kept a low profile, the LAPD had their backs for a cut of the action.

Crawford was well connected to the LAPD. Assistant Chief Frederick Walsh was rumored to be the LAPD senior corrupt cop and tight with Crawford. Completing this cabal of graft was the Los Angeles County chief deputy district attorney and the chief of staff of the newly elected mayor.

Under the previous mayor, Crawford along with political boss Kent Parrot effectively ran Los Angeles. The electorate falsely thought that having rid themselves of Mayor Cryer and the shadow mayor Parrot in the last election, they had also rid themselves of the corrupt 'City Hall Gang'. But only the front men changed. Charles Crawford still wielded his control over Southland vice while remaining even more influential within the LAPD.

The new mayor, John Porter took on a Kent Parrot protégé as his chief of staff. As for Porter, he was a certifiable screwball. A Bible-quoting teetotaler, evangelizing Protestant, former used-auto parts dealer, former senior member of the Ku Klux Klan, he styled himself a reformer. Of what was not clear. Like his predecessor, his Honor the Mayor was oblivious to the vortex of official corruption swirling around him.

After several weeks of investigative work, Fraser was ready to contact this woman district attorney recommended by Carmody. He wanted to give her something as a test of her commitment. He had what he thought was enough evidence for the district attorney's office to open an investigation against a businessman doing extensive business at the harbors. If it became an official investigation then Fraser stood a better chance of publicizing his findings without flirting with libel. If she turned out to be an ally, all the better. At the least he might get a better understanding of the appetite of the district attorney's office to pursue indictments for graft.

CHAPTER 4

Abigail Blumenthal was an attractive young woman in her late twenties in spite of her austere professional gray suit, hair pulled back into a bun, and dark-rimmed glasses. Fraser would also add that her expression when introduced was anything but cordial.

"You're a reporter with the Examiner, right? The message said that Captain Carmody suggested you pay me a visit. Why's that?"

"I'm working on a story. It has to do with corruption. Probably involving public officials."

"You have evidence?"

"Some. Probably not enough to obtain an indictment?"

"I don't understand. Why are you here rather than Carmody? Is this about an ongoing police investigation?"

"No. At least not yet. I'm here to ….."

Blumenthal cut him off. "Then I can't help you, Mr. Fraser. Not sure why you came to me."

This certainly was not going well. Fraser now questioned why he was here.

"Let me back up, Miss Blumenthal."

"It's *Mrs.* by the way."

"Ok. Sorry. As I was saying, I met Captain Carmody after I was stabbed. According to Carmody it was a couple of cops. But I never made a statement about the incident."

"Why not?"

"Because I didn't trust what might happen. If Carmody was right, and I believe him, then I might have a bigger problem. The guys that attacked me were LAPD detectives. Actually tried to kidnap me. They suffered some physical injuries themselves in the scuffle."

"What happened to them?"

"Broken noses. Badly wounded pride. Handcuffed to their car. But of course I'd never admit to any of that. You can see how that might turn out to my disadvantage."

Blumenthal cracked a thin smile.

"Interesting. Captain Carmody told me about you. So what is it you wish to discuss, Mr. Fraser?"

"We both know that corruption is widespread in Los Angeles, including within this office. Your former boss, District Attorney Keyes, was found guilty of accepting bribes in the Julian Petroleum scam just last year. Your new boss Fitts was once Keyes' chief deputy. Doesn't mean he's corrupt but it doesn't instill confidence. Add to that the known reputation of your boss chief deputy DA Henderson Burke, friend to everyone that has money and needs an ally in the justice system."

"I'm hardly going to comment on that. And you've not answered my question about why you are here."

"Simply this. Carmody appears to be an honest cop. More than that he's willing to stick his neck out to do something about the graft. Since he directed me to you I assume you have the same motivation.

"So I'm proposing to help where I can. Feed you anything I uncover. Try to help you make a case where possible. Get information back from you that will be helpful in my investigations. In short, unofficially team with you to get indictments. If you get indictments, my stories become that much bigger with no legal issues over libel. I need to know what kind of evidence will constitute a good criminal case. Without insider help in the DA's office, anything I write about may serve more as a warning to the bad guys. I need the legal help."

"Very well, Mr. Fraser. So is this just a get to know each other meeting or do you have something you want to share with me?"

One tough broad this Abigail Blumenthal, thought Fraser. She appeared to be more than just the token female in the district attorney's office. He suspicioned her male colleagues found that out the hard way.

"I came here not just hat in hand, Mrs. Blumenthal. Take a look at these," Fraser said, handing her a sheaf of typewritten notes and some photo enlargements.

Blumenthal studied the materials for several minutes.

"And the gentlemen in these photographs?"

"The young women I don't know. Hired for the evening I determined. Taken at a restaurant in Long Beach. The others include the Port of Los Angeles executive director and the Port of Long Beach managing director. Haven't yet identified the guy on the left. But the bald guy on the right is Richard Kerner, CEO of Pacific Shipping & Logistics. Shipping, trucking, cargo transloading, warehousing, import, export, you name it. If it has to do with moving merchandise in the Southland, Kerner has some stake in it."

Blumenthal picked up Fraser's notes. "You're alleging bribery to these two harbor officials. You claim it's from Kerner. Bribery for what?"

"For starters preferential access within the harbors. No labor issues with the longshoreman. Kerner's trucks get the best loads and quickest loading, unloading. No-bid contracts for all manner of services contracted by the harbors. Combined, they're the biggest employer in Southern California. Staggering amount of purchases. No questions asked by customs officials. That's of course where the real money comes from. Foreign bootleg liquor."

"What's your evidence?"

"The kickbacks come in the form of periodic payments to the heads of operations at both ports. The payee is a private real estate investment fund, Cal South Investments. Essentially a Kerner subsidiary through another subsidiary. The fund pays a quarterly dividend to the harbor execs for fund shares they supposedly own. The amount varies to appear as a product of actual fund profits. The amounts are deposited directly into their respective bank accounts at Bank of America."

"And how did you come by this information, Mr. Fraser?"

"I'd rather not go into that. Confidential sources you understand. But let's just say I have insider information. Kerner has a lot of enemies as you might image. Some even work for him."

"So how is it you know these payments are bribes?"

"My source says that Cal South Investments is a shell corporation. I've confirmed that through other sources. It may well have actual investments but no one knows anything about them. No one knows any of its investors. The fund doesn't advertise. It doesn't do business with any major financial institution. It appears to be a Kerner-held financial entity created for distributing bribes. Could be a means to obscure the origin of bootleg money, but that's just a guess at this time."

"There's still no evidence these payments are bribes. What makes you so sure?"

"Because the average annual payments to each of the harbor heads amounts to around a hundred thousand dollars a year. That would suggest investment far beyond either of these gentlemen's means."

Blumenthal said nothing for several moments.

"You are most enterprising, Mr. Fraser. I can make no promises other than to make sure any information you bring me does not get to the *wrong* people. I certainly can't promise to be your source within the DA's office. But I will give you a piece of information to establish my bona fides as it were. This man seated to the left." Blumenthal pointed her finger to the man Fraser had not yet identified. "This is LAPD Lieutenant Sven Borgstrom."

"LAPD? Ok, makes sense. Police protection is essential to moving bootleg liquor. How is it you recognize him?"

"Only because Captain Carmody told me what you were probing that led to you being attacked. Carmody found out the name of the suspected LAPD lieutenant that may have murdered that prostitute."

"Borgstrom?"

"Yes. I looked him up out of curiosity. But there's no mention of his name connected with that homicide. If he is the murderer you and Carmody have a long way to go in proving it. Thought you'd like to know that though. Might want to watch your back if you're digging into something else where he's involved."

Abigail Blumenthal was everything Captain Carmody had said. He neglected to comment on how attractive she was. Tall, shapely, outstanding legs. Raven colored hair, intense hazel eyes, angular face with a narrow patrician nose, perhaps a bit too long to be a classical beauty. While a potential valued ally within the district attorney's office, it was Abigail Blumenthal that Fraser could not get out of his thoughts. Working with her was an inviting prospect even though she was married.

Where to begin with developing the story of graft at the harbors into a front page story? Of course that meant finding enough evidence for criminal indictments. The means was always the same. Whether a reporter or a cop you tried to find someone to rat-out the target. The motive for that was self-interest, hatred, greed, or fear. Fraser was talented in finding those perspective sources then effective at persuading them to give up information. It was about finding vulnerability.

With the help of other Examiner staff, it took several days of exhaustive research to identify a possible source associated with Pacific Shipping & Logistics. The story was a page-four, one paragraph filler from months earlier.

'Los Angeles --- In a bizarre incident at Pacific Shipping & Logistics headquarters in Long Beach, a disgruntled employee, William Kel-

logg, age 43, attacked an executive with a letter opener. Apparently Kellogg had just been terminated. Returning to clear out his desk, Kellogg returned to Vice President Karl Dressler's office and stabbed him in the arm with a letter opener before other employees wrestled Kellogg to the floor. Kellogg was arrested and booked on assault charges. A company spokesman indicated that Mr. Dressler's injuries were not serious. Kellogg was reportedly terminated for job performance reasons. The spokesman added that PSL was saddened by Mr. Kellogg's apparent mental breakdown.'

No mention that Kellogg, an accounting manager, was engaged in low level embezzling to finance a gambling habit that led to his firing. That came from Kellogg's embittered ex-wife.

The incident occurred seven months ago. Kellogg received a sentence of six months in jail and five years' probation. Should be out of jail by now. Captain Carmody provided an address.

The address was a low rent apartment complex badly in need of repair in the city of Wilmington near the port. According to the parole officer, Kellogg's wife had divorced him and sold the house while he was in jail. Kellogg was broke and out of work.

Kellogg answered the door in a dirty flannel robe and slippers. Even at ten o'clock in the morning, Fraser could smell the cheap booze on Kellogg's breath.

"Who the hell are you?"

"Name is Fraser. I'm a reporter for the Examiner?"

"Fuck off."

Kellogg attempted to close the door but Fraser stepped forward putting his shoe in the way.

"Just need a little of your time Mr. Kellogg. It's not about what happened at PSL. But it's about PSL. I think the company is engaged in illegal activities. Maybe we can help each other."

Kellogg's eyes cleared. After a moment of consideration he said, "Ok. Come in."

Fraser spent the next two hours with Kellogg in his dingy kitchen. After hearing Kellogg's probably biased version of his firing, Fraser was eventually able to turn to his agenda. Blaming his circumstances on Dressler, Kellogg was eager to reveal anything damaging, especially after Fraser produced a bottle of good Scotch.

Kellogg managed PSL payables. He was able to recall considerable details of PSL's business partners, contracts, and what he suspected were dubious payments. "Dressler set me up by accusing me of embezzling those funds. I never got a cent."

While that was a goldmine of insider information, it was what Kellogg revealed about his boss that opened up another potential possibility for Fraser.

"That fucking little Dressler. Suffers from little-man syndrome. Stupid little mustache, slicked back hair. Arrogant. Liked to touch the girls at the office. Slapped their behinds, put his hands on their shoulders. They all hated it. They found him repulsive but they needed their jobs. What he really liked though were young girls. Fucking pervert."

"How do you know that, Mr. Kellogg?"

"Because I paid his pimp. A madam actually. Disguised as business entertainment expenses. She runs a brothel in LA. Specializes in young girls. *Very* young girls. Saw some naked photos on Dressler's desk one time."

The brothel checked out. Carmody confirmed it had a reputation for underage girls, reportedly as young as thirteen. Unconfirmed reports of girls even being procured from orphanages. Well protected by the LAPD.

It cost Fraser several uneventful evenings following Dressler as he left work. One night instead of going to his home in Long Beach, Dressler drove north toward Los Angeles. The destination turned out to be the brothel.

Fraser followed shortly after Dressler entered the lobby of the Excelsior Hotel. It was a modest five story structure in downtown Los Angeles' Bunker Hill area. By all appearances it was a cheap hotel.

At the desk, Fraser said to the clerk, "I was told I could perhaps find some female companionship here."

"Not sure that I can help you with that, Sir. This is a hotel. Unfortunately we have no rooms available tonight," the clerk said.

"Really? I'm a colleague of Karl Dressler. It was his recommendation that for the right price one could enjoy the company of young attractive women here."

Fraser slid a twenty dollar bill across the counter.

"Mr. Dressler you said? I believe he's here tonight."

"I hope so. Said he was coming. Suggested I join him."

The clerk pocketed the money. "Go up the stairs to the second floor. Someone there will help you."

There was a large sitting area with a small bar off to the side. Shabby furniture with several well-dressed men holding drinks. All were engaged in talking to young women wearing lingerie with heavy makeup. The women were young but seemed of legal age. Several unattached women lounged in chairs. Fraser was approached by a middle-aged woman.

"I believe you're new to our establishment? I'm Lydia. I manage the hotel. And you are?"

"Arthur Doyle, mam. A colleague recommended this place." Fraser had always been intrigued by the forensic details contrived by the author of the Sherlock Holmes adventures.

"Excellent. Look about, choose who you like. The price is twenty dollars for an hour."

Lydia held out her hand. Fraser counted out the money.

"I think I'll have a drink first."

As Fraser walked over to the bar, he identified Karl Dressler sitting with drink in hand and a woman sitting on his lap. A few minutes later Lydia approached Dressler and motioned with her finger for him to follow. Dressler got up from his seat after pushing away the woman on his lap. Lydia said something into his ear. Dressler nodded.

Sensing Dressler was about to commence whatever sexual revelry he had planned this evening, Fraser approached one of the girls and offered her a sip of his whisky. He was eyeing

Dressler, ready to follow behind to determine where Dressler was going.

Lydia soon returned to escort Dressler to the stairs leading up a level. Dressler was not accompanied by a prostitute. Fraser selected the closest prostitute's arm and motioned her to lead the way. They headed upstairs just behind Dressler.

As the prostitute guided Fraser to continue up another floor, he glimpsed Dressler entering the second room on the left down the hallway on the third floor.

Fraser didn't have a plan. This was about opportunity. Only if Dressler were engaging with an under aged girl would this foray into LA's underbelly prove useful. He had to stall for a little time. But once inside the room the prostitute quickly shed her clothing and lay naked on the bed.

"You're a handsome one. We can have some real fun. What kind of sex do you like?"

"Well I don't know. My first time here. I'm a little nervous. Give me a few minutes to finish my drink."

"Well come over here while you finish your drink. You like what you see don't you?"

Fraser came to the side of the bed. The woman unbuttoned his fly. Fraser couldn't help himself from growing hard. The prostitute was pretty with large breasts. Once she pulled his cock free from his pants he was fully erect.

She took him into her mouth and began teasingly stoking him with her lips and tongue. As she progressed with an ever tightening grip of her lips with rigorous strokes, he felt himself soon approaching a point of no return before climaxing.

Practiced as she was, she too sensed his elevated state and stopped. Looking up at him she said, "Want to come in my mouth or in my pussy? Got to wear a condom if it's my pussy."

Fraser took this as his opportunity to escape. "Tell you what. You're really something. Don't want this to be over in a flash. Let me go down and get us both a couple of drinks. Then I'll come back. You can do more of what you were just doing and we'll go from there."

Fraser reached into his pocket and peeled off some bills. "Here's a tip in advance. I'll also pay for another hour downstairs. Make a night of it."

Fraser put himself back into his pants. "Don't go anywhere."

He descended the stairs. Seeing no one in the hallway, he approached the second door on the left. A man's voice could be heard inside.

Fraser extracted his Leica camera from his inside coat pocket, checked the exposure settings for the low light then opened the door.

Dressler looked toward the door. He was lying on the bed naked. Two clearly preadolescent girls were also on the bed. They too were naked. Fraser was almost physically sick by the sight of this disgusting pedophile. He took six photographs in rapid succession before an enraged Karl Dressler bounded off the bed and came toward him.

The guy was only five foot four and a little overweight, but blind with rage. Fraser stopped him with a hard blow to his midsection, dropping him to his knees. The breath knocked out of him, Dressler could only muster a weak groan following by vomiting. Fraser said nothing. Wanting to kick this vile creature in the head, he instead eased quietly out the door.

A few days later Karl Dressler opened an envelope sent to his office marked *personal & confidential*. Inside was a photo enlargement. A note read to meet at a nearby restaurant.

Fraser sat down across from Dressler.

"You!"

"Good to see you again, Dressler."

"What is this, blackmail?"

"Guess you could call it that. But it's not about money. I don't need to tell you what happens if these photos become public? Know who I am?"

Dressler shook his head.

"Newspaper reporter. So I can get these pictures published all over. Your boss Mr. Kerner wouldn't take kindly to the bad publicity. At the least you'd be fired. Go to jail most probably. This is evidence of statutory rape. Then of course in jail some inmates don't like child molesters. And maybe besides being butt-fucked by some big smelly guys, the LAPD might not be happy with you upsetting one of their operations. You see this story will feature the Excelsior Hotel under LAPD protection. Ruin their business there. Fact is you might not survive in jail.

"Now, you could just commit suicide. Can't stop you from doing that. Actually I'd be ok with that alternative. But you have another way out."

Dressler was pale. Maybe he was contemplating suicide. But Fraser assumed he didn't have the courage.

"Which is what?" Dressler said weakly, barely able to utter anything.

"You're going to get me enough information to hang Kerner and all the crooked officials you guys support. You're going to be my spy. Tell me everything. Get me hard evidence."

"You're crazy. If I did that I would be killed. These are big players. You don't know who you're tangling with."

"Yes I do. And you won't be killed. I have people I'm working with. You'll get police protection. Not crooked cops. You'll also get immunity. After you testify you get out of town. Get yourself a new name. Either that or I go with what I've got right now. That's enough to destroy you and make a pretty good story. So what's it going to be?"

Dressler was breathing hard almost hyperventilating. Eventually he was able to say, "Ok. What do you want me to do?"

"I told you. Get me evidence. I need documents. If you can't steal them without discovery bring them to me and I'll photograph them. Do it quickly. I want something in five days or these photographs get circulated. When you have something put a personal ad in the Examiner reading *middle-aged man looking for young female companion to share in athletic activities*. The following day meet me at the restaurant at the Biltmore downtown."

Dressler's ad appeared in the personal section on day four.

"I need some assurance that I get immunity before you get anything," Dressler said.

"That's not going to happen until I've got something to give the authorities."

"No deal then."

"I don't think so, you piece of shit. I'll just give the district attorney the photos and you get arrested. End of discussion. You'll make the front page. We'll use enough of the photo to maintain public decency but enough to make the point. It's your call."

Dressler said nothing for several moments just staring down in his lap. Eventually he pulled two envelopes from his brief case placing them on the table.

"What you wanted. The envelope marked in red contains originals that I need to return to the files. Can I have these back tomorrow?"

"No problem. I will have them couriered to you in a sealed envelope marked confidential. So what have you got for me?"

"Enough to implicate a lot of important people. Enough to get me killed. About that immunity? When do I meet someone from the district attorney's office?"

"If what you're giving me is all you say it is then I'll set a meeting soon. I'll telephone you. I'll use the name Doyle. A personal friend if your secretary asks."

After Fraser went through Dressler's documents, he knew he had struck journalistic gold. This stuff alone would be enough for a major story and probably enough for indictments. But not yet. Dressler's access could be exploited to provide even more damning information on illegal activities going in many directions.

The next day Fraser called Captain Carmody. Could he arrange a meeting to include Abigail Blumenthal?

While waiting on Carmody, Fraser also learned that like the Pacific Club whorehouse, the Excelsior was also owned by vice kingpin Charles Crawford. Somewhere in this LAPD Lieutenant Borgstrom and his cop thugs might be involved as well.

CHAPTER 5

Captain Carmody selected a small Italian restaurant in Hollywood for the meeting. He wore his signature rumpled gray suit with an ugly tie. Fraser was waiting at a table toward the back. They discussed Dressler while waiting for Blumenthal.

She entered minutes later. Unlike Carmody, her gray suit was tailored, probably expensive. White blouse, gold necklace. Smart heels. Hair still up but now with more makeup. No glasses this evening.

"The Captain says you have some information we might be interested in," she said launching immediately into the reason for the meeting.

"That's right. It has to do with the ports. Both LA and Long Beach Ports. Graft and all sorts of illegal stuff. Very incriminating material." Fraser said.

"And how did you come by this material?" Blumenthal said.

"Somebody high up in Pacific Shipping & Logistics. Richard Kerner's company. Kerner himself is implicated."

"So why would this person give such material to a newspaper reporter rather than the police or the district attorney's office directly?"

"Come now Miss, I mean Mrs. Blumenthal. How would that person know who to trust? Especially this person knowing people in high places are involved, including the police."

"So why you then, Mr. Fraser?"

"I work just like you do. Find a weak link then push on it. In this case a disgruntled ex-employee who wants revenge on the guy that fired him. Knows things about his former boss."

"What sort of things?"

"The guy likes young girls. Underage girls. *Very underage*. I have pictures of him in the act of committing statutory rape. Pretty disgusting."

"So you're blackmailing him to do your bidding?"

"That's right. Just like you and the cops do to get a conviction. You turn one bad guy against another by lying and threatening. And none of us should feel sorry for this low life pedophile. Here look at these." Fraser handed Blumenthal the photographs from the Excelsior. "All he wants is immunity and a chance to get out of this with his skin intact."

Blumenthal had a sharp intake of breath when she looked at the photos. Shaking her head she said, "How did you possibly get these pictures?"

"A professional secret I'm afraid," Fraser said.

Looking first at Carmody then turning to Fraser she said, "All right. Let's see what you have. If it's as good as you say then we'll agree to limited immunity for your snitch. Not on the sex charges though. What's this creep's name?"

Fraser handed Blumenthal the envelope. "Karl Dressler. A vice president for Pacific Shipping & Logistics. Reports to Kerner directly. Some of the materials were originals. The photographed documents had to be returned to PSL's files. I've clipped my comment notes to some of the stuff. Also typed up a summary of what this cache tells us. How things are possibly connected. How the various parties I've identified are connected. Tried to guess at the unknown gaps. I also included a target list for our spy's next foray into the enemy's files. Could use your help there."

Blumenthal took her time scanning through the documents individually then passing each along to Carmody. Neither said anything until they were done. Both looked up with expressions of astonishment.

Blumenthal said, "This is extraordinary, simply extraordinary. I had no idea, Mr. Fraser."

"Christ, Fraser. I trust you know what you have here," Carmody said.

"Yeah I do. A hell of story. A chance to put some major rats away."

"And for that reason this is dangerous stuff," Carmody said. "We all must remain careful. Look at the names we'll be going after. They carry a lot of juice. Not above resorting to muscle. Look what happened to you, Fraser. So the important thing is for us to keep this very tight. We can't trust anyone we aren't absolutely sure of. That includes you, Counselor. You understand?"

"I'm aware of the sensitivity of this, Captain."

"No, I mean that political flunky your boss Chief Deputy DA Burke. He's tight with city hall's fixer and big-time crook, the mayor's own chief of staff, Robert Knowles. There're not mentioned in these documents directly but I can tell you they must be connected in some way. There's too much money involved. Too much protection to pass around."

"I understand, Captain. Burke is a piece of shit. I'm the token woman DA. I get the low key white collar crimes not the sexy Hollywood murders. But DA Fitts likes me so I've got some maneuvering room. I'll be able to keep this away from Burke until I have enough that will make it a fait accompli when I take it to Fitts. I'm not a virgin at this game, Captain."

Virgin? Carmody winced at the sexual reference. Fraser concealed a smile. Mrs. Blumenthal was certainly unusual.

Taking charge, she said, "Ok. Let's play it this way. We'll flesh out additional things we'd like from your Mr. Dressler using the threads you've identified, Mr. Fraser. In fact let's do that right now. Then you go back to Dressler. Tell him to deliver on this new batch of evidence. If it's as good as the first round then he gets his immunity."

Fraser said. "Tell me something, Captain. If Mrs. Blumenthal gets enough for indictments and Dressler turns state's evidence, can you protect him to get him to trial?"

Carmody nodded. "Sure. I've got enough of my boys I can trust. Like I told you, not all the LAPD is on the take."

Ninety minutes later they were done. Carmody left first. Outside Fraser told Blumenthal he would be in touch when Dressler had something more.

The following day Fraser met with Dressler again. After scanning the typed note of things he was expected to deliver, Dressler blanched.

"This is ridiculous. I don't even have access to some of this. What the hell do you expect me to do?"

"I expect you to do whatever it takes. That's what it takes to get your immunity from the DA. If not, you go down with the others. That's what the DA said. And of course you have this other special legal problem too."

"Listen. If I'm caught stealing this information it'll get me killed. Behind these big shots are some very nasty people."

"That's your problem, Dressler. So don't get caught. When you've got the material, use the same signal through the personal column. I'll meet you here the same time the following day. You've got two weeks."

It took only one week before Fraser saw the ad. He immediately arranged to meet with Captain Carmody and Abigail Blumenthal the evening the response appeared in the newspaper. Carmody pointed out this could be a trap. Dressler may have turned or been discovered. He suggested he and Fraser would meet Dressler with several trusted detectives as backup. If Dressler delivered the goods then they would meet with Blumenthal at the LA central library.

Dressler arrived on time. Even Fraser was impressed with what he presented. The creep had indeed delivered not only enough to indict a whole host of public and private big shots, but enough to probably convict several on just the accumulated evidence they now had. Satisfied, they left through the back taking Carmody's car to the library.

After looking over this new material from Dressler, Blumenthal said, "Very well, Mr. Dressler. This is indeed valuable evidence. Good enough to give you limited immunity."

"What do you mean *limited*?"

"I mean you need to continue to cooperate until we feel we have enough to file charges."

"You never said anything about that you sonofabitch," Dressler said to Fraser.

Blumenthal responded, "That's my deal for the immunity, Mr. Dressler. Are you in or out?"

Dressler lowered his head and nodded affirmatively.

"Good. Now it's up to you on what you bring us. But make no mistake, Mr. Dressler, you will bring us useful material on a regular basis."

Fraser said, "And I'm the bag man, Dressler. No more personal ads, just a regular schedule. I think the central library here is good place. Nice and public. So the deal is to be here at six o'clock every Friday evening."

"That's a long drive up here to downtown," Dressler said.

"Doesn't seem to be too long a drive for your other pleasures."

Dressler looked as if he'd been slapped.

"Perhaps Captain Carmody can return Mr. Dressler to his car at the restaurant. I'll drive you back, Mr. Fraser. I need a word with you."

Once Carmody had escorted Dressler out of the library, Blumenthal said to Fraser, "We shouldn't let this go too long. We've got quite a lot already to make some strong cases. Enough to seek indictments. Enough to turn the city upside down with search warrants. But Dressler on the witness stand corroborates everything. If we keep throwing the dice too many times, he might end up dead. I want everything he gives you each Friday that very night so I can determine when we pull the plug. Here's my office and home phone number. I'll meet you immediately after you're done with Dressler."

That was an interesting prospect meeting Abigail Blumenthal every Friday night.

"Tell me something, Counselor, does Dressler get off raping these young girls with his immunity?"

Blumenthal smiled. "Of course not. The immunity offered was *limited*. Only related to bribery, fraud, theft, all the charges that will accrue from his material assistance and testimony. We never discussed immunity for statutory rape. I couldn't in good conscious allow him to continue molesting girls. So the pervert can go to hell after he's served at least some good purpose."

Holy shit thought Fraser. Wouldn't want to get on her wrong side. As for Dressler, hard to feel much compassion for the child molesting creep.

Dressler proved remarkably productive over the next couple of weeks by obtaining more evidentiary documentation of criminal activity, implicating a lot of people. His material also suggested other avenues of wrongdoing to investigate. Evidence piled up. It was the mother lode of news stories. Fraser's editor was falling all over himself anxious for things to come to a head so he could break the exclusive story. It would run for weeks as front page. And the Examiner not only had the scoop but the inside track with the ability to flesh out the backgrounds of all the participants when the story broke. As the fallout grew into criminal trials, the story would continue to provide news for months. It would be the biggest scandal in the Southland in years.

After receiving the latest packet from Dressler each Friday for the last several weeks, Fraser had the pleasure of seeing Abigail Blumenthal. Her aggressive façade evolved into a softer interaction. On their fourth meeting at the library after concluding business, Blumenthal shocked Fraser by saying, "Perhaps you know somewhere where we can get a drink. Some place nice, not some noisy, smoke-filled speakeasy?"

"Ah. Sure. That sounds great. How about the Writers Club on Sunset? It's not too far."

"Where you got stabbed?" She smiled. "Sure. I'll follow you in my car."

What the hell was this about? Looked like she was coming onto him? She was married, wasn't she? No question he was attracted to her. He'd never met a woman this intriguing before.

Drank her Scotch neat just like he did. Over drinks, Blumenthal commenced to candidly share her background. Jewish, daughter of a federal judge. Two brothers also lawyers in San Francisco. Stanford Law School graduate 1921, making her a couple of years older than Fraser. Passionate about women's causes.

"Sounds like you're angry at men," Fraser said.

"And why not? More precisely at male dominated conventions. Men are afraid of women. Afraid they'll lose their power over everything. Christ, women only got the right to vote less than ten years ago. Even freed male slaves in the last century could vote, but not women. It's time to set things straight. Women are just as capable as men at *everything*, probably better at most things."

"No reason I see why they wouldn't be. Do you think there would be any less graft if more women were in office or heads of corporations?"

Fraser meant it too. Women certainly couldn't be any worse than male dominated power in every facet of life. But he wasn't sure they wouldn't be just as corruptible.

"Might be. At any rate it would be different. I don't seem to intimidate you do I?"

"No you don't. Do you try to intimidate, Mrs. Blumenthal?"

She smiled broadly. "Of course I do. Obvious, isn't it? Seems necessary in this male dominated world, especially for a professional. But I admit I probably overdue it. Pushes people away. I'm a little better with other women. And by the way, call me Abigail, Marc."

"Ok, Abigail. How'd you come to drink whisky under Prohibition?"

"My father. First it was to be like my brothers then I came to like it. I like good wine too. Dad still drinks. Thinks the eighteenth amendment was the single stupidest thing the government ever did. Look at all the crime it's bred."

"Couldn't agree more. I acquired a taste for Scotch from my father also. But then again he is Scottish"

"And your mother?"

"French. So I acquired a taste for good wine also. Bordeaux and Burgundy especially. It was part of dinner even as a child. She died a couple of years ago. Wonderful woman. Strong minded like you. Intelligent. Ran counter to convention if it was her wish. Married Dad in Paris when he was there on banking business. That too was her decision over her family's objections. Not only was she to marry an American and move to New York, but he wasn't Jewish."

"Your mother was Jewish?"

"Yes. And father is Protestant if you want to call it that. At least that's what you would call him because of his cultural background. Neither Mom nor Dad went to church or synagogue so it's just a cultural label as far as I'm concerned. So I would think of myself as Scotch-French-American. How about you?"

"Well American first. Third generation. Before that my ancestors came from Germany. I'm not religious but I still identify culturally as being Jewish. My parents still observe Jewish traditions. Even though I don't, I'm still connected with the Jewish experience. It's hard to explain. I'm very much aware of anti-Semitism here just as elsewhere in the world."

"And your husband? Is he Jewish?" Fraser had to understand her marital circumstances. Widowed perhaps? Divorced? Neither?"

"You're dying to understand why a married woman is here having drinks with you. Truth is I'm still married but separated.

One year now. I have my own place. Yes, he's Jewish. Nice guy. Maybe too nice. Something just lacking in our relationship."

"Sorry, I didn't mean to pry. Can't help being attracted to you. Never met a woman like you before."

"You mean I'm not like those sexy actresses you normally date?"

Fraser was taken back for a moment.

Smiling mischievously, she said, "I'll confess, I had Carmody check you out rather thoroughly. Your father's a big shot at MGM. Naturally gives you access to a lot of pretty women. A perfect opportunity for a good looking smart guy with connections."

Fraser swallowed. Was this going where he thought? That would be a delight.

"I want to spend the night with you," Blumenthal said, placing her hand over his. Leaning across the table, close to his face, staring into his eyes, "Interested?"

"Absolutely. Interested from the first time I met you even though you acted like a bitch."

"Well I am a bitch. But I think you like that, so that works."

Abigail Blumenthal was uninhibited in bed. She clearly liked sex.

Fraser had taken her back to his place. The attendant at the club assured him her car would be safe overnight. Before entering his car she kissed him while pressing against him. During the ride home she first rubbed his crotch until he was fully erect then unbuttoned his trousers and grabbed his cock. The sensation was electric.

Once they entered the house they kissed and hurriedly undressed while still in the living room. Once naked, Blumenthal stood back to allow Fraser to admire her. She knew she had a good body. Long legs, erect full breasts. She reached up and undid her hair letting it fall to her shoulders as she shook her head.

"Damn that looks good," she said walking up to him then taking his erection in her hand. "Hope you're a good lover, Marc. I haven't been with a man in a long time."

For the next couple of weeks Fraser and Blumenthal spent at least every other night together.

After the last delivery by Dressler, Blumenthal announced she was ready to seek indictments. Time to bring Dressler into protective custody after he showed next Friday. She would take her whole case directly to DA Fitts the following Monday. Chief Deputy DA Burke would raise a stink complaining that Blumenthal had circumvented procedure. Fitts would mollify him. Fitts was a headline seeker. As the district attorney he could grab media center stage even while acknowledging the extraordinary work of one of his junior prosecutors. This would be the major prosecution of his first term. Perhaps enough to win a second term two years from now.

On Thursday before the final meeting with Dressler the next day, Fraser received a terrible personal shock. A call at his desk at the Examiner offices from his stepmother. Distraught, she told him his father had collapsed at the studio. An apparent heart attack. He was rushed to the hospital but just pronounced dead.

Unable to make his rendezvous with Dressler on Friday, Carmody assured Fraser that plans were in place to safely hide Dressler until he was called to testify as the state's star witness.

Late that Friday night, Carmody called Fraser at his father's home.

"Dressler never showed at the library. I waited until closing," Carmody said. "After that I drove to Long Beach with a couple of my detectives. He wasn't at home. One of my guys is good with locks. We looked around inside. Clothes still in the closet along with a suitcase. Toiletries in the bathroom. Doesn't look like he took a lamb. Left one of my guys there to see if he returned by the morning."

"So what's your guess, Captain?"

"I think Dressler was made. Probably slipped up. Caught stealing something. He's a weak piece of shit. He'd talk his head off at the first threat of violence. Of course after he talked they'd kill him. Chances are he's in some landfill."

"Shit. Does Abigail know yet?"

"No. I'll let you break the news to her."

"You think this will jeopardize making cases against all these guys?"

Carmody had seen all the evidence to date. "Well it's not as tight as having an insider to testify, but she has enough to file charges and get search warrants from the right judge. I assume you'll make it a big deal in the press. Your publisher Hearst likes this sort of thing."

Blumenthal was devastated by the news when Fraser called her. She promised to meet him at his house the following evening. It would give her the day to assess the strength of her several cases without having Dressler as a witness.

As invested in the story as he was, Fraser put it aside temporarily. His grief too consuming. He had loved his father just as he had his mother. Both died unexpectedly while too young. Both seemingly in good health. His relationship had evolved from father and son to friends especially after his mother's death. Even with the generation apart, they shared a range of intellectual interests.

Fraser's sister made the journey to Los Angeles leaving her husband back in New York to care for the children. She returned the day following the funeral. Fraser's stepmother, the former Mexican singer and actress also left Los Angeles to be with her family in Mexico City. To counter the depression of his loss, Fraser forced himself back into work. The shear scope of the graft proved such a compelling story it consumed all his attention.

Working with Abigail Blumenthal helped too, both professionally as well as personally. It was becoming more a relationship than a transient affair.

A few days after the funeral of Fraser's father, Captain Carmody called.

"We found Dressler. Dead of course. Not in a land fill. Body turned up in a toilet on the docks. Found him sitting upright on the toilet seat with the stall locked. Talked to a detective that was on the scene. Not a pretty sight. Face was worked over badly. All his fingers were smashed. Cause of death was having his throat cut. Bled out down his front with the blood running into the toilet. Wasn't obvious that the feet visible under the stall door was a dead guy sitting on the can. An employee came back again later and got curious.

"So he gave up everything they asked for. The brutalized body was left for discovery to send a message to any other would-be witnesses. They'll be expecting charges to be filed after Dressler told them what he turned over. You need to watch yourself, Fraser. Tell that to Blumenthal too. Can't tell how far these guys might go. Even though they're white collar criminals and corrupt public officials, they're partnered up with some violent types."

Blumenthal was devastated by the news of Dressler's death. A professional setback tinged with some guilt for having been the cause of his grisly murder. She had gotten greedy. Underestimated the risk. She now confided to Fraser her uncertainty about the strength of some of the cases without Dressler as the state's witness.

"Well that's just fine. You never told me that this rested so heavily on Dressler's testimony." Fraser was more than irritated. Had he known that he would have cut short Dressler's continued spying sooner. Blumenthal over-reached. "So what do you intend to do?"

"I guess I'll take it to Fitts. See what he thinks. Take my lumps about not going through channels. If he agrees, we can seek search warrants since we know some of the places to look."

"Wonderful. Search warrants. Scoop up a lot of paper hoping to find incriminating material. Stuff they've now destroyed. That'll take months. No reason not to go to press with my story. My editor was right. Should have done this weeks ago. Thought teaming with the DA's office would give the story more weight when it broke."

"I'm sorry, Marc. Listen. Can you give me a couple of days? Let me talk to Fitts first. Better he hears from me that I was working secretly with a reporter rather than learning about it from the newspaper."

"Ok. Only until Friday. It'll be Sunday's front page headline. All the names. Got the paper's ass covered from any libel since I have photographs of all the documents Dressler provided. Safe in a vault at the Examiner. Maybe this'll flush out more pissed off whistleblowers. It'll certainly keep the pressure on while the DA's office decides to shit or get off the pot and seek indictments. Personally I don't know if any public official in LA County can be trusted."

"Agreed. I'll talk to Fitts tomorrow. We'll still salvage this. Can I see you Friday, Marc?"

"Of course. Pick you up at seven at your place. We'll have a nice dinner," Fraser said. He hoped she would have encouraging news about her meeting with Fitts. He also hoped for a romantic evening.

It would be the first night she would spend the night since the ordeal of his father's death and funeral. While Marc Fraser was deeply saddened by the loss of his father, he felt inadequate to comfort his stepmother in her grief.

Before dinner, Blumenthal gave him a detailed recounting of her discussion with District Attorney Fitts. As she anticipated, he jumped at the chance to take charge of the investigation with the prospects of multiple high profile prosecutions. Her bypassing of the chief deputy did not become an issue. She would work directly for Fitts and a team of additional prosecutors. Fitts even found advantage of being allied with the Examiner. Preferred that they did not break the story but Blumenthal said that would happen on Sunday.

After strategizing with Fitts she was more confident about the strength of many of the cases. They had what amounted to a mountain of evidence. However a lot depended on how high the graft extended, how much the crooks were willing to pay, and the extent of fear they could exert over potential witnesses, even jurors.

"So I must be in the office first thing tomorrow morning to get things moving. Can we order dinner now? I'm spending the night but I've got to get some sleep. We can have *dessert* at home if you don't keep me up all hours."

Fraser smiled at the prospect. After all that had happened, he needed a pleasant evening with Abigail.

Both anxious to get home, they left the restaurant in West Hollywood at 8:30, driving east on Santa Monica Boulevard then turning north onto Highland Avenue. Fraser's house was just below where Highland merged with Cahuenga Boulevard before entering the pass climbing through the mountains to the San Fernando Valley to the north.

The grade increased. Fraser shifted down a gear. Few cars on this dark night except for the one behind him. Less than a mile from his house, the car behind repeatedly tuned its headlights off and on. Fraser wondered if the car was trying to signal him that something was wrong but the car then pulled over to the side of the street.

Moments later Fraser was surprised by the sudden glare of headlights coming fast down the grade in the center of street only a few hundred feet away. A large truck? Shit!

At the last instant the truck veered further into Fraser's lane. Fraser attempted to turn away to the right but too late. The truck's large bumper caught his roadster in the left front quarter panel with an indirect blow but enough to stop the car dead. The truck proceeded to scrape down the side of the roadster catching the roadster's rear bumper then spinning the car 360 degrees as the truck accelerated away never stopping. The crippled roadster coasted slowly downhill smashing into a utility pole.

Fraser and Blumenthal were both unconscious. Blumenthal was wedged on the floor under the dashboard. Blood streamed from a gash on her head. Her left arm was bent at an unnatural angle. Fraser too had a bad laceration to his cheek. The steering wheel pressing into his chest was bent from his hands.

Fraser came to as someone was pulling him from the vehicle. His thoughts immediately were for Blumenthal.

"Help Abigail …. Please. Is she ok?"

"No she's not ok, Fraser. Neither are you by your looks," a man said.

"Got to help her," Fraser said. He fell out of the car onto the pavement. Rising up on all fours he gasped with the intense pain in his chest. Blood spewed from his mouth as he coughed.

"You don't seem to understand, Fraser. You both died in the crash. Trouble is you're just not dead yet. But we're going to fix that. I'd say you broke some ribs. Maybe punctured a lung by the look of the blood you're coughing up," the big man said.

Fraser looked up. What was he saying? An ugly face with a deformed nose.

"We'll just finish you off with a few blows to your chest with this," the man said holding a nightstick which he slapped repeatedly into the palm of his hand. "Maybe break your nose just for fun while I'm at it. Stand him up against the car, Dombrowski"

Dombrowski? The cop that knifed him? Now he recognized the big guy. Felgenhauer.

Dombrowski attempted to lift Fraser to his feet. Fraser cried out in pain, dropping back down on one knee. As Dombrowski struggled to get a hold under Fraser's left arm Fraser saw the cop's revolver under his jacket in a shoulder holster. His only chance or he was surely dead. Abigail too.

With nothing to lose Fraser drove his right fist into Dombrowski's groin. The force enough for him to feel the compression of the guy's genitals. Dombrowski's eyes widen as his body went slack. Fraser reached inside the jacket and pulled out the revolver before Dombrowski collapsed.

Fraser pointed the gun at Felgenhauer.

"Drop the nightstick."

Felgenhauer stood dumbstruck. This couldn't be happening again.

"Do it you sonofabitch. No reason why I won't shoot you."

Felgenhauer dropped the nightstick.

"Now take out your gun. Slowly. Two fingers. Put it on the ground." Fraser coughed up more blood. What to do? Must get help. Not sure how long he was going to last before passing out. "Kick it over here."

Dombrowski curled into a fetal position on the pavement began shrieking in agony. Between cries of agony he was retching repeatedly.

"Now go get help. Run down the street. Find a phone. Call an ambulance," Fraser said to Felgenhauer.

"Why the fuck would I do that?"

"Because you stupid shit, if you don't sooner or later a car comes by and your friend here has some difficult explaining. So will you. This way you get back and take him away with you. I'd say he needs to get to a hospital. Of course you could just leave him but he might resent that. Might implicate you if he's pissed off enough."

Not sure he was convincing, but after a slight hesitation Felgenhauer ran down the street to the nearest house.

Fraser crawled back over to the car's front seat and touched Blumenthal's neck. Did she have a pulse? He couldn't tell with his own heart pounding. He stroked her head, careful to avoid the wound.

Several minutes later Felgenhauer returned out of breath. Once Fraser could hear ambulance and police sirens approaching he allowed Felgenhauer to haul Dombrowski into the back seat of their car.

A police car arrived on scene just before the ambulance. Fraser threw the two revolvers onto the back seat floor of his car. Once on the stretcher he blacked out.

CHAPTER 6

New Year's day, 1930 again saw Marc Fraser convalescing in a hospital after surgery to repair the damage to his right lung. The prognosis was encouraging. His stepmother had returned from Mexico to be with him as did his sister from New York. Both remained for the two weeks it took for the doctors to pronounce that he was out of danger. He was still bedridden as was Abigail Blumenthal.

Among his visitors was the great man himself, his employer William Randolph Hearst. He came with Marion Davies who burst into tears when she saw Fraser bandaged in bed with oxygen tubes to his nose.

"Damn these people. Randal told me the whole story." Randal Schmidt was the Examiner's managing editor. "I called up your friend Captain Carmody to hear the details directly. Unbelievable. Audacious beyond belief. Means they're running scared. Once you're well enough I told Randal to get a secretary up here to your room so you can write up each day's story. He's to print your byline in larger than normal type. You can stick it in their face. For somebody at this only a few years you've done a thoroughly outstanding job of investigative journalism, Fraser."

"That's true, Marc," Marion Davies said. "W.R. can't get over what you've exposed. Now you must get well. When you're back on your feet we want to see you." She bent down and kissed his forehead.

Once he was able to leave his bed in a wheelchair Fraser made his first visit to Abigail Blumenthal also convalescing at the hospital. Even expecting that first sight of her to be distressing, it was still a shock. She had suffered a broken arm and broken ankle along with a severe concussion. The severity of the concussion still concerned the doctors. She had recovered sufficiently to allow for a sustained conversation without her tiring although still heavily medicated to alleviate the constant head pain.

With the complicity of the nursing staff, subsequent visits avoided those times when Blumenthal's estranged husband would be at her bedside. Her husband knew that she was a passenger in Fraser's car the night of the collision. He either knew or must suspect more than a professional relationship. No point in making the situation more difficult. He was a nice guy by all accounts, including Blumenthal's own comments.

"Getting along better today, Abby?" Fraser said. It had been two days since his last visit.

"Yes. The pounding headache is better. Don't have to take the pain medication as often which puts me to sleep. Listen, Marc. I've come to a big decision. About me, about us, about being a prosecutor. About Walter too." Walter was her husband. "This isn't for me. I'm a good lawyer. Better than most men. I'll do fine in private practice. Commercial work, corporate law. Not this cesspool you swim in. Never thought all this stuff you uncovered with graft involving the ports would lead to such violence. Naïve I guess. They tried to kill us, Marc.

"All this has made me rethink what I'm doing. What I'm doing with you. I'm very fond of you, Marc. Maybe even in love with you. But you're an adventurer. It's clear that will be your life. You're smart, good looking, a wonderful lover, but the other part of your life isn't for me. It's made me rethink how I feel about Walter. He knows about you yet he still wants me back.

Not sure I'm ready for that but I don't think you're the alternative, Marc. I guess I see things differently after what happened."

Fraser was stunned. Yet another unexpected personal loss. Maybe in love with Abigail Blumenthal, certainly deeply attached to her. Knew that he also avoided thinking seriously about committing to a future together. Would she divorce Walter? Did he even want to get married? They never talked about that. Yet the prospect of losing Abigail left a terrible void.

"I..... I don't know what to say, Abby. I understand what you're saying but I can't bear the thought of not being with you. We are good together."

"Sure we are. We connect. Our lovemaking is terrific. You so much want to please me in bed. Yet our professional lives will not be compatible. I'm getting out of criminal law. I'm not a crusader. You're a newspaper guy. Ambitious. You thrive on the adventure, the challenge of figuring things out. You're a romantic wanting to fight bad guys. What are you going to do in the future? Become a newspaper editor? Are you going to ever write like you've talked about? Do you want to settle down like normal people? I don't think that's you, Marc."

Fraser did not respond. Because she was right.

"Let's not talk about it right now," Blumenthal said. "My head is hurting something awful. Did Fitts talk to you?"

Preferring also to avoid this personal issue, Fraser said, "Yesterday my editor called him and told him we're going with the story tomorrow so he paid me a visit. Thanked me for the investigative work that will become the foundation of his cases. Wouldn't give me the specifics. Said he wasn't ready yet to make that public. Promised to announce seeking indictments soon."

"Didn't give me much more than that either. He's going to grab the credit and the headlines. It'll get him elected next election. But I don't care. Told him I'd be resigning."

Fraser chose to stick to the professional side of the conversation. "Captain Carmody gave me a lot more. Whatever his motives, it seems that Fitts is fully committed. Carmody's boss, Deputy Chief Monahan has been personally tapped by Fitts and the chief of police to head up a special investigation unit. Carmody is part of that unit. So the whole official side of the probe has legs. I'll still continue to look around the edges. I don't think either the LAPD or the district attorney's office is very good at investigating this sort of thing. Especially without you."

Blumenthal smiled weakly. Her face showed the strain of physical as well as emotional pain.

"By the way. Carmody said that our *accident* was being treated as a hit and run. Told Carmody what happened. The truck intended to smash into us. But just like before when these two thugs jumped me a year ago, neither of us could file any charges without the other filing counter charges."

Fraser did not tell Blumenthal about their second close brush with death had Felgenhauer and Dombrowski completed their assignment. Nor did he tell her that according to Carmody, Dombrowski too remained in the hospital suffering substantial damage to his testicles and even his pelvis. Felgenhauer must at least have a damaged reputation among his colleagues, and his crooked nose as a reminder of his failures.

By the spring of 1930, what was quickly becoming known as the *Harbors Scandal* dominated media attention in Los Angeles. District Attorney Fitts made the investigation his signature objective. He produced indictments against all the big fish and a fair number of the second tier people. Enough evidence that plea deals were being cut right and left by the lesser players to lighten their criminal charges or escape with immunity all together. The whole mess at the twin Ports of Los Angeles and Long Beach was unraveling in a great public display of populist disgust.

Major trials dates were set for late summer. Included were Richard Kerner, CEO of Pacific Shipping & Logistics, the PSL chief financial officer along with two vice presidents, two Los Angeles County Supervisors, LAPD Assistant Chief Frederick Walsh, the president of the local longshoreman's union, and the managing directors of both ports. The probe also netted criminal charges for a police commander, the CEO of an oil company, and two county auditors. The chief deputy district attorney and the chief of staff to the mayor were unnamed in the scandal but both unexpectedly resigned for personal reasons. Fraser thought there might be hope for Los Angeles yet to avoid becoming another graft-compromised city like Chicago.

Fraser's coverage spanned the next couple of months in the run-up to the criminal trials. Even though the top culprits were facing trial the scandal continued to feed on itself. Peripheral stories abounded. Lower level participants had become complacent since the corruption reached so high up that there was widespread sloppiness in concealing evidence of illegal activities. An incriminating paper trail abounded once the house of cards came apart. New names immerged faster than the district attorney's office could file charges. Plea deals cut with lower level perpetrators produced new evidence adding fuel to the conflagration.

Fraser pursued leads to new stories providing a depth to the scandal in the form of how such corruption could take hold. His reporting read like a crime novel. The lesser participants, seduced through greed or fear to engage in criminal activity, each had their own story. Fraser was developing a particular writing style that drew much praise. His stories were featured as front page in all the Hearst Publications newspapers throughout the country. He even appeared in a Hearst Metrotone News short film discussing how he broke the story of the Los Angeles Harbor Scandal.

Just before the trials took place, Fraser received news from Captain Carmody that provided a measure of personal satisfaction. It further proved his theory that vulnerability of organized wrong doing lay at the bottom of the criminal hierarchy. Somebody will always give away somebody above if it's to their benefit.

"That old case of the murder of the prostitute you were investigating. The alleged perp, LAPD Lieutenant Borgstrom. Well, we arrested him."

"You're kidding? What happened?"

"Your recurring nemesis, that asshole Felgenhauer. Seems he was implicated in the fallout of the Harbor Scandal. All sorts of people talking to save themselves from going to jail. Anyway, he cut a deal to save his ass. He gave up Borgstrom as the murderer of the prostitute. Drove Borgstrom away from the scene. Said Borgstrom told him what happened."

"And?"

"Felgenhauer gets a walk. Immunity deal. Kicked off the force of course."

"Borgstrom?"

"He will be indicted on second degree murder charges."

"Will he be convicted?"

"I think so. You see the other witness is Detective Dombrowski. He didn't get as good a deal from the DA as his partner Felgenhauer but he probably won't serve any time. If it's any satisfaction, Dombrowski is still in a bad way physically. Walks with a limp I understand. Might not be having much sex from what the doctors say. You apparently did some real damage between his legs."

The year 1930 was both triumph and tragedy for Marc Fraser. The breaking of the Harbor Scandal story was a professional achievement beyond his wildest dreams. Critics remarked that he had gotten lucky. But finding the means and co-opting the degenerate creep Dressler into spying was first-rate creative work. Fraser now had celebrity status. How could he top the success of the Harbor Scandal? Just like the movies after having starred in a major hit, what next?

Against that success was the untimely loss of his father and of course Abigail Blumenthal.

That initial conversation with Abigail at the hospital never changed direction. After she left the hospital, she announced to Fraser that she would be moving back to live with her husband. She said a clean break was the best. He would remain a special interlude in her life but they had no future. Interlude? That was her word. She would cherish their time together and wished him well. It was not that easy for Marc Fraser. Abigail Blumenthal was the first woman that he had ever cared so deeply about. The void she left was profound.

1930 was also the beginning of the dark days of the Great Depression. The excesses of the prior decade reached their climax in the last months of 1929. The entire world was now poised on the brink of economic catastrophe. Only a very few saw the dangerous fault lines in the unbounded prosperity of the past decade. A cascade of events in financial markets trading began in September that brought a close to the Jazz Age and ushered in the Great Depression. It would last for the next decade.

On September 3, 1929, the Dow Jones industrial average hit 381, its peak for the bull market of the 1920s. But on October 24th, Black Thursday, the Dow Jones fell 13% in a mob-like panic as investors tried to sell off their holdings. Thousands of investors and brokers were ruined since their holdings were often purchased on margins of as little as 10-20%. A fall in price placed an immediate cash call on the investor to make up the margin shortfall. Banks across the country failed as they too had invested in the market on margin and could not satisfy depositors' withdrawals.

The disaster accelerated as trading resumed on the following Monday, October 28th. The Dow Jones fell another 13% to 260. The following day, Black Tuesday, October 29th, it fell another 11.7% to 230. By the middle of November, the value of all New York Stock Exchange stocks had dropped from $80 billion to $50 billion. Every successive trading day deepen the loss.

The ripple effects from this economic collapse of the world's greatest industrial nation rapidly moved outward quickly enveloping the entire world. In 1930, the world was already sufficiently interconnected economically that the ill-conceived, unsustainable financial underpinnings that lead to the Wall Street crash depressed commerce everywhere. Whether economies were based upon manufactured goods, agriculture, or natural resources, everything and everyone suffered. Capital, the fuel that drove industrial enterprise, dried up. Without industry the need for raw materials shrank. Without commerce and money in circulation, agricultural prices declined. The entire structure of global economics became fundamentally crippled.

The Great Depression called into question the social viability of capitalism and therefore democracy. It provided a basis of desperation that drove millions to the extremes of Fascism and Communism. These opposite poles of the political right and left would themselves clash. Democracy became the third leg of an unstable stool that would lead to shifting alliances and inevitably to the brink of another global war.

So much of one's life results from circumstances of chance. Sometimes those random variables led to opportunities, sometimes unintended consequences, sometimes disaster. That is where one's own intellect and skills could direct outcomes. Fraser had learned to go with the flow while recognizing then exploiting opportunities. That's what made him a talented investigative journalist.

One such opportunity had been meeting Marion Davies. That led to an introduction with William Randolph Hearst, in turn leading to his first newspaper job. He managed that opportunity spectacularly. Only a few years in the newspaper business, Fraser had made a name for himself as a tough, clever reporter.

Davies called again. After exchanging pleasantries and asking about his recovery, she said, "W.R. talks about you a lot. Calls you his favorite reporter. And he has a lot of great reporters at all his newspapers. Your coverage of the Harbor Scandal was *superb* to use W.R.'s own word. Anyway, he wants to see you, Marc. Suggested you come up to San Simeon next weekend if you can. Spend a few days. What do'ya say?"

Of course. When the Chief called you made the time.

"Sure, Marion. Love to. That's way up the coast, north of San Luis Obispo isn't it?"

"Yup. Too long a drive. Tell you what. Why don't you take the train up with me? I'm leaving Friday morning. I'd love the company."

"That's sounds great, Marion."

"Good. I'll come by with my chauffeur and pick you up about ten. By the way. Do you have a girlfriend you might want to bring along? San Simeon would certainly impress her."

That was a painful reminder. He would have loved to take Abby but that was clearly over. Having never returned to her prosecutor job, Fraser had not spoken to her since she declared they were through.

"No. I'm unattached at the moment. But thanks for the offer."

The train pulled into the small San Simeon station on the coast. Once disembarked, Davies and Fraser were met by several servants in two cars. One was to drive them up the hill, the other for Davies considerable luggage. Looking up, Fraser could see the towers of the enormous Cass Grande building in the distance looking like a cathedral. Hearst himself still called it the Ranch, harking back to his days of youth when the family camped on the hilltops of hundreds of acres overlooking the Pacific Ocean. Everyone else called it Hearst Castle. It was arguably the grandest estate in all of the United States at the time.

Arriving at the estate, the effect was overpowering. Only one of Hearst's many palatial homes both in California and New York, it spoke of unrestrained spending not only on the architecture but on vast quantities of art and antiques decorating each residence. Inside, Casa Grande with its over one hundred rooms, was like being in a museum. Even the smallest elements of construction materials came from ancient buildings in Europe. It was hard to image such wealth existed.

Fraser was assigned a room in the large eight bedroom guest house named the Casa del Sol close by to the outdoor Roman-inspired Neptune Pool. After unpacking, he strolled about the vast grounds until the cocktail hour. A butler located him then escorted him to the large house to meet his boss and host.

William Randolph Hearst was a gracious host complimented by his paramour the charming Marion Davies. There were a number of guests seated in the magnificent Assembly Room. The walls were walnut paneled covered with Renaissance and Baroque tapestries and paintings. The fireplace itself was a sculpture. Objets d'art were everywhere. It was late November on a sunny but chilly afternoon with a breeze coming on shore from the ocean. A fire was lit. Even though huge, the room felt cozy.

Upon Fraser entering, Hearst came over to him straight away extending his hand.

"Fraser, so good of you to come. Everyone. Let me introduce Marc Fraser my best reporter on any of the papers. As you know, Mr. Fraser is the reason that Los Angeles experienced this great public catharsis this past year by exposing what has become known as the Harbor Scandal."

Hearst personally introduced him around to each guest. Fraser knew only one person, the actress Pola Negri from their meeting the first time he met Hearst and was offered as job on the Examiner.

"Darling, of course I remember you. I always remember handsome men," Negri said and gave him a kiss on the lips while touching his face with her hand. She was a striking beauty with her black hair and creamy pale skin. But in an age awash with beautiful women on film, Negri was also a genuine accomplished actress. Having finished her last silent film the year before, she was undaunted as she planned to enter the world of *talkies* even with her pronounced East European accent. "We met just before Rudy died a few years ago. Such a sad time for me. But life goes on."

Rudolph Valentino died only months after Fraser briefly met him with Negri in 1926. The incomparable Negri had indeed moved on making publicity induced headlines about her personal romances.

Once introduced, Hearst took Fraser by the arm and guided him out of the room. "Let's have a word." Hearst was typically impatient. "According to Marion you're part French? Speak the language fluently I understand?"

"Yes, Sir. My mother was French."

"Do you know wine, French wine?"

"Fairly well. My father fancied French wine. He had the means to still have a supply of good vintage even with the restrictions of Prohibition. We enjoyed a good bottle often. I inherited access to his illicit source of supply."

"Prohibition. The national curse. But let's go to the wine cellar. Since you can appreciate a good Bordeaux and Burgundy please select some bottles for dinner this evening."

They descended a spiral staircase to the underground cellar which maintained the cool temperature required of wine storage. Fraser was surprised when they reached what looked like a bank vault steel door. Hearst spun the combination lock then pulled the heavy door back. Certainly eccentric to protect vintage wine in a vault with the unimaginable value of the art upstairs so accessible.

Like everything else at this place, the cellar was huge.

"Take a look around," Hearst said.

Fraser did just that, reacting with amazement as he discovered cases of the best vintages from all the first growth Bordeaux estates and foremost Burgundy Grand Crus of the Côte d'Or.

"My God. I've seen bottles of many of these but never tasted them. An extraordinary cellar, Sir."

"Good, good. Then you'll enjoy the evening all the more. Marion says you also like good Scotch whiskey. Single malts. I'm a fairly modest drinker but how about a small taste before we return upstairs. I'd like to discuss something with you."

Sitting at a small table, Hearst poured a couple of fingers from a bottle of twenty-five year old Scotch into two glasses.

"Ready for something bigger, Fraser? News business I mean. You've proven to have a remarkable talent at finding out things. An engaging writing style."

"Thank you, Sir."

"But I'm not talking about the Los Angeles Examiner, or even LA. I'm talking about publishing your stories throughout Hearst Publications. And I'm talking about from Europe."

Fraser nearly choked on his whisky. "A foreign assignment, Sir? That's going to mean writing about politics. I don't have any experience in that area, especially foreign affairs."

"Few do in the world's current state of turmoil. Those that think they know look at it through the lens of an earlier generation. The same generation, my generation, that brought about the Great War in Europe followed by this deepening economic depression.

"Europe and the Far East are besieged with nationalistic demands that may easily lead to another great military conflict. America knows nothing about the affairs of the rest of the world. There's every chance we could again get drawn into a foreign war. Therefore, that's the next front line of important journalism. You're a quick study obviously. What do you think?"

"I'm flattered, Mr. Hearst. It's an intriguing thought. I studied in Paris. Spent a lot of time there since I was a child. I like Europe. At least France. Haven't been to many other places."

"Paris was exactly what I was thinking as your base of operations. Like you said, you know the city, read and speak French like a native. I asked Randal Schmidt what else he knew about you. Said you could speak passible Spanish from being around your father's second wife. Have at least an academic working familiarity in German from your school days. Seems you have a linguistics talent that makes you perfect for this role. What do you say?"

Fraser would have preferred a chance to consider the implications longer but that wasn't Hearst's impulsive style.

"Thank you, Sir. When do you want me to start?"

Hearst smiled broadly. "Soon as possible. Let's say after the first of the year. Unfortunately, Paris in January won't be as warm as Los Angeles. Now that that's settled, please pick the wine for our dinner guests."

Unattached and suffering a malaise, the first ever in his life, Marc Fraser assessed his circumstances. Gone was his father. Gone was what he concluded was his first real love. Found his calling as an investigative journalist but was still chastened by the attempt on his life. Three months to fully recover from his injuries perpetrated by corrupt public officials. The Harbor Scandal while a spectacular personal success bred an anxiety of what to pursue next that could compare. Did he want to continue reporting on the underbelly of Southern California? Even Los Angeles had only so much headline generating opportunities. Fraser was suffering a mix of emotions that left him anxious and a little disoriented.

Now this offer to go to Europe. Not only Europe but a different type of journalism. Under different circumstances he may have balked but nothing now tied him to Los Angeles. The prospect of a new challenge he could sink his energies into held an enticing prospect. And of course returning to Paris. Why not?

PART TWO

EUROPE

CHAPTER 7

Although Marc Fraser did not possess a particular background in foreign politics, he did have some academic background in world history having taken a minor in history while pursuing his journalism degree. Spurred by the Great War in Europe he took a personal interest in European history during his high school years being part French. Therefore, he possessed a working understanding of what was transpiring at the beginning of the 1930s. He had also learned that most things that appear complex became not only fathomable, but understandable in the context of their cause and effect relationships once one got inside the fundamentals of the subject. The prospect of covering turbulent European politics took the form of an intellectual challenge rather than an intimidating task.

Hearst explained that Fraser's job was to write from a broader perspective by trying to frame the pan-European state of affairs understandable to Americans. The geopolitical scene in Europe was rapidly changing since the Great War. Most of the old governing institutions were swept away or coming under increasing attack. The rise of Fascism and its antithesis Communism threatened European democratic states in the form of dictatorial strongmen. Hearst had foreign correspondents in all the major capitals. Fraser's job was to collaborate with them to write engaging material outside their more provincially rooted perspectives. Present Americans with a broader understanding of European events.

After several weeks at his sister's in New York over the year-end holidays of 1930, Fraser had filled his reserve of all things American before embarking on this new adventure in Europe. Manhattan in wintertime served to acclimate him to colder temperatures forgotten over the past years in California. Paris in winter could be cold but it was still Paris.

Being an urban creature, he embraced the unique character of all three of the great cities he had lived in. However, not only did he have a particular fondness for Paris, this new job would have the added allure of being able to experience other European cities. All things considered, 1931 was starting off with renewed anticipation.

He embarked from New York on the great transatlantic Cunard liner *RMS Aquitania*. He and his family had actually sailed the great ship several times before in their many crossings to visit his mother's homeland. The great ship was the successor flagship of the Cunard fleet to the earlier *Lusitania* sunk by a German U-boat in 1915. Considered the most attractive ship of the time, she was nicknamed the "Ship Beautiful". Her interior could rival that of her White Star competitor, the ill-fated *RMS Titanic* launched two years earlier which sank on her maiden voyage in 1912.

The Atlantic crossing afforded Fraser a brief opportunity to reset his mind to this new life venture. With little to do during the day and too cold to enjoy being outside, he settled into the first class bar at a corner table with his portable typewriter. Until the cocktail hour the bar remained sparsely populated. With no reporting assignments he immersed himself in working on his first novel. He had been at it for the past year. Abigail Blumenthal had challenged him into actually beginning what he so often talked about. He still wasn't over her as evidenced by not responding to advances by at least two flirtatious females.

Arriving at the French port of Le Harve on the English Channel, he was already mentally realigned to a new life, both professionally as well as personally. Paris still felt every bit as much *home* as New York or Los Angeles so it was not to be that much of an adjustment. Endless memories. Had his mother not died unexpectedly, he would have completed college at the Sorbonne and might have stayed on in France to pursue a career. It had been years since he left Paris. So much had happened. Even though a cold overcast day, stepping outside the Gare St. Lazare rail station in Paris' 8th Arrondissement, it felt good to be back.

He booked a room for an extended stay at the Hotel Madison on Boulevard Saint-Germain. It was centrally located on the Left Bank of the River Seine as it bisected central Paris. The Left Bank, actually the south side of the river and home to the 5th and 6th Arrondissements, was historically populated by intellectuals, artists, and students. He knew the neighborhood from his days at the Sorbonne since the Madison was across the wide boulevard from his favorite haunt, the Café de Flore.

The Left Bank was the grittier part of old Paris. He preferred this to the more upscale Right Bank of the Seine where as a child he stayed with his family on their typical twice-annual visits. While his father came from modest means, his mother came from wealth as part of the French branch of the Rothschild clan. She did not indulge by staying at the prestigious Ritz, but preferred the more modest yet elegant Regina across the street from the Louvre Museum.

He still had extended family on his mother's side in Paris. Once he announced to the family in Paris of his relocating there, his mother's closest cousin had done considerable research toward finding him a suitable apartment for rent. Her last cable provided three possibilities. Wanting a couple of days to himself before trying to fend off her invitation to stay with her and her husband until he got settled, he wired a later arrival date.

Actually the research was done by her daughter. Fraser wasn't sure what their relationship was called but was happy to have her take charge of showing him properties. She was three years his junior and in graduate school at the Sorbonne pursuing a degree in economics. Not surprising for someone in the extended Rothschild banking family. She was smart and attractive. Attractive enough to be a little disconcerting since she was related even if somewhat remotely. Reminiscent of Abigail Blumenthal with softer edges. He was consciously aware of his attraction to smart, strong-minded, pretty women. But leaving aside the fact she was his cousin first removed or some such label, it was still pleasant to have the company of a pretty woman that took charge of getting him settled domestically.

The apartment selected was on Rue du Sabot, a small street a few blocks south of Boulevard Saint-Germain in the 6th Arrondissement. It was one floor up with windows facing both the street and an interior courtyard. It was ideal but Harriet decided that they must do some redecorating to make it habitable. It became evident that Harriet de Rothschild Sauveterre had an eye for style. With new colors, new window coverings, and a few new furniture acquisitions, the apartment truly transformed. His favorite piece was a grand mahogany desk that took four workmen to carry up the flight of stairs. A writer needed a proper place to be creative she declared.

After a week, Fraser got down to the business of his new job. Whatever that was exactly. The Chief had been vague about what he expected. Fraser sensed that WRH probably had no specific expectations therefore it was up to Fraser's initiative to shape the assignment into something meaningful.

Another Hearst-owned news service, Universal, maintained a small office at 4 Rue de Cirque. It was a small suite of a couple of offices on the third floor located close to both the French President's Élysée Palace and the U.S. Embassy next to Place de la Concorde, in the 8th Arrondissement. The Paris bureau was headed by C. F. Bertelli, a staff correspondent manning the post since the Great War.

Bertelli was a jovial sort in his fifties. Short and on the stout side he evidently enjoyed his creature pleasures. On the first day in the office, Bertelli spent the remainder of the morning chatting mostly about his own background, about the Great War, all the while puffing on a cigar that permeated the cramped office with smoke. Abruptly at noon, he escorted Fraser off to lunch.

Lunch was not the quick sandwich and coffee taken on the run when he worked in Los Angeles. Every meal in France was an important event of the day. More important than work. Having been in Paris for twenty years, Bertelli embraced everything Francophile, particularly the food, even more so the wine.

"Along with briefing you on what is going on in Europe, at least from a Paris perspective, the Chief wired that I should take good care of you. So for our first business lunch, welcome to Bernard's."

Bernard's was elegant. Obviously Bertelli was expensing what must be a costly lunch. Over several courses and two bottles of good Bordeaux, he regaled Fraser with his take on Europe.

"Let me start with what I know best - France. The Third Republic is under great stress at this time like all the other democracies in Europe. Despite the inability to collect on war reparations from a bankrupt Germany, the French economy still grew steadily in the 1920s. Until now. The Depression caused by the Wall Street crash in '29 has caught up to France."

"And the French government?" Fraser said.

"Ah, the government. Floundering I should say. Just like all the parliamentary governments in Europe. It's the economy. The lack of capital causes the lack of industrial output resulting in widespread unemployment just like the United States. The working class everywhere is suffering. Starving in some places. When people don't have enough food they do desperate things."

"Like turning to Communism?" Fraser said. "There seems this widespread fear in the U.S. about the spread of Communism. Is that a meaningful threat to France?"

"Not as much as the Chief likes to portray. The Communists have been around in France for a long time. Stalin's excesses in the Soviet Union have cooled some of the attraction here in France. But there are other even more radical far-left movements. People are becoming more desperate. Who knows what might happen if things do not change economically."

"And things are much worse in Germany I understand," Fraser said.

"By far. The Weimar Republic cannot even be considered a governing force. Formed after the Armistice of the Great War, it became a caretaker government."

"What do you mean caretaker?" Fraser said.

"Caretaker in the sense that Germany was beaten. The Weimar government was expected to oversee a broken state. Governing has not really been possible with the punitive conditions imposed by the armistice. The Allies had won. Badly depleted, but nonetheless still the victors. The Entente Powers sustained far more casualties than the Central Powers but the Germans still lost. All the combatants were exhausted by the time the United States entered the conflict. Fresh troops. Unlimited materiel."

Fraser said, "That seems the crux of the matter here on the continent. It's about the Great War. Were the conditions imposed on Germany too severe? What's your view? France pushed for the more severe measures against Germany didn't they?"

"Yes they did. Can't blame France though. The Germans annexed the French provinces of Alsace and Lorraine after the Franco-Prussian War. The French felt justified to take it back after the Great War. This attempt at rewriting history by the Germans in order to say they had no choice but to go to war is utter nonsense. The Germans invaded first. Simple as that. Thought they could do again what they did in 1870. March all the way to Paris. But the truth is, with this downturn of the entire world economy, it may end badly for all of Europe. Germany is coming apart. No telling where that will lead."

"The Chief thinks there is real concern about the Communists staging a revolution in Germany like they did in Russia. Then on the other side there is this Hitler fellow. I'm off to Berlin next month to get a closer view."

"Berlin is certainly the center of everything right now. It's crawling with foreign correspondents. The Chief has several there already. The most senior is my colleague Karl von Wie-gand. Look him up first. He'll take good care of you. Been over here in Europe longer than me. Born in Germany. Knows Germany better than anyone.

"I don't envy your task, Fraser. Going to be hard to distinguish your reporting from the clutter of everyone else."

Fraser smiled. How well he knew that. "And what about this Hitler and his right wing nationalist party that seems to be gaining strength?"

"Ah, the National Socialist German Workers Party. In German, the *Nationalsozialistische Deutsche Arbeiterpartei*, the NSDAP for short. Lead by Herr Adolf Hitler. Most troubling to the French. They fear Germany as the real threat, not some Western European Communist revolution like in Russia. A Germany led by a strongman. A new Kaiser. Someone like this Hitler. Look what's happened in Italy. Mussolini started this Fascist movement now he's building a substantial military. This National Socialist German Workers' Party is gaining strength in Germany. A rearmed Fascist Germany is a terrible prospect."

"But Italy was part of the Entente Powers, along with Britain and France in the Great War. Are they now seen as a threat?"

"Who knows? But not like Germany. There you have the festering resentment of war reparations to be paid to France. Italy was not happy with their share of the spoils of the armistice. They wanted a bigger share of territory out of the former Austrian-Hungarian Empire who allied with Germany. Mussolini appears to harbor resentment against the Brits and French for this past injustice dealt the Italians. Mussolini has ambitions for a new Roman empire. Read his articles published in our own newspapers."

"What about the other major powers?" Fraser said.

"Better that you go to Berlin, Rome, London, and maybe Moscow to learn first-hand. I know how the French view things, but I'll give you my take on these others. Let's take the Soviet Union. They're equally at the heart of this turmoil. The bloom is off the rose since the 1917 Revolution. What with Stalin's stupid five-year plan that included collectivization of all agriculture to speed industrialization, the entire Soviet Union is on the verge of some awful famine. Add to that the purge of god knows how many tens of thousands of peasants to force the five-year plan. To keep control, Stalin has created the ultimate police state. On the one hand you have this Western fear of international Communism, but the Soviet Union poses a more direct threat to Germany from the east."

Fraser interjected with, "Which brings into focus the overtures to Stalin by Britain and France."

"Correct. Seems you already have a good understanding of things over here, Mr. Fraser."

"So Italy is then an unknown. What about Spain?"

"Well Spain is not as important economically as these other European powers, but it too is in political chaos. A backward poor country. Dominated by the Catholic Church and wealthy landowners. On the other side are a vigorous Left comprised of Communists, socialists, and anarchists as well as others. Spain had a monarchy until 1923, followed by a military dictatorship that toppled just this year. Things were bad economically in Spain even before the Depression. Spain has now established a so called Second Republic. Spain has lurched all over the political spectrum. It's an ungovernable mess. Fortunately it appears as no military threat to the rest of Europe."

"Sounds a lot like of what's going on in Germany though," Fraser said.

Bertelli reflected for a moment. "Yes, I see what you mean. But to the French, Germany is the real threat. It's about geography and too much bad history between them."

Marc Fraser found himself immediately attracted to the swirl of competing variables. He loved the challenge of complexity. History, economics, political ideologies, virulent nationalism, and personalities were seemingly converging into an array of possible collision vectors. This was analogous to predicting several moves in advance in multiple chess games. Each new event

created different sets of possible strategies with differing proba-
bilities. Heady stuff for a young journalist.

So different to view the situation from the perspective of Europe. He could understand the isolationist attitude in the United
States with years spent in Los Angeles. Partly from the United
States being separated from the political turmoil engulfing Europe and the Far East by two vast oceans. Partly from apathy
bred of preoccupation with domestic issues. Especially hard to
look beyond provincial concerns with most people struggling
economically to just get by with basic life necessities during the
Depression.

Here in Paris an entirely different mood existed from that of
Los Angeles. Anxiety about everything was pervasive. The government of the French Third Republic was struggling to contend
with the threatening forces of the worldwide Depression, competing political ideologies, and of course the perceived military
threat of a resurgent Germany.

Before leaving Paris for Berlin, Fraser had made the rounds
of various European embassies in Paris, interviewing the most
senior career foreign service officers and military attachés. These
officials were typically more candid than the politically appointed ambassadors. Expanding on Bertelli's briefing, it became clear
why Berlin was the center of concern. The rise of this National
Socialist German Workers' Party, now being referred to as the
Nazi Party, stood out as something to be feared if it ever came to
power in control of Germany. As the second largest political
party they already had a significant number of seats in the German parliament. Herr Hitler's publically proclaimed objectives
left little doubt that Germany would become a threat to Europe
if he came into full power.

More than democratic elective success, the Nazis' militaristic
fervor visibly emphasized their objectives. Hundreds of thousands of adherents paraded around in paramilitary uniforms.
The *Sturmabteilung*, the SA, known as Brownshirts, or Stormtroopers wore arm bands with the *Hakenkreuz*, or swastika Nazi
Party insignia. They loved the spectacle of parades. Banners and

flags evocative of medieval pageantry. They also loved violence evidenced by increased attacks against political opponents. The ranks of the Nazi SA were largely populated by the less educated, with substantial numbers of simple thugs that found license to commit violence. Not only France but other countries bordering German had good reason to fear a German-styled Mussolini in the form of Adolf Hitler.

While Fraser would have enjoyed spending more time in Paris, Berlin was the hotbed of news. After all, news was about bad things and what better place of origin for bad things than Germany in 1931.

By June, 1931, having spent three months in Paris, Fraser was ready to step into the snake pit of Berlin. He was already sending dispatches based upon the collective impressions gathered from the diplomatic corps safely positioned from Paris. From here diplomats and businessmen could construct narratives based as much upon their own biases as any real attempt at intellectual explanation of the complex interlocking factors. The only consensus being a geopolitical storm was coming. The Great War of 1914-1918 never completely ended. The Armistice of 1919 only laid the foundations for the current troubles.

From this wide-ranging material Fraser fixed on a style for his weekly filed stories. With all the reporting of dry facts and ever changing opinions from a remote Europe, his reporting read like the beginning of a serialized novel. His writings dealt heavily on the personalities, their backgrounds, their opinions, the origins of what might be their bias. Protagonists and antagonists. These he set against those espousing entirely different opinions. Fraser's objective was to illustrate rather than attempt to tell his American readers what this all meant. Obviously, no one knew where events would lead. It was now time to go to the source of all this foreboding – Berlin.

A good time to leave Paris for at least a few months for personal reasons as well. His attractive cousin Harriet de Rothschild Sauveterre had become more than just kissing kin. From the on-

set she pursued him, getting him into bed at the first opportunity. Harriet was what men fantasized about with French women
and sex. She also had a talent for subterfuge, using a mutually
shared excuse with a married friend having an affair as reasons
for both to account for their overnight absences. It seemed an
arrangement developed before Fraser came on the scene.

Obviously Marc Fraser liked women. To his good fortune,
women found him attractive and interesting. In a bit of self-
appraisal, he realized that he enjoyed more than just random
sexual encounters. While their covert liaisons were a delight of
carnal pleasures, Harriet did not represent a sustainable relationship. Although intelligent and witty, they did not click intellectually. She did not share the same appreciation of the arts as
he did. Her pursuit of a graduate degree in economics pointed to
a career in the family banking business. His talk of European
politics often led to arguments based upon economic theories
she declared outweighed all other factors. He soon realized she
was not broadly read, not open minded, not interested in intellectual discourse. In the long run, they were not good for each
other. Good time to separate.

CHAPTER 8

In June Fraser embarked by rail from Paris' Gare de l'Est headed for Berlin. A twelve-hour trip arriving in the morning. Before walking out to the platform, he looked up at the monumental painting by Albert Herter in the main hall illustrating the departure of French soldiers for the Western Front in the Great War. Prophetic of another such war with Germany?

Wiring ahead, he arranged to meet the senior Hearst correspondent in Berlin, Karl Henry von Wiegand in the bar at the Adlon Hotel for lunch upon his arrival. Fraser had booked a room for an extended period at the Adlon, Berlin's premier hotel. Hearst was generous with his expense account allowances.

Upon arriving at the Lehrter Bahnhof rail station in Berlin Fraser was taken with the marked differences between Berlin and Paris. The short taxi ride the mile to the Adlon gave him a brief glimpse of the oppressively heavy architectural style of the German Republic's capital and the capital of the earlier Duchy of Prussia. This was the seat of historic German militarism. The architecture reflected that sense of solidity, strength, purpose. A seeming contradiction of mood to the freewheeling decadence of sexual freedom, drugs, and avant-garde intellectual adventurism that characterized Berlin during the twenties. Those liberties were now under threat.

The Weimar Republic came about as a result of the Great War. A defeated Germany struggled with the privations inflicted by the aftermath of the war, easily turning to diversions of the spirit. The government of the Republic was far left-leaning in direct contrast to Prussian conservatism that governed prior to the war. Therein lay the foundation of the developing political turmoil.

But the Adlon Hotel did not disappoint. It was not unlike the Ritz in Paris, even to a similarity in the exterior architectural design. Located on the main boulevard Unter den Linden, it stood opposite the imposing Brandenburg Gate. After a shave and a wash-up in his room, Fraser entered the bar to look for Wiegand.

Asking at the bar if Herr Wiegand was present, the bartender pointed to a corner table with a man and woman.

"Herr Wiegand?" Fraser said approaching the table.

"*Ya*. And you must be Herr Fraser," Wiegand said standing up to shake Fraser's hand. "And allow me to introduce Frau Bella Fromm. Frau Fromm is a fellow journalist, a diplomatic correspondent for the German Ullstein papers."

Wiegand was in his late fifties and Fromm probably in her forties. Both were well dressed.

Fromm extended her hand and smiled at Fraser. "So good to make your acquaintance, Herr Fraser. Karl has provided something of your background. I believe you had quite a success in exposing a major corruption scandal in Los Angeles. Several bad officials went to jail I understand. We should be as fortunate here in Germany to be able to clean out the criminals."

"Please, let us adjourn to the dining room and have lunch," Wiegand suggested.

"Please excuse my poor German," Fraser said. "It has been some time since my college years. I read it more fluently. Hope it will improve with use and perhaps my accent will lessen."

"Not at all, Herr Fraser. Your German is entirely adequate," Bella Fromm said giving him a smile.

After the obligatory European pleasantries, Fraser got down to business. "Germany has a rather curious mix of political ideologies at play. The Reichstag is decidedly left-leaning and you have an old guard Prussian general as president, a throwback to the monarchy of the Kaiser. Then of course you have these National Socialists, Mussolini-styled Fascists led by this charismatic leader, Adolf Hitler."

"Yes, it's a witches' brew. I fear it can only end in some broader catastrophe. Let us hope not as cataclysmic as the Great War. That would be the end of Europe," Wiegand said. "At the root of Germany's ills is the dire economic situation. Worse than anywhere else in Europe. Germany has four million unemployed. The hyperinflation and economic collapse after the war had just started to turn around when this worldwide Depression virtually eliminated all access to capital. Economic activity here has slowed to a crawl. Germany is in the throes of a terrible banking crisis. Banks are failing at an alarming rate as people attempt to withdraw their money."

Fromm jumped in with, "And this economic strife has done much worse, Karl. It has given the National Socialists the perfect excuse from which to climb to power."

Fraser said, "We hear about Hitler's anti-Semitic rhetoric in the United States. How's that received?"

Fromm smiled condescendingly. "*Rhetoric*? It is far more, far worse than mere rhetoric. Herr Hitler has tapped into the latent anti-Semitism that apparently exists everywhere, even the United States. But the Nazis have gone much further. It serves Hitler's purpose to give a face to Germany's failings. Provides a rallying cry to recruit his army of thugs, the SA. Do you know the SA now numbers in the hundreds of thousands? Some estimate maybe a million strong. His rants about the nature of this economic depression, the Jews as instrumental in the defeat in 1918, then conspiring with foreign powers to subjugate Germany has swelled their ranks."

"Yes. The SA, the *Sturmabteilung*, Brownshirts they're called. Am I correct?" Fraser said. "How are they connected with the Nazi Party?"

"They're the muscle behind the Nazi Party. A private army," Fromm said. "They dress up like boy scouts in brown uniforms. They go about intimating people but do much worse to Jews. Acts of SA violence are on the rise. The police typically do nothing to intervene. Violence against Jews is unofficially condoned."

"Why? Where does the Nazis' power come from?"

Wiegand said, "Lots of reasons. Fear, victimization. Hitler particularly preaches to the German sense of nationalistic identification. It's a perfect set of circumstances for him. And make no mistake, it is Hitler. There are other prominent Nazis but it is Hitler that is the visible symbol. His speeches rise beyond oratory to something resembling religious fervor."

"If you look beyond the words at his speaking style you see a consummate demagogue," Fromm said. "All is choreographed for affect. He arrives late. Let's the anticipation of the crowd build. Strides to the podium and basks in the applause while saying nothing. When the venue becomes totally silent he starts. At first you can barely hear him as he speaks softly and deliberately standing with his hands placed on the podium. In the middle of his speech his tone rises. He now looks down at his notes sparingly. The words are simple. The sentences short. Inflammatory words are punctuated with emphasis. As he reaches the climax he is nearly yelling, the message becoming ever more virulent. And when in the throes of the heart of his message, he articulates with hand gestures befitting a performance of Hamlet. And his eyes. When you look at the films, the close-ups, it's the eyes you notice. At the end they reveal the wildness of a zealot in the throes of a religious experience like Karl alluded to. It's quite a performance."

"Yes, I've seen a couple of newsreels," Fraser said. "But is this someone that could actually rise to prominence in the government? I've read about his background. Hardly impressive."

Wiegand said, "Neither is Mussolini's background. Now he's the Fascist dictator of Italy. It's conceivable in times such as these."

Fromm said, "And regardless if events eventually lead to another European war, German society will still suffer terribly. I fear there is little hope for German Jews. And Jews represent so much that is vital to German society. I should tell you that I am Jewish so you can consider that perspective when I get off on a rant against the Nazis."

"No need to add a disclaimer, Frau Fromm. I have been briefed by others that have provided similar opinions of this Adolf Hitler and his Nazi Party," Fraser said. "But your perspective as a German journalist experiencing these events from so close is helpful."

"You don't know how close, Mr. Fraser," Wiegand said. "Can you imagine Bella is even on personal terms with an intimate within Adolf Hitler's inner circle?"

"Interesting. For the record, my mother was Jewish. Would that make me Jewish in the eyes of the Nazis?" Fraser said.

Following Wiegand's suggestion, Fraser purchased a copy of Hitler's *Mein Kampf* written while serving a sentence in prison for treason after instigating the abortive Munich Beer Hall Putsch in 1923. Reading it in the span of a week, it proved a ghastly piece of semi-coherent socio-political ramblings. Hitler was not a literary artist but a political pamphleteer. But for all its literary flaws, it clearly laid out the ambitions Adolf Hitler had for a Germany under his control. No question that such control would take the form of a dictatorship. Beyond the anti-Semitic racial nonsense and assignment of blame for Germany's ills since the Great War, the pragmatic political objectives for a resurgent Germany are clearly spelled out. Apparently others were discounting these grandiose schemes as unrealistic rhetoric designed to win support from a disaffected population. Many simply marginalizing Hitler. After all he was only a low ranking soldier in the war, a failed artist, a one-time derelict in Vienna, a non-intellectual with a talent only for oratory.

From the hard facts, Hitler and his National Socialist Democratic party, the Nazis, were not going away. They already held eighteen percent of the seats in the Reichstag parliament from the 1930 elections. Nazi membership was reputed to be close to two hundred thousand. Behind them was a paramilitary-organized cadre of hundreds of thousands of uniformed marching thugs, several times larger than the regular Wehrmacht German military forces. In the presidential elections just a couple of months prior, the old general Paul von Hindenburg was elected President. Adolf Hitler came in second in the voting. The Nazis were not going away. Furthermore, Adolf Hitler was the Nazi Party.

Mein Kampf made Hitler's ambitions for Germany clear. Amongst the autobiographical drivel and the various racial polemics toward Jews and Slavs were very clear pragmatic policies that threatened all of Europe. Two themes dominated Adolf Hitler's vision for Germany. The first was to rid itself of the onerous terms of the Treaty of Versailles of 1919 that set out crippling restrictions on Germany. War reparations, as pressed aggressively by France, injured an already war- weakened German economy. Failure to maintain these payments led to France and Belgium occupying the resource-rich Ruhr Valley in the early 1920s in retaliation.

Under the terms of the treaty, Germany was also severely restricted as to the strength of its armed forces. The German military was to be reduced to substantial inferiority relative to the victorious French and British. The army was limited to only 100,000 troops. The General Staff dissolved. Offensive weaponry was prohibited. The navy dismantled.

The second theme articulated by Hitler involved territory. The treaty stripped Germany of 25,000 square miles of territory, populated by 7,000,000 people. The Treaty demilitarized the German Rhineland and Saar regions. To compensate for destruction of French coal mines, the output of the Saar mines was ceded to France. Belgium acquired sovereignty over the Eupen-Malmedy area. Czechoslovakia became independent including the heavily ethnic German population of the Sudetenland region. Portions of Upper Silesia were ceded to Poland. German colonial protectorates were granted their independence.

The dominating tone to Adolf Hitler's political platform was German nationalism. Nationalism in the most extreme. Throughout *Mein Kampf* and reinforced in his speeches, the Germanic people were held to be a superior race. A race therefore with special entitlements. A race that had been unfairly disenfranchised by criminals, envious other nations, Communism, and sub-races in the form of Jews and Slavs. It was a Wagnerian form of German nationalism, a mystical Teutonic fable.

Hitler's philosophy was routed in a fundamentalist Darwinian view applied to mankind. Survival of the fittest among races applied not only to the lower species but to man as well. A continual competing for space and wealth among races. His demented rationalization placed Jews as a non-race. The Jews were antithetical to this natural process of racial competition. The Jew therefore corrupted the process whereby through their unnatural manipulation the weakest might dominate the fittest.

To Hitler's perverted logic this holistic philosophy perfectly justified his promoting a racially justified territorial expansionist Germany, *Lebensraum,* along with the repression of Jews.

Fraser's journalistic approach in the face of so many American correspondents reporting from Germany was to give his readers a sense of place, people, and what life was like in these foreign places. That meant interviewing less obvious public figures yet still people of importance. These would include the intellectual and scientific community, artists, businessmen, both critics and supporters of the Nazis. And of course Jews of all walks of life since they were becoming the focus of hostility of the Nazis and their uniformed SA thugs.

Fraser planned to work those sources over the remaining months of 1931 to flesh out a compelling narrative of what it was like to be German, why Germany was the focus of so much concern for Europe. He would then venture to other countries to explore their respective views on a resurgent Germany. That meant London, Rome and Moscow. Once he completed that itinerary, he would return to Paris to reassess the depth of French concerns against their historic enemy.

The French had good reason to mistrust Germany. In 1870, the North German Confederation led by the Kingdom of Prussia successfully invaded the northern portion of France. In what became known as the Franco-Prussian War the German military overwhelmed French forces in a war lasting less than one year. Eventually laying siege to Paris, the French were forced into agreeing to an armistice. An armistice that was signed in Versailles with France forced to pay war reparations, along with ceding the border region of Alsace-Lorraine. Then came the twentieth century horror of the Great War in 1914.

Again France was invaded by Germany but this time with a different outcome. Four years of unprecedented carnage in a war of attrition fought from defensive trenches on the Western Front. Although more fluid, the Eastern Front ranging over a large area was equally brutal. The poorly equipped poorly led Russian troops suffered disproportionate casualty rates to the Germans and Austrians. The carnage was appalling in both theaters of the war. Casualties ran into the millions. An entire generation of French and German manhood was decimated.

Both countries along with Great Britain were economically crippled. In Russia the last Romanoff Tsar was deposed before war's end and replaced with a Bolshevik Communist government. With all the European warring nations exhausted, the war was brought to conclusion only because of United States intervention on the side of France and Britain. The French then took their revenge on Germany at the Treaty of Versailles in 1919.

The legacy of the Great War had metastasized into a new European malignancy by 1931.

CHAPTER 9

Within several weeks of arriving in Berlin, Fraser had learned as much about the German political situation as any of the longer-term foreign correspondents. It was now time to set about an interview schedule of a cross section of German society to paint his more humanized reporting for the American public. However, this did not mean talking to the average person on the street in some adhoc-type opinion poll. This wasn't a research project. He was just reporting news colored with his interpretation for daily publication of current events. His byline was titled *Notes and Pictures from an American in Europe.* A thoroughly vacuous title contrived by an unimaginative editor.

Fraser would set out to target businessmen, religious leaders, scientists, artists, generally avoiding the more well-covered political figures. If the Nazis were to come to power, it would largely come from votes from the working class but it was the German middle class that formed the framework of German society. Yet he still had to find a niche to differentiate his writing from the many well regarded American foreign correspondents reporting from Berlin. And of course produce interesting photographs. Even if the material did not make for compelling reading he could still attract attention with interesting photos.

How did Christian religious leaders view the Nazi Party? What was their position on anti-Semitism? Germany was an overwhelmingly Christian country split two-thirds Protestant with the remaining third Roman Catholic. Jews represented less than one percent of the population.

Fraser's research suggested a fairly widespread sympathy among the Protestant denominations, principally the largest, the German Evangelical Church, for a tradition grounded in loyalty to the state. Here too was an historic anti-Semitic undercurrent that embraced many of the racial aspects of Nazi ideology. From the 1920 Nazi Party platform, article 24 read:

'We demand freedom of religion for all religious denominations within the state so long as they do not endanger its existence or oppose the moral senses of the Germanic race. The Party as such advocates the standpoint of a positive Christianity without binding itself confessionally to any one denomination. It combats the Jewish-materialistic spirit within and around us, and is convinced that a lasting recovery of our nation can only succeed from within on the framework: The good of the state before the good of the individual.'

Many Christians took this as a positive jester toward Christianity, ignoring the slander to Jews. So Fraser went to look for a Protestant member of the clergy. After making inquiries it was easy to settle on someone of interest. By his background, Lutheran Minister Martin Niemöller came to his ministry by a most unusual background. Born into a conservative Prussian family, his father a Lutheran pastor, he pursued a military career as a U-boat commander during the Great War. For distinguished combat service Niemöller was awarded the Iron Cross First Class.

Fraser met him at his rectory office in the Berlin suburb of Dahlem. A modest man of medium stature maybe ten years older than Fraser, hair beginning to thin, glasses.

"I fear not only the socialist policies of the current government but their lack of leadership," Niemöller said. "In these times of economic hardship they are a disgrace to Germany. I come from a conservative background and am ardently opposed to the socialists. Communists are an even worse danger. Their allegiance is not to Germany."

"Are you in agreement with the National Socialists? Specially Adolf Hitler's views on not complying with the provisions of the Treaty of Versailles?"

"Completely. The Treaty is an abomination that has unfairly punished Germany. Architected by the French. Continuing under those burdens will eventually lead to another military conflict. Germany will not suffer indefinitely."

"Who do you feel was responsible for the Great War?"

"The answer to that is complicated. Since Germany was defeated it is easy for the world to accuse Germany of responsibility. It even forced that acknowledgement from Germany in the Treaty of Versailles. The same as a forced confession."

"But since Germany invaded Belgium, didn't she strike the first blow?"

Niemöller clinched his jaw before responding, "The first conflict perhaps, but not the start of the war. The rest of the world forgets the circumstances that preceded the clash on the Western Front."

"So you are arguing that Germany was justified in attacking Belgium?"

Niemöller paused before answering. His demeanor suggested he was wrestling with an awkward intellectual argument.

"Herr Fraser, the circumstances that led to the hostilities were complex. International alliances escalated beyond controls of governments. Events in Sarajevo caused a cascade of unfortunate events."

"At the least do you see Germany equally responsible?"

"Herr Fraser, I am not going to debate history with you. Let me state my position in direct terms. Germany was threatened by France. Old antagonisms. France and Britain colluded in an effort to diminish Germany. Their alliance with Russia left Germany surrounded by hostile states. The assassination of the Archduke of the Austrian-Hungarian Empire was just the spark to set loose latent hostilities. To your question, Serbia was to blame for the Great War."

"You're speaking of the interconnecting alliances of military support? The assassination in Sarajevo did not need to escalate into a broad European conflict. It was still Germany that first acted with aggression."

"I do not agree. Germany acted preemptively for its security. To you the war is what is portrayed by the victors. I lived that time. I fought for Germany in a just war to protect our national interests against the increasing threat by other countries. Events following the assassination in Sarajevo made those threats immediate. Russia mobilized. France and Britain threatened by backing Russia. Germany was under a gun."

No point in pursuing an argument about the past war that ended thirteen years ago. Fraser's interest was the near-term future of Germany.

"What about the Nazis' racial policies, particularly related to Jews?"

Niemöller took a deep breath and sat forward in his chair. Obviously considering his response carefully it was several moments before he answered.

"In unequivocal terms I do not agree with their so-called Aryan racial policies. It is entirely un-Christian. German Jews present no threat to Germany. They are just as much German as anyone. So while I see the National Socialist political agenda as positive for the future of Germany, I cannot support their social views."

"But if they come to power, which might be a real possibility, won't their repressive social policies be put into practice?"

Niemöller again hesitated. "I would hope not. Politicians say outrageous things to get votes. The National Socialists need to make strong impressions to win popular support. Regrettably they play on latent anti-Semitic prejudices. Although Jews are a small minority in Germany they occupy many important positions in German life. Business, banking, science. The list of prominent Jewish Germans is just as important today as in German history. While the prejudice cannot be eliminated, it is simply not possible to rid German society of Jews as Herr Hitler advocates."

At least here was a German that could separate the demented racial rantings of the Nazis from the pragmatic business of economics and foreign affairs.

The Catholic Church was inherently more suspicious of National Socialism. German nationalism was not as deeply embedded in the Catholic culture. Certain Nazi leaders were also rabidly anti-Catholic. So Fraser assumed at least a critical assessment from the Apostolic Nuncio in Berlin, Archbishop Cesare Orsenigo. He was also close to the former Italian Cardinal Achille Ratti before Ratti was elevated to Pope Pius XI.

Fraser said, "The United States has a large Roman Catholic population so the Church's views on the political turmoil existing here in Germany is important to Americans. Your Excellency, from the Holy See's perspective how is the emergence of this ultra-right National Socialist Party, the Nazi Party, viewed?"

Speaking in excellent German, the Italian prelate said, "Viewed? The Church strives to rise above the secular arena of politics. With the world's Catholics spread amongst so many countries their secular lives are dictated by all manner of governing systems. The Holy See however attempts to use the Church's influence wherever possible to promote social reforms and justice. The Church cannot be seen as competing politically with governments."

A diplomatic non-answer. And the Church itself is a monolithic, absolute monarchy not given to any form of democratic process Fraser thought to himself. The Nuncio was reputed to be a diplomat with sympathies to Italian Fascism therefore inherently receptive to the Nazi brand. Perhaps Orsenigo's views were not surprising since his mentor the current Pope Pius XI had architected a rapprochement with Benito Mussolini's Fascist government of Italy. Maybe Orsenigo could arrange an audience for Fraser with the Pope?

"The National Socialists could easily come into power in the near future. Is that good for Germany?"

Considering the question carefully for a moment before answering, Orsenigo said, "I would not be the best judge of that. I would offer that the increasing appeal of the National Socialists to the population stems from offering a renewed sense of national pride. In fairness to the current government though, these economic problems being experienced worldwide make governing difficult. Every country, including the United States, is in difficult economic straits."

More non-committal diplomatic evasion.

"And would you agree with Herr Hitler that the terms of Treaty of Versailles must be eliminated?"

"In hindsight, the punitive measures of war reparations and the loss of German territories with important resources are inhibiting German prosperity. In so doing those victorious countries are creating a more antagonistic Germany, a more dangerous Europe."

"And what is the Vatican's position on the Nazis' virulent anti-Semitism?"

"The Church abhors the persecution of any group. Unfortunately anti-Semitism has a long history in Europe. These latent hatreds need little encouragement to come to the forefront."

"Some would even say the Catholic Church itself is anti-Semitic."

By his expression Orsenigo was clearly not pleased with this comment.

"Certainly not as part of any official Church doctrine. But let me be frank, Herr Fraser. Judaism sets itself apart from Christian tenants therefore frictions will naturally develop.

"The Jewish fundamental belief in what we recognize as the same God takes a very different path. Obviously Jews do not believe in the divinity of Jesus Christ, nor the resurrection. This is basic to Christians by representing the cleansing of one's sins for entry into heaven. The Old Testament, the foundation of the

Jewish faith, deals very sparingly with the afterlife. Perhaps this is why Jews seem more preoccupied with present life."

Orsenigo's guarded ambivalence to the Nazis extreme anti-Semitism was perhaps expected as a diplomatic representative of the Pope. But the clergyman went even further.

"Historically Jews have set themselves apart from other cultural groups. Admittedly as a race they have been economically successful. This often provokes the un-Christian response of jealousy but nonetheless it further isolates the Jews. Their success in business, banking, and the arts, areas that so fundamentally effect cultural life, makes non-Jews apprehensive."

Race? Even this educated intellectual views Jews as a race as if they can be identified by some biological distinction. His rationalizations border on Adolf Hitler's own interruptions in *Mein Kampf* of why Judaism threatens the natural order of racial competition.

Two Christian clerics with unexpected viewpoints. A lesson to avoid stereotyping. The real world is always more gray than black and white. Both clerics seemed to ignore the plain fact that religion of any stripe runs counter to the tenants of the Nazi Party. Under National Socialism all social discourse was directed toward the state. German nationalism was everything to the point of mysticism that replaced conventional religion.

While intrigued with being in Europe at center stage of events that might shape world events, this business of foreign reporting was decidedly different from the investigative journalism that had formed his career. Not likely that he would dig out a headline breaking story in Europe as he had done in Los Angeles. The interviews with the two religious leaders were revealing but would still make only boring copy. Interviews with these types of influential people would not yield the material that would form his narrative of how the average German felt about these larger controversies. He had to be more creative to sell newspaper back in America.

Movies. Of course. He would start there next. German film-making was perhaps second only to Hollywood. Well received even in America. Several German stars like Marlene Dietrich were now international celebrities. With his MGM connections, it would be easy to get inside the German filmmaking industry. Americans would inherently be interested in the views of German movie stars and filmmakers.

A quick reply by telegram from his former boss at MGM's publicity department provided several names. One name was familiar to Fraser, a producer named Harry Sokal with his own production company HR Sokal-Film GmbH right here in Berlin. Fraser recalled his father talking about the spectacular alpine background films produced by Sokal and directed by Arnold Fanck. Fraser knew the movies his father was referring to. The MGM cinematographer that introduced him to photography had shown him a couple of Fanck's movies to illustrate the striking impact of cinematography. But it was the pretty female star that captivated Fraser at the time. Her name was Leni Riefenstahl.

Since he had arrived in Berlin, his excursions by public tram were mostly around the city center. Besides being an uninspiring city architecturally, evidence of the economic depression added to a somber mood. People moved about with downcast expressions. Long lines for food handouts were a common sight. A foreigner felt guilty eating a good meal imagining the envy of even the waiters. The impression seemed of utter despair. There was little conversation as people queued for just a meager ration of bread.

The location of Sokal's studio was in a Berlin industrial area. It would be Fraser's first venture further afield. Once the taxi left the city center, Fraser got a sense for the origin of the depression. It appeared as if half of the industrial buildings were shuttered. For those still operating, signs posted on closed gates read *keine arbeit verfügbar*, no work available. Unemployment was far worse here than in the United States or France.

Sokal's studio was housed in a warehouse building with an attached office building. Fraser assumed the high-bay warehousing building probably served as sound stages. The surrounding buildings appeared to be warehouses. The neighborhood was probably relatively quiet therefore conducive to filming with adequate soundproofing in this new age of sound production.

Harry Sokal greeted Fraser warmly. Yes of course he remembered Fraser's father. So sorry to hear of his passing. Sokal explained that he met Douglas Fraser in Los Angeles a couple of years ago while trying to put together a joint project that never developed. Sokal was distinguished looking, older than Fraser, perfectly fitting into the Hollywood look with open shirt, scarf, dark blazer, with light colored slacks.

"I have seen your alpine films, Herr Sokal. Spectacular cinematography. I worked for a brief time at MGM. A friend at the studio introduced me to your work. I was hoping to also interview your director Arnold Fanck and maybe your star actress, Leni Riefenstahl."

Sokal smiled. "You are in luck, Herr Fraser. Both are here in the studio today. They are working on the editing of our newest film, *Der Weisse Rausch, The White Ecstasy*. We completed filming in April. Looking to release it by year end. We shall all have lunch together."

What a stroke of luck. He would actually get to meet Riefenstahl. Her film images were vivid in his mind. That face, the penetrating eyes of course, the gorgeous legs. Some women have an inexplicable effect on a man. Now he would see if her film image held the same attraction in the flesh.

"Excellent. I would enjoy that very much, Herr Sokal. Even though my pieces are not entertainment features, perhaps I can make helpful references to your new movie. I assume it will be released in the United States?"

"Oh yes, most definitely. I fear that I might have to consider even working abroad if things continue to worsen here. Hollywood would be my first choice."

"Worsen in what why, Herr Sokal? You mean the difficult economy?"

"That is certainly bad enough but movies are still doing well. Escapism from hardship perhaps. But no, I mean if the National Socialists come fully into power. You see, I am Jewish. Already there are difficulties. Herr Hitler has left no doubt about his feelings about Jews. To the Nazis it is not just historic German anti-Semitism. Hitler advocates what sounds like the destruction of all Jews in Germany. We are to be gone or maybe even killed."

"But do you actually think it would come to that if the Nazis came to power?"

"I think it is possible. If it should come to that it may then be too late for a Jew to escape. One cannot just immediately abandon one's home and livelihood."

"The National Socialists have the second most seats in the Reichstag. What would constitute them coming into full power as you put it?"

"I am no expert on politics but it is obvious that the parliament does not run affairs in Germany. It is the President and his appointed Chancellor. So if the Nazis gain more seats in the next election, who knows? Right now Chancellor Brüning heads only a minority coalition. That means the real power lies with President Hindenburg. He is too old to last that much longer. If Adolf Hitler were to ever become Chancellor then I fear that would be the end for German Jews."

Sokal escorted Fraser to the small viewing theater at the end of the office area. As they entered the darkened viewing room, a close-up shot of Riefenstahl dominated the screen. A man turned from his seat to see who entered leaving the door open with light streaming into the room. Seeing Sokal, he turned off the projector and switched on the room lights.

As the lights came on Fraser looked at the real Leni Riefenstahl now turned in her chair.

"Leni, Arnold, let me introduce Herr Marc Fraser. He is a correspondent for Hearst Publications from the United States. I knew Herr Fraser's father from Metro Goldwyn Meyer in Hollywood."

Fraser shook the director Arnold Fanck's hand first since he was nearest. Riefenstahl rose from her seat. She was wearing a tailored ivory-colored silk blouse with dark gray slacks. Her hair was styled yet still with a wild look much like in some of her film roles. Fraser was immediately seduced. It was Riefenstahl's deep expressive hazel eyes that drew him in.

"I am delighted to meet you, Fräulein Riefenstahl. I have seen several of your movies. Quite taken with your extraordinary athleticism. Filming those scenes must have been arduous."

"Yes they were. Arnold is a demanding director. But the mountain scenery he captures is truly spectacular," Riefenstahl said. She was still holding Fraser's hand.

A grinning Fraser let go her hand and turned to Fanck. "That is certainly so. The friend at MGM that introduced me to your work is a cinematographer by the name of Clyde De Vinna. Highly praises your work. Perhaps you know his name."

"Of course. He won the academy award for cinematography for *White Shadows in the South Seas* a couple of years ago. I have also been privileged to work with a number of excellent cinematographers. They have developed innovative techniques for working in the mountains under difficult filming conditions."

"Clyde also taught me photography. As a journalist it has proven a helpful tool. Might I take a couple of photos of each of you for publication?"

Fraser took several shots of all three filmmakers with his Leica, getting a couple of close-ups of Riefenstahl. Sokal then suggested they depart for lunch. Fraser could continue his interview over wine.

Lunch stretched over two hours and a couple of bottles of wine. Although Fraser was distracted by Riefenstahl he still managed to ask questions about Fanck's and Riefenstahl's views on the political questions raised by Hitler's National Socialist Party's growing influence.

"I make movies. Politicians are a disgusting lot," Arnold Fanck said. "These Nazis are particularly a bad lot. Herr Hitler is perhaps a good actor but these Brownshirt SA are a bunch of mad dogs. Hitler just wants power."

"And how do you feel about the Nazis extreme views on Jews?" Fraser said to Fanck.

Fanck was dismissive. "Well, just so much talk to gain votes. Jews are a minority so he doesn't have to curry their support. Better to make them the enemy and capture votes from those that have always hated the Jews."

"Easy for you to dismiss that threat, Arnold since you're not Jewish," Sokal said.

Fraser turned to Riefenstahl, "And your views on Adolph Hitler and his political party, Fräulein Riefenstahl?"

"I'm even less political than Arnold. Each political party paints the others as villains that will destroy Germany if they come to power. Germany isn't doing very good with the current government. Hard to see things much worse if there should be a change. Besides, much of Germany's economic problems are caused by other countries. Isn't this terrible depression caused by the Wall Street Crash in New York?"

"And how do you feel about the Jews?"

"I have nothing against Jews. Harry is Jewish. It doesn't matter. I agree with Arnold that all of Hitler's talk about the Jews is political nonsense to win votes."

Harry Sokal shook his head. "You both miss the point. If the Nazis come to power they will persecute the Jews. If they succeed then there is no reason they will not attempt to control everything. Industry, newspapers, films. Listen to Hitler's words. He wants to be a dictator. We'll have something just as bad as Russia with Stalin. Absolute power is the same no matter what the name."

To change the subject, Riefenstahl said, "I am also interested in photography, Herr Fraser. I would like someday to work on the other side of the camera. Arnold is teaching me the techniques of editing. Taking all the raw film footage and constructing it into a movie is like a sculptor molding a block of clay. It's the difference between capturing pretty scenes and creating an artistic work."

"Same for still photography," Fraser said. "Some shots are just images. Others are art. As in motion pictures it's about angles, composition, and of course lighting effects. Even news photos can be more interesting with artistic technique."

Riefenstahl held her eyes on Fraser for several moments accompanied with a small smile.

The next day, Fraser's phone rang early in the morning.

"Herr Fraser, this is Leni Riefenstahl. Hope I am not disturbing you?"

"Not at all," he said disguising his delight.

"I wanted to call and tell you how much I enjoyed meeting you yesterday. As I said, I am becoming more deeply interested in the cinematography side of filmmaking. At some time in the not too distant future, I will no longer have the youth to play a leading actress. Need to look to the future."

"That will certainly be a long time off, Fräulein Riefenstahl."

"Nonetheless, I am intrigued more by the art of filmmaking from behind the camera. If I may be so bold I would like to discuss photography with you. It seems we both share that interest parallel to our other work. Perhaps you are free for lunch?"

He wasn't but he would change that.

"Absolutely. I'd love that, Fräulein Riefenstahl."

"Wonderful. I shall meet you at your hotel at noon. The Adlon I believe you said. And please, call me Leni."

Fraser was waiting in the hotel lobby like a nervous suitor. Sharply at noon, Riefenstahl walked into the lobby. She looked even better than on screen. Dressed in cashmere overcoat with fur collar, she wore a matching beret-style fur hat. She was wearing a skirt with heels. Once she removed her overcoat, Fraser looked at a daringly low-cut blouse. A gold chain hung down drawing the eye to her cleavage.

Over a bottle of chilled white wine, they chatted mostly about their respective backgrounds, filmmaking, eventually coming around to photography. Fraser was enthralled by her recounting her evolution from dancer to actress. And not only acting but the rugged physical demands of learning to mountain climb without stunt doubles. For her part, she was more enthused about her editing work, and a personal new film project.

She was about to leave for a shoot on location in the mountains of northeastern Italy where she would make her directorial debut as well as star in the movie. It would also be the first movie with sound filmed entirely on location in rugged terrain.

Riefenstahl was interested in both his insider Hollywood stories as well as their shared interest in the artistic aspects of photography. He explained how he had come to using the small Leica camera, compensating for no artificial flash lighting by manipulating exposure settings. That forced him to consider every aspect of light, exposure settings, shadow, and angle. Riefenstahl was genuinely intrigued asking technical questions.

"And besides photographs for newspapers, you said you do artistic photography. What kind of subject matter, Marc?"

By now they were Marc and Leni. Both sensed a strong physical attraction.

"Two subjects particularly interest me. Architectural shots. Not just famous buildings but buildings with character. Especially if I can do something interesting with the light. Even the most mundane subject can yield interesting art."

"So manmade subjects rather than landscapes, spectacular scenery, that sort of thing?"

"I guess. Never thought of it that way."

"And the other subject?"

Fraser hesitated a moment before answering, unsure of Riefenstahl's possible reaction. "The female form. Again it's all about light, shadows, angles."

Riefenstahl smiled. "Interesting. Do you mean capturing women in various natural settings, or like models in fashion photography?"

He shook his head. "No not that. That's to show the fashion. I want to show the female form artistically. Create impression, even be provocative."

Riefenstahl smiled even more mischievously. "Marc, are you saying you photograph women in the nude?"

He sheepishly acknowledged yes with a nod of his head.

"Now that is *interesting*. Is your work any good?"

"Every artist thinks so. Do you think you're a good actress?"

"Now don't change the subject. Let's get back to your naked women. Where do you recruit your subjects?"

"Well, as circumstances just arise I guess. Some women enjoy seeing themselves portrayed in an artistic manner."

"These are girlfriends?"

"Some have been but others just friends. It really is about the art not sex."

It did not matter to Riefenstahl. She too saw art in the human form. But this wasn't about art at the moment. She was attracted to this handsome American.

"Would you like to photograph me, Marc? In the nude?"

Fraser swallowed then answered, "Very much. I have admired you from afar. Your athletic body would make a remarkable subject."

"I have never posed in the nude before."

"Well, it's all somewhat clinical. Just like going to the doctor."

"My doctor is a woman, not a handsome man."

Fraser did not know what to say. The thought of a naked Riefenstahl was already consuming his thoughts.

Riefenstahl stared into his eyes. "Then let's do it. Right now. In your room. What do you say?"

Fraser hurriedly laid money on the table not waiting for the bill.

Once in the room, Riefenstahl said teasingly, "Ok, Herr Director, what should I do as your model?"

Thinking of soon seeing a naked Leni Riefenstahl distracted his thoughts from setting the improvised shoot. First of course was to create the lighting for effect.

"Bear with me. I need to stage how to capture you. Ah, the light coming through that window. That offers some dramatic possibilities."

He pulled the sheer curtains to diffuse the bright sunlight. Then he pulled the heavier opaque curtains to narrow the stream of light. With the room lights off, he now could photograph from the shadows into the light. He then positioned Riefenstahl. Yes. Standing, the sunlight was catching her hair just right. Before he could find a tactful way of telling her to remove her clothing, she preempted him.

"Yes, I see what you are arranging. Should I now remove my clothes?"

He nodded. He was distractedly aroused as she removed first her skirt, followed by her slip. Proceeding to remove the fasteners on the garter belt securing the nylons, he said, "Wait. Leave the stockings on for the moment."

"The blouse?"

"Yes. Remove it."

After removing the blouse, she said, "And this?" touching her brassiere.

He nodded.

She disconnected her bra and slowly lowered it exposing her breasts. "And now?"

"Put the blouse back on but do not button it. It's sheer enough that the light will come through."

Positioning himself behind her, he dropped to one knee. Turning her slightly, he could capture the outline of her body including her left breast with the light filtered through the blouse. Then he posed her with one foot raised onto an ottoman.

He captured her from different angles using various camera settings for a range of effects.

Now he would move on to full nude shots.

"Now you can remove everything. Leave just the heels and the necklace."

After twenty minutes of posing not only standing by the window lighting, but in a chair with her legs draped over the arm, another with her knee raised onto the small table showing off her shapely legs and athletic behind, he had exhausted his ideas for staging poses. All the while she was asking a stream of technical questions to understand what he was trying to achieve. Throughout he was becoming increasingly aroused.

Riefenstahl came over to the bed and sat down. Making no move to put her clothes back on, she motioned him over toward her with a finger.

Standing in front of her she pulled him closer by grabbing his pants by the waist. He bent down and kissed her.

As he began unbuttoning his shirt she said, "Let me help."

His erection was clearly visible through his trousers. She touched him then unbuckled his belt. As she unbuttoned his fly the touch of her fingers only increased his state of arousal.

She dropped his trousers then pulled down his underwear.

"Now that is a pretty sight. Certainly would make an interesting picture.

She grabbed his cock pulling him toward her then took him fully into her mouth.

Minutes later sensing he could not take much more she pulled back onto the bed. "Now maybe you would like to reciprocate to get me to the same state of arousal although I'm already very wet."

The afternoon was an endless round of sexual exploration. Hungry later, room service delivered a bottle of Taittinger champagne in an ice bucket along with imported French foie gras, Russian caviar, and toast. The Adlon had no food shortage for those that paid well in foreign currency.

It proved not only an afternoon of sexual delight with the attractive Fräulein Riefenstahl, but another lovemaking session followed after dinner. She didn't leave until the following morning.

CHAPTER 10

His affair with Leni Riefenstahl was intense but brief. For the next two weeks neither did any real work. Champagne lunches were typically followed by afternoons of lovemaking. Dinner together every night often followed by late into the morning partying at what remained of the decadent Berlin cabaret scene. But then Riefenstahl declared she must leave for the Dolomites, the mountain range of northeastern Italy, to begin shooting her next film, *Das Blaue Licht, The Blue Light.* Since she was also directing the movie, she chastised him for seducing her away from doing proper last minute preparations.

Fraser had also neglected his reporting. They separated with her off to the mountains in Italy and him heading south to the German state of Bavaria. His first destination was to be the architecturally interesting old city of Nuremberg then on to Munich. Both held special significance to the National Socialist German Workers' Party. The movement was born in Munich, coming to national prominence with Adolf Hitler's abortive coup attempt in 1923 labelled later as the *Beer Hall Putsch.* Nuremberg was the ancient seat of power of the Holy Roman Empire. This thousand-year, Middle Ages Germanic empire was the ideological basis for Adolf Hitler's National Socialists' envisioned next Germanic empire the Third Reich.

Just as well that both he and Riefenstahl had professional demands that forced a return to reality after their interlude of debauchery. Once she left, he was glad for the opportunity to leave drab Berlin.

Arriving by train in Nuremberg, he was hoping for a more interesting architectural experience. His first impression was encouraging after exited the rail station. This now was an interesting city. The buildings and waterways reminded him of Amsterdam. Old Germany. A setting for a Wagnerian opera. Nuremberg had charm to rival any in Europe. His hotel room was something out of the Belle Époque era.

For the next several days Fraser set about interviewing local businessmen, clergy, and even a women's literary group. Little of the avant-garde evident here in Bavaria. This was southern Germany steeped in historic Germanic tradition. Conservative. The consensus of all those he interviewed was contempt for the left-leaning Weimar Republic's Reichstag, the German parliament. There was overwhelming support of traditional German values. France was universally despised. To their thinking, the Great War was forced on Germany by France allied with Britain and Russia. The oft articulated view that a surrounded Germany was forced to fight for its very sovereignty. France continued to repress Germany. Right-wing political parties found a receptive populace here in Bavaria. That included Adolf Hitler's *Nationalsozialistische Deutsche Arbeiterpartei*, the NSDAP, in English slang the Nazi Party.

Nuremberg was a pretty place but Fraser was tiring of the oppressive feeling pervading Germany. Germans were markedly angry. Angry at their government, angry about the Depression. Blamed everything on outsiders. Particularly antagonistic toward their old enemy the French. Since Fraser thought himself as French out of heritage as well as a love of France, it was difficult to continually hear invectives directed toward the French.

After a week in Nuremberg, Fraser took the train further south to Munich. This is where Adolf Hitler and his National Socialist German Workers' Party came to national attention ten years earlier in the ill-fated *Beer Hall Putsch*. It was a premature, ridiculously ill-conceived maneuver to declare Bavaria to be under their control. Hitler had certainly come a long way from those old days of street brawling.

Hitler survived the violence of that day following his proclamation in the beer hall in 1923. Sixteen of his fellow conspirators died in a march when confronted with Bavarian troops. Arrested for treason, he then survived a trial with only a light prison sentence imposed. That in turn was truncated after serving only nine months. During his time in Landsberg Prison Hitler drafted his political polemic *Mein Kampf*. The debacle provided a mystical basis for the Nazis.

Fraser's first stop was where it all began, the large beer hall known as the Bürgerbräukeller. It was located on the east side of the Isar River on Rosenheimer Street. Fraser knew it was not the type of drinking establishment found in the United States or for that matter most anywhere. Like all drinking places around the world, these served as places of social gathering but German beer halls were often on a different scale.

The Bürgerbräukeller was a vast hall capable of seating a couple of thousand drinkers. More an auditorium. Long wooden tables with benches allowed the convivial Germans to sit butt to butt as they quaffed large steins of beer delivered by buxom waitresses with arms like wrestlers.

After settling into his hotel he walked to the Bürgerbräukeller mid-afternoon. He wanted to take photos both inside and outside before dark. Being Saturday, the evening should prove lively with weekend drinkers. Good way to get comments by buying a few beers. Maybe he could find a few people that were here that night in November, 1923 when 600 Brownshirts, the *Sturmabteilung*, the SA surrounded the beer hall. Inside, the Bavarian Prime Minister, Gustav Kahr was addressing 3000 businessmen at the Bürgerbräukeller. Hitler's screwball plot was to take over Munich then use it as a power base from which to launch a take-over of the German government in Berlin.

Entering the beer hall, Fraser sought out the manager to explain who he was. Large numbers of Americans of German descent would be interested in his famous establishment. Provide a sense of their heritage.

"*Ya, ya.* Most happy to be of service, Herr Fraser. I was here that night in 1923 you know. I was chief barman at the time," the manager said motioning Fraser to a table and signaling a waitress.

"The SA Brownshirts came in from the back and lined up along both these walls," the manager said pointing down the vast hall. "Some had guns. Led personally by Ernst Röhm."

A waitress brought two steins of beer and a bowl of pretzels.

"Then Herr Hitler took the speaker's platform. A couple of SA troopers pushed the Prime Minister away. To gain silence Hitler fired a shot into the ceiling then jumped on a chair and yelled *the national revolution has broken out. The hall is surrounded.*"

"Then what happened," Fraser asked.

"Nothing much. Hitler and Röhm ushered the Bavarian Prime Minister, the Bavarian police chief, and the local army commander off into a side room. The SA stood guard in the hall but the businessmen raised a hell of fuss. About ten minutes after leaving the hall Hitler returned.

"Hitler spoke, nearly yelling. According to him the coup was complete. Bavaria was in the hands of the National Socialists backed by his personal army of SA."

"But all that changed the next day I understand."

"Ah yes. I was not at the march. Had to work that day since it was Friday, always a busy night to prepare for. Hitler's march, even with old General Ludendorff alongside, turned out badly for the National Socialists. Sixteen were killed by the police and army. Seems that the Prime Minister didn't honor whatever Hitler thought he had agreed to. Hitler was arrested and charged with treason."

"Do you support Hitler and the National Socialists now?"

"Wholeheartedly. Adolf Hitler is the only one that can restore Germany. Didn't see it that way back in 1923 though.

Thought they were just another political party. Then Hitler went to prison. Should have been the end of him yet now look how far he has come. It is destiny that he should come to power. Restore German power."

"Some would say that would be at great expense. Hitler's distain for parliamentary process would mean personal liberties would be curtailed. And for German Jews, much worse," Fraser said.

"Herr Fraser, you are American. You hear only the enemies of Germany. Perhaps not the American people but your government sides with the French. It is the French that are enemies of Germany. They continue to bleed Germany. They want Germany to forever remain weak. It is time for a strong leader to lead us. Not those socialists in the Reichstag."

"How do you feel about Jews?"

"Vermin. Bloodsucking parasites. While our enemies from the Great War still rob us, inside Germany we have the Jews. The Jews control all the money. They're not Germans. Keep to themselves. Germany would be better off without the Jews."

Similar sentiments were voiced by others interviewed that evening at the Bürgerbräukeller. Hitler was the hometown favorite. No one voiced any qualms about Hitler's vehement anti-Semitic rhetoric.

After a couple of more days, Fraser concluded that Munich and Bavaria were lovely interesting places. Berlin was drab. But they were all Germans. Most portrayed themselves as victims. Everything that happened in the last twenty years was the fault of others. German Jews were an all too easy a scapegoat based upon latent European anti-Semitism. Fraser had experienced enough of Germany.

He also rethought his upcoming plans to travel and report from other European countries. His pieces and photos were intended to portray the mood of the political turmoil infecting Europe. Had to be careful to avoid looking like a travel column. While Eastern Europe was suffering the ubiquitous unrest that seemed to perpetually plague the Balkan states, the center of threatening uncertainty remained Germany. And while the Communist dictatorship of the vast Soviet Union loomed to the east, Germany was buffered on their eastern border by Poland. The Poles hated the Russians. It was more about France and Belgium on Germany's western border.

On this border lay the center of German heavy industry in the Ruhr Valley and the disputed Saar Basin. The principle antagonists were again Germany and France. Everyone else was in the corner of one or the other. So he decided to ride that vein of emotional intensity between these historical adversaries, both imbued with strong nationalistic underpinnings. No need to take the measure of the typical Italian or Brit, much less other countries like Spain. As for Moscow, that could wait. Not on his favored list of places to experience anyway. Therefore he would complete this swing through Bavaria then return to France perhaps via Belgium.

The Belgians were unfortunately linked to France as the gateway for German aggression in the past. He would make his pieces centered on how the Germans and the French populaces viewed the escalating tensions between their two countries.

CHAPTER 11

Fraser returned to Paris for a respite after his foray into Germany. It was now the first week of January, 1932. It was cold, gray, with drizzling rain, though still good to be back in Paris. He had amassed notes enough to satisfy weeks of submittals before venturing out again. Then it would be to parts of France never visited.

In February, Fraser took a train south to Marseille. Cold also in the south with the winter mistral winds blowing across the elevated terrain of the Massif Central. For the next several months, he would direct his interview questions for French comments on the growing influence of Adolf Hitler. What that meant to France.

He could also devote serious writing time to his novel in progress. What better environment than the French south of Provence, the Cote d'Azur, and Gascony? Then he would make his way back north to Loire and Normandy. He would conclude his itinerary with Burgundy and Alsace-Lorraine, the area of so much Franco-German dispute. Did they now feel secure from a German invasion with the massive fortifications of the French Maginot Line?

The remainder of 1932 passed pleasantly. It was like a holiday roaming about France. Stays at quaint locales. A gastronomic adventure with the continued plenty of French agriculture in spite of the effects of the Depression just starting to be felt in France within the last year. Wine from Burgundy, Bordeaux, Châteauneuf-du-Pape on the Rhone, Chinon in the Loire Valley, crisp white wines from Alsace. Foie gras in medieval Sarlot in the Dordogne. Bouillabaisse in Marseille. Simple but rich cream dishes in Normandy, elaborate delicate sauces in Lyon. Cheeses from every French region. France was a delight.

But the hard times of the Depression were starting to intrude and an ever darkening political storm threatened from the east. As for the consensus feeling among the French he interviewed, there was deep seated resentment if not outright hatred of Germany. It was Germany that started the Great War, invaded Belgium then France. Decimated a whole generation of French manhood with millions killed and maimed in those terrible trenches. None of the French interviewed questioned punitive retribution. The more pragmatic alternative of fostering a German economic recovery to lessen a growing threat was too nuanced. As for Hitler, he was just another German radical. If not him than someone else just as bad. Fraser thought they were missing much in that assessment.

Events in Germany in 1932 continued to foretell the rising influence of Adolf Hitler. Running against President Hindenburg in March, Hitler polled 30% of the vote behind Hindenburg's 49%, dictating a runoff. While Hitler lost that election to Hindenburg, it clearly placed him at the head of German politics. The aging Paul von Hindenburg was already eighty-five. He held office only because of the veneration of his leadership at the head of German armed forces in the Great War. Hindenburg served as a symbol of traditional Prussian leadership for the struggling Weimar Republic that came about with German capitulation in 1918 after the overthrow of the previous monarchy.

Hindenburg had no political successor. He did not head a political party. A figure-head, a pseudo-monarch over a fractious imperfect parliamentary system. A head of state already suffering bouts of senility. During the parliamentary elections in July, the National Socialists German Workers' Party captured 230 seats in the Reichstag giving them the largest representation in the Reichstag. While disliking Hitler and his paramilitary SA rabble, Hindenburg could no longer ignore him.

But neither the Nazi Party nor President Hindenburg had a governing majority. The other parties refused cooperation to form any majority coalition government with the Nazis. Hindenburg refused to appoint Hitler as Chancellor as the President was allowed to do under Article 53 of the constitution. Therefore, the ineffectual minority-led parliament would continue until new elections scheduled for November, 1932.

Fraser wrote a piece in late 1932 that would soon prove prescient.

'Adolf Hitler is the most powerful political figure in Germany. His National Socialist German Workers' Party has more seats in the Reichstag than any other political party. President Hindenburg is incapable of leading Germany for much longer. Why would anyone think that Herr Hitler will not soon ascend to a position of full power in Germany? From time spent in Germany, I think that is a virtual certainty.

Given that premise it is difficult to understand why there is not greater fear about what that might mean for Europe. The German people are blind to the dangers represented by Adolf Hitler. He heads more than a political party. Imagine the Democrats or Republicans in the United States being backed by uniformed para-military units numbering in the tens of thousands marching in the streets, intimidating anyone in opposition with violence. These are the Sturmabteilung, the SA, Storm Troops, commonly known as the Brownshirts. In reality they are Nazi muscle, street thugs. German police already turn a blind eye. And Hitler will come to power. The SA will then be integrated in some manner into the military or worse yet, into the police.

Germany is therefore poised to become a police state with all that means. A constant state of fear. No free press. Imprisonment for political opposition. Imprisonment without trial? Worse? Look at Stalin's Soviet police state.

And if you are Jewish? There is simply no place for you in Germany. Imagine attempting to remove 500,000 people from your soil. That is the Jewish population of Germany. There are those that say this is just electioneering rhetoric. No one would go to those lengths in practical terms. And why not?

Reading Hitler's own political autobiography **Mein Kampf** *provides passages that reveal a pathological hatred for Jews that goes far beyond political posturing. Here are some excerpts:*

....they were not Germans with a special religion, but an entirely different race.

....international Jewish world finance needed this bait in order to carry out the longed-for plan of a destruction of Germany.

....The activity of the so-called liberal press was the work of grave-diggers for the German people and the German Reich. One can pass by in silence the Marxist papers of lies; to them lying is as necessary to their life as catching mice is to the cat; but its task is only to break the people's folkish and national spine, in order to make it ripe for the yoke of slavery of international capital and its masters, the Jews.

....The Jew forms the strongest contrast to the Aryan. Hardly in any people of the world is the instinct of self-preservation more strongly developed than in the so-called chosen people.

....If the Jews were alone in this world, they would suffocate as much in dirt and filth, as they would carry on a detestable struggle to cheat and to ruin each other, although the complete lack of the will to sacrifice, expressed in their cowardice, would also in this instance make the fight a comedy.

....When judging Jewry in its attitude towards the question of human culture, one has to keep before one's eye as an essential characteristic that there never has been and consequently that today also there is no Jewish art; that above all the two queens of all arts, architecture and music, owe nothing original to Jewry. What he achieves in the field of art is either bowdlerization or intellectual theft. With this, the Jew lacks those qualities which distinguish creatively and, with it, culturally blessed races.

....the Jew possesses no culture-creating energy whatsoever, as the idealism, without which there can never exist a genuine development of man towards a higher level, does not and never did exist in him. His intellect, therefore, will never have a constructive effect, but only a destructive one.

....his spreading is the typical symptom of all parasites; he always looks for a new feeding soil for his race.

....the Jew is the great master of lying.

....the Jew cannot possess a religious institution for the very reason that he lacks all idealism in any form and that he also does not recognize any belief in the hereafter.

According to Adolf Hitler the Jew therefore can never be a real German. He is anti-Christian, pro-Marxist, believes in no after-life, therefore is dominated by only the basest of pursuits in his present life. The Jew lives a life dedicated solely to self-preservation, living apart from any civilized society while feeding on that society as a parasite, to use Hitler's own terminology. After continually preaching this theme it will be difficult for Hitler to avoid carrying through with the persecution of German Jews given the rampant anti-Semitic that already exists.

And for the rest of Europe, look also to Hitler's Mein Kampf. *A Nazi controlled Germany will clearly pursue territorial ambitions through the same aggressive tactics.'*

Fraser's correspondence from his sister in New York provided an antidotal view of how Americans viewed the political turmoil in Europe. Clearly the dislocations of the Great Depression overshadowed everything. Other countries' politics barely got noticed. As for Europe, it was always a quarrelsome place according to her husband. His articles appearing in the Hearst newspapers were interesting but entirely foreign. The way he shaped each story around a particular person made his pieces good story reading. She liked the photographs. Perhaps she was not a reliable indicator but Fraser sensed he still might be pissing into the wind.

America certainly had its own problems. 1932 was a presidential election year. Would Franklin Roosevelt beat incumbent Hubert Hoover seeking his second term? How vulnerable was Hoover being cast with the blame for the Wall Street Crash of 1929, and his entire first term dominated by the onset of the Great Depression? And what about what Japan? Wasn't their invasion of Chinese Manchuria last year a bigger threat to the U.S. than European squabbling? Japan was descending into a military dictatorship. Resource-poor, they were already invading their neighbors. Japanese aggression in the Far East seemed more a threat than Germany in 1932.

1932 however concluded on a personally pleasant note for Marc Fraser. Travelling the breadth of France further enriched his love of the country. An opportunity to experience its varying regional foods, wine, architecture, its intellectual culture, and the universal French zest for appreciating life. He also finished his novel of muckraking journalism and somewhat fictionalized daring exploits in Los Angeles. This first novel would fit into the gritty noir-fiction genre coming into vogue in early 1930s Los Angeles.

His love life however remained unsettled. Upon his return to Paris was a letter from his cousin Harriet among the pile of unopened mail accumulated during his months-long stay in Germany. She wrote:

Hope you are well my dearest Marc. Don't know where you are off to but I believe you are doing what you like. I have the fondest thoughts of those sweet times we spent together before you left Paris. But it was never meant to become more than that. I must now tell you that I have found someone. We are engaged to be married in the fall. You'll understand if I cannot invite you. Your loving cousin, Harriet.

That was as it should be. She was right. It was never going to be more than just the sex. Fortunate not to have an awkward situation. Nonetheless, self-examination still suggested some sort of character flaw that drew him to doomed relationships. A mix of impossible personal aspirations mutually conflicting to fostering a relationship? His journalism career, travel, and the solitude of a writing life did not create an easy basis to meld with that of an equally driven partner. An independent thinking partner would add her own set of aspirations. Children were not in the picture. That alone was a non-starter for a good many women.

The introspection was intellectually useful but did not curtail his appreciation of women's company. Since he was good looking, urbane, with the exotic profession of foreign correspondent, a writer, an American yet fluent in French, and in a country with progressive attitudes toward sex, female company abounded. Yet clearly he could do a better job managing his love life.

Paris was now home. Perhaps without a consistent female companion but he had made a circle of friends from different walks of life that made for a rich social life. He even had what he would term as a best friend, something he hadn't experienced since his college days.

He met Henri Marchand, a filmmaker in his rounds of interviews. Marchand was the managing director of a Paris film production studio, Productions Artistiques Cinématographiques. With Fraser's connections to the American film industry they shared much in common beyond discussing the European political situation. Both loved literature. Both were engaged in artistic pursuits with an appreciation for all forms of photography. Marchand seemed to know everyone in Paris and introduced Fraser to an eclectic mix of Parisians.

While 1932 was a very good year for Marc Fraser, it would be his last year of settled life for some time to come. Depending upon how he looked back on impending events, he was either in the wrong place at the right time, or the right place at the wrong time. Europe was about to become unhinged.

CHAPTER 12

The year 1933 was to prove the birthing of the Nazi malignancy that would soon envelop much of the world in events of staggering enormity. Events never experienced in modern times. In the years ahead, another world war would harvest millions of lives with modern weapons of mass destruction. Depraved despots would inflict acts of barbarism not seen since the middle ages upon countless more millions. In 1933, the world was descending into a dark valley.

Marc Fraser's prediction about the rise to power of Adolf Hitler came true in January, 1933. With no real choice after the resignation of the short-term sitting Chancellor, a reluctant President Hindenburg acceded to appointing Hitler as Chancellor of Germany to provide for a functioning government. A rapid succession of events soon followed propelling Hitler into a position of absolute dictatorial powers.

The rest of Europe did not realize the monster that was rising anew from the ashes of the Great War. Any doubt as to the direction of the new leadership was quickly dispelled in a matter of only two months.

On February 22, forty thousand SA, along with Hitler's personal bodyguard the *Schutzstaffel*, the SS are sworn in as auxiliary police.

Working against attempts of opposing political parties to form a majority coalition, Hitler forces President Hindenburg to dissolve the Reichstag and call new elections for March.

On February 27th, the Reichstag's parliamentary building burns. Ostensibly a Dutch communist found inside the burning building under incriminating circumstances is accused by the Nazi Party. Many believe the Nazis are actually responsible. As a result of Hitler's pressure, the following day President Hindenburg issues the Reichstag Fire Decree invoking emergency powers as allowed under the Weimar Constitution. The decree gives Hitler as Chancellor the authority to administer by edict. Many key civil liberties are suspended, including imprisonment of opponents of the Nazis, and suppression of any unfriendly publications. Germany now became a one-party Nazi state. Much worse was to immediately follow.

With the suppression of all political parties other than the Nazis the SA became further emboldened to exercise power in the streets. With free reign from interference from any police authority bands of SA began committing acts of increased intimidation and violence. Their victims were no longer just Communists but even passers-by, especially after a night of drinking. Jews of obvious identification as Eastern European immigrants with beards and black hats became particular targets.

Nazi courts were set up to deal with political dissidents. To incarcerate those political opponents and others deemed undesirable, the Nazis created special internment facilities termed concentration camps. The first of these were in Dachau near Munich in the south and Oranienburg near Berlin in the north. Over the next few years they would expand this penal gulag with Buchenwald near Weimar in central Germany, Sachsenhausen near Berlin in northern Germany, and Ravensbrück for women outside of Berlin. By the end of the year, the courts were bypassed altogether. Not only political dissidents were being incarcerated in these concentration camps but common criminals, beggars, gypsies, and alcoholics.

With SA storm troopers intimidating non-Nazi Party members of the Reichstag, the Reichstag passed the Enabling Act, subsequently signed by President Hindenburg. The Act granted the cabinet, Hitler's appointed cabinet, the authority to enact laws without the participation of the Reichstag for four years. Parliamentary government ceased to exist in Germany. Through this act, Adolf Hitler legally obtained plenary powers and became Führer.

Once in unrestricted control, the Nazis left little doubt as to the fate of German Jews. Any rationalization that the Jews were only a convenient scapegoat to attract votes was quickly dispelled. In April the Nazis staged a boycott of Jewish shops and businesses. This was followed by a decree defining as non-Aryan anyone descended from even one Jewish parent or grandparent. Later in the year Jews are excluded from the arts. Jews are prohibited from editing newspapers. More restrictive yet is the edict prohibiting Jews owning land. And this is only the beginning of this modern-day Jewish pogrom. For Jews, events will continually worsen. Hitler fully intends to make good on his genocidal racial threats.

Wasting little time to reshape Germany society into their fanatical vision, the Nazis stage mass books burnings of any literature inconsistent with their narrow views of philosophy, history, and political ideology. Unrestrained uniformed SA paramilitaries roam the street free to intimidate without hindrance from any official police. For any imagined offense against the Nazi government anyone could be subject to summary arrest and indefinite imprisonment. For even the majority non-Jewish Germans their well-ordered society had descended into a police state. In the span of less than a year the nascent attempt at parliamentary government had dissolved into an absolute dictatorship. With a leader far more extreme than even the aggressive monarchy of the Kaiser at the turn of the century that took them into the Great War.

In early April, 1933, Fraser received a telegram from the Chief himself. It read, *Proceed Berlin immediately – stop - Interview arranged with A. Hitler following Wed – stop - Wire results – stop - WRH.*

Not thrilled to return to Germany at least the sunny spring day held promise as he disembarked the train in Berlin. That mood quickly changed as he exited the station to make his way once again to the Adlon Hotel on the Unter den Linden. Loud-speakers blared a Hitler speech. Loud enough to be irritating by volume alone, worse by listening to his protracted rant.

Before entering a taxi he saw a contingent of jackbooted SA storm troopers marching in formation on the street. As the SA passed, several people on the sidewalk stopped and gave the raised outstretched right arm Nazi salute. The militaristic spectacle was a visual symbol of how much things had changed since his first trip here a year and a half ago.

"Is this sort of thing normal?" Fraser asked the taxi driver.

"What do you mean, Sir?"

"I mean, broadcasting political speeches at a deafening volume. And why should anybody salute a bunch of men in uniform that aren't even army or police?" Fraser refrained from saying provocateurs and thugs.

In the rearview mirror, Fraser saw the taxi driver grimace.

"That is the Führer speaking, Sir. Still so many problems he must fix. He must make his thoughts known. All Germans must be behind him. That is why we offer a salute. To show our solidarity."

What nonsense. But looking in the mirror at the driver's face, Fraser saw fear rather than the fervor of an acolyte. Were things so bad that people feared comments made to strangers?

Fraser had wired ahead to his old colleague Karl von Wiegand to join him for dinner at the Adlon that evening. His appointment with the new German Chancellor Adolf Hitler was scheduled for mid-morning the next day at the Reich Chancellery.

Describing the scene outside the rail station to Wiegand, Wiegand said, "Ah, it is so much worse, Herr Fraser. Those stormtroopers you saw are free to create all sorts of trouble. People on the street are accosted for any reason. It is their way of exercising power. The Nazi SA and Hitler's personal guards the SS are now the police. Above the law. If people do not offer that hideous Nazi salute they may be attacked. Even foreign journalists are not immune. You must be careful, Fraser."

"Has Germany descended into a lawless place where people have no rights?"

"Not lawless, but only the laws set down by the Nazis for their own purpose. As to rights, there are no longer any civil rights. That's the real definition of National Socialism. Socialism in the sense that everything is subservient to the good of nationalism in the form of the German state. And the German state is now the Nazis with its singular leader, and dictator, Adolf Hitler."

"And it's because of Herr Hitler that I have returned to Berlin. The Chief personally arranged an interview for me with Hitler. You have interviewed him in the past. What can I expect?"

"Expect to ask few questions. Hitler likes to do all the talking. And it will be his agenda. He may answer something entirely different to your question to launch into some diatribe of a subject of his choosing. No question he has extraordinary oratory skill but I think he is unstable. I'd be interested in your impression."

"Why would the Chief want me to interview Hitler? Why not you or one of the other Hearst correspondents?"

Wiegand smiled and took a sip of his wine. "I don't pretend to know the Chief's mind. He's got some quirks of his own. Probably some impulsive thought. But I hear your pieces are well received back home, Herr Fraser, so you might have a fresh perspective to convey."

The German Chancellery was a former 18th century palace on Wilhelmstraße. Armed guards in black uniforms and polished helmets flanked every door. Fraser was ushered into a grand waiting room by a military officer. On one collar was an insignia of two lightning-bolt like symbols. On the left upper arm was the distinctive orange armband with Nazi swastika. These were Hitler's personal bodyguard the *Schutzstaffel*, the SS.

He waited an hour by himself in the vast high-ceiling room. Eventually a large thickset man in a simple double-breasted tan colored uniform entered. From photographs, Hermann Göring was unmistakable.

Göring extended his hand, "Herr Fraser, the Führer will receive you now. A rare opportunity for a journalist. I personally arranged this interview with your publisher Herr Hearst."

As Göring led Fraser down a long hallway he said, "Herr Hearst shares an enlightened view about the real political threat to the West. He rightly realizes it is the Soviet Union. The Slavs harbor a barbaric eastern culture that threatens the West with the disease of Communism. They are the true enemy. The National Socialists German Worker's Party came into existence to fight Communism. To preserve German culture."

"Perhaps after I interview the Chancellor, you might also consent to an interview, Herr Minister?"

"Yes. I think that may be possible," Göring said.

Göring ushered past two more SS guards through another set of twelve-foot high doors. Hitler's office consisted of a massive desk at the end of the room with comfortable upholstered chairs arranged in a more informal setting before large windows facing unto the inner palace courtyard gardens. Although sunlight streamed in from the windows, the room was oppressive. The walls were gray stone, the window draperies heavy dark green velvet. A large chrome-plated emblem called a *Parteiadler*, consisting of an eagle with outstretched wings astride a swastika hung on the back wall. Flanking this emblem of the Nazi Party were oversized Nazi flags in their garish orange with black swastika on a white field.

Adolf Hitler stood behind his desk looking down with both hands on the desk. For a couple of moments Hitler did not acknowledge Göring's and Fraser's presence appearing to study something on the desk. Both Göring and Fraser stood silently.

Eventually looking up, Hitler looked questioningly at Göring.

"Herr Fraser, Mein Führer. The American journalist working for the prominent American publisher William Hearst," Göring said.

"Ah yes," Hitler said coming around from the desk. He offered a limp handshake then said, "Let us sit and talk, Herr Fraser," motioning Fraser to a chair. Göring also took a seat.

Hitler was of average height, dressed in a dark suit. A lock of hair frequently drooped across his forehead which he pushed back with his hand. His complexion was pasty. And of course his strange but distinctive toothbrush-mustache.

"Herr Chancellor, many Americans are troubled by your strong position on Jews. There is anti-Semitism in the United States but nothing approaching the extreme positions you have advocated. Jews make up only a small percentage of the German people. Do you believe that strongly that Jews represent a danger to Germany?"

Hitler smiled condescendingly. "I have studied the Jewish problem. Not only does the Jew represent a threat economically and culturally, but they side with the socialists and the Communists, those actively bent on destroying Germany. The Jew exerts a threat well beyond their numbers.

"But the world makes too much of this Jewish problem. I must confront more pressing problems. While the vile conditions of the Treaty of Versailles wrongfully punishes Germany, its real intent is to forever subjugate Germany to second class status among the nations of Europe. France, Belgium, Great Britain, Poland, and of course the Soviet Union conspire in this. They surround Germany, pressuring us from all sides. This artificial state of Czechoslovakia created in 1919 serves to enslave Germanic people under Slav rule.

"Versailles redefined the geopolitical boundaries of Germany, ignoring populations of ethnic Germans living in Poland, the

Sudetenland, and Alsace-Lorraine. This was the doing of the French and British. It robbed Germans of their historic right to resources in the west and agricultural lands in the east."

Fraser attempted to interject a question but was cut short by Hitler raising his hand.

"German history has been a continual fight to protect German soil. Territory occupied by the Germanic race for a thousand years. Germany's enemies have constantly sought to deprive Germany of those rights. Those enemies wrongly condemn the concept of *Lebensraum* as imperialistic. It is nothing more than asserting ancient Germanic rights."

Fraser new that *Lebensraum*, living space, was a German ultra-nationalist concept of territorial expansion. For the Nazis the concept meant expansion by aggression into Eastern Europe, the basis of which was the inherent right of a superior race, Aryans, to displace inferior peoples. Slavs in this case.

Hitler continued talking as if rehearsing a speech rather than specifically addressing Fraser. Göring sat silent with a subtle expression of bored tolerance. Fraser assumed Göring endured these Hitler monologues frequently.

"This new German Reich, the Third Reich shall undo all that. We will forge a return to German greatness. Once again the German people will take their rightful place among nations. Germany is no threat to its neighbors. It asks only for justice of equality. We can no longer abide by these oppressive restrictions imposed at Versailles in 1919. German lands confiscated. Reparations that thwart German economic progress. Restrictions on military capabilities to insure Germany remains inferior to its neighbors thereby providing the means for those countries to politically extort Germany. But that is to be no more!"

Hitler slammed his fist into his other palm for dramatic effect. Fraser could see a drop of spittle at the corner of his mouth. And his eyes. Fraser understood what Bella Fromm meant by the wild look of a zealot. Hitler was as passionate as a tent-evangelist. But there was no mistaking his message. *Reich* is German for empire. Hitler believed he was creating a third Germanic empire, a successor to the Holy Roman Empire and the second German empire formed by Chancellor Bismarck in the nineteenth century. Empires by definition were expansive, furthering their dominion over other lands by military aggression while ruled by a singular sovereign. Hitler saw himself as the successor to Frederick Barbarossa and Otto von Bismarck.

Abruptly Hitler signaled the end of the interview if it could be called that. But for Fraser that didn't really matter. There was nothing new to learn from interviewing Adolf Hitler. He was not circumspect about even his most extreme views voiced in public and print. But seeing Hitler up close gave Fraser a more intimate appreciation for the personality. The impression was chilling. No one adjective accurately describes Adolf Hitler, however terms such as fanatical, messianic, unstable, dangerous, all seemed well founded.

Hermann Göring agreed to give Fraser thirty minutes the following day in his office within the Chancellery building. That proved to be an equally revealing experience.

Göring was a former fighter pilot ace of the Great War. Credited with downing twenty-two Allied aircraft, he was the last commander of Jagdgeschwader 1 Squadron, Manfred von Richthofen, the Red Baron's fighter squadron. Göring was awarded with two Iron Cross decorations and the coveted *Pour le Mérite*, known informally as the Blue Max. Although arrogant and vain Göring was by deeds a true military hero. Still handsome with magnificent hair, the once slender dashing aviator had now gained considerable weight.

Göring was an early member of the NSDAP and a close associate of Adolf Hitler. He was wounded in the failed Beer Hall Putsch of 1923 that led to Hitler's conviction for treason. The wounded Göring was smuggled out of Germany to Innsbruck, Austria where he underwent surgery.

After Hitler was named Chancellor, Göring was appointed as minister without portfolio, Minister of the Interior for Prussia, and Reich Commissioner of Aviation. He immediately moved to expand police control in Prussia by creating the *Geheime Staats-*

polizei, or Gestapo. Göring might be derided behind his back for his personal excesses but he was the second most powerful person in Germany.

Göring said, "The Führer spoke of military restrictions imposed by the Treaty of Versailles. That lies at the heart of the problem. Without a powerful military no country can maintain its sovereignty. Those restrictions will now be set aside."

"Is that in the process of happening?"

"Of course. We are proceeding with acquiring an effective air force. The last war proved that air power is essential for defense."

"How is defense separated from offensive capability?"

"The answer to that lies not with weaponry but politics. Any weapon can be used for either. Germany's enemies have rebuilt their armies and navies. They would claim for the cause of defense. Yet Germany is to be deprived of that same defense? No, the British and French could mount an attack on Germany with those same weapons claimed for defense. Germany is surrounded by hostile nations. She must rearm. The Führer has been clear on that."

"What about the French Maginot Line of fortifications? Surely those cannot be other than defensive?" Fraser said.

"Herr Fraser, the Maginot Line of fortifications is not really a weapon. It is an entrenchment of the kind seen in the last war. These are installations to hold the Alsace-Lorraine region taken from Germany. They are a means of repression to place Germanic people there under the thumb of France."

"You speak of repression, Herr Minister. Some would say that is precisely what is being done now with the National Socialists in power. Rumor is that numerous detention facilities, called concentration camps I believe, have been established throughout Germany. Are these intended to jail political opponents?"

"Not for political opponents but for those illegally engaged in acts that threaten the government. And yes there are such facilities. They are a legal recourse essential to maintaining order in these turbulent times. The Communists burned the Reichstag. They are not political opponents but terrorists. That has led the Führer to invoke emergency powers."

Fraser intended to write a fiery piece on these *emergency powers*. Nothing more than a cover to indefinitely detain anyone thought to be a political threat. This regime was only months in power and already they had established a concentration camp in Oranienburg near Berlin. Another in the south in Dachau near Munich. Kemna in the east near Düsseldorf. What kind of government immediately needed new prison facilities to incarcerate thousands if not for political opponents?

"Perhaps I could be allowed to visit one of these facilities? I understand there is one not far from here?"

To Fraser's surprise, Göring said, "Yes, I believe a visit can be arranged. That would be Konzentrationslager Oranienburg just north of Berlin. You shall see we have nothing to hide. But the world should understand that Germany will deal decisively with enemies of the State."

The questions and answers tilted back and forth. Fraser again learning nothing new except a more intimate feel for Göring the person. Unlike Hitler who seemed to stand back from interpersonal exchanges, Göring was a skilled debater. For all his extravagant habits and arrogance he seemed to operate from a position of intellect as compared with Hitler's emotion-based erratic outbursts. The contrasts would make for interesting copy in his next published commentaries.

Fraser's contemplated assessment of the Nazi leadership as a monstrosity of deranged fanatics that had deluded the populace to gain power would probably get him banned from Germany. The frightening part was these aberrant personalities were not the political fringe. These people now controlled Germany with unrestricted powers. The world didn't see it that way. Most Germans only saw the potential of immediate redress to their grievances. What they now had was a monstrous, uncontrollable dictator that was hell-bent on carrying out his megalomaniacal visions. Having seen Hitler and Göring close up, Fraser was convinced a European conflict of some sort must be imminent.

With a pass authorized by Göring personally, Fraser took the train north to Oranienburg the next day. In less than an hour he arrived in the small town. The stationmaster at the quaint rail station informed him the detention facility was right in the town, walking distance from the station.

Konzentrationslager Oranienburg consisted of a fenced compound surrounding a large brick factory building. Two armed SA stood guard a the wooden gate. After showing his pass another guard was summoned from inside to take him to the camp commandant.

He was made to wait in an anteeroom to an office with a window. Inside the office an SA officer sat at a much abused wooden desk. The whole place looked like what it probably was, the office of a former factory. The cinder block walls were painted a drab light green, considerably scuffed. Bare light bulbs cast uneven illumination. Even for a prison it looked like a dump.

Evenually the door opened and the officer addressed him. "I see Minister Göring has personally authorized your visit, Herr Fraser. I would not agree with allowing foreign journalists to interfere with strictly Germany affairs. However, I obey orders. I am Commandant Sturmhauptführer Ritter. I will personally escort you through the facility. That must however be brief as I have more important duties to attend to."

The former factory had been haphazardly modified into a prison consisting of what appeared to be dormitories. Double bunks with only one foot clearance filled the spaces to optimize the inmate density. No one was in the living quarters as Fraser walked next to the Commandant. The place stank of unwashed bodies. It was gloomy with only a couple of bar light bulbs that even in the daylight provided only a twilight with the filthy windows, some broken, prevented from cleaning by heavy-gage steel mesh.

Fraser took out his camera.

"What are doing!" the Commandant yelled.

"Taking photographs. Please read the Minister's authorization. It expressly allows me to take photographs."

The Commandant read the pass.

"Very well. But quickly. We must move on."

Fraser adjusted for the poor light. This wasn't art but it was certainly atmospheric.

"Toilet facilities?" Fraser asked after snapping several shots.

"This way."

Fraser recoiled at the stench as he stepped through a doorway. The toilets consisted of two rows of suspended planks with holes over galvanized buckets. This perhaps for hundreds of prisoners? No running water. Breathing through his mouth it was even difficult to stay long enough to get photos. All the time the Commandant stayed well outside the disgusting area.

"Where do the prisoners bathe?"

"Outside of course."

"Of course, since there is no running water inside. And where are the slop buckets emptied?"

"You sound like someone with the Red Cross. A reporter interested in hygiene?" He smiled sarcastically.

Outside, hundreds of inmates milled about, huddled in small groups. The inmates apparently wore their own clothing. Now considerably filthy, evident even from a distance.

"The showers. You are interested in the showers, Herr Fraser." The Commandant pointed to an area outside one of the buildings. The shower consisted of a single one-inch pipe over a few planks on the ground sitting in a pool of muddy water.

Fraser took a continuous roll of photos then reloaded his Leica.

"May I speak to some of the prisoners, Hauptsturmführer?"

Before answering the Commandant made a show of reading Fraser's authorization.

"Out of the question, Herr Fraser. It says nothing here about allowing interviews."

"Can I ask you questions about what offenses these men are here for?"

"No. That information must come from the Ministry. Since you are close to the Minister, I am sure he would be glad to help you. Now if you are through, I believe I have shown you what you require."

"Very well, Hauptsturmführer Ritter. Perhaps a few shots here in the yard. A couple of you of course."

The Commandant actually posed. The perfect Nazi asshole poster figure to appear in American newspapers alongside pictures of this pesthole. The stupid shit. Then again, maybe the Commandant knew that nobody would care. Having to wait in Oranienburg a couple of hours for the next available train gave Fraser time to brood on that possibility.

The last few days since returning to Berlin left Fraser depressed. As an investigative journalist in Los Angeles he dug into criminal wrongdoing of corrupt officials. In the United States there were consequences for criminal behavior. In 1933 Germany there was no rule of law. The equivalent of mobsters held official power. The realization that Germany had descended into something so potentially dangerous was profoundly unsettling. How could he convey these unbelievable extremes in mere words? Even in photographs? One needed to be here to see up close that reality. There was simply no way to portray the true gravity of what this meant to the rest of Europe much less to Americans.

That evening at the Adlon Hotel bar, Marc Fraser was having a Scotch while making notes recounting his interviews with Hitler and Göring. He would compose his copy over the next couple of days. Contrary to the Chief's admonition to report immediately, this would take some time to draft. And the text could not be sent by telegraph. It might land him in a concentration camp. Certainly would prevent him from future reporting from Germany. Besides, all he obtained from the interviews was a sense of their personalities. Nothing really newsworthy. He would relate those impressions into the broader context of recent events in Germany.

The photographs from within the Oranienburg concentration camp were however real news. Certainly must file those from outside Germany after developing the negatives.

Into the Adlon's bar walked two men. Fraser recognized one as Hamilton Armstrong, the editor of the prestigious American journal *Foreign Affairs*. He had been introduced to Armstrong at an American embassy press function in Berlin during his first trip in 1931. The man with him looked vaguely familiar but Fraser couldn't place the face. Maybe because the two men looked remarkably similar. Same age, dark hair, both with mustaches.

But as they passed his table, the man he didn't recognize stopped abruptly.

In terrible German with some indistinct accent the man said, "Excuse me, Sir. Did I not see you leaving the Chancellery yesterday?"

Fraser now vaguely recalled passing the man on the steps.

Deciding on English, Fraser answered, "Yes. I was there."

"Ham, a fellow American. This is my friend Hamilton Armstrong. And I'm Allen Dulles."

Dulles offered his hand as did Armstrong.

"I'm Marc Fraser, a correspondent for the Hearst Publications. I believe we met briefly a couple of years ago here in Berlin, Mr. Armstrong. And now I remember passing you yesterday, Mr. Dulles."

Dulles said, "Yes. Then we should compare notes, Mr. Fraser. May we join you?"

Dulles and Armstrong sat down at Fraser's table and motioned for the waiter. After ordering whiskies, all three briefly explained what they were doing in Berlin. Armstrong was obviously in the business of foreign affairs journalism. Dulles and Armstrong were old friends from college at Princeton. Armstrong explained that Dulles was a partner at a New York law firm that had substantial client interests in Germany. Dulles' role within the law firm managed by his brother centered on his extensive experience in Europe from his prior career in the U.S. diplomatic service. Sullivan & Cromwell provided unique expertise to clients with foreign business interests. Allen Dulles also spoke both German and French although badly.

Dulles said, "I'm here as part of a disarmament conference delegation. I was accompanying a diplomat from the State Department. I had some experience with that sort of thing after the Great War. We had a meeting with the new German Chancellor."

"My guess is that probably did not go well," Fraser said.

Dulles was a little taken back and looked at Armstrong.

"Did you also have an interview with Adolf Hitler?" Dulles said.

"If you could call it that. I asked the Führer one question to which he answered with a diatribe monologue outlining all the injustices heaped upon Germany. Frankly I was not impressed with anything about Hitler. Small fellow. Unassuming. Off the podium without a crowd it is difficult to see how he captivates anybody. To call him strange is a gross understatement. Much of what he says is just nonsense. Themes based upon Germanic myths, or screwball racial theory. Hermann Göring appears smarter but he's a real piece of work too."

"You spoke with Göring as well? How did you arrange that?"

"Well the Hitler interview was arranged by Mr. Hearst personally. I simply asked Göring who was present if I could also interview him. He agreed. Testing the boundaries, I asked to see one of their detention facilities, these concentration camps people are calling them. Surprisingly Göring agreed to that too. The guy is arrogant beyond belief."

Fraser didn't care who knew his feelings. He was thoroughly disgusted with Germany.

Dulles and Armstrong again exchanged glances.

"That is impressive, Mr. Fraser. I don't know of any foreign journalist that's been to one of these camps. The Nazis just recently constructed them I understand. When will you be going?" Armstrong said.

"I've been. Yesterday actually. Town of Oranienburg just north of here. I was even allowed to take photographs."

"My god! What was it like?" Dulles asked.

"Something awful. It's not like a regular prison. The inmates are more like cattle in a pen. The Nazis say they are political agitators. I suspect simply political opponents. No trial, no charges. Just locked up. Worse than primitive toilet and hygiene facilities. Disgusting. Wait until my photographs are released. Hope it wakes up people back in America."

Dulles said, "That is truly remarkable, Mr. Fraser."

All three men hit it off. Through more drinks and dinner they discussed the complex interplay of factors plaguing European stability. All agreed that the various heads of states in Europe were ill-equipped to deal with the likes of Adolf Hitler. Dulles and Armstrong were repulsed by the anti-intellectual composition of the Nazis. Armstrong in particular sided with Fraser that a military conflict of some sort in Europe seemed inevitable with the belligerence of Adolf Hitler. Armstrong too had read Hitler's *Mein Kampf*. Dulles was a little more guarded. The lawyer and former diplomat still harbored the possibility of negotiation.

Leaving the Adlon dining room late that evening, all were a little tipsy with too much alcohol. Dulles and Armstrong were leaving Berlin in the morning. Both gave Fraser their office addresses in New York.

Fraser wired Hearst: *Will arrive Paris in four days - stop - Will write regarding interviews but have much more including photos - stop - Best to transmit from Paris – stop - Fraser.*

Four days would allow a little personal time before catching the train to Paris. He couldn't leave Berlin without trying to contact Leni Riefenstahl.

CHAPTER 13

Fraser never had Riefenstahl's address when they had their intense but short-lived affair two years earlier. They met at restaurants and ended up in his room at the Adlon. They wrote briefly for a couple of months, but at the time Fraser sent his letters in care of Harry Sokal's studio since Riefenstahl was shooting a film on location in Italy.

Her last letter suggested nothing was to come of their short time together. Riefenstahl confessed she had met someone while working on the film. She thanked Fraser for the special time they shared in Berlin. Unfortunately they had different lives. Events conspired to separate them. She would fondly remember their passionate interlude.

The same ending as with Harriet. Why then was he still interested? Because Leni wasn't Harriet. Because she was still stuck in his thoughts. He couldn't leave without attempting to make contact. If she was married or involved he would graciously retreat.

No one answered calls placed to Harry Sokal's office. So he took a taxi to see what he could find out. The studio still displayed a sign. A single automobile was parked outside. The glass in the front door was smashed. Fraser stepped on the broken shards on the floor. The office area was a mess of overturned chairs, emptied files, and papers covering the floor.

"Anybody here?" Fraser shouted.

"Who's there?"

"It's Marc Fraser. Is Herr Sokal here?"

Sokal came out of his office carrying a box which he set down on a desk. "Ah, Herr Fraser. What brings you here?"

"What happened?"

"A visit from the SA. A final visit of warning it would seem. Didn't take their prior threats seriously enough. Unless I want to end up in one of their camps, I have no choice. I'm leaving Germany. I told you what might happen to Jews. Didn't expect it be this bad so soon. The Nazis have been in power only months and this," he said spreading his arms to convey the destruction. "It's worse in the studio. All the equipment, cameras, lighting, everything is all wrecked. Why are you here, Herr Fraser?"

"I'm so sorry, Herr Sokal," Fraser said. "Since I could not reach you by telephone I came to inquire if you have an address or telephone number for Leni Riefenstahl."

Sokal fixed Fraser with a glare.

"Sure, I'll give you her number. When you see her, tell the bitch she can rot in hell. She's probably fucking some Nazi these days."

"What did she do to make you feel that way?"

"She knows I'm Jewish. Says she doesn't have anything against Jews yet now she is working for the Nazis. For Hitler himself. She's directing some propaganda film to glorify these monsters. Working with that malignant clubfooted dwarf Joseph Goebbels. Minister of Public Enlightenment and Propaganda. Can you image a more stupid title? I tried to get her help to use her influence before all this happened. Wouldn't even take my calls."

Sokal returned to his desk and scrawled a note which he handed to Fraser.

"Here's her number. Don't know your relationship from before but count yourself lucky that nothing came of it. Leni's only out for herself. Always has been. She'll fit right in with the Nazis."

Fraser left bewildered. Leni was a creative artist. The Nazis in every way rejected real art. What the hell was she doing working with them? He decided not to ask Sokal if she was currently involved in a relationship.

He called after returning to the Adlon. "Leni, this is Marc. Marc Fraser."

"Oh my god! Marc? So good to hear from you. Where are you?"

"In Berlin. The Adlon of course."

There was silence for a moment before Riefenstahl said, "Of course. Fond memories, Marc. So much has happened since our time together. I assume you're still living in Paris?"

"Yes. Spent most of the last eighteen months travelling throughout France."

"Yet here you are back in Berlin. Perhaps just to see me?"

"Well I would like to see you, but I can't lie. I came back to interview Adolf Hitler."

"Have you met the Führer yet?" She sounded excited about that.

"As a matter of fact I have. A couple of days ago. Listen, Leni, I'm not intruding into your personal life am I? If you're involved with someone I'll understand."

"No, I'm not involved with anyone. The affair I wrote to you about never worked out. Should have come back and reconnected with you. But that's life. What about you? Is there someone back in Paris? Even if there is can we have dinner for old times' sake?"

"Absolutely. And no there is no one special back in Paris. Are you free tonight?"

"Oh yes. That would be nice. The restaurant there at the Adlon, about seven?"

"Wonderful. I'll see you tonight, Leni."

By her tone he could easily see how the evening might end up. Both were still affected by the memory of those two weeks. He could sense it in her voice. He hoped Sokal was wrong about her working with the Nazis. No matter his physical attraction to Riefenstahl, that would be difficult to overlook.

He was waiting at a secluded table as she walked into the restaurant. She looked spectacular in a black knit dress that showed her trim figure and long legs. A black felt hat with a white feather and smart black pumps set off her outfit. Men's' heads turned as she walked over to his table.

They kissed carefully to preserve her lipstick then embraced tightly for several moments before sitting down.

"This is marvelous seeing you, Marc. I forgot to ask, how did you get my new telephone number."

"From Harry Sokal. I paid him a visit."

"Oh." That was all she said then looked down to avoid eye contact.

"His placed was wrecked. SA thugs paid him a visit. Said he had been threatened before they destroyed his studio. He also said you were now working with the Nazis. Didn't tell me what that meant. So I guess I'll just ask. Are you working with them, Leni?"

She hesitated before answering. Tilting her head back and chin out somewhat defiantly she said, "Yes, I suppose you could say that. In a couple of months I'll be directing the filming of the National Socialists German Workers' Party rally in Nuremberg."

"My god, Leni, how did you get involved with such a thing? Working with these Nazis?"

"Circumstances beyond my control, Marc. I was working on a project financed by Harry Sokal. Since he was a Jew he felt he must leave Germany. Production on the project was immediately discontinued. Harry abandoned the entire crew and cast."

"What are you saying? You're blaming Sokal? Wasn't it the fault of the Nazis? Their stupid anti-Semitic racial policies? They're a bunch of thugs, Leni. How the hell could you blame Sokal?"

"Harry was just using that as an excuse."

"An excuse? Christ, I just saw what these assholes did to his studio. You're blaming Sokal for saving his life over financing a movie?" Fraser tried to contain his anger by still raised his voice.

"Of course not. He shut down production because I wouldn't succumb to his romantic advances. He's pursued me for years."

Fraser was dumbfounded with her ridiculous rationale. He just shook his head conveying disbelief.

"Marc, the Führer himself demanded I do it. How could I not agree with my other work on hold? The Führer was so taken with my directing of *Das Blaue Licht* that he said I was the only one to capture the spectacle of this year's largest of all party rallies now that he was Chancellor. Besides being Chancellor the Führer is most persuasive. You met him. Did you not feel his magnetic personality?"

Fraser took on a fierce expression. "Magnetic personality? More like mentally disturbed. Unstable. Demented even. Certainly scary. Anything but magnetic. He's the head of this monstrous regime. Do you have any idea what the hell is going on, Leni?"

"I didn't come here to be lectured, Marc. I thought we'd have a nice dinner, talk about art, enjoy each other's company. You apparently want to argue politics."

"Listen, Leni. I visited one of the Nazis' concentration camps. The prisoners were not criminals, simply people the Nazis saw as political opponents. No trials just locked away. You should see this place. Every German should see this place. Farm animals have better living conditions."

"If it's so bad why would they let a foreign journalist tour the place?"

Good question. Fraser could only image it was Hermann Göring's carelessness bred of extreme hubris.

"Because the Nazis no longer care what anyone thinks. They're in complete power. They want to invoke fear. Your dear Führer now rules by decree. No parliament, no courts to worry about. A dictatorship."

Riefenstahl grabbed her hat and handbag then stood. "Sorry you feel that way, Marc. It was a mistake seeing you again. Good luck, but goodbye."

Devastated that Riefenstahl had so completely gone over to the dark side, Fraser did not even stand as he watched her stride out of the restaurant. How could he have so misjudged her? Was she that venal or conveniently naive? She certainly wasn't stupid. But no one living here could ignore what was going on in Germany.

He looked her up vaguely hoping to maybe rekindle their brief love affair. Prepared that she may have moved beyond whatever they had momentarily shared. But not this. Discovering her collaboration with Adolf Hitler was incomprehensible. Unforgiveable. His anger made it easier to dispel any latent feelings for Leni Riefenstahl.

In no mood for dinner he decided to take a walk. The night was clear and warm. Get a last impression of Berlin before leaving the next morning. This brief trip was enough to provide a sensational series of pieces of how far Germany has descended into a society unrecognizable from just a few years ago. The interviews with Hitler, Göring. The photos from Oranienburg Concentration Camp. The list of prominent Jews of science, the arts, business that felt compelled to leave Germany. Leni Riefenstahl's acceptance of the new regime in spite of its obvious criminal underpinnings was all too typical. The vituperative stories he would send off for publication once he was back in Paris would make it unable for him to return to Germany. That suited him just fine.

He walked south from the upscale Unter der Linden Boulevard with no particular destination in mind. Leni Riefenstahl was upsetting on many levels producing an increasingly foul mood. How could he have misjudged her so badly? It would take some time to sort out.

Eventually he came to a bar. He would have a drink. Bid farewell for good to Berlin. Maybe see what the barkeep thought about things. Could he find one good man among these Germans that had not fallen into step with Adolf Hitler?

He was surprised to encounter two *Sturmabteilung* Brownshirts outside as he left the stylish bar. Their type seemed better suited to the working class areas of Berlin. Perhaps they were officers. He wasn't familiar with the SA's insignia of rank, but recognized their unit affiliation because of their all-black kepi caps with a stupid skull and bones insignia like fucking pirates. They belonged to Hitler's personal contingent of guards, the *Schutzstaffel*, the SS. Both men appeared slightly drunk, smoking cigarettes.

Fraser walked past them when one reached out and grabbed his arm.

"Why did you not salute?" the one still holding Fraser's arm said. His speech was slurred.

Fraser decided to play the foreigner feigning he did not speak German.

"I'm sorry. I don't speak German. I'm an American," he said in English. "*Ich spreche kein Deutsch.*"

The other SA officer responded, "That is fine. I speak English. What kind of American are you?"

"I'm sorry, I don't know what you mean. I'm a journalist." The SA officer's English was poor so he may have misunderstood.

"Ah, a journalist. The Jews run the newspapers in American. You work for a Jew?" The tone was belligerent. The other SA officer still clutched Fraser's coat sleeve.

"No. I work for William Randolph Hearst. He's not Jewish. Do you know the name?"

"Sounds like a Jew name. Maybe his family name is Hearstein. Changed it to sound less Jewish."

The two SS laughed.

Fraser said nothing, trying to present a passive expression as much as he wanted to punch these assholes in the mouth.

"Your name?"

"Fraser."

"Are you a Jew? You look Jewish."

"No. I'm not Jewish."

"They all say that. Papers."

"You're not police. Why should I?"

The two SA officers looked at each other in disbelief that someone was talking back to them. The one holding Fraser's sleeve removed his hand and drew a Luger pistol from his holster.

"So I believe you are a Jew. Hans, keep your gun on him."

"Papers. Now!"

Fraser took his passport from his coat pocket and handed it over. Didn't think they had stooped to arresting foreign journalists yet. But he was not so sure his status would protect him from physical attack.

"Herr Marc Fraser. American passport. Ah, and what is this? Ah, a French visa. You live in Paris, Herr Fraser?"

"Yes."

"The French are pigs. A decadent race. Homosexuals, perverted art. Jews run things in France just like in America. I still think you might be Jewish, Herr Fraser. You will come with us."

"Where to?" His tone more defiant.

The SA officer doing the talking swung his right hand hard in a backhanded blow across Fraser's right cheek.

The blow stunned Fraser but did not knock him down. It did mean he was in for a bad time. The same officer then grabbed his arm and pulled him along the sidewalk.

"Shoot him if he tries to escape, Hans. We are going to find out who Herr Fraser really is."

The blow had not done much damage but Fraser faked a more pronounced effect. After walking a short distance down the block, Fraser was shoved down an alley. They were not detaining him for questioning. This was to be a beating. Shades of those dirty cops in Los Angeles. The difference here being the SA had free reign to do as they pleased.

"That's far enough. Up against the wall," the officer that struck him said.

"I say you're a Jew. An American Jew. Living in decadent Paris. Maybe a homosexual Jew. How about we see if you're a Jew? Let's see if you've been circumcised. Undo your pants and show us you cock, Herr Fraser."

Fraser shook his head no.

"Easier on you if you do it. If we have to strip off your trousers we will make it most painful. Now drop your pants!"

The other officer still held the Luger on Fraser. The one doing the talking now extracted a weighted sap, a beaver-tailed leather-bound weapon with lead shot in one end. A nasty device capable of breaking bones with relatively little force. Fraser knew of the weapon often carried by Los Angeles police. He was in for a very bad beating unless he could talk his way out this.

"Listen, I'm an American journalist. I even have a letter here from Minister Göring."

The SA with the sap said, "I think you're a lying Jew. That will make it all the worse on you."

"No, here's the pass to inspect one of your detention facilities." Fraser produced the paper from his coat pocket and handed it to the SA.

The one called Hans with the gun said, "What's it say, Otto?"

The SA with the sap looked up from reading the paper then proceeded to tear it up.

"Like I thought, a lying Jew."

Like his old boxing mentor had taught him about street fighting, look for an opening to seize advantage. As the officer tore the paper into small pieces Fraser kicked him viciously in the knee. Heard the joint give way with a sickening sound.

The officer screamed in pain. Fraser caught him from falling backward by grabbing his necktie near the knot at the collar then pushed him hard into the second officer with the drawn gun. As the injured officer collided with his colleague, the Luger discharged. At point blank range, the 9mm round exited the lower abdomen of the officer narrowly missing Fraser.

The wounded officer fell back toppling then landing on top of his colleague. Fraser quickly retrieved the sap. Still holding the Luger, the trapped officer tried to dislodge the dead weight of his companion. Before he was able to free himself and take aim on Fraser, Fraser swung the sap as hard as he could catching the officer over the ear. The impact made a sickening impact sound. The man was immediately knocked unconscious.

Now what to do? The man shot in the abdomen was semi-conscious, evident by his muted groaning. The exit wound was disgorging a copious amount of blood by the look of his soaked shirt and pooling on the ground. Feeling the chest of the man he knocked unconscious, he too was apparently alive but his breathing seemed shallow to Fraser. Better if they did not live to tell who attacked them. Although he had no remorse for these two thugs, it was not in Fraser to finish them off.

However, Fraser's sense of morality did not extend to getting them help. Even if he were to make an anonymous call, he still had to successfully get out of Germany. There could be no justi-fication for his actions. At best, he would end up in a Nazi con-centration camp. He needed to buy as much time as possible. Best if they did die of their injuries.

Fortunately they were in the shadows well into the alley from the street. No one walked by at the end of street but he still needed to conceal the bodies as quickly as possible. The alley was L-shaped so it seemed better to pull the bodies around the corner further yet from the main street. Trash cans and empty crates filled this unlit part of the alley.

Fraser removed the neckties from both wounded men. He tied their wrists behind their backs. Their ankles were secured by the leather shoulder straps that connected to their waist belts. Handkerchiefs were ripped in half then knotted together as gags should either recover full consciousness.

Best he could do to give himself time to escape Germany. It might provide him several hours before their discovery by someone dumping trash in the morning. Then again it was only an issue if either man lived and was able to provide the name of their assailant.

Like so many other German Jews even in 1933, Marc Fraser would now have to leave Germany to save himself from the Nazi police state. He could never return while the Nazis remained in power. Would have to fabricate a less extreme reason for leaving than the failed assault and perhaps his killing of two SA officers. Even in safe circumstances outside Germany he did not want to advertise what happened.

Returning to the Adlon Hotel, he settled his bill claiming he had an early train to catch in the morning. Packing quickly, he descended the stairs and left through a back entrance avoiding the front desk. It was only ten o'clock at night so taxis were available, but he wanted to leave as little a trail as possible so he walked the two kilometers to the Lehrter Bahnhof rail station.

He was looking for the next train out of Berlin, hopefully heading west, but at least out of Berlin. Unfortunately it was many hours to the German border. If either of the wounded officers were found and able to talk there might be a nationwide alert for him.

Checking the train schedules he was in luck. There was a train at midnight leaving for Hamburg. Arriving in Hamburg at four in the morning, there was a train leaving an hour later for Amsterdam. That was another five hours, mostly within German borders. Within that time the SA officers would surely be found. If they were able to identify Fraser by name then it was a matter of how efficiently the borders could be alerted. Should have killed the bastards. But he wasn't going to be captured. For that eventuality he brought along one of the assailant's 9mm Luger pistol.

The trip was tense, particularly the layover in Hamburg, but uneventful. The conductors checking his papers made no facial reaction indicating that he was a person of any interest.

Looking up the SA insignia of rank once back in Paris, Fraser realized that the officer shot was a Sturmbannführer, the other a Sturmhauptführer, like the Oranienburg commandant. Mid-level ranks equivalent of a major and captain respectively. That would mean a significant challenge to the new ruling party and their paramilitary storm troopers. Fraser realized with dread that it would probably mean reprisals on some innocent group, most probably the Jews. A troubling thought.

CHAPTER 14

Germany in 1934 was in the throes of a fast changing political transition from a republic to a right-wing dictatorship. Once Adolph Hitler was appointed Chancellor the effective dismantling of the parliamentary power of the Reichstag followed with the Enabling Act. This allowed Hitler and his appointed Cabinet to enact laws without the involvement of the Reichstag. Accordingly, the Chancellor could govern by degree, quickly solidifying the Nazi hold on power. Hitler had his sights on soon establishing total power once the senile eight-six year old President Paul von Hindenburg died. As President, Hindenburg was the official head of state and supreme commander of the armed forces. Once Hindenburg died, Hitler could consolidate the remaining elements of authority by command of the armed forces and assume full foreign affairs authority as head of state.

The first order of business was to seize firm control of all policing functions. As Interior Minister of Prussia, Herman Göring created the *Geheime Staatspolizei*, or Secret State Police, commonly called the Gestapo. Another old-time Nazi, Heinrich Himmler, was already the chief of police for Bavaria in the south.

Göring had ambitions to make his Gestapo the overriding secret police for all of Germany. However he was out maneuvered by Wilhelm Frick, the Reich Minister of the Interior, along with Himmler, convincing Hitler to expand Himmler's police authori-

ty over all German states other than Prussia. Within two years
Heinrich Himmler would consolidate all police functions under
a unified Germany-wide Gestapo, as well as absorbing all conventional criminal policing of the *Kriminalpolizei*.

The other element of German state power was the military.
The *Reichswehr* was the reconstituted and substantially diminished German armed forces established in 1919 under the restrictive conditions of the Treaty of Versailles limiting Germany to a
100,000-man army and 15,000-man navy.

Unlike most political parties that come into power, Hitler
and his National Socialist German Worker's Party was backed
by its own highly organized paramilitary wing. The *Sturmabteilung*, the SA by 1934 numbered three million. It dwarfed the
size of the regular professional military thereby neutralizing the
army as any political threat. Accordingly, Hitler could secretly
begin increasing the strength of the *Reichswehr* to rearm Germany without posing a political threat to his new regime. Historically, the army represented a potential independent threat to any
government. Military coups were the principle means of toppling political regimes.

While Hitler did not fear a coup d'état by the *Reichswehr*, the
SA itself was however becoming a difficult instrument to control. SA members were widely being appointed as auxiliary police, asserting their authority as they pleased over official police.
While Hitler was the nominal head of the SA, its chief of staff,
Ernest Röhm, an old Hitler crony from the Beer Hall Putsch
days, wielded broad power.

Röhm had been arrested and convicted of treason along with
Adolf Hitler for their failed Munich coup. He was the only Nazi
official that addressed Hitler by his first name. But Röhm was
increasingly exercising his own agenda to the irritation of Hitler.
The rank and file SA were still prone to unprovoked outbursts of
street violence. Röhm himself was an outspoken advocate of
redistributing German wealth. Hitler had grander visions of
power that did not include fulfilling the socialistic motives of
National Socialism. Conciliatory overtures to the military along

with industrialists and bankers formed a basis for Hitler's grand vision for a powerful Germany. That required both a firm economic underpinning and a disciplined professional military. The SA was now proving counterproductive to Hitler's larger ambitions. Their bloated ranks, led by Ernst Röhm with increasing independence, made for difficult control by Hitler.

Röhm was even lobbying for control over the regular military, the *Reichswehr*. That was contrary to Hitler's planned enlargement of the size of the military well beyond the limits imposed by the Treaty of Versailles. Along with this he intended to rearm with armor, artillery, aircraft, and war vessels. A singular benefit of the forced reduction in military forces in 1919 insured that only the best officer corps remained in uniform. It was a strong foundation on which to build a modern German military capable of achieving Hitler's imperialistic ambitions. He could not sacrifice this in favor of a general staff populated with SA officers with no practical military experience, leading an army of ill-trained street fighters.

While the SA served as an invaluable asset in the rise of Adolf Hitler over the previous ten years, Hitler always harbored a concern. He was well aware that the SA was swollen with men of all sorts of motivations. Difficult to control, perhaps prone to cliques that might even pose a personal threat. Therefore, early on Hitler formed a small elite personal body guard and dedicated to his personal service rather than the political ideals of National Socialism. The *Schutzstaffel,* or SS was formed. In 1927, Hitler promoted a slight, bookish, bespectacled SA officer, Heinrich Himmler, to command the growing SS guard contingent of the SA. Himmler was loyal to Hitler and melded his service to also further his own ambitions. Those eventually included ultimate control of all policing, intelligence functions, as well as creating a viable combat military force reporting outside the regular military directly to Himmler.

A key subordinate to Himmler's ambitions was an ex-naval officer, Reinhard Heydrich, hired to set up a counterintelligence unit within the SS. Heydrich set up the *Sicheheitsdienst,* or SD in

1932. Admired by Hitler, Heydrich was equally ambitious and quickly became the number two man in the SS.

Among the most influential of Hitler's lieutenants, all hated Ernst Röhm. Himmler and Heydrich saw Röhm in competition for the independent power of the SS. Hermann Göring had his own ambitions of heading the military. Joseph Goebbels because Röhm's actions ran counter to his propaganda efforts shaped in concert with Hitler's grander ambitions. Adding to this was Röhm's well-known homosexuality running counter to virulent Nazi theories of degeneracy. Only Hitler remained loyal to his old comrade of the early days. But these enemies of Röhm increasingly counselled Hitler that his own ambitions were being threatened by Röhm's independence.

In April, 1934, things came to a head. Those aligned against Röhm increased their lobbying of Hitler to get rid of Röhm. They used Röhm's published anti-Hitler rhetoric to support their allegation that Röhm was plotting to overthrow Hitler. Röhm certainly had the military means with three million SA under his command.

Himmler and Heydrich compiled a dossier of fabricated evidence suggesting that Röhm had been paid twelve million marks by France to overthrow Hitler. Additionally, a high-ranking SA officer that was plotting against Röhm secretly reported on Röhm's anti-Hitler sentiments directly to Hitler. Indirectly, Hitler was eventually informed by someone close to President Hindenburg that Hindenburg was close to declaring martial law and turning the government over to the Reichswehr if Chancellor Hitler could not reign in Röhm and his Brownshirts. That sealed Röhm's fate.

Hitler ordered his deputies to prepare a list of potential enemies both within the SA as well as outside. Falsified evidence that Röhm planned to use the SA to launch a coup against the government was assembled. This planned *Röhm-Putsch* would be presented to key SS officers just prior to moving against Röhm and those on the target list.

To this background of plotters newly promoted SD Sturm-bannführer Heinz Konrad Leitner reported to the office of his immediate superior Reinhard Heydrich in Munich in June, 1934. Leitner was a principle architect of the contrived *Röhm-Putsch* evidence under Heydrich's direction.

"Today we will present this material to a select group of senior *Schutzstaffel* officers. I want you at my side to answer any questions," Heydrich said.

Leitner thought how remarkably poised and calm Heydrich appeared. This was a dangerous gamble they were embarking upon. Any number of things could go wrong. That could mean that Röhm might launch a retaliatory attack bringing about the very event Himmler and Heydrich had invented. But then again, that was Reinhard Heydrich. A perpetually calm demeanor with cold menacing eyes. The Führer was even said to have described Heydrich as 'the man with the iron heart.'

"Yes, Sir. Am I to understand the planned action will be imminent?" Leitner said.

"A detailed plan has been created for immediate execution. You are to take part directly, Leitner. Are you up to the task?"

"Yes, Sir. Absolutely. What are my orders, Sir?"

"Everyone will be given their orders individually. Nothing committed to paper. Your assignment will be to go to Bad Wiessee, a resort town on a lake fifty kilometers south of Munich. You will drive down to Bad Wiessee with other selected *Schutzstaffel* officers next Friday. Rooms have been booked at a modest hotel not far from the Hotel Hanselbauer. You are to wear civilian dress. Early Saturday morning you will drive to the Hanselbauer and rendezvous with other *Schutzstaffel* accompanied by Bavarian police. At the Hanselbauer will be the entire *Sturmabteilung* leadership including Röhm. All are to be arrested."

"Who will be in charge of this raid, Sir?"

Heydrich smiled with that sardonic smile more threatening than his normal passive expression. "Why the Führer himself of course."

Leitner came bolt upright in his chair as if responding to a call to attention.

Heydrich continued, "Actually, the senior SS officer commanding will be Obersturmbannführer Lippert. You will be second in command. Very early Saturday morning you and Lippert will assemble your strike force some distance down the road leading to the Hanselbauer and wait for the arrival of the Führer. Consult with Lippert and work out the tactical logistics."

Leitner left Heydrich's office with his poise and swagger now replaced with a real fear for the first time in his career. This was not only the equivalent of going into combat but failure would render it a suicide mission. This was Hitler potentially pitting his fanatically loyal but much smaller *Schutzstaffel* forces against the vast numbers of the *Sturmabteilung*. First they would need to be successful in decapitating the *Sturmabteilung* leader. Then it would rest on the *Sturmabteilung* rank and file's devotion to Adolf Hitler to follow his direct leadership.

Heinz Leitner was born in 1904 to a Bavarian farm family. Too young to serve in the Great War, his formative years were still shaped by the war and all that came after. The second of three boys and a girl, Leitner, along with his younger brother, sister, and mother worked the farm for four years while the father and oldest brother fought on the Western Front. The father rose to the rank of captain before taking a debilitating wound in 1917 at Passchendaele in Belgium. The serving brother was killed earlier in the war at Verdun.

Embittered by the capitulation of Germany his father embraced many of the rationalizations of the growing nationalistic political movement of the National Socialist German Worker's Party in Bavaria. He was particularly taken with the fiery nationalistic-themed rhetoric of its charismatic leader, Adolf Hitler. Already harboring anti-Semitic feelings the father accepted the conspiracy concept of Jews, Socialist, and Communists having undermined German military forces in the war. The collapse of the German economy that followed was again the fault of the left-leaning Weimar Republic. The onset of the world-wide Depression was evidence of Jewish manipulation of financial institutions. The Great Depression had its origins in the American collapse of their stock market in 1929. Everyone knew that the United States was dominated by Jewish Wall Street banking.

Although Heinz Leitner and his family weathered the deprivations better than most during these difficult times since they produced their own food by bartering the surplus for other necessities, his nationalistic fervor and anti-Semitic views were firmly established by the time he graduated from gymnasium.

Money was tight and the farm could still use his labor but Leitner's father insisted he attend university. Leitner had a particular aptitude for mathematics. Displaying an inherent understanding of the farm machinery he therefore settled on studying engineering. However after only two years at the Munich Technische Hochschule, he was forced to leave for lack of money. Returning to his family home in 1923, he took a sales job with a farm implement manufacturer to support himself as well as contribute to the rest of the family.

It was a bitter pill to swallow for Leitner. Forced to live in his childhood bedroom along with his younger brother while working for a commission-based salary that was spotty at best in these bad times. Further insulting to his pride, the manufacturing company was owned by a Jewish family. The owner's son was in charge of sales, therefore Leitner's immediate boss. Adding further insult, his younger boss possessed the arrogance of wealthy privilege, grating against Leitner's own arrogance of his perceived racial superiority. These forced circumstances cultivated hatred within Leitner with no immediate outlet.

Leitner stuck out the demeaning situation for almost two years. By 1925 hyperinflation brought industrial commerce in Germany to an almost virtual halt. Out of necessity the company terminated their entire sales force including Leitner. Leitner however took it as another personal affront of Jewish origin.

Adding further insult Leitner now was forced to revert to manual labor to support himself while also assisting his family.

His aging father with his lame leg from the war was relegated to administering the farm business. Mother did the cooking and cleaning, the younger brother and sister the heavy farm work. Leitner added his own labor but was soon freelancing his skills at repairing farm machinery for others in the region. He was good with engines, a skilled welder, with the ability to keep failing machinery running where there was no money to buy replacement parts. Payment was often in the form of barter.

Leitner was intrigued by the message of this rabble rouser Adolf Hitler so admired by his father. Hitler had miraculously resurrected from the ashes of his failed coup in Munich years earlier. Now he headed this growing political movement the National Socialist German Worker's Party. Attending a Munich rally in 1928, Leitner was mesmerized by Hitler's oration that night. Shaking Hitler's hand after the event, he immediately joined the Party. Soon after, he joined the military wing of the NSDAP, the *Sturmabteilung*, the SA Brownshirts.

Leitner had risen in rank within the SA when approached two years later at a subsequent NSDAP rally. He recognized the small man with the round-lens spectacles. Various divisions with the SA were designated by color displayed on the front of their kepi caps. The small man with the round-lens spectacles approaching wore the all-black kepi with the deaths-head insignia denoting Hitler's personal body guard the *Schutzstaffel*, the SS. As Deputy Reichsführer-SS with the rank of SS-Oberführer, Henrich Himmler was well known to all within the SA.

Himmler extended his hand to Leitner saying, "Sturmhauptführer Leitner?"

"Yes, Sir," Leitner replied coming to attention then shaking Himmler's hand. "An honor, Oberführer."

"I have excellent reports on you, Leitner. I understand you also attended the Munich Technische Hochschule. I too studied there. The *Schutzstaffel* has need of dedicated men such as you, Leitner. Does joining the *Schutzstaffel* interest you?"

Leitner was overwhelmed. Interested? He couldn't imagine his unexpected good fortune. What he was doing within the SA was simply venting his social frustrations along with others of the same political persuasion. The *Schutzstaffel* was perhaps something much more. A possible career even. A career within a growing political movement that might come to power. No longer working for meager wages in jobs of no stature with no dignity and no future. Right now he still lived with his parents and siblings, made his living through manual work, had no prospects for a future, for marriage, for a real life.

"I am very interested, Oberführer. And very honored."

"Excellent. Report to my adjutant at my office in Munich tomorrow morning."

Heinz Leitner found a professional home within the elite *Schutzstaffel* corps. Increasingly Henrich Himmler was shaping the unit into a highly disciplined independent military unit growing in size. Himmler's vision of an almost medieval quasi-religious fraternity was designed to further differentiate the SS from its mother organization the SA. Based upon mystical concepts harking to Germanic fables, with a hierarchy resembling the fictional construct of King Arthur's Knights of the Round Table, Himmler was fashioning a military-like cadre of hundreds of thousands. With this he intended to subsume all control over security, policing, counter-intelligence, and judicial processes in Germany.

To critics the SS appeared a mix of fanaticism, screwball racial theory, deified devotion to Adolf Hitler, questionable recruits with unremarkable backgrounds, bound together by symbolic rituals. It was all those things, but proved effective in creating a zealously dedicated organization. An organization of such menace as to eventually inflict unspeakable horrors well beyond the borders of Germany.

Leitner found an outlet to apply a broad range of personal skills. While promotion within the SS was to a large degree merit-based, other factors came into play as with any organization. He was equally ambitious therefore alert to any opportunity.

His boss Reinhard Heydrich had a music background. Heydrich asked if he would like to accompany him and his wife to a

philharmonic concert by escorting Heydrich's niece. The niece
was taken with the handsome SS officer that evening. A short
romance eventually led to marriage. While the bride was rather
plain, she came from a modestly wealthy family. Leitner's financial circumstances dramatically improved. The family association with Heydrich gave him added stature.

   After leaving Heydrich's office, Leitner met with Obestur-
bannführer Lippert to work out the plans. They would be leading a fifty-man contingent of selected SS officers. They would
dress in civilian clothes for the trip south to Bad Wiessee but
present themselves in uniform for the assault the following
morning. Ernst Röhm and several SA colleagues were on holiday
in Bad Wiessee. On Thursday Hitler would personally call Röhm
and order him to assemble all the SA leadership at Bad Wiessee
on Saturday for an important conference.

   The plan was simple. All of the SA leadership was to be arrested. They would be transported by lorry back to Munich's
Stadelheim Prison. The Bavarian police would be under SS orders.

   "Then what, Obersturmbannführer?" Leitner said, knowing
the answer.

   "They're to be executed of course. They are conspirators preparing to overthrow the government. After all, you created the
brief for those charges, Sturmbannführer Leitner. Drastic action
is called for to protect the State wouldn't you say?"

   "Of course, Obersturmbannführer," Leitner said. He was up
to it although this remained a nerve-racking high-stakes gamble.
If successful then he was in the very circle of power. If it went
wrong he would save at least one bullet for his own end.

   What was to become known as the *Night of the Long Knives*
began in the earliest hours of Saturday, June 30, 1934 with Adolf
Hitler arriving in Munich by air at 4:30 in the morning. Hitler's
entourage drove to the Bavarian Interior Ministry where they
assembled the local leaders of an SA rampage of violence the
previous night. Hitler was so enraged that he personally ripped

the epaulets off the shirt of the chief of the Munich police for failing to keep order. Hitler shouted that he would have the chief shot. Later in the day the man was executed.

As prearranged, Hitler and his entourage sped off south to Bad Wiessee to rendezvous with the SS contingent to make the assault on the Hotel Hanselbauer.

Heinz Leitner accompanied Hitler as they entered the hotel. As planned, Leitner's superior Obersturmbannführer Lippert entered Ernst Röhm's room number 70 along with Adolf Hitler. Leitner accompanied by a junior officer entered room number 71. With pistol drawn, Leitner looked upon his target, a senior SA leader recognizable from photographs, lying naked in bed with a very young man. At gunpoint, Leitner ordered them outside without allowing them to put on any clothing.

With all the SA leaders assembled outside for transport, Hitler personally asked Leitner about the circumstances of the two naked men. Leitner told Hitler he found them in bed together that way.

"Disgusting degenerates," Hitler screamed. "Shoot them!"

"*Jawohl, mein Führer*," Leitner said then immediately obliged by first shooting the senior SA officer in the forehead. The younger man was shot in the face as he sank to his knees begging a reprieve. Leitner followed with a coup de grâce shot to the head.

"*Das ist gut*," Hitler said and turned away.

The purge of the SA lasted three days. Ostensibly maintained as a thwarting of an imminent coup, it was labelled by Nazi propagandist Joseph Goebbels as the *Röhm Putsch*. Back in Munich, Hitler denounced the conspiracy to an assembled group of Nazi Party members and SA. Simultaneously, Goebbels telephoned Hermann Göring that same morning to let loose execution squads to liquidate other unsuspecting targets deemed a threat to Adolf Hitler.

As for the captured SA leaders now housed in Munich's Stadelheim Prison, none would escape execution. As for Ernst

Röhm himself, Hitler had ordered he be allowed the dignity of committing suicide. Obersturmbannführer Lippert walked into his cell, laid a pistol on the table with a single bullet and told Röhm he had ten minutes.

"If I am to kill myself, let Adolf do it himself," Röhm said to Lippert.

Returning after hearing no shot fired within the allotted time, Lippert entered the cell to find a defiant Röhm. Without preamble Lippert shot Röhm three times in the chest.

Leitner's assignment was a less prosaic delivering of death. He was to supervise the execution of the remaining eighteen arrested SA leadership. Thirteen were dispatched by a bullet to the head in the exercise yard. But the remaining five most senior officers were to be decapitated by guillotine which remained as the method of execution for common criminals. Several of the SS officers vomited at the gruesome spectacle. To Leitner's own surprise he was not repulsed by the heads dropping into buckets as the blade cleanly severed the heads.

With no way to keep the purge secret, on July 13, 1934, Hitler justified the purge in a nationally broadcast speech to the Reichstag:

'In this hour I was responsible for the fate of the German people, and thereby I became the supreme judge of the German people. I gave the order to shoot the ringleaders in this treason, and I further gave the order to cauterize down to the raw flesh the ulcers of this poisoning of the wells in our domestic life. Let the nation know that its existence — which depends on its internal order and security — cannot be threatened with impunity by anyone! And let it be known for all time to come that if anyone raises his hand to strike the State, then certain death is his lot.'

Hitler had successfully removed the threat of his own Stormtroopers thereby placating the established regular military, the *Reichswehr*, by assuring that their power would not be usurped by the SA rabble. He was now free to enlist the *Reichswehr* in enthusiastic participation in his quest to rearm Germany.

One month later, Adolf Hitler ascended the final step to power with the death of President Paul von Hindenburg. Hitler swiftly moved to combine the offices of President and Chancellor making his position as Führer of the German Third Reich one of absolute dictatorial power.

CHAPTER 15

Since the harrowing events that led to Marc Fraser's abrupt departure from Germany he needed a break before pursuing further reporting from other countries in Europe. Without telling anyone about what happened in Berlin he requested a leave to return for a visit to the United States.

He had not been back for some time. That now seemed appropriate. It would partly satisfy an obligation to see his sister. A short side trip to Guadalajara to visit his step mother would be enjoyable. Professional reasons as well. After living and working in Europe for the last several years he needed to regain perspective. After all he was writing for an American audience.

Most of the time spent back in the United States was in Southern California visiting old acquaintances. A few drinks with is old boss at the Examiner, Randal Schmidt. A tearful meeting with Guido Leopardi. The little ex-boxer was retired from the MGM studio living in a bleak boardinghouse. Rheumatoid arthritis had reduced him to a near-cripple. He was overjoyed to hear that the skills he had taught Fraser had proven useful.

LAPD Captain Carmody looked a little older. Still the cheap suit with an ugly tie. Bought him a couple of drinks now that Prohibition had ended. Still the honest cop looking to retire in a few years in a small bungalow up the coast with the wife.

Abigail Blumenthal declined an invitation to lunch. Wished him well over the phone.

Marion Davies was delighted to hear from him immediately inviting him to a dinner party. Fraser accepted having a sweet spot for the crazy film industry. All good memories.

Hollywood now fully transitioned to talkies was growing every year. Marion had made that transition as well and was still making movies. The Great Depression if anything was driving the industry. Going to a movie offered a diversion from the difficult circumstances of the time. Even the impoverished working class could occasionally afford the admission price for a couple of hours escape into a world of adventure, drama, or laughter.

At Marion's dinner in the vast mansion in Santa Monica, she invited the actress Greta Garbo. Garbo notoriously shunned Hollywood social functions preferring the company of a few close friends. Marion said to him, "You'll like Greta. She's smart and witty. I like her independence. She just came off doing two pictures for MGM, *Mata Hari* in 1931, and *Grand Hotel* in 1932."

"You introduced me to her some years ago at one of your parties when I met you for the first, Marion."

"Oh yes. I forgot. Well Greta's come a long ways since then. Her screen success has given her a degree of clout in selecting roles. I was in one meeting with her and Louis Meyer who can be a real belligerent jerk if someone gives him an argument. Well Greta gave as good as Meyer did. He eventually backed down. She got to do *Queen Christina* last year. Period piece about a Swedish queen. Being Swedish the part was obviously meant for her. She might like to hear your views on what's going on in Europe."

It turned out to be a wonderful evening. Better that William Hearst was not there to dominate the conversation. He remembered Garbo from that earlier Davies' party he attended years ago. Apologetically, Garbo apparently did not.

Greta Garbo was strikingly beautiful to the point of distraction. She was dismayed over his recounting of what was happening in Germany. He was impressed by the caliber of her questions.

Garbo said, "All of Europe is like a dysfunctional family forced to live in the same house. The borders of countries often do not reflect the mixed cultures within those boundaries. In Sweden most everyone is of a common culture. Little conflict. But of course we are a small country so we can be damaged by the arguments of our larger neighbors. The Baltic affords little protection from the turmoil on the Continent. A Germany led by this Adolf Hitler and his Nazis is a frightening thought."

Political talk gave way to movie talk over dinner.

Garbo said to him, "Marion just gave me a copy of your book this evening, *Provoke the Devil*. Impressive accomplishment. What's it about?"

"Thanks for asking. It's a novel about political corruption in Los Angeles. As a newspaper reporter I had a lot of real-life material to work with."

"Yes, I know. You helped put away a bunch of bad guys a few years ago. I looked you up when Marion invited me to dinner."

Garbo was about Fraser's age. Unescorted that evening. Was she flirting? Chasing beautiful women was still a habit.

She added, "I read a lot of novels. They're a lot more engrossing as stories than screenplays. But Marion says your book would make a good movie. I like the author Ernest Hemmingway. Just finished his bullfighting novel, *Death in the Afternoon*. Before that I read his *Farewell to Arms* about love and war in Italy. Is your work anything like his?"

Fraser smiled. "No. Hemmingway has a terse, sparse style. My style is somewhat different. He tells a good story though. You can feel his characters. Hope my work is viewed as favorably.

"I actually met Hemmingway while I was attending the university in Paris ten years ago. I was studying journalism. He may have given me the bug to explore writing fiction. We also share the same publisher."

A great evening but any fantasy about a fling with Greta Garbo was only fleeting. Los Angeles brought back memories but it was no longer home. Two days later he was on a plane to New York.

The remaining days spent in New York with his sister were strained. He and his brother-in-law were never close. Politically they were an ocean apart. The brother-in-law was a fervent isolationist. The United States must not be drawn into another European war. No amount of Fraser's explaining the broader implications of Europe descending into armed conflict would affect his position. It wasn't about squabbling European countries as his brother-in-law categorized them collectively, it was about a pent-up kennel of mongrel cultures led by one rabid dog, Adolf Hitler that was at the heart of the problem. Like so many Americans, his brother-in-law was dismissive of the threat of Germany. Too bad Germany was chaffing under the terms of the Treaty of Versailles. That was the penalty for causing the Great War.

Fraser pointed out that Germany only lost because of the United States entry into that war on the side of Britain and France. That could happen again. To which his brother-in-law countered that was way too premature to consider. To which Fraser countered that when it became a real possibility it might be too late. So it went back and forth.

The argument was symptomatic of the general American attitude. Americans simply did not think in international terms thereby fostering pervasive isolationism. Perhaps that was the American psyche or just a function of its geographic remoteness from Europe and Asia. Not only did the Atlantic and Pacific Oceans render a natural defensive buffer against foreign aggression, it also promoted a provincial attitude. As the most powerful economic country in the world since the Great War it was probably only natural that its preoccupation was domestic.

In sunny Southern California with its beaches, its citrus groves, and most of all its movie industry, it was easy to see how Americans felt detachment from events abroad. But even given these rationalizations of the American perspective, Fraser was frustrated with the underlying self-absorbed attitudes of America during his return to the United States. They didn't even acknowledge that the failure of the United States financial system led to the market crash of 1929, which rippled outward causing economic grief to the entire world.

Equally disturbing were displays of approval for the new government in Germany. There was no moral backlash of any strength directed at the virulent anti-Semitism of the Nazi government. If anyone dismissed Adolf Hitler as just another European aberration like Mussolini, they only had to look at the newly released documentary film, *Triumph des Willens, Triumph of the Will*. Both a remarkable artistic film as well as a darkly foreboding warning to the world. Produced and directed by Leni Riefenstahl. Fraser lamented her deluded conversion to the Nazis while admiring her extraordinary cinematic talent.

Fraser left New York by steamer to Europe in May of 1935. Paris was now home. There remained a degree of sadness brought about by his disappointment on his return to the States after three years. He felt like an outsider. There was a storm brewing yet he still wanted to return to Paris.

CHAPTER 16

After returning from his visit to the United States, Marc Fraser spent most of the prior year venturing out to other countries to write from these differing perspectives of events shaping Europe.

In Great Britain there was a general level of ambivalence not unlike that in the United States. All the more surprising with the experience of the Great War waged against an earlier militaristic Germany led by someone as outspokenly aggressively as Adolf Hitler.

A visit to Dublin made clear the Irish were still consumed with gaining full independence from the Britain. The Irish Free State established at the end of the Irish Civil War over ten years earlier did not heal the wounds of hundreds of years of British domination over Ireland. The Irish still chaffed under the British yoke.

Brussels and Amsterdam viewed Germany with the same distain and mistrust as the French. No country suffered worse devastation during the Great War than Belgium. Geographically it sat between Germany and France. If Germany and France were to ever come to blows again, Belgium would again be caught in the middle.

Italy proved an interesting mix of competing opinions. No one of course would speak against *Il Duce*, Benito Mussolini, but this was clearly not the same type of police state that Nazi Germany was becoming. To the typical Italian, family and the good things in life were paramount. Inherently not militaristic like the Germans they wound up with Mussolini and his Fascism out of economic desperation. Mussolini had delusions of a new Roman Empire with expanded international power and colonies that were not universally shared by most Italians. Italians were notoriously provincial viewing themselves first as Roman, Venetian, Florentine, Milanese, or Sicilian before identifying as Italian. The opposite of the efficient Germans, the Italians were bureaucratically dysfunctional. Fraser instinctively liked the Italians.

If he thought Berlin was a disturbing environment, Fraser quickly realized that the Soviet Union was in a class of its own. He was forewarned to be careful since foreign journalists enjoyed no special protections from the repressive police state run by Joseph Stalin. Requiring a special Soviet visa he was chaperoned by a minder, assumed to be NKVD, the secret police, from the time he disembarked the train in Moscow. After a week of frustration with no one willing or allowed to speak to him, he left in disgust.

He garnered no first-hand material on the mood of any segment of the Russian people except by observation, but enough to paint a startling picture living life in perpetual unrelenting fear. Fear of unannounced arrest for bizarre charges with no basis other than the whim of someone powerful. Worse than Nazi Germany. There you knew what not to say. In the Soviet Union it simply didn't matter how careful you might be. For some never revealed reason you might be sent to a brutal labor camp in Siberia for ten or twenty years. If you were of some importance you might simply disappear for good.

If that wasn't bad enough, with few exceptions Moscow was a depressingly ugly city as Soviet inspired architecture increasing dominated. Inspired did not mean creative. To the contrary, Soviet buildings were uniformly gray, utilitarian, designed with absolutely no appreciation for aesthetic appeal. Prison-like architecture suitably fit for the rotten climate and a depraved social order.

His parting shot before leaving Moscow was to present a list of people he would like to interview. He anticipated the response but he might be surprised. He wasn't. The list had been prepared after considerable research. It consisted of a range of prominent Russians in the arts, literature, and science. They were not even known to be dissidents of the current regime, just individuals of some reputation in the West. The following day his government minder informed him that all those he had listed were not in Moscow. All were known to reside in Moscow.

As he left Moscow he wondered if Nazi Germany would descend so far. The Soviet Union was a dystopian monstrosity. All sense of normalcy was contorted into some unrecognizable perverted social condition. Witnessing Stalin's complete control, Fraser could better understand the unease of many in the West of the threat of Communism ever spilling into populace inspired revolutions elsewhere in the world. Hitler's boogey man was all too real.

Germany however was rapidly transforming into something far worse than Fraser had experienced just two years ago. Hitler had successfully purged the SA leadership bringing the ranks of millions under control thereby winning favor with the established German military. With President Hindenburg's death, a plebiscite approved Hitler becoming absolute dictator with the title of Führer. The SS became separate from the diminished SA and assumed control over all policing functions including the secret police, the Gestapo. Persecution of Jews increased.

Fraser concluded that Hitler had now reached a position where he had not only consolidated all power of the state but he had successfully brought the military and industrial base into his sphere. They were successfully seduced by the vision of his ambitions which coincided with their own. No influential sector remained to counter Hitler's nationalistic vision for a greater German Reich.

Reporting on political events was however losing Fraser's interest. He began seriously considering leaving journalism to write fiction full time. A compelling lure of spending afternoons at the typewriter looking out his apartment window. Strolling Paris to one of his many favorite restaurants for dinner. Sometimes with friends. Perhaps with a lady friend. Discussing literature and art. Waking late. Breakfast or an early lunch before resuming writing in the afternoon. Holidays by train to other parts of France. Only two problems. Given his past career would he become bored? A damn good journalist, was he good enough to make it as a novelist? Did he have more than one book in him?

The pursuit of a real story was addicting especially if it had bad characters involved. Maybe his sense of justice in exposing wrong doing. But writing his first novel had proved particularly fulfilling. Creating his own stories with vivid characters by portraying whatever suited his interests was enormously gratifying. Yet so was crafting a compelling newsworthy story derived from his own investigations. Nothing was more satisfying than sitting in front of the typewriter. The questioned remained, journalism or fiction? Or continue to pursue both?

The independent writing life offered much appeal when contrasted with the demands of investigative journalism. He would give it more consideration after the upcoming remaining European trip to troubled Spain. That idyllic scenario as the life of a writer in Paris might also be disrupted if this demented German Führer made war again against France. But things might develop differently. Hitler also had designs on territory to the east. All of Europe was suffering dangerous uncertainty. He had to try to make sense of what was going on. Spain was yet another brewing powder keg.

Spain was in more political turmoil than any other European country. Not unusual since Spain seemed always in turmoil for at least the last hundred years. It was a European backwater. Primarily an agrarian economy their natural resources were also concentrated more in the north in the politically antagonistic Catalonia and Basque regions. These regions historically wanted independence from the government in Madrid. Culturally they did not regard themselves as even Spanish. Adding to this was a retrograde Spanish society where power rested with large land owners allied with a bloated military officer corps and supported by the powerful Catholic Church. The rural working classes were not only peasants but near serfs with circumstances not much better than the Russian proletariat that overthrew the Tsar in 1917 Russia.

Spanish landowners enforced a subsistence living through withholding work backed by brutal repression of a militarized Civil Guard in their pay. Spain had turned particularly violent with the clash of the privileged right and the impoverished left. The leftist political parties had united into a Popular Front now poised to win the next general election scheduled for February, 1936.

Unexpectedly, Fraser received a telegram a few weeks before his scheduled departure to Spain. It was from Allen Dulles. *Travelling Paris Monday next - stop - Can we meet? - stop - Leave message Ritz Paris - stop - A. Dulles.*

At the Ritz bar, Dulles said, "I've read your articles in the American papers. You have a good feel for what is going over here."

"By over here you mean Germany?" Fraser said.

They were both enjoying whiskies.

"Of course. I've just come from there. Last time. I persuaded my brother, our law firm's managing partner, to close our Berlin office. A hard sell but Cromwell & Sullivan can no longer be supporting German business and banking with what's going on. The Nazis persecution of their Jews is unacceptable."

"Anti-Semitism exists everywhere. Here in Paris, even New York." Fraser didn't necessarily accept a non-Jewish law firm having those kinds of ethics.

"True, but the Nazis have gone beyond just prejudice. I suspect that it will soon take on a much more virulent form. Perhaps wholesale harm to Jews. Mass deportations perhaps. Apart from the ethical implications of such policies, ultimately that will lead to investment risks. We can't be recommending German investment to American firms and we fear entanglements representing our former German clients."

All about profits after all. But he wouldn't hold that against Dulles. At his core Dulles was an intellectual pragmatist. But one with a cultivated charm. Fraser liked him. At least he was doing the right thing even if not as altruistic as it might appear.

"By the way, I read your book, *Provoke the Devil*. A good read. A lady friend recommended it. I believe the appeal for her might have been the racier parts. That notwithstanding, I was intrigued by the investigative ingenuity of your protagonist. So I looked into your earlier professional career in Los Angeles. How much of the book is autobiographical?"

Fraser smiled. "Obviously the skeleton of the story was based upon real events. Some of the stuff came directly from my work when I was with the Examiner. As to the larger than life escapades of my protagonist, romances and all that, well let's just say I employed considerable fictional license."

"From the newspaper archives you were apparently involved in a real event similar to the character in your novel. The scene where the protagonist kills the thugs that caused the accident killing his girlfriend."

"That's what I mean by fictional license. Pretty sure that real event was not an accident but I could never prove anything. Obviously I didn't kill the real-life bad guys. The woman, the prosecutor I was working with survived although badly injured. In the end I was successful in causing prosecutions for corruption in the so-called *Harbors Scandal* that put away some bigshots."

Dulles smoked his pipe and sipped his whisky nodding his head in acknowledgement.

"I take it you like it over here?" Dulles said.

"Here?"

"I mean Europe."

"Not exactly all of Europe. I like Paris. For that matter lots of other places in France. I feel French. I'm French-American. As for the rest of Europe, I'm more discriminating. Amsterdam is lovely, London boring, Dublin lively, Rome interesting, Berlin absolutely not. Not going back there. Frankly I'm thinking of resigning from reporting. Might try my hand at another book. I am scheduled to go to Spain to cover what's happening there. Probably because I speak Spanish. Not thrilled with the assignment. I'll reassess my future plans when I return from Spain."

"Spain, huh. That's interesting," Dulles said. "When we met in Berlin in '33 I did not elaborate as to what I actually did."

"You mean you're not an international business lawyer?"

"Oh yes. That I am. But perhaps with a different twist. When I was with the State Department I did a lot of work over here with disarmament issues after the Great War. I was still assisting State when I met you in Berlin.

"When I left government service to join my brother's law firm, I did not wholly give up my involvement in foreign affairs. That is actually my role within the firm. Advising clients on international business from the perspective of the prevailing political winds. My contacts from my diplomatic days are a valuable resource when matching clients to foreign officials. That of course works both ways."

"So you're saying that you still play an unofficial role with the U.S. government? A spy perhaps?"

Dulles laughed. "Nothing quite so glamorous. Let's just say that I am a facilitator, a conduit to funnel useful information to those in Washington. All the great powers of the world have foreign intelligence agencies. All except the United States. Part of our national naivety. Espionage is not gentlemanly or whatever silly rationale. But that is where we stand. In a world that almost certainly will explode soon into some sort of military conflict. The only official means currently to gather vital intelligence from which to plan strategic responses to events happening in the world is through our military attachés."

"And how do these attachés obtain information without engaging in espionage?"

"Rubbing shoulders with diplomats and other military attachés. And from people like you. Remember, the vast majority of useful intelligence is just out there for the harvesting. It doesn't require furtive spies passing along state secrets."

"So you'd like me to pass along information. Sounds like spying to me."

"Semantics. Intelligence is everything. The point being the United States is blind to anticipating events until they happen. Not a good perspective for a world power in these insecure times."

"So what are you suggesting, Allen?"

Dulles leaned in toward Fraser. "First, I'd like to introduce you to Lt. Col. Sumner Waite. He's the assistant army attaché here Paris. He'll be especially interested in your trip to Spain. Things are so bad there politically that a larger conflict seems inevitable. There's already considerable violence. The United States is very interested in what is happening in Spain. There seems a distinct demarcation between Left and Right political movements. A microcosm of larger antagonisms playing out elsewhere in Europe."

"Listen, Allen, I have no intention of passing along military information. Wouldn't know what's important anyway."

"Think about this, Marc. If you were reporting from Germany right now it would be difficult even dangerous to communicate material critical toward the Nazis to your publisher. You might encounter the same problem in Spain. Waite might be able to offer some ideas to *disguise* your material. Might prove useful journalistically. If any of your reporting has broader intelligence value then that's just a bonus."

"Ok, I'll talk to your Lt. Col. Waite. No promises though."

"Excellent. Another whisky?"

Before parting, Dulles provided Fraser with a New York address and telephone number. "In case you find it safer to forward information ostensibly to your *lawyer*."

"Safer? I'm not doing anything that requires a *safer* means of communicating. Whatever that even means."

"Poor choice of words," Dulles said. "All I'm suggesting is talk to Waite. He might be able to provide you some useful ideas for bypassing the censors when filing your stories.

Three days later, Fraser was seated in front of the desk of Lt. Col. Sumner Waite at the newly constructed United States Embassy on the historic Place de la Concorde in the heart of Paris. Although U.S. military attachés received no special training in intelligence gathering, Dulles told Fraser that Waite in particular knew something about what was called tradecraft.

Fraser hit it off with Sumner Waite. A first-rate intellect, Waite gave him a surprisingly well-informed overview of the political dynamics in Spain. He candidly told Fraser there existed the real possibility of a military coup. After coming to power in 1933, the right-wing government brutally suppressed an armed rising of desperate, starving workers in late 1934. As a result, an energized leftist coalition has been growing in strength. Civil war was a real possibility. He thanked Fraser in advance for any service Fraser might provide to the U.S. in the way of information.

"What sort of information might be helpful?" Fraser asked.

"Obviously military related information. That is of course if things move beyond the current political violence. The Spanish military is still conservatively Right politically so the situation could descend into civil war. But of course you can't provide that kind of information if you're still in Spain. You'd be shot as a spy. That is something for authorized observers, namely military attachés like me. You'd be surprised how much information can be gleaned by just rubbing shoulders with the host country's military officers."

"That's what Dulles said. But I don't expect to be interviewing military types. Not even political figures. My assignment is a little different."

"Of course. We're just looking for the same material you want to publish, Mr. Fraser. In your case, particularly your photographs."

"Not sure I understand, Colonel. Just get it then from the Hearst newspapers."

"I'm not sure you understand, Mr. Fraser. The kind of violence being perpetrated by both sides will make anything you write, certainly any photographs you take, subject to censorship to whatever side you're reporting from.

"You were in Germany since the Nazis came to power I understand. Image if you were there now how difficult it would be to get anything out that would be damaging to them. Well, it's probably worse in Spain. The place in not under any consistent governmental control. Violence is localized. Hard to tell who is in control. No one is held accountable. I suspect it's even dangerous for an accredited foreign correspondent."

Fraser had not realized that the situation was so extreme in Spain. What the hell was he getting into now?

"How do you normally file your stories, Mr. Fraser?"

"If I'm outside of Paris, usually by post to an office here in Paris used by European Hearst correspondents. Sometimes by telephone, occasionally by telegram. Photographs by post or hand delivered."

"You can imagine the difficulty if you are among those that may not trust what you're doing. None of your material will be secure. First time you step over some line you'll be thrown out of Spain. Maybe worse if you offend the wrong people. Things are pretty chaotic down there."

"Ok. I see what you mean. So what are you suggesting?" Fraser had never been in the equivalent of what Waite was describing as a near warzone.

"I understand you develop your own photographs?"

"For my personal photography I do."

"Then the answer is micro-photography. According to a person familiar with the technical side it should be fairly simple for someone already familiar with developing negatives. I understand the equipment necessary is fairly minimal, just the chemicals become awkward. You can use your standard 35mm camera. The process produces exceedingly small format negatives.

I'm told the size of a typewritten page can be reduced by some-thing like 200 to 1. Small enough to conceal the negative in any manner of ways. In a hat band, inside the seam-fold of clothing, under a postage stamp."

What was he getting himself into? "Dulles called this trade-craft. So this *is* spying, Colonel."

"Depends on your definition."

"If I'm caught smuggling out photos then it will certainly be considered spying."

"What about your normal journalistic materials? You wouldn't consider those espionage materials. How do you ex-pect to get your material to your publisher? Unless of course you're going to be in Spain for only a short period and write your story after you leave. Even with that scenario you may have difficulty getting undeveloped photographs past a censor."

A short stay was probably not going to be the case. He was expected to file weekly for a protracted period. How long de-pended on what happened there. Of all the places he had visited, Spain sounded the most complicated. It would take some time to canvas the different regions undergoing their own localized turmoil. It would probably also be the most compelling for his continuing series on life in Europe. This Spanish assignment had the same tinge of adventure as his days in Los Angeles. There was real danger in sticking himself in the middle of what he knew to be wholesale murders and torture being committed by the competing factions. Was he up to this?

"Well I guess it won't do any harm to learn this *tradecraft* as you call it, Colonel."

Waite sent him to an address in Montmartre north of central Paris. This was the bohemian artist and prostitution quarter. The nondescript sign over the store front read *Kovač Photographie*. It was a suitably sleazy hole in the wall along a street of cheap re-tail goods and sex related merchandise. Surprisingly the proprie-tor was a neatly dressed well-groomed middle-aged man who escorted him into the back room after Fraser told him Colonel

Waite sent him. An innocuous phrase corroborated Fraser's authenticity.

Fraser guessed the man to be East European by his accented French. Looking at the display of the suggestive nude photographs in the small lobby, Fraser was taken by the photographic quality going beyond the prurient sexual impact to something approaching art. He could see the same impressions that he tried to achieve in his own photography of the nude form. Once they began discussing the aesthetics of photography as art not simply a means of reproducing a likeness they quickly developed a rapport.

"You're a talented artist, Monsieur Kovač. Why this pornographic work?"

Ladislav Kovač, stated the obvious, "Sex sells better than art."

Over a glass of wine Kovač explained how to develop micro-sized negatives using an improvised set-up. The only special equipment required was a two-inch diameter plano-convex lens to substitute for the condenser of a conventional enlarger. A bargain at 100 francs. Fraser had his own supply of photographic developing chemicals. Lastly, Kovač sketched out how Fraser could construct a homemade platform to mount onto a standard tripod to hold the lens at a distance of one meter from the camera.

It was a two-step process involving developing a second negative. Tedious but necessary to achieve good image resolution because of the light required with this jerry-rigged equipment. The result was a reduction of a page of text or a photograph to a negative of only 1.0 x 1.2mm. Assuming varying circumstances, the trick will be to create an adequate incandescent light source directly above the condenser lens and the conventional 35mm negative for the second-stage photographic reduction.

While the set-up was comparatively simple, the process sequence was complicated, laborious, and required precision. Fraser paid attention while asking questions and making careful notes. He would have to experiment at the apartment to determine if he could do this under unknown circumstances. Even developing regular sized film might be difficult. Lugging chemicals would be a burden. Would he even have access to creating a dark room for developing his film? The obvious place was a toilet. But would hotels encountered in Spain have toilets in every room?

Was all this necessary? Waite had suggested it might very well be. Spain was in social chaos. It would be a situational case of what he was reporting. If it ran counter to whoever was the host authority then it would be censured. Fraser was well aware of the difficulties for long-term resident correspondents in Germany filing material critical of the Nazis now that they were in heavy-handed control of everything in Germany. However, Spain was still a republic, at least in theory. Would the international press be censured? Waite suggested that might be the case with the situation so factionalized.

Made sense at any rate to have this trick as an option. Armed with this clandestine process he still needed a means to secretly transmit the material out of Spain.

The solution seemed simple. He would send seemingly personal correspondence to Allen Dulles in New York, addressed to his sister but using Dulles law firm address. The micro-reduced negatives would be concealed under the postage stamp. Dulles would forward the inflammatory copy and photographs to predetermined news outlets for publication. Anything of intelligence value could be forwarded to his friends in the Army's Military Intelligence Division.

There was the dilemma. How could he disguise himself as not being the origin of the photographs? Publication must also be other than Hearst Publications so as not to be easily connected to him.

The difficult trick would be to conceal his identity as the only obvious source by reason of connection to the content. Attribution would be an anonymous freelancer, a dissident Spaniard. He must therefore radically alter his writing style in these secret dispatches. Maybe mimic Hemmingway. Disguising the photographs presented a much greater challenge.

Dulles would act as the middleman collecting any submission payments. As part of the bargain to funnel information to U.S. Army Intelligence, Dulles would agree to shop his freelance material to the various news services, UPI, API, Reuters, and even Fraser's own Hearst news service, INS. Helping his own government was fine, however getting information to the public was of greater importance. Even the U.S. government was self-serving. Not always in the best interests of the citizenry they pledged to serve. So he would not tolerate any censorship on Dulles part.

He explained all this in a letter to Dulles then packed for Spain. Fraser felt a certain thrill in this cloak-and-dagger tradecraft not to mention the adventure of sticking his nose into a dangerous place. He still doubted that he would uncover anything of intelligence value. Not his concern. However having this means of secreting his material out of Spain did make sense.

As physical protection, some time ago he had a holster fashioned out of kid leather for the switchblade. It could be worn by buckling a strap just above the calf so it would not slip down his leg. Might be missed in a sloppy hand search. The weapon itself was a beautiful piece of craftsmanship with a mother of pearl handle. A blade sharp enough to shave with. A useful souvenir forfeited by that thug-cop Dombrowski who stabbed him with it back in LA. The knife was for just in case. He hadn't worn it that night a couple of years ago in Berlin. Wouldn't make that mistake again if he was going someplace potentially dangerous. Spain sounded like that kind of place.

PART THREE

SPAIN

CHAPTER 17

The Spanish seemed to possess a cultural trait for settling political differences through violence. Provoked by economic circumstances, the early 1930s saw a succession of political upheavals. The aspirations of a privileged entrenched wealthy class to retain their historic subjugation over an impoverished peasant and working class forced into subsistence conditions had been ever present in Spain for generations. Violence escalated from both sides as the poor organized for greater political influence. Two political poles emerged. No one could remain neutral. Acts of incomprehensible brutality became commonplace. It was the worst of times for the Spanish.

From 1923 to 1930 Spain was ruled by the inept military dictatorship of Miguel Primo de Rivera. He lacked clear ideas and eventually alienated his supporters including the Army. Rivera's long standing support by the discredited king, Alfonso XIII, further deepened social tensions with Spain's poor majority. Lacking support of the Army, Primo de Rivera resigned in 1930. Faced as well by an Army that declared they could no longer support the monarchy, King Alfonso left Spain in early 1931.

The fall of the monarchy led to elections that ushered in the Second Republic with a populist socially progressive majority in the parliament. A new constitution was drafted moving against much of the conservative tenants of the former ruling elite.

Those included the large landowners, the Army, and the Catholic Church. The constitution now gave freedom of speech, freedom of association, the vote to women, legalized divorce, and disestablished the influence of the Catholic Church. With the constitution removing much of their official prerogatives such as controlling education, the Church moved even further politically to the right.

The Left proved equally unsuccessful in governing Spain. A military coup originating in Seville in 1932 failed only through lack of support across Spain. By 1933 a resurgence of a more organized Right came together. A new Catholic-based conservative party with the acronym CEDA was formed drawing into its ranks all the right-leaning political factions. Even progressive parties dominated by traditions of the Church were drawn to the CEDA umbrella.

CEDA would function as a propaganda vehicle giving cover to the more violent right-wing parties under the guise of the Church. Chief among those was the extremist *Falange Española*, the Spanish Phalanx. A nationalist party inspired by Italian and German Fascism, it was launched by the eldest son of the disgraced former dictator Primo de Rivera. The Spanish right-wing parties then went on to successfully win a majority in a general election in November, 1933 against a divided group of leftist parties.

With power now shifted back to the Right, violence on both sides escalated. The following year saw continued bloody exchanges of localized violence. To punish rural peasants, landowners selectively withheld work. Literally starving, peasants marched against landowners only to be brutally suppressed by the military-controlled Civil Guard supported by privately hired mercenaries.

As a harbinger of things to come, what started as a miners' strike in Asturias in northern Spain turned into a major revolutionary uprising in October, 1934. Under the command of General Francisco Franco, the government crushed the revolt. Using naval bombardment in support, elite battle-hardened Spanish

Foreign Legion and indigenous colonial troops known as *Fuerzas Regulares Indígenas,* or simply *Regulares,* were brought over from Morocco.

The revolt portrayed by the Right as a Jewish-Bolshevik conspiracy resulted in 3,000 miners being killed and over 30,000 taken prisoner. Constitutional guarantees were suspended. Torture within the prisons was widespread. This was the first use of the elite battle hardened Spanish Legion. Use of the colonial *Regulares* schooled in the brutality of the wars against Islamic Moroccan Berbers during the 1920s on the Spanish mainland was intended for effect. The *Regulares* knew nothing of European accepted conduct related to prisoners of war.

With the horrific excesses perpetrated by the Right, backed by the guns of a sympathetic civil policing authority, the political Left eventually came together in a Popular Front. The coalition consisting of the *Spanish Worker's Party* (PSOE), the *Communist Part of Spain* (PCE), the *Worker's Party of Marxist Unification* (POUM), the *Republican Left* (IR), the *Republican Union Party* (UR), the socialist *Worker's General Union* (UGT), and the anarchist trade union, the *Confederación Nacional del Trabajo* (CNT). Further support came from regional nationalist parties from Galicia (PG) and Catalonia (ERC) seeking autonomy from Madrid rule.

This was the same collection of warring Left political parties that lost the elections in 1933. They were now coming together at the end of 1935, still with no common collective purpose other than to defeat the entrenched conservative power of the Right. But now they would appear on the ballot as a single *Popular Front Party.*

Spain was clearly a more complicated political environment than Germany. But as with most social strife the underlying issue was always economic. For Spain the demarcation of the haves versus the have-nots was profoundly more acute. The disparities were bred into Spain's history. The landed aristocracy historically supported a monarchy enforcing rule through a strong military. With the exception of the less than two years governance of the First Republic over sixty years earlier, Spain had always been a monarchy or military dictatorship until the coming of the Second Republic in 1931.

With the Iberian Peninsula returning to Christian rule in the sixteenth century after driving out the Ottoman Moors, the Roman Catholic Church ordered Jews and Muslims to convert or leave Spain. To insure its power, the Church, in league with the Spanish monarchy, embarked upon the repressive *Inquisition* lasting a hundred years. From that time the Church maintained a firmly integrated official position within Spanish society. For self-serving reasons, the Church sided with the conservative elements in Spanish society, frequently ignoring the suffering of their peasant congregants.

An agrarian economy with some natural mineral resources, Spain did not yet process a strong industrial sector. The workforce was overwhelmingly unskilled. Spanish society had less of an independent middle class compared with most of Western Europe. Spanish peasants whether farmers or miners were the poorest in Europe.

Getting into the fractious politics of Spain would put Fraser's American readers to sleep. His pieces had to show simply but dramatically what was going on, what life was like for the Spanish. Fraser needed to show the underlying factors that gave rise to so many competing political factions.

※

Fraser arrived by air on an Air France Latécoère 28 single propeller aircraft on the newly inaugurated Paris to Madrid route. Certainly the fastest way to travel long distances but uncomfortable. The constant drone of the engine noise. Cramped into the eight-passenger low fuselage for several hours meant a trip to the washroom to relieve yourself. A task just getting to the washroom by walking hunched over. Once there you needed the skills of a contortionist not to urinate all over the seat around the relief hole or down your own pant leg. Not sure how a woman managed.

By prior arrangement, his point of contact was a woman journalist in Madrid, Loretta Elizalde. She came recommended by his fellow Hearst correspondent in Paris. Elizalde worked for a socialist newspaper, *El Liberal*. The well-established *Liberal* was recognized for its more objective journalism compared to the radical publications of the various far-left political parties. Fraser did his own research by reading several of her articles on the brutal suppression of the uprising of striking miners in the north of Spain the previous year. Good writing. She made the moral case for the strikers. Conveyed a real sense of outrage at the atrocities inflicted by the Spanish military. Why the use of brutal colonial forces?

Arriving in the afternoon, Fraser set off for the nearby compact old section of Madrid not far from his hotel. This part of Madrid was a pleasant place with interesting architecture. It was a sunny October day. Of particular delight was the rectangular Plaza Mayor with its balconies, pinnacles, dormer windows.

He read in a guide book of the colorful history of this plaza. Mostly a violent history it seemed. Other than the staging of bullfights and pageants, it was the site of public executions and public trials of the Spanish Inquisition. This was the heart of *Leyanda Negra*, the Black Legend that painted the Spanish Empire as cruel, bigoted, and exploitive. Fraser wondered if that applied to twentieth century Spain?

He met Loretta Elizalde at a café in the lively Puerta del Sol for lunch.

"Señor Fraser?" a petite woman some years older than Fraser in a business suit said in English after approaching the outdoor table where he was seated.

Fraser rose from his chair, "*Si*. And you must be Señorita Elizalde?" he said in Spanish. "You must excuse by poor Spanish. I am much more fluent in English or French."

"Not at all. How is it you even speak Spanish?"

"My stepmother. She is Mexican so I'm sure that colors my pronunciation as well."

"Perhaps just an accent."

They made small talk about their respective backgrounds then ordered lunch. Fraser learned that Elizalde was from the northern coastal city of San Sebastian, in Basque Country.

Elizalde said, "There is another complexity adding to political strife in Spain. The Basque, Catalonia, and Galicia all have ambitions to be separated from the rest of Spain. Very different cultures, particularly from those in the south. Distinct languages separate from Spanish. My place of birth, San Sebastian is *Donostia* in Basque."

"What's your personal view on independence for your native Basque Country?"

"I would prefer autonomy but still within a greater Spain. Separate regional governance. Preservation of the Basque culture. Something like your states have in America. Full independence doesn't make sense to me. We would become an insignificant backwater like tiny Andorra.

"According to your letter you are writing on life in Europe from various perspectives. More focused on how people view what is going on, rather than reporting on the overarching politics."

"In a manner of speaking," Fraser said. "But the origin of those politics becomes much more complex in Europe than in America. Europe is a collection of so many different countries and cultures with different experiences. All within an area the size of the entire United States. The U.S. is diversified but nowhere to the extent of Europe. Not only do people need to contend with their more immediate problems, but the actions of neighboring countries become directly significant. The United States doesn't have any troublesome neighbors. Everyone pretty much speaks English. I want to give my readers a sense of what it's like to live within the turmoil of Europe."

"That's certainly ambitious, Señor Fraser."

"Perhaps, but at least it gives me a perspective for my stories that separates me from the army of foreign correspondents reporting on the latest developments. If I am numbed by this constant barrage of political goings-on in every country, I suspect the American reader is even less interested. I try to write material that gives them a sense of feeling rather than trying to tell them information. Since I take my own photographs that helps. Everyone is drawn to pictures."

Elizalde nodded in agreement.

"I saw those photographs you took of that concentration camp in Germany a couple of years ago. *El Liberal* published them. Current reports out of Germany suggest that things have become much worse. There are more of those camps I'm told. That's what we fear might happen in Spain if the Right continues to remain in control of the Cortes, our parliament. Spain might be a token Republic but widespread violence by the Right goes beyond even what is happening in Germany. There is outright murder, rape, and torture committed in many areas of Spain. Especially where local governing councils controlled by extreme right-wing groups are backed by the Civil Guard."

Fraser nodded but then responded, "What about violence committed by leftist groups? Riots and rampages by workers. Murders are reported there as well. Even priests and nuns. Especially here in Madrid, the capital."

Elizalde clinched her jaw, nodding vigorously. "Yes. Certainly. There can be no excuse for such outrages. It's the unfortunate reaction to a history of repression by the privileged class. Case in point is the miners' strike in Asturias last year. The working class finally became fed up and tried to demand a living wage. The strike was suppressed by the military using colonial troops from Morocco. It was unimaginably savage. The Army fought fellow Spaniards as if they were Rif savages from North Africa."

Fraser said, "The world press reported that it was more than just a strike. The miners were armed. They occupied towns by force seizing local police barracks. In any country that would be considered armed insurrection. How could the government not forcibly suppress that threat?"

"At the root of all such rebellion is injustice. Rebellion usually turns violent. The morality is for each person to weigh. The miners like the rural peasants and the factory workers work for starvation wages in horribly unsafe conditions. Throwbacks to the last century. The Spanish economy is ruled by a privileged elite."

"As it is in most countries. Are you a Communist, Señorita Elizalde?"

"Certainly not. Socialist perhaps but not a Bolshevik. I am Basque. I am also Jewish by ancestry. There are only a handful of Jews in Spain by the way. The Jews were either forced to convert to Christianity or driven out of Spain hundreds of years ago. Not many Freemasons either. As for Bolsheviks, well the various Communist parties have only a small membership, and not all are Bolsheviks. The Right paints all of the Left with the Communist label to propagandize the threat against traditional Spanish culture.

"The Roman Catholic Church is an integral part of supporting the Right. The Church is virulently anti-Communist of course. Rooted in conservatism the Church aligns with the Right for shared power. In Spain it's a class thing. Many in the working class have no personal association with the Church. That's especially true in the more industrialized areas such as here in Madrid.

"The Right uses the same tactic of giving the enemy a name as Adolf Hitler uses the Jews in Germany. The same emotional cause of nationalism based upon their interpretation of exclusionary tradition."

Fraser needed Elizalde's assistance so he chose to avoid debating politics. He was cynical enough to find some fault with most political ideologies.

"Ok. I'm certainly no supporter of the far-Right. Had my fill of the Nazis while in Germany. France is having the same clashes between the Right and Left. Riots in Paris last year were instigated by right-wing groups challenging the leftist government. Nothing quite like the Fascist paramilitary SA in Germany however."

"We have our own Fascists here in Spain, the *Falange Española*," Elizalde said. "They even wear similar uniforms. Blueshirts to be different from Hitler's Brownshirts and Mussolini's Blackshirts. They're strongly aligned with the Catholics of the *Confederación Española de Derechas Autónomas,* CEDA, and the monarchist parties of both the *Alfonsinistas* and *Carlists.* All the parties with wealth and power. And of course, the military with its bloated officer corps. Most are from the ranks of the privileged class of course."

"Is there a real fear of a military coup bringing a dictator or a king back into power?"

"Constant concerns. After all, for most of Spain's history we have been governed by kings or dictators. This current Second Republic came on the heels of the failed dictatorship of Primo de Rivera only in 1931. A year later another general, José Sanjurjo attempted a coup. After it failed he was tried and sentenced to death. But of course he had powerful friends. The sentence was commuted to life in prison. Then just two years later he was granted amnesty going into exile in Portugal. I'm sure there is still support among the senior military for another try."

"Where is the worst of this friction between the Right and the Left?"

Elizalde thought for a moment. "Different circumstances all over Spain, but if you want to go into the lions' den, I'd suggest the south. Andalusia. Try Seville."

"Why is it so bad there?"

"The region is dominated by wealthy landowners. The rural peasants are the poorest of the Spanish working class. The landowners have brutalized the peasants for ages to discourage union organizing. They have circumvented the new employment laws about employment. Even went to the extent of withholding land from cultivation to starve what amounts to a feudal working class. People sometimes forced to scavenge for acorns and the leavings of harvest grain crops for survival. The landowners enforce authority through an entirely coopted Civil Guard. People literally starve in large numbers there. And of course the Church supports the landholders. The southern peasantry is less religious than in the north of Spain. So the Church guards its status routed in tradition by siding with landowners."

"Very well. Do you have a suggested starting point?"

She smiled. "How about the Marquis de Morón de la Frontera? His name is Carlos Antonio Cabrera Fuentes. Old aristocratic family. Big landowner southeast of Seville. Into all sorts of things. Horse breeding. Cattle. Prize fighting bulls for the ring. Belongs to the syndicates that own the two great bullrings in Spain, the one in Seville, the other in Ronda. Olives, wheat, leather goods, you name it. Politically active. Heads the local *Falange* in Seville. Younger brother is an army officer in the Spanish Legion serving in Morocco."

"How is it you know so much about Cabrera?"

"He's frequently in the news. All of it bad news. Over the last several years almost a hundred peasants have been killed on various Cabrera estates. Has his own group of armed security thugs. Because of his connections he has free reign of terror when it suits his purpose.

"The younger brother was part of the Legion forces that put down the strikers in Asturias last year. An officer in Colonel Juan Yagüe's command. Yagüe is a butcher. Read the accounts of his terror tactics against the strikers. Brutality seems to run in the Cabrera family. Sound like the right place to start?"

Fraser smiled. He liked Elizalde. "Sounds perfect."

Actually sounded worse than the Germany assignment.

"What about here in Madrid? What's the situation here?"

"This is the center of the Left. Militant working class aligned with various political parties. The Left has seen the result of trying to follow their independent agendas. They're coming together in a Popular Front. That's the situation in Madrid.

"President Zamora got fed up with the right-wing CEDA party, the largest party in the Cortes. It was formed to protect religion, family, and property. Traditionalists. Decidedly nationalistic. Their leader Gil Robles even declared that *either parliament submits or we will eliminate it.* Clearly no friend to a democratic republic. Zamora will not let CEDA form a government so he has called for new elections at the start of the new year. The Popular Front sees a real chance to win a majority in the Cortes.

"Unlike the rural areas such as Andalusia where the *Guardia Civil* represents the police authority, in the larger cities there is the newly formed *Guardia de Asalto*. The *Asaltos* were police units formed under the Second Republic in 1931 to deal with urban violence. The rural *Guardia Civil* are led by army officers therefore more a tool of the Right. The *Asaltos* are typically loyal to the government."

"Does that mean these *Asaltos* support the Left?"

"Not exactly. But as an institution they generally support the Republican government. Unlike the *Guardia Civil* which seems an extention of the conservative elements of the military."

"Let me see if I understand, but I doubt anyone can truly understand Spain," Fraser said. "A Byzantine mix of every imaginable political ideology confronting severe social problems. A real challenge to try to explain Spain to my American readers.

"You have more political parties than any other country. The entire population seems divided toward one political extreme or the other. Unlike in the United States where the political center is the largest bloc, here it has little influence. An officially sanctioned state religion in the Roman Catholic Church bent on preserving traditional conservative society. Then you have a military with its own sense of power. Military dictatorships not that long in the past. Add to that a divided civil police authority that unevenly enforces laws or takes political sides regionally."

Fraser shook his head to convey bewilderment. "This must all end soon in a military coup or a civil war depending upon how the two extremes align themselves. God help the Spanish."

"Not sure about God's help. For most Spanish if there is a God he has long since abandoned them. The popular activism in Madrid, Barcelona, and other major cities gives hope for some kind of future for the Spanish working classes. In the cities the land owners cannot hold sway."

Fraser said, "Many in the world fear a socialist revolution. Overturn traditional institutions. Wreck the existing economic structures. Is that what you hope for?"

"I don't know about revolution. Spain is going through a democratic process. But of course I hope for a change in the economic structure. The Spanish working classes are the poorest in Europe. Life should not be that way."

Fraser nodded in sympathy with her statement. "I couldn't agree more. But from what I understand if the military sides with the Right then the democratic process may be terminated. A military coup could mean civil war. How can the elected government defend against a mutiny of the military?"

"It's not that clearly demarked where the allegiances fall. The military officer corps for example is by no means wholly supportive of the Right. Let me give you a name of someone to talk to. He's a middle ranking army officer right here in Madrid. Although it's ostensibly a secret organization, I know that Major Martell is active in the *Unión Militar Republicana Antifascista*, the UMRA. It's the anti-fascist counter to the pro-fascist *Unión Militar Española*, the UME. I know, more acronyms. But that's the way it is here.

"Anyway, you should talk to Martell. I'll give you a note of introduction. He knows me. Don't discuss the UMRA directly. He'd deny any such organization exists. But get his take on the political situation within the military before you venture into the Andalusian pro-fascist stronghold."

Elizalde scrawled a note from a page of her reporter's notebook. She handed the note to Fraser.

"Here's his office. Also the address for getting your Spanish press credentials is close by. You'll need a press pass before going anywhere. Good luck, Señor Fraser. Hope you can make sense of Spain. We Spaniards can't."

CHAPTER 18

On the way to the Ministry of the Interior to register as a foreign correspondent, Fraser stopped to watch two separate street demonstrations. Hundreds were marching with banners singing or yelling slogans. He was taken with the number of women among the demonstrators. As he took photographs the idea struck him that the more compelling method of telling the story of Spain was through photographs. If the peasants in Andalusia were so desperately poor that many risked starvation that could only be told visually.

He was able to walk the short distance from the interior ministry to the war ministry both located on the wide boulevard Paseo del la Castellana. Government officials were not his usual sources to shape his stories about life among the peoples of Europe. All governments distorted circumstances to support their position. But Loretta Elizalde had been extremely helpful so if for no other reason than professional courtesy he would talk to this Major Martel. And the military seemed key to what would happen in Spain. The officer corps was not sitting on the sidelines. Yet according to Elizalde, there were political divides even in that traditional institution. Worth his time to talk to an insider.

At the Ministry of War Fraser was ushered into Major Felix Martel's office after telling an aide that he was here at the request of Loretta Elizalde.

Martel was a short trim man in a well-tailored olive green uniform. Probably early forties, sporting a close-cropped mustache. Marring what otherwise would be a handsome face was a nasty scar on his left cheek.

"Please be seated, Señor Fraser. And how is it you know my cousin?" Martel said.

"Loretta Elizalde is your cousin? She had not told me. Just that you were someone I should talk to. She came recommended as a journalistic contact here in Spain. I'm a correspondent for an American news service doing pieces on life in Europe. About the political turmoil in Europe."

"Loretta says in her note that you were in Germany. Wrote some anti-Fascist articles. Published photographs of one of their concentration camps. I take it you are a critic of Adolf Hitler?"

"Critic would be an understatement. He is a malignancy. A pied piper leading Germany to war. There seems no effective counter to a resurrected belligerent Germany. What about Fascism here in Spain?"

"I agree that Fascism is a disease," Martel said. "I'm not a socialist like my cousin but I share her views on Fascism. It's founded on ultra-nationalistic concepts. Mussolini and Hitler both talk of empire. Here in Spain it is the same. Spain, like Germany and Italy lost most of her colonies in the last fifty years.

"But the face of Fascism is not as well defined in Spain as it is in Germany and Italy. The true Fascists, the *Falange Española Tradicionalista*, have little power as a political party. However as even the name *Tradicionalista* implies, they are part of powerful right-wing confederation of political groups all with similar ideologies. Nationalism, social tradition, the Catholic Church, the protected interests of the privileged wealthy, and most of all, fear of the working class. They are anti-democracy. For the first time we have a real republic in Spain so that threatens the far-Right."

Fraser said, "Like most new republics Spain is clearly struggling. Germany certainly is. Even Mussolini started out as prime minister of a parliamentary government. Spain's democratic experiment may also fail. In most of these situations what happens depends on the army. Where does the Spanish Army stand politically?"

Martel took a few moments before responding. Fraser assumed he was measuring how far to go with an unknown foreign journalist.

"The Army is by no means aligned totally with the Right. Unfortunately many senior officers are but there is probably an equal number that have opposing views. Probably not very far to the left but still supportive of the concept of Republic. There are many officers of conscience that see that something must be done to elevate the plight of the poor Spanish worker."

"What about the Chief of the General Staff, General Franco? Where does he stand?"

"Hard to say exactly. He did not support General Sanjurjo's attempted coup in 1932. He's a devout Catholic so he has strong traditional values. Certainly does not embrace the Left. Concerned about the intrusion of Communism taking root in Spain. Unfortunately, like many others he does not make the distinction between the Moscow-directed Communism from other Marxists, socialists, and anarchists. The Moscow directed Comintern Communists have a comparatively small political following in Spain.

"Franco is a good soldier. He'll support the Republic I believe. I served under his command in Morocco during the Rif War ten years ago. That's how I got this," Martel said turning his head slightly to show the cheek with the scar. "A Berber's knife. The fighting was often at close quarters. A barbaric enemy. A vicious war. Colonel Franco always led from the front of his soldiers. I respect him."

Asked about leftist violence, murders, arson, desecration of Church property, Martel shook his head while clinching his jaw.

"To be expected but unfortunate. Pent up anger over generations of desperate poverty."

"Why is the violence directed at the wealthy and the Church worse in the larger cities like Madrid, Barcelona, Valencia?"

"Spain is a collection of regions. Each very different. People often identify more with their region then a greater Spain. The Right controls the governments in much of the northwest and southwest. The Civil Guard, the police in rural areas, often does the bidding of landowners, businessmen, and mine owners. The cities you mentioned have more progressive governments. The urban police, the *Asaltos* are more sympathetic to these working class protestors. So civil unrest is uneven throughout Spain."

"Your cousin suggested I look up someone in Andalusia if I wanted to explore the excesses of the far-Right. His name is Carlos Cabrera. A titled aristocrat. Big landowner. Do you know him?"

Martel grunted as a sign of disgust. "Know of him? Certainly. Cabrera is a true Fascist. Active in the *Falange*. But I'm more acquainted with his brother, Eduardo."

"In what way?"

"Fellow officer. Major Eduardo Cabrera. Spanish Legion. I served with Cabrera in Morocco. He's a disgrace to the uniform. A barbarian, not a soldier."

"What happened?"

"I mentioned the war in Morocco was ugly. The Moors from the Rif Mountains were a fierce enemy. Well disciplined, they could shoot well and fought as a fighting unit. But they were also barbaric animals like something from ancient time. They took few prisoners. Those they did were horribly tortured until they died. The torture was not to extract information just to inflict pain.

"Fighting alongside the Spanish Legionnaires were our local Moroccan troops. Moors themselves called *Regulares*. They had the same inclinations about mutilation and torture as the Rif natives. Some of these practices contaminated Spanish soldiers, even officers. Cabrera was one such officer that turned to acts of sadistic torture of prisoners. Had I been in command, I'd have shot Cabrera for the things I saw him do. His own Legionnaires were often repelled.

"But enough of old war stories. I wish you well, Señor Fraser. Be careful however in Andalusia. Spain can be a dangerous place for someone asking uncomfortable questions."

Just because he had this Cabrera's name didn't mean he would get any cooperation. Fraser certainly wanted to interview someone in the Spanish Fascist movement. Maybe someone even to be coopted to provide photo opportunities. It worked with Göring. Why not the same tactic?

With his influence perhaps Hearst could arrange a meeting. But that would take too long. The Chief would want to know more background. Difficult to convey with the poor reception over the transatlantic telephone cable. They would both shout themselves hoarse. Mail would take a month. The solution was simple. Fake a telegram to the Marquis de Morón de la Frontera from William Randolph Hearst. That should get Cabrera's attention. Fraser placed an overseas call to his New York editor.

After dictating the brief telegram, he laid the bombshell about signing it W. R. Hearst. "George, I'll take full responsibility. For Christ sake the Chief got me an interview with Hitler. This is no different."

"That's not the point. It's what your telegram implies. Makes the Chief out as cozy with Hitler and Mussolini," George Walberg said yelling back to be heard over the static-ridden transatlantic cable.

"Well he is, George. Thinks Communism is the world threat, not these asshole dictators. Just send the fucking telegram. You know the Chief appreciates initiative. You'll look indecisive if you force me to go to him directly for something so minor."

After a long pause. "Shit. Alright. But it's your ass, Fraser if there's any blowback."

Fraser was in no mood to cover political demonstrations in Madrid. Instead he decided to search out photographic subjects in Madrid's working class suburbs that would convey a sense of the deprivations of the poor. He had four days before his hoped-for rendezvous with Carlos Cabrera in Andalusia.

The Madrid photographs were uninspiring. Poor underfed people but visually no worse off than others in the world suffering the Great Depression. Just more sad images.

Within a couple of days a telegram arrived at his Madrid hotel. Señor Cabrera would be glad to receive him in Seville.

CHAPTER 19

From the moment he stepped off the train in Seville, Fraser knew something was terribly different here. Exiting the rail station he was accosted by several beggars. Ragged clothes, emaciated. Not panhandlers like everywhere in the States, these appeared to be genuinely starving people. He'd never seen anything like this. He gave each a couple of pesetas in paper currency then had difficulty evading their thanks until their attention was diverted by a man screaming insults at them.

A young man in a uniform of a blue shirt, tan trousers, and cap with a red tassel fixed with the unmistakable five arrow-insignia of the *Falange* approached at a quick pace. He was now screaming threats.

Once the beggars scattered, the Falangist approached Fraser. Stopping he came to attention clicking his heels as smartly as any German SS.

"Are you Señor Fraser from America?"

"Yes, I am Fraser." Guess he must stand out as a foreigner to the other passengers exiting the rail station.

"Excellent. I am instructed to take you to Don Cabrera. He is staying in the city today to meet you. Come, I have a car. I regret that you were bothered by that scum."

The Falangist took his suitcase while Fraser carried his portable typewriter to a large black Mercedes-Benz sedan. The short drive revealed a most pleasing city. Motoring down the wide boulevard of well-appointed buildings they passed the elaborate gardens on the backside of the Alcázar Palace. Minutes later the sedan turned in front of the beautiful University of Seville building. Just beyond on the opposite side of the street the Mercedes pulled into the front driveway of the Hotel Alfonso XIII, a singularly elegant building surrounded by tall trees. As Fraser exited the Mercedes after the door was opened by a footman, he could see the spire of the great cathedral to the west. This seemed an extraordinarily beautiful city. Hard to reconcile with it being the center of Spanish Fascism. But then Munich is also a beautiful city.

After depositing him at the front desk, the Falangist said, "Don Cabrera has arranged a room for the night. Once you are settled, he requests you join him for dinner in the hotel dining room at eight o'clock."

The Falangist clicked his heels again and departed.

Fraser looked about the hotel lobby. To say it was spectacular was an understatement. It outdid even the Ritz in Paris. Large glass windows offered a view into the interior courtyard garden. Ornately scrolled woodwork. Moorish influenced tilework. No evidence of the Great Depression here. He had no idea why he was being feted in such style.

Promptly at eight, Fraser strolled into the dining room telling the maître d' he was meeting Don Cabrera. Might as well use the honorific *Don* since the guy was actually an aristocrat with a title.

Effusively the waiter guided him toward a table off to the side. Seeing his approach, the middle age man seated at the table stood up. He was dressed in a light gray suit, white shirt with red-striped tie. Salt and pepper hair with a matching close-cropped beard. Elegant, distinguished.

"Señor Fraser, how good of you to join me. Please be seated," he said in Spanish after shaking hands. He assumed Fraser must know his name since he never introduced himself. "Might you allow me to speak English since I get so little opportunity?"

"But of course, Don Cabrera. Your English appears better than my Spanish."

Cabrera motioned for a waiter who appeared instantly.

"I am having a glass of cava. What might you like?"

"Perhaps a Scotch whiskey?" Fraser said to the waiter in Spanish. "A single malt."

The waiter rattled off several labels. The Alfonso felt it was the most elegant hotel in all of Europe therefore it offered the best of international liquors.

"Ah yes. I will also join you. Two of the Macallan 25 Year," Cabrera said to the waiter.

"I know of your publisher, Señor Hearst. He has considerable influence in America with his newspaper empire. And of course America is important to Europe. I was honored to receive his telegram requesting my assistance to be of service to you."

"I will convey that to Mr. Hearst, Don Cabrera."

"Señor Hearst also recognizes the political realities that Europe faces. The threat of the Bolsheviks and their plague of Communism. His newspapers give voice to those that stand for Christian traditions. I believe that Adolf Hitler and Benito Mussolini have even written articles for the Hearst newspapers?"

"That is correct. Mr. Hearst likes to give voice to the whole range of political discourse."

That was bullshit. The Chief, once the champion of the common man, had turned surprisingly sympathetic to Fascism, cloaked when necessary as anti-Communism. Not only had he published paid-for articles by both Hitler and Mussolini, Hearst actually attended the 1934 annual Nazi rally in Nuremberg.

"I recognize Señor Hearst's true concerns over the threat of Communism," Cabrera said. "Bad enough that Russia has descended into Communism led by Bolshevik criminals. Could anything be worse than that monster Stalin? Now the threat of their intention to export Communism to the rest of the world. Even America is not immune."

"I do not see Communism as that much of a threat. What is often called Communism is really just socialism, or more simply just the lowest of the economic class trying to get a better deal in life."

"I understand your viewpoint, Señor Fraser. However it is naïve not to believe that given fertile ground, Communism will thrive. What are called progressive reforms often come at some unfair expense to others. At real risk is the very fabric of any culture losing its identity. Its customs, its history, its religion, its language."

"Would you not agree that some change is inevitable, Don Cabrera? Especially where people are struggling to secure the basics of life."

"Unfortunately, change is always painful. Those areas in which we might all agree should be improved often are accompanied by more far reaching changes which are not acceptable to those of us that respect tradition."

"I understand you are an influential member of the *Falange Española*. Some consider the *Falange* pro-Fascist. How would you characterize that?"

Cabrera expression hardened. "Nonsense. A mistruth from the Left to malign not only the *Falange* but other tradition-based parties by comparison to Italian and German Fascism. We do not embrace any of that. I am also active in the *Confederación Española de Derechas Autónomas*. CEDA is certainly not Fascist. What we do embrace is a traditionalist version of Spain.

"We differ from Hitler and Mussolini in that we do not seek territorial expansion. Nor do we subscribe to a conspiracy of Jews, Freemasons, and Communism. There are very few Jews in Spain. As to Freemasons, that is a ridiculous construct. The common thread is Communism. In that, the *Falange* recognizes that as the true threat. No one needs to invent a Communist conspiracy since they openly speak of spreading Communism throughout the world.

"Therefore, I have no quarrel with providing you the opportunity to write about Spain. You see I researched your articles after Señor Hearst wired requesting my assistance. You were not kind to Adolf Hitler. He does seem to be ill-suited to lead a great nation. His persecution of German Jews is misplaced, counter-productive."

"Thanks for clarifying your position, Don Cabrera. But explain this widespread violence between the peasant farmers and those like yourself that own large agricultural estates?"

"Communist agitation. Provocateurs. Part of the international Communist conspiracy. That is why. They convince ignorant peasants to join trade unions then they instigate strikes. When that does not get results they destroy property. They convince these people that the Church is the enemy. Priests have even been killed. Nuns raped.

"In the northern cities it is the factory workers. Last year in Asturias it was the miners. Peasant farm workers here in Andalusia. These people are not spontaneously rising in rebellion. They are being led by Communists or Communist sympathizers intent on overthrowing Spain. We will not become another Russia."

Fraser thought to himself that the desperate circumstances of today's Spanish working class looked a lot like Russia at the turn of the century under the last Tsar.

"Do you support a parliamentary form of government, Don Cabrera?"

"To be candid, Señor Fraser. I am doubtful. This Spanish Second Republic is not proving successful. Germany's Weimar Republic is no longer functional. Italy is now ruled by one man. France is struggling. The Communists and the rest of the Left are gaining power there. And of course if Communism prevails you again have a dictatorship of one man. Stalin is proof of that."

"So what does that leave as a workable form of government?"

"Perhaps a return to a monarchy. A constitutional monarchy. Maybe something like our neighbor Portugal. A parliamentary government but in the hands of a strongman like Salazar. The key is a strong leader that keeps things under control. Benevolent rule but firmly in control. Like your President Roosevelt even."

Now there was a stretch. How little the Europeans knew of the United States and vice versa.

Fraser said, "The problem always seems the eventual transition of power. That strong leader never wants to leave. Or if he dies there is a power struggle. People usually die."

"I concede that is the inherent weakness of an autocratic government. But for that tradeoff you get productive periods of stability."

Tradeoff? Sounded not much different in practice than the Nazis to Fraser. Depended on what type of strongman a country wound up with. Nothing to be gained however by pursuing a debate with Cabrera.

"But enough of politics for the moment," Cabrera said, seeming to agree to move to a more neutral topic. "Let us enjoy our dinner. You can tell me about America. And since tomorrow is Sunday, I would be pleased if you would accompany me to the bullfights. Have you ever seen a bullfight?"

"I'm afraid I haven't but I would be honored to join you."

"Excellent. The bullfights are an old tradition. An art form. Our Plaza de Toros is the grandest in all of Spain. Afterwards we shall dine with a couple of business associates. I admit that we are politically conservative but you will see Spain is vastly different than Germany. I am also aware you are here on business not socializing, Señor Fraser. If you would therefore permit me, I would like to show you around my beloved Andalusia. Allow you to form your own opinions."

To his guilty surprise, Fraser enjoyed the spectacle of the bullfight. Yes it was bloody. Arguably cruel with the inflicting of injury by the mounted picador's lance before the death dance phase of the spectacle with the matador. At the end, the bull is dispatched with the sword imbedded between the horns. If the kill is quick the bull drops immediately with the matador awarded an amputated ear as a grisly token. Still, the pageantry was engrossing.

The evening proved unexpectedly informative. Cabrera's associates included the provincial commander of the Civil Guard and the representative of the U.S. giant oil company Texaco.

Fraser and Cabrera were driven by the same Falangist driver to a flamenco club across the river where they met the other two guests. Another captivating experience enjoyed over tapas and a lot of wine. Little serious talk could be exchanged since the performance interludes were brief in duration. Impossible to talk over the castanets and the staccato punctuations of the dancers' pounding heels. Cultural imperatives also dictated extended socializing before discussing business.

It was ten o'clock at night when the party returned to the Hotel Alfonso for dinner. Europeans typically dined late in the evening but the Spanish took that to an extreme. Suited Fraser since he was nocturnal, never favoring the early morning hours.

"As a fellow expatriate what do you think of Seville?" the American representing Texaco said.

"Magnificent," Fraser said. "Very medieval from what I saw walking about for a couple of hours. Narrow streets meandering with no sense of having been laid out by some modern city planner. Absolutely charming. I make my home in Paris. While Paris has its own charm it's still a modern city. In Seville, you can feel the history of hundreds of years."

"Well said, Señor Fraser," Cabrera said. "You can see what those like me feel when we speak of Spain. There is much to protect and preserve in our national identity, our way of life."

"I can understand those feelings. But apart from the ideological differences of those that hold conservative views with the various leftist political elements there still appears a real problem with the plight of the working classes," Fraser said.

"I do not believe any worse than many other places in the world during this time of great economic depression," Cabrera said. "However, those working classes you speak of want to change the very fundamentals of Spanish society. For them to have more they are intent upon destroying everything. Redistribute land ownership. Create trade unions for unreasonable wages that leave nothing for profits. Those left-leaning political elements come in various forms. Socialists of every stripe, anarchists. A mostly disorganized Left with different political aims. But behind them, unifying them, subverting them to their own purpose is the internationally affiliated Communists."

The Civil Guard commander, Major Santiago Garrigós interjected, "Communism does not respect the culture of a people. It rejects Spanish history, religion, and our traditional customs. It only subscribes to its own political ideology. It rejects anything nationalistic. What Don Cabrera says is true. The Communists are behind the agitation all over Spain. We see it most vividly here among the farm workers. Behind every march, every attack on some establishment target, every attempt to organize trade unions, there is a Communist agitator leading these illiterate peasants."

Fraser reflected that for the Nazis, their initial raison d'être was constructed on being a counter to Communism. They later found a better scapegoat in the Jews. Here in Spain there were very few Jews. The Catholic Church saw to that in the Spanish Inquisition four hundred years earlier. So the propaganda nemesis for the Spanish Right remained international Communism.

Cabrera said, "I am a businessman, Señor Fraser. All these claims of starving workers are greatly exaggerated. Admittedly it is a hard life. The unfortunate fate of birth. But consider this. It is not in my best interest to maltreat my workers. They are a valuable asset. Yet I cannot stand by while this rabble rises up to tear down generations of Spanish culture."

Fraser said, "I have read of incidents where laws passed by the parliament to improve the conditions of the working population have been ignored here in Andalusia. Has that not provoked an inevitable backlash from the working class?"

"Those incidents are inflated by the liberal press," Cabrera said. "Chief among these is *El Liberal* based in Madrid. The editor is a prominent socialist. Worst of all is their leading reporter, a woman by the name of Loretta Elizalde. She writes articles based upon selected facts that distort the true events. The newspaper even has an edition devoted to Seville. From her articles she must have many sources among the agitators here."

Major Garrigós added, "I can attest to what Don Cabrera means. Certain local officials of the political Left routinely misapply the laws. These little men think their office gives them power to act as they wish. They expect my Civil Guards to enforce distorted interpretations of the law. It is nothing more than personal greed to steal from businessmen like Don Cabrera. As the head of the police I refuse to be a party to their corruption. Furthermore, I will keep the order. Unionists cannot agitate here."

Spoken like a true Fascist. I see what Elizalde meant about Andalusia. The political opposite of Madrid. The landowners here ran things backed by the regional police.

"As a correspondent for the Hearst newspapers, Señor Fraser, you must be able to appreciate what Don Cabrera complains about with the distortions of the leftist-press," the Texaco man, Roberto Sanchez said. Sanchez' Spanish was excellent albeit with a Mexican pronunciation the same as Fraser. "Señor Hearst certainly sees the dangers of international Communism."

Fraser knew what Sanchez meant. William Randolph Hearst had become outspoken about the threat of international Communism. Just the previous year, he had launched a journalistic anti-Communist witch hunt attempting to discredit many of Roosevelt's New Deal supporters. The Chief's political leanings troubled Fraser sufficiently to consider abandoning journalism, at least for Hearst Publications. But it proved an asset for this Spanish assignment.

"Unfortunately truly objective journalism is hard to find. As for myself I try to portray the facts as plainly as I see them. My photographs are intended to capture descriptive images. The impression conveyed by those images depends on the viewer's perspective. I've been writing now for a couple of years on life of all sorts of people in Europe. Giving the American reader a sense for the circumstances. But I avoid editorializing. For me that defines my journalistic objectivity."

"But you must draw conclusions. How can you not express your own feelings in your reporting, Señor Fraser?" Sanchez said.

Fraser smiled condescendingly. "Of course I draw conclusions. Based upon my observations. Based upon the facts and circumstances. If someone kills another person then I can report that as a fact. But attempting to ascribe motivation is an act of speculation. Hard not to let your own biases intrude when you get into those murky waters."

"But would you not conclude that anti-leftist regimes might hold better prospects for economic success? For example, you see the success of the National Socialists in Germany in dramatically reducing unemployment and establishing effective economic underpinnings. In the face of this worldwide economic depression Germany is making real progress where the United States continues to struggle with Roosevelt's New Deal leftist schemes."

"Under the extremes of the Nazis, many would argue success at what expense? So as not to appear evasive however, Señor Sanchez, let me put it this way. All governments throughout the world are flawed. Behind that the mechanisms of all the forms of governance are inherently flawed. In all examples some of the people will be disadvantaged. The perfect ideology has not yet been conceived by man. Never will be. I personally view the level of civil rights as the best measure of a government. So it's a situation of push and push back. Unfortunately that often turns violent."

"But the United States has its own civil rights problems, Señor Fraser," Cabrera said. "The problems with your Negros. Food shortages among the poor."

"My point exactly, Don Cabrera. The U.S Constitution may spell out the rights that everyone should enjoy but delivering on that within society has not proved possible even in the United States."

All of this was just intellectualizing obfuscation to avoid argument. He wasn't about to condescendingly agree with their ultra-conservative views and couldn't very well articulate his contempt for Fascism to this group.

Fraser certainly was not pro-Communist which he found an equally repugnant ideology. But he did hold the personal view that those with wealth, therefore with the power, would always abuse that power. He certainly introduced his own attitudes into his reporting, even his photographs. No journalist could avoid that seeping into the work. What was objectivity after all?

Before having to further deflect the conversation away from his own political views, they were interrupted by a Civil Guard officer approaching to whisper something to Major Garrigós.

"Excuse me for a moment," Garrigós said as he left the table striding briskly away with the junior officer.

Several minutes later, Garrigós returned. "Don Cabrera. I have some distressing information. An informant has advised us that a large group of farm workers will descend on your properties outside of Coria del Rio early tomorrow morning. It has been organized by provocateurs of the *Federación Anarquista Ibérica*. They are the worst of the anarchists and communists."

"And what is it you plan on doing, Major?" Cabrera said.

Garrigós looked first at Fraser before answering. He seemed to be carefully selecting his words.

"I have ordered a contingent of the *Guardia* to the area. They shall be in place by dawn. We may be confronted by an unexpectedly large mob according to the information. If I may suggest, Don Cabrera, it would be wise to insure we have sufficient resources to suppress any trouble."

"I agree, Major. If confronted with a large enough force perhaps violence can be avoided," Cabrera said. "I shall insure that you have adequate resources. Now, gentlemen, I believe we must cut short our evening. We have much to do. Señor Fraser, assuming you do not mind leaving in the early hours of the morning, you may accompany me to Coria del Rio. It is only twenty kilometers but I'm afraid I must leave the hotel at four in the morning."

"Thank you, Don Cabrera. As a reporter I wouldn't miss the opportunity."

CHAPTER 20

Promptly at four o'clock in the morning Fraser met Carlos Cabrera in the hotel lobby. Cabrera was dressed in calf-length laced boots, a loose working shirt with a felt hat. Surprisingly he was wearing a holstered revolver. Two rough-looking armed men joined us in the lobby as Cabrera gave them instructions. They lugged a box of food and jugs of water prepared by the hotel kitchen which they placed into the trunk of the Mercedes parked in the front of the hotel.

Standing outside next to a sedan with the markings of the Civil Guard was Major Garrigós. After Cabrera exchanged a few words he returned to the Mercedes saying to his men, "We're ready. Let's go."

One of the men got behind the wheel, the other in the front passenger seat. From the back seat, Fraser could see two shotguns propped between the knees of the man in the passenger seat. Behind the Civil Guard car was a large lorry with a canvas top loaded with Guard officers. Following Cabrera's Mercedes the convoy left the hotel travelling across the Rio Guadalquivir then headed south through the darkened deserted streets of pre-dawn Seville.

As Cabrera announced they were within a few kilometers of his property they began seeing the occasional peasant walking along the side of the road. Further on, the numbers increased.

Men and women of all ages. In the dim moonlight, Fraser could see faces drawn with the ravages of hunger. Shabby clothes, rope sandals. An occasional rake or pitchfork. Most of the women carried empty wicker baskets strapped to their backs.

It was still dark when the convoy of vehicles pulled in front of a gated compound surrounded by a low stucco wall. A modest estate house stood back at some distance. At the gate were two Civil Guards in uniform along with half a dozen other men armed with revolvers and shotguns. Once the lorry emptied out the additional Civil Guard contingent there were over twenty armed men.

Cabrera conversed with a man who appeared in charge. Obviously working for Cabrera, he removed his hat in deference to the boss.

Fraser took out his Leica and made setting adjustments for the low light condition. As he proceeding to take photos Major Garrigós hurried to his side and placed a hand on his arm.

"No photographs, Señor Fraser. This is a police matter."

"I am an accredited journalist. Why am I here if not to report whatever may happen?"

"I understand, Señor Fraser, just no pictures."

"Why?"

Before Garrigós could respond, Cabrera approached. "Allow Señor Fraser to take photographs, Major. We have nothing to hide. We are simply defending our property. The Civil Guard is here to uphold the law.

"Attacks on property have been a constant threat for years, Señor Fraser. Here in the rural areas it is worse since our assets are spread over large areas. Subject to attack by our own workers who are deluded into thinking they can dictate higher wages by force. Outside Communist agitators come here with promises that they know cannot be achieved. Their real purpose is to foment revolt. It is for political gain not to help the workers."

As daylight broke onto a nearly cloudless sky birds began to chirp promising a magnificent early November day. The scene of a few workers walking the road did not suggest what they were now seeing. Across the fields which had been recently harvested of the wheat crop, dozens of peasants roamed the fields.

Cabrera and Garrigós surveyed the scene with binoculars.

Fraser screwed in a long focal length lens to take long range shots giving him a magnified field of vision.

"They appear to be scavenging the leavings on the ground from the harvest." Fraser said. "Are things that bad for these people, Don Cabrera?" He was taking photographs with good resolution with the larger lens.

"Times are difficult this year because of the draught. Unemployment is understandably high. There is simply less work available. Yet these people chose to join a union. They stopped work as a means of economic threat. A foolish move with work at a premium. The workers brought in to work the harvest have plenty of food. These people created their own plight."

"But now it's not political. People that are hungry will do anything. Especially if their children are starving," Fraser said.

Cabrera becoming progressively angrier as he surveyed the people in the fields. Turning, he shouted at his local overseer, "Ernesto. Release the pigs into that field. These people are not entitled to food they did not earn."

Ten minutes later a herd of hundreds of Ibérico pigs trotted into the field for a rare feast. Encountering the people some of the pigs turned aggressive. Shouting ensued. Pitchforks found their mark. Terrible screeches came from the wounded pigs.

The first shot rang out. Fraser brought up his viewer to survey the scene in the distance. A man lay on the ground attended by a woman of indeterminate age by her weathered face. It made a telling photo as she looked up with an expression of horror on her face with her arm raised in supplication. The photo could have many interpretations.

That rifle shot was quickly followed by others. Fraser swung his camera to capture the Civil Guards firing. Cabrera's civilian gunmen sprinted into the field closing on the workers to within effective shotgun range. Fraser too rushed forward. Suddenly one of Cabrera's men fell forward not far from Fraser.

Fraser rushed to his side. No question what happened. Part of his face was blown away. A rifle shot apparently not a shotgun. A sniper?

Fraser hit the ground as sustained firing erupted from both sides. The roar of shotguns was punctuated with the sharper crack of rifle rounds. In a prone position, Fraser could not tell what was happening. Rising up he chanced exposure to capture the chaotic scene.

The unarmed majority of workers were running away. However, a makeshift skirmish line of armed peasants took up kneeling positions in a line. Mostly armed with old double barreled shotguns along with a few ancient rifles, they were firing on the attacking police and Cabrera's private militia.

The peasants put up a brave fight but they did not have the firepower to match the Guards and Cabrera's armed men. The firefight lasted no more than ten minutes. Fraser had been close enough to capture extraordinary photos. Photos of the wounded and dead. What could lead these people to such desperation?

Provocateurs were a propaganda excuse of the Right. There may be instigators inciting these peasants but at the root was something as basic as food for subsistence. These people were starving. This day of violence brought absolute clarity to Fraser. Spain's problems were not political, they were social. The same as the 1917 October Revolution in Russia that brought down the Tsar. It may have been led by Bolsheviks but it was social economics and repression that gave voice to that revolt. Germany on the other hand was more a political issue fueled by nationalistic aspirations.

The peasants retreated leaving behind at least a dozen dead and wounded. Snapping continuous photos Fraser moved forward to within a few meters behind the advancing Guards and Cabrera's men. He had never been in a war zone witnessing wounds from gunshots. Not the sanitized images of the movie screen where shootings appeared bloodless. Here there were not only holes in the human body but ghastly sights of faces torn away by shotgun pellets. A hole in the eye from a rifle bullet.

The agony of the wounded suffering not only their physical injuries but anticipating perhaps an even worse fate.

No peasants were captured other than those wounded and unable to flee. Fraser reloaded a new roll of film into the Leica. This aftermath of the violence would potentially yield even more compelling images of the close up faces of the victims.

A shotgun discharge rang out to the left of Fraser. Turning in surprise he saw the terrible sight. One of the wounded men had been dispatched with a shotgun by a Cabrera gunman. The blast was point blank to the face, no longer recognizable as such. Fraser's stomach lurched as he took several photos. So gruesome it probably couldn't be published in American newspapers.

A second shotgun blast rang out some distance away. Since they were shotguns it meant the shooters were Cabrera's men not the Civil Guards.

"Is this what the police do here, Major? Shoot arrestees?"

The Civil Guard Major barked an order to all the armed men to cease any further firing on penalty of arrest. Turning back to Fraser he said, "This is what happens when these mobs are led by agitators. They purposely force violent confrontations."

"At the least, are you going to arrest these men? Executions of wounded victims go beyond defending property. Have you no rule of law in Spain?"

"Señor Fraser, things are different here. I have insufficient Guard forces to police the region. It therefore is necessary that landowners such as Don Cabrera protect themselves with their own security. Unfortunately confrontations such as today may get out of hand. One man was killed and two others wounded today by this mob. One of those was a Guard doing his duty to keep order. Don Cabrera's men were supporting the police." Major Garrigós looked Fraser in the eye to convey his point when he said, "No charges will be brought against Don Cabrera's men."

Before Fraser could continue to argue a woman's screams came from a distance away. Three of Cabrera's men were standing close together. Fraser took off at a run to investigate. The Major and a number of his Guards followed.

Arriving at the spot first Fraser understood what was going on. Lying in the field was a completely naked young woman. Not pretty but with large breasts. Blood seeped through her fingers covering a bullet wound to her thigh. She was sobbing uncontrollably. The men had laid down their shotguns. One was unbuttoning his trousers. Fraser took photo after photo.

Noticing Fraser, one of the men lunged at him trying to grab the camera. Fraser pushed back with a hand to the man's chest. Not backing away, the man swung at Fraser who ducked under the blow. Straightening up, Fraser drove his foot hard into the man's knee sending him down in pain. From the ground, the man attempted to draw his revolver from the holster at his waist. Out of breath, Major Garrigós slammed his boot into the man's hand.

Garrigós took control. The naked woman was order covered. She and the other two wounded were accorded some rudimentary treatment to their wounds consisting of bandages to stem the bleeding of gunshot wounds. Garrigós ordered the bodies of the dead to be brought together for removal.

"Señor Fraser. I will trouble you for the film."

Fraser was about to protest when Cabrera approached.

Fraser immediately confronted Cabrera, "Major Garrigós wants to confiscate my film. Are you ashamed to have this event made public in the American press, Don Cabrera?"

Garrigós said, "This is police business, Señor Fraser. Your film is evidence."

"That's interesting. I have been involved with many police related events in Los Angeles. Never once have the police confiscated photographs. Does the Civil Guard have something to hide?"

Garrigós reddened and was about to say something when Cabrera interceded.

"It is alright, Major. I asked Señor Fraser to accompany me as my guest. We simply put down an attack by an armed mob.

They were intent on confrontation since they brought weapons. Our actions were entirely justified. Let the pictures show what happened.

"I once considered these people part of our extended family, Señor Fraser. Before this accursed Republic there was nothing like this. They are misguided, ignorant, but nonetheless they represent a threat to society when enlisted into rebellion by anarchists, Communists, that whole breed of scum."

"Don Cabrera, several of your men were about to rape one of the wounded peasant women. Do you condone such reprisals?"

"Reprisals? I think that is perhaps too strong a word, Señor Fraser. These men were just fired upon. Emotions get out of hand. However I do not sanction such action. But these are rough men, used to responding with simple reactions. They shall be disciplined. I am glad it did not go further thanks to you."

A fucking lying hypocrite. No different than the goddamn Nazis.

Fraser was surprised that he was not asked by either Cabrera or Garrigós how he would report this event back to America. Nor did they mention the photographs which would be far more provocative. He realized they were sufficiently self-assured as to not care about outside criticism. Cabrera was the equivalent of a modern-day feudal lord.

Cabrera spent the next two days showing Fraser around his vast estate spending in Morón de la Frontera southeast of Seville. Cabrera was especially proud of his horses and fighting bulls. Not once was the massacre discussed. Nothing of any political nature was discussed around Doña Cabrera. She was either shielded or preferred to ignore any of these unpleasantries. Life within the great estate house seemed frozen in the last century. Servants flitted around as Doña Cabrera supervised the household which probably would run just fine without her interference.

Doña Cabrera was a refined but rather severe looking woman. While everything around the home felt from another time she however dressed impeccably in the latest fashion. She warmed to Fraser, even becoming quite animated discussing movies after Fraser explained his early background in Hollywood. As Fraser described living in Paris she lamented the hardships of living the rural life. Their home was even some distance from Seville which she pointed out was only a provincial city. Everything revolved around the business of agriculture. How she loved Paris. Even attending cinema was difficult here.

Don Cabrera was delighted with having provided his wife an interesting guest. Fraser departed with great expressions of friendship. Uncharacteristically for such a stiff aristocratic bearing, Doña Cabrera even kissed Fraser on the cheek wishing a return visit whenever he might again come to Andalusia.

As beautiful a place as it was Fraser had no wish to return. Scratch the surface and under that mask of beauty was a layer of true ugliness. If Spain erupted in a civil war Andalusia would become a violent place.

Fraser was anxious to return to Paris. While he could file his articles by telephone or telegram, the photographs could only go by post. And it was those photos that made the story powerful. Even so, he decided to pay a brief return visit to Loretta Elizalde in Madrid to thank her. Had to stop in Madrid on the way north anyway. On the train he wrote up his piece on the events in Andalusia.

'Andalusia, Spain – Byline Marc Fraser: Titled Massacre in Andalusia: Humankind is doomed to an endless contest of those in power exploiting those without. Nowhere is this more evident than in Spain. A throwback to the last century. The rural peasantry and working class live a subsistence existence. Often less than subsistence. Starvation is not an abstraction but an ever present cloud of imminent disaster. Politics has little meaning as an ideology. It is rendered irrelevant by the simple urgency of existence; food, shelter, security. For the poor of Spain, securing these basics is a daily challenge.

When they rebel against injustice they are brutally put down with guns. Imprisoned, tortured, or killed depending largely upon who is rendering judgement. Justice plays no part in their fate.

I witnessed firsthand today an event that I understand is not unique. Starving peasant farm hands excluded from working the fields because of their affiliation with union organizing had been locked out of work. That means starvation. The land owners have resisted negotiating what we in America would consider a normal exchange of compensation for labor. The demands of these Spanish peasants is far more basic to just survival than the demand of workers in the United States that result in labor related strife. Here that strife means people being gunned down while scavenging for food. Spanish children suffer malnutrition beyond comprehension for a western European nation.

The event of which I speak was the forcible repression of a group of workers invading a field of harvested wheat in a place called Coria del Rio. Looking for nothing more than the remnants of grain lying on the ground as a desperate food source. Scavenging. They encountered the landowner backed not only by armed thugs but the official backing of an armed contingent of police. Admittedly, some of the group of a hundred workers came armed. A futile misguided effort but understandable if one's very existence hangs in the balance. When things have come so far there can only be a bad ending.

The landowner, Don Carlos Cabrera ordered a herd of pigs unleashed into the field. The pigs saw a feast. The workers saw the loss of this meager source of survival. Violence was inevitable.

A pig was skewered by a pitchfork. The man wielding it was then shot. Then a barrage of gunfire erupted from both sides. Out gunned, the workers quickly retreated as armed civilian security backed by the Civil Guard unleased an overwhelming rain of gunfire. The casualty count was one dead, one wounded of the landowner's men, twelve dead of the invading farm workers with three others wounded.

However, adding to this tragedy was the barbarity inflicted on these starving peasants. Of those dozen dead, several were executed after suffering wounds. One wounded woman had been stripped as she was about ready to be raped by three men. Had I not been photographing the scene, it is doubtful that any of the wounded would have survived.

There seems to be a common thread of justification for any act in defense of these ultra-right nationalists throughout Europe. Whether Germany, Italy, or Spain, the enemy was Communists, anarchists, socialists, and of course Jews. Reduced to non-humans, any violent excesses were justified. The hubris of these arrogant power brokers is remarkable. Göring let me photograph a concentration camp. Now Cabrera and the Civil Guard commander here in Spain allowed me to photograph what amounted to extra-judicial executions. They simply do not care what the rest of the world thinks.

After the Bolsheviks came into power, millions died in the subsequent Russian Civil War not that many years ago. Similar conditions exist in Spain. There is no middle ground. God help Spain if it ever descends into a full blown civil war.'

CHAPTER 21

After arriving in Madrid Fraser telephoned Elizalde. Meeting at the same café, he thanked her for the lead to Carlos Cabrera. Over dinner, he recounted how he manipulated an interview. While he sipped his wine she read his typed recounting of the events in Coria del Rio.

"You witnessed this? And you have pictures too?" she said.

"Exceptional photos. Some are too lurid for publication but it shows people being killed. Haven't had the opportunity to develop them. It'll have to wait until I get back to Paris."

"We could get them developed here?"

"Thanks but I don't want to trust the politics of whoever might do the developing work."

"And Cabrera and this Civil Guard commander knew you took these photos? Why did they not confiscate them?"

"Cabrera's arrogance maybe. His sense of aristocratic etiquette since he invited me along. Not sure. These are raw images so I'm anxious to get this stuff off to New York. I'll frame it against the contrasting background of circumstances here in Madrid."

"The good and the bad as it were?"

"You think Madrid is the *good*? I'd hardly call it that. The Leftists in control in Madrid have blood on their hands too. They seem just as extreme as the Right. Every act of barbarism justified by their own corrupt ideology. Spain is going to explode when these two poles collide. Is this the way things are in all of Spain?"

Elizalde held her instinctive response deciding against political debate with Fraser. While she sympathized with the plight of the Spanish working classes she was a social activist, not decidedly political. At least not enough to defend excesses of the Left. She also had her own political baggage as a Basque nationalist.

She said, "Regardless of the political ideologies, it's the exercise of extreme brutality against people wanting nothing more than enough to eat. A life often no better than conditions of domestic animals. That is at the root of Spain's problems. You saw that in Andalusia. That was what happened in Asturias last year. The scars are still fresh. Buildings destroyed. Thousands killed. Moroccan foreign troops used to put down the miners' insurrection. The brutality was beyond comprehension. Rape, torture. Tens of thousands imprisoned. The torture continues for those still in prisons."

Elizalde turned silent for several moments.

"If you had photographs of that torture, could you get them published?" she asked.

"I suppose so. You have photos?"

"Yes."

"I'd need the story behind it. No one in America would even remember that far away event. How did you come by these photos?"

"A family friend. A doctor in San Sebastian. Treated the wounded from those terrible two weeks. Continues to treat them in one of the main prisons. Treats the effects of their continued maltreatment in prison."

"And why haven't you been able to publish these photos?'

She shook her head. "First of all I was afraid it would expose my doctor friend to danger. People get murdered in Spain for less. But he encouraged me to try. So I took a cautionary step to select only photos that we thought might not implicate him as the source."

After a pause, she resumed, "But I did not count on the timidity of the managing editor of *Liberal*. He refused to publish not only the photos but my story. Too provocative. Couldn't corroborate without identifying the source which I wouldn't do. He simply didn't have the courage. Sign of uncertain times."

"Do you have your story written?" Fraser asked.

"Yes."

"Ok. So if you're wondering if I could get it published then of course I'll try. I'll give you full attribution."

"God no! Don't do that. I would be in trouble. And my source especially."

"Very well. But I am leaving early tomorrow morning."

"Then accompany me to my apartment. It's not far."

Elizalde's apartment was an exhausting four flights of stairs. Small, neat, with Spartan furnishings. Books and papers were piled on a battered desk with a typewriter. A working environment. He guessed she had no live-in man in her life.

From atop the tiny kitchen cabinet reached by her standing on a chair, she brought down an envelope. Handing it to Fraser she said, "Tell me what you think."

There were perhaps twenty photographs along with as many typed pages. He would read her copy later. The first photograph made him wince. It showed a man badly bloodied from a terrible beating. The face was not recognizable. One eye seemed only a dark hole. The torn shirt was soaked in his blood.

The next photo was a pair of hands. The fingers broken and pointing in unnatural angles. Additional photos captured other victims of torture. The range of injuries suggested a sadistic creativity in inflicting pain.

The last phot was a hanged man. With his feet only inches from the floor it was obvious a death by slow strangulation.

"These are inmates in a prison?"

"Yes. Fortaleza de la Concha in San Sebastian. The place is more like an eighteenth-century dungeon. I'd rather you didn't identify it specifically. Just say it is in the north."

"Quite a risk your doctor friend took getting these pictures."

"A brave man with a conscience. Photography as a hobby. Developed these himself so he didn't have to trust anyone."

"Extraordinary. Had to take these probably in difficult light conditions. Knows what he's doing with a camera. I'll do my best to see they get published. I'll send them off along with my own stuff to New York. I'll assume there's nothing telling in your written copy to point to you?"

⁂

Fraser had some powerful material, especially the photographs, both his own plus these torture victims from the Asturias rising. Better reportage than he'd seen from anybody else covering Spain. Fraser sensed Spain must be facing some imminent social upheaval. And it would be violent with the widespread politically motivated violence across the whole of Spain for the last several years. Right on Left, Left on Right violence depending on the region, the city, even down to the village level. However, Spain was a mere ripple to seemingly larger events going on in the world.

Germany continued to scare the hell out of Europe. From a defeated foe in 1918 thought to be sufficiently subjugated under the Treaty of Versailles to a resurgent military power. Germany now led by a belligerent dictator represented a clear threat to its former enemies. The coal-rich Saar region officially rejoined Germany earlier in the year. Hitler officially announced German rearmament effectively negating the Treaty of Versailles. Conscription of all able-bodied German men reaching nineteen was implemented to rapidly increase the number of men under arms.

The world was shocked by the virulent anti-Semitism pervading Nazi Germany taking the form of continued persecution of the German Jews. In September, the Nuremberg Race Laws against Jews was decreed. Jews are to be denied the rights of German citizenship. Marriage and extramarital relations between Jews and Aryans are prohibited. Jews cannot work or conduct commerce outside their Jewish communities. Hitler was making good on his campaign to rid Germany of Jews as foretold in *Mein Kampf.* What might be the next step? News reels made their way out of Germany. Even so the plight of German Jews was largely ignored by the world.

An equally growing threat to the West was exported International Communism loosely directed from Moscow. The towering economic success of the Bolshevik Communist Soviet Union made the former backward Russia-dominated confederation an international power with five-fold growth in industrial output in only twenty years.

Fearing a rearmed Germany, a leftist French government signed a treaty of mutual assistance with the Soviet Union attempting to pressure their historic adversary from both eastern and western fronts.

Mussolini's Italian army invaded Ethiopia. Although the aggression involved colonial Africa it served to focus attention on the other Fascist state in Europe that was rapidly rearming. Hitler and Mussolini are friendly. Both shared outsized nationalistic ambitions.

The United States and President Franklin Roosevelt were wrestling with the intractable Great Depression. Domestic economic issues overshadowed foreign political frictions. Internationally, the U.S. government viewed an ambitious military dominated Japan in the Far East as a greater threat to U.S. interests.

By the close of the year 1935, Spain's irreconcilable political strife is lost in the weeds to the rest of the world's concerns.

Upon returning to Paris Fraser worked feverishly for several days compiling his materials. Developing the photos himself he was astounded when he first saw the negatives. More dramatic then he could have hoped given the hurried circumstances of taking the shots. He would use Elizalde's photos and copy to provide a counterpoint from a Spanish view. An anonymous Spanish source fearing government retribution. The two stories, one in the north the other in the south would portray a pervasive climate of violence in Spain.

This Spanish work product was powerful. Better than his material from Germany. Powerful reporting that revealed more than mere information. Not the lukewarm material of life in Europe to be read over breakfast coffee in American homes. The photographs provoked a range of superlatives; riveting, poignant, gruesome, distressing, wrenching. They would force the viewer to read the copy for explanation. Whether it stirred real interest or not it was still good reporting.

The bulky envelope was posted using the newly inaugurated transatlantic air mail service of just a year ago. Using sea planes, it was a circuitous route leaving from Marseille to Rio de Janeiro, Brazil. Then flying north with stops in Puerto Rico and Miami before arriving in New York.

Fraser knew that it arrived because two weeks later he received a rare overseas telephone call from his editor, George Walberg.

"Got your package. Interesting pictures," Walberg said.

"Thanks. When will the first piece run?"

There was a long pause before Walberg said, "Probably next week. Listen. I sent your copy to the Chief. To put it mildly, he was unhappy."

Fraser was stunned. This was first-rate material. "What the hell do you mean, *unhappy*?"

"Come on, Fraser. You portray the Communists running Madrid and their attacks on the Church as some inevitable revolutionary movement of the downtrodden working class. Your words even. You paint this armed peasant mob bent on destroying property as victims when they're confronted by the police. Your writing sounds like that of a Commie sympathizer."

"What the fuck are you talking about, Walberg? Can't you read what happened? Look at the fucking pictures for Christsake!"

"Listen, Fraser, it doesn't matter what I think. Those are the Chief's sentiments. Told me to tell you to get your head on straight. He was worried about your perspective after your German reporting. Liked your middle of the political road material that followed better. Your piece trashing Stalin's police state after visiting Moscow redeemed you. But now you seemed to have gone over to the Left."

"You're telling me you're not going to print my story?"

"After editing. Lots of editing."

"And the photographs? What about the ones about the torture of prisoners?"

"Some we'll use. They're good with a different narrative."

"You are a real prick, Walberg. As an editor you don't know journalism from dog shit. I'll go around you right to the Chief."

"You know, Fraser, you're a real pain in the ass. You only have this cushy overseas assignment because the Chief liked you. I'd watch your step from here on out. So go ahead. Call the Chief, write the Chief. I don't give a damn."

Fraser was livid with rage. He wanted to be standing in front of Walberg and throttle the little shit rather than arguing over a scratchy sounding international connection.

He was not one to react rashly but what Hearst had done, assuming Walberg was not lying, was too fundamental to continue unchallenged. Not only did Fraser have journalistic integrity, he didn't need this job for his livelihood.

"Tell you what Walberg. I won't bother calling the Chief. You can do that. You can tell him I quit. Have a nice fucking day, asshole."

With that he slammed down the receiver. Over a couple of whiskies and a good bottle of Bordeaux at *Les Deux Magots* he not only felt better but relieved. Better if it had not ended this way but he was becoming less interested in this type of journalism anyway. Digging for dirt on bad characters, fighting the good fight for truth and fairness was his passion at one time. Idealistic perhaps, but he still found success along with personal satisfaction that what he was doing mattered.

These last years as a correspondent covering mostly European politics didn't do that. Only a few isolated events like the massacre in Coria del Rio engaged his passion. Now his interests increasingly turned to writing fiction. He had enough life-experiences for many novels. Remembered Hemmingway sighting that when they met over ten years earlier in Paris. Taking inventory, he had as much interesting life-material as the now famous Hemmingway.

Still, it was hard to let go. Apart from the rebuke of his reporting from Spain he wanted to know what sort of surgically altered crap became published. He had an obligation to explain to Loretta Elizalde. Her doctor friend's photographs would either not be published or the context altered to convey a different message. Contacting his Hearst colleague in Paris, C. F. Bertelli, he asked him to get copies of the San Francisco Examiner and his old paper the Los Angeles Herald Examiner when his recent series of articles and photographs about Europe appeared.

The editing hatchet job was worse than he could have imagined. Not only altered beyond a bland middle of the road reporting of just facts, whoever did the editing created a decidedly pro-Right coloring to the circumstances. Reading only this reporting, one would get the impression that Spain was threatened by Communists, socialists, and anarchists bent on destroying the Church and traditional Spanish culture.

He wrote to Elizalde. Included were the newspaper clippings along with his written submission and a full set of photographs that he took in Coria del Rio. Told her the censorship of his own publisher caused him to quit. Good luck to her. Good luck to Spain.

As the new year of 1936 got underway, Marc Fraser felt relaxed for the first time in years. He loved Paris. Now he could enjoy living here without continually leaving on assignment. Even the cold gray of Paris in winter didn't dampen his renewed enthusiasm to pursue writing fiction full time. Spring was only a couple of months away. Only the continued menace of a belligerent Germany intruded to darken his spirits as it did for everyone in France.

CHAPTER 22

Back in Paris life was good for Marc Fraser. At least until July. That was when a military mutiny in Spain instigated what would become three years of a brutal civil war. From the onset it would have far reaching implications. Fighting beset by atrocities typical to civil wars where people living in the same village or region turn upon one another. But unlike most civil wars this twentieth century conflict would prove to be a preliminary round to an even greater European conflagration.

Fraser remained acutely aware of events in Europe. Even though he yearned to retreat into his own world of writing fiction he could not ignore events that foreshadowed some larger cataclysm that seemed inevitable.

In February the Spanish leftist parties cooperated to form a unified Popular Front thereby narrowly taking a majority in the newly called elections. Their victory ended two years of a right-leaning coalition government. As a result the far-Right became more militant. What little political center existed in Spain evaporated.

The newly elected Popular Front coalition government wasted little time in consolidating control. A campaign was launched against the opposition Right. Fearing a military coup, Army Chief of Staff Francisco Franco was demoted and reassigned to a remote command in the Canary Islands. The ultra-right *Falange*

Party was banned. Riots, strikes, and civil anarchy in different forms broke out in various parts of Spain. Not waiting for government action, some socialists groups forcibly freed political prisoners.

Everywhere people were compelled into choosing between the two extreme alternatives. Choosing might be coerced or simply necessary for surviving within the prevailing community in which one lived. Fear became pervasive.

The Popular Front coalition may have effectively joined together to win the election but they immediately fell into infighting. From the onset collective governance fell apart with the various socialist parties not willing to cooperate with the republican factions.

Shocked by losing their majority in the Cortes the political Right now voiced alarm about a Socialist-Communist takeover they claimed to be inevitable. Extremists began to seriously conspire as to how to overthrow the Republic.

Elsewhere in Europe the continuing political strife in Spain appeared nothing new. Spain had always been a mess. Whatever happened there was unfortunate but would not impact the rest of Europe according to prevailing opinion.

Fraser was not so sure. Having seen Spain from the inside he knew the continued antagonisms must eventually escalate into something far worse. Certainly bad for the Spanish. Yet might such a civil war also have implications for the rest of Europe?

His first hand experiences in Germany and Spain left a profound disgust of the ultra-Right. Their self-serving justifications, anti-republicanism, abiding nationalistic fervor was nothing more than a play for power. First Italy, then Germany, now Spain. Politics seemed now a contest between Fascist nationalism and struggling republican forms of government. The democratic process was inherently a crucible for competing ideologies therefore seen as ineffective. These Europe republics were all new to the process. For the far-Right the great antagonist was Communism. Communism in the form of the threateningly virulent Soviet form.

To no surprise, things came apart in Spain in 1936. In July four Fascist gunmen murdered a police lieutenant of the Assault Guard in the afternoon in front of his home in Madrid. The victim was a known member of the anti-Fascist UMRA military organization. In retaliation the following day a fellow Assault Guard officer and friend of the slain officer ostensibly arrested a prominent right-wing politician. Shot dead in the police van, the body was later dumped at the entrance to a cemetery in Madrid. The next day Assault Guards and Fascist militias engaged in a shootout at the cemetery where burials for both of the murdered victims were taking place. Four people died.

Three days after those events in Madrid the Army mutinied in Morocco. From the Canary Islands, General Franco declared a state of war. He then was flown to Morocco to take command of the Spanish African Army.

This was the same army Franco commanded in crushing the Asturias Miners' Strike two years earlier. The battle-hardened troops consisted of the Spanish Foreign Legion along with indigenous Moroccan troops, the *Regulares*, led by Spanish officers. The Spanish Legion was the elite troops with combat experience fighting North African Berber rebels. Those colonial wars instilled in them a behavior for horrific brutality toward the enemy.

Within days the Nationalist rebels seized control a third of Spain. The major cities of Pamplona, Oviedo, Salamanca, Avila, Segovia, Cadiz, and Seville came under rebel control. Whereas a military coup is a quick attempt to seize power this immediately developed into civil war. Opposing armed forces immediately arrayed in open confrontation.

The Nationalist rebels established a strong foothold in the south with the importing of Spanish troops from Africa. This was accomplished with the assistance of German aircraft ferrying them from Ceuta in Morocco to the mainland, thereby circumventing the Spanish naval blockade manned largely by mid-rank officers that remained loyal to the government.

Heavy fighting commenced throughout Spain. Rebel forces represented the most effective fighting troops. Within months they controlled Andalusia in the south as well as a good deal of northwest Spain. But Spanish military allegiances split setting in place the prospect for eventual pitched battles. Loyalist forces laid siege to the great stone fortification known as the Alcázar in Toledo defended by Nationalists. They prepared to defend major Republican strongholds, particularly Madrid and Barcelona.

Fraser was reading all this in the morning edition of *Le Figaro* over coffee in his apartment when his telephone rang. The French operator asked if this was Monsieur Marc Fraser. An overseas call from the United States.

"Marc? This is WR. How have you been?"

What the hell? Why was Hearst calling him?

"Marion sends her love. She was sad to hear you left us."

"Doing fine. Writing. Working on another book. Another novel."

"Good, good. I have to apologize for the way things happened after you got back from Spain. I understand why you were upset when I read what they did to your submittal."

What the hell was this crap? "I was told you ordered the rewrite. Is that true?"

"Well, yes. But I didn't intend for it to be so radically altered. That idiot Walberg made it sound like you were condoning police brutality. What I didn't like about your draft was its lack of balance. After all, these people came armed, trespassed onto property with the intent of confronting the police. You neglected to identify the source of the unrest as the Communists and socialists."

Fraser held himself in check. Why bother arguing? The former champion of the people, Hearst now clearly embraced the Right. Not only in the United States but in the world. Even Fascism could be accepted against the new enemy, Communism. Fraser's silence made his point.

"Listen, Marc. You're a talented journalist. You know how to dig out front page news. Know how to capture powerful photographs. I'd like you to go back to Spain. Cover this growing civil war."

The arrogance of William Randolph Hearst was astounding. Why would he think that Fraser would be even remotely interested?

"No."

"Hear me out, Marc. You're made for this kind of reporting. They're all sorts of correspondents in Madrid that are covering from the Republican government side. No one that I know of yet is covering from the Nationalist rebel side. Not only do I have some leverage there but you now have a powerful contact in this Carlos Cabrera. His army officer brother must be with the rebels if he was serving with the Spanish Legion in Morocco."

"And of course if they saw that crap you published over my byline they now think that I'm sympathetic to their cause. Was that your intention all along, Chief?"

"No. Certainly not. I didn't know it would come to this. But here we are. It's a singular opportunity."

"The answer is still no."

"Do me the favor of just thinking about it. I know you're angry. I would be too. But I would bet that reporting from a war zone must pique your interest. Perfect way to gather more material for your fiction. I'll pay you three thousand dollars a week if you'll take this on. I know it's not about money but that shows you how badly I want you there. Will you at least think about it?"

Fraser's defenses had been partly breeched. It wasn't the money. Partly getting back into a real reporting adventure. And something in him had changed. No longer was chasing after wrongdoing just an abstract endeavor. He now had strongly developed opinions on social questions. Jews being persecuted in Germany. People starving in Spain. The distressingly crude justifications of Fascism. Their appeal to the base instincts of anti-intellectuals. The rank and file enlisted from the stupid and thuggish. Nationalism everywhere was as an excuse for any excess.

An opportunity to exercise his newfound sense of social consciousness? Hearst was correct. Those like Cabrera would now think him sympathetic with the published articles attributed to him. It gave him immediate credibility. Of course he would have to report under strict censorship. Perhaps that cloak and dagger tradecraft that he got from the military attaché Colonel Waite might now have application? Sticking it to these characters certainly was enticing.

"I'll think on it. I'll wire you in a few days. No promises."

"That's all I can ask, Marc. Hoping you accept the assignment, I have already taken the liberty of making arrangements. I know the chairman of the big oil company Texaco. Name is Torkild Rieber. They do extensive business with Spain. Rieber's personal sympathies side with the Nationalists."

An understatement. Fraser knew of Rieber. A well-known supporter of Fascism. Friendly with Hitler, sure to be a friend to Franco. The rebels would need gasoline for their mechanized forces. A marriage of convenience.

"Rieber has a representative in southern Spain by the name of Roberto Sanchez. Rieber wholeheartedly agreed to have his man act as a go between for transmitting your copy out of Spain."

"I've met Sanchez. He's a friend of Cabrera's."

"Excellent. See what I mean. This is a perfect arrangement for you and INS."

Fraser hated himself for caving to Hearst's manipulation. The prospect of covering this war was however enticing. Even more so if he could circumvent the rebel censors to get out material damaging to their side. Maybe circumvent Hearst's censorship also. The problem would be to disguise that it was not him secreting out the contraband material, especially the pictures. He'd have to work that out before agreeing to this potentially dangerous adventure.

He had already convinced himself to go back to Spain if he could find a way to get his material published without implicating himself. A certain death sentence if accused of spying. Thousands had already died within the first weeks of the civil war. Most were not combatants just on the other side politically from someone with a gun. The outlet for his material was obvious. *El Liberal*, Elizalde's Madrid newspaper. Along with *Paris-Soir* in Paris. *Paris-Soir* adopted the unusual practice of publishing both sides to politically charged stories. How to route it out of Spain remained the question.

His old acquaintance Allen Dulles was the answer. The United States military wanted intelligence on Spain. Their military attaché in Madrid would see things only from the Republican side. Fraser could provide information from the Nationalist side. The quid pro quo was getting his uncensored material in print under an autonomous attribution. But could he sufficiently disguise himself as the source? That could only be determined later within the context of actual circumstances.

If Dulles would participate then Fraser made up his mind to give it a try. If it didn't work out he would simply abort the mission and tell Hearst to screw himself. The following day he placed a call to Dulles at the law offices of Sullivan & Cromwell.

Fraser explained the background of events of his trip into Spain last year. Tried to explain his agreement to return although it sounded somewhat self-righteous when he articulated it. Regardless, Dulles was ecstatic. He relished this stuff. Knew of Fraser's visit to Lt. Col. Waite last year. Fraser explained the tactics Waite and a technical *consultant* had contrived. Had not tried it but it would be vital to this venture. The key was getting the stuff repeatedly published without being identified as the source. The photographs would be the most difficult to disguise.

"Here's how it works, Allen," Fraser said. "I'll send my dispatches intended for publication under my byline to my old newspaper editor at the Los Angeles Times. That will be the censored material. Separately I'll send a letter addressed to my sister in New York. Except it will be to your home address, Allen. Under the postage stamp will be micro dots. Photos, typed stuff photographed then reduced. All for publication anonymously. Anything of intelligence value you can pass along to your friends in the military or State Department. Still not sure who you work for though."

Dulles dodged the question answering, "My God. That's impressive, Marc. You've the makings of a real spy. Can you develop these micro dots in the field?"

"I think so."

"This is a war zone. How do you intend getting your material out of Spain?"

"The Nationalists apparently have a lot of international friends. Some in the United States. William Hearst himself. He's arranged to get me accredited by the rebel army command. You know a guy by the name of Rieber? Heads Texaco."

"Sure. Outspoken Fascist sympathizer. He was featured on the cover of *Time Magazine* a couple of months ago."

"Well Hearst has arranged through Rieber to use Texaco's Spanish representative as a conduit. I've met the guy. He's cozy with these Spanish Fascists in the south."

The following day Fraser placed a call to Hearst. He agreed to take on the assignment on condition his copy and photographs would not be edited. Easy enough for Hearst to agree since he knew it would already be censored by the rebel army to exclude anything damaging to their propaganda.

"I'll use the Texaco guy in Spain to send out my material. Have your friend Rieber communicate to him. Need to know where to contact him. Wire Carlos Cabrera I will be coming to Seville within the week. The city's already under rebel control I understand. Also, my material goes to my old editor in Los Angeles, Randal Schmidt not that weasel Walberg in New York."

CHAPTER 23

Marc Fraser arrived at Seville Airport on Saturday the first of August. It took two days to make the multi-stop indirect routing now that civil war had broken out. Paris to Toulouse with Air France, followed by a long hop to Lisbon, Portugal with Aero Portuguesa out over the Atlantic to avoid unknown hostilities in northern Spain. Under the corporatist authoritarian virtual dictatorship of Portuguese Prime Minister António Salazar there was official sympathy for the Nationalist rebellion in Spain. So it was easy to charter a flight from Lisbon into rebel held Seville.

Disembarking the small aircraft he lugged his two canvas duffle bags with shoulder straps. One held a bare minimum of clothing. The heavier other bag held his camera gear, developing supplies, and typewriter. Expecting the summer temperatures, he was dressed for field work; cotton shirt, cotton twill pants, ankle-high hiking boots, and a denim tropical hat. Still he wasn't prepared for the ninety-degree heat with humidity.

Approaching the terminal building he recognized the same Falange officer from before. After saluting smartly, he shook hands with Fraser and took one of the bags. "Don Cabrera is staying at the Alfonse as before. I am to take you to him. Seville is secure but unfortunately his home in Morón de la Frontera remains under Republican control. But not for long."

As they entered the terminal building a loud speaker was blaring a speech. Same as in Berlin however the words stopped Fraser in his tracks. It was a Hitler-like rant but the substance was chilling. The words were a warning. '*Communists, socialists, anarchists, unionists, will be shot. The more the better. Summary execution for anyone resisting. As a deterrent, the valiant soldiers of the Spanish Army of Africa are directed to commit rape on women collaborating with the enemy. Those that opposed the Nationalist forces are less than human. Spain must be purged of such vermin. Let terror precede our advance.*'

"Who the hell is that?" Fraser asked the Falangist.

"Ah, that is General Queipo de Llano. Colorful is he not?"

"General?"

"Yes. He commands the Nationalist forces here in Seville."

Good God. What kind of barbarity would this lead to if the commander himself openly encouraged violations of international law? Violations of basic humanity. Fraser did not realize the extent to which wholesale atrocities on both sides had already begun.

Arriving at the Hotel Alfonso XIII the Falangist escorted Fraser to a meeting room off the lobby. After knocking, the door was opened by a Spanish officer in battle dress.

The Falangist saluted and introduced Fraser. Before the officer could say anything, Carlos Cabrera shouted from within the room, "Show Señor Fraser in if you will, Eduardo."

A beaming Carlos Cabrera embraced Fraser. "It has started. We shall now take back Spain and rid it of this Communist scum. We have the Army. We have help from our German and Italian friends. Come, let me introduce you."

Several men sat around a rectangular dining table covered with maps.

"Gentlemen, let me introduce Señor Marc Fraser. An American like our good friend Roberto Sanchez. He was here last year. Witnessed that incident with the mob in Coria del Rio. I read his article published in the Hearst newspapers in the United States.

An objective piece of reporting. Clearly pointed to the necessity of maintaining order in the face of armed outlaws.

"Madrid is crawling with correspondents reporting censored government lies to the rest of the world. I believe as does General Franco that we need our own conduits to present our side to the world. Especially to the United States. Here is the General's personal authorization, Señor Fraser."

Cabrera handed Fraser two documents; a letter of safe conduct and a letter authorizing wide latitude of access to military operations. Censorship to be confined only to *obvious militarily sensitive material*. Cabrera also included his own letter signed as commander of the local *Falange*.

Roberto Sanchez, the Texaco representative quickly rose to shake Fraser's hand. "Good to have you with us, Señor Fraser."

Carlos Cabrera said, "Let me introduce you. First my brother, Major Eduardo Cabrera. Eduardo commands the 5th Bandera of the Spanish Legion from Ceuta in Morocco." Bandera was the Legion designation for a battalion-sized infantry unit.

"And this officer is Colonel Juan Yagüe. Some say the most capable field commander in all the Spanish Army."

Yagüe remained seated acknowledging Fraser with a nod.

"General Franco placed the Colonel in overall field command of the forces here in the south."

Fraser looked at the remaining person in the room. A German recognizable by his SS uniform. Fraser knew the rank insignia, a Hauptsturmführer, equivalent to a captain in the regular army. This war had only started and here were the Nazis like flies on shit.

Fraser would not have been surprised to see the Italian military also represented. Just a few days ago the first squadron of Italian war planes arrived in Spain. The Italian Navy was also reported to be maneuvering warships into the western Mediterranean. Portugal was officially neutral but sympathetic to the rebels. Fascist Europe was uniting. Everyone else better watch out. Spain now, what might be next?

"And this is Hauptsturmführer Heinz Leitner of the German *Sicherheitsdienst des Reichsführers-SS*," Carlos Cabrera said, mangling the pronunciation. "The SD, the Security Service of the SS is the easier acronym."

Like Yagüe, Leitner nodded without rising, smoking a cigarette in the German fashion between upturned thumb and forefinger.

"Hauptsturmführer Leitner is here as an observer for the Director of the Reich Main Security Office, Reinhardt Heydrich. The support of the German Reich has proved essential to establishing our early successes."

Major Cabrera said, "Well Colonel, I must be leaving to prepare my troops for tomorrow. We are leaving at dawn for this pesthole Arahal. It's only an hour's ride with our lorries but I want to strike early."

"Then on to Morón de la Frontera," Carlos Cabrera said. "That is why I am going with you, my brother. To free our properties from these Communists."

Colonel Yagüe seemed focused on larger strategic matters. "Major, when you are finished freeing up the Cabrera estates, take your Bandera north to link up with my main body. We then march on Badajoz. Thousands of laborers have confiscated property throughout the area. The entire province is a leftist stronghold."

"I would like to accompany Major Cabrera as well, Colonel," Hauptsturmführer Leitner said.

The meeting adjourned with everyone going to prepare for the early morning departure. But even a cool shower and the fan couldn't alleviate the oppressive evening heat for Fraser. A couple of whiskies sent up from the bar helped. At four in the morning the alarm clock terminated a fitful sleep.

Fraser joined Carlos Cabrera and Leitner for coffee in the dining room. Shortly thereafter the younger Cabrera picked them up in a sedan driven by a Legionnaire. Outside of Seville, they rendezvoused with Major Cabrera's troops loaded into a convoy of lorries. Several lorries pulled field artillery pieces.

Fraser wondered if they were going into a pitched battle with an opposing armed force of regular military.

Approaching the small town east of Seville, Cabrera dispersed his troops along the only two roads into Arahal effectively encircling the town. Fraser noticed that the majority of the soldiers were Moorish Moroccan *Regulares*, recognizable by their weathered dark complexions and uniforms. The same colonial troops that Franco and Yagüe used to brutally suppress the Asturian Miners' Strike two years earlier.

Arraying his eight 75mm Howitzers, Major Cabrera commenced a bombardment of the town. There was no armed resistance in evidence. What was this about? Fraser snapped photographs but they really didn't convey much about what was going on.

After thirty minutes of heavy artillery fire Cabrera's troops marched into the town with many buildings now in ruin. Several bodies were visible in the main street as Fraser followed the soldiers. No one fired on the soldiers. It was quiet except for some distant sounds of wailing. Then a Moroccan soldier shot a man coming out of a building. That was followed by other sporadic small arms fire.

Still no armed resistance from the town. The artillery barrage militarily unwarranted. Coming around a street corner a burned out church stood two blocks away. Closer inspection revealed the fire was days old, the blackened timbers cold. Apparently not the result of the recent artillery fire. Arrayed in front in a line were twenty-three charred bodies.

An old man in his seventies was roughly hauled before Major Cabrera who stood staring at the burned bodies.

"You are the mayor of this town?" Cabrera said.

The old man was shaking. "Yes."

"Who are these burned people?"

The man started to weep. Cabrera motioned to the Moroccan *Regulare* behind the man. The soldier slammed the butt of his rifle into the small of the man's back sending him to the ground.

"Once more I will ask."

The old man now in great distress said, "They were Nationalist sympathizers. Rounded up on orders of the town council.
We feared they would attempt to support ....."

"Support us you mean? Are you a Communist?"

"No. A socialist."

"The same thing."

"But we did not harm them."

Cabrera turned angry. "What the hell do you call this Comrade Mayor? You burned them alive! In the church which you
also spit on."

"No, no! We were only holding them. They had food and
water. Some were even released. The others feared it was a trap
to shoot them escaping. We did not set the fire."

"You insult me old man."

Cabrera withdrew his Astra 9mm automatic service pistol.
Walking up to the old man kneeling in the dirt he fired a round
into his forehead. Fraser captured the execution with his Leica.

Carlos Cabrera came up to his brother within minutes of the
execution. Upon seeing the burned bodies he turned his head
away and retched. Recovering after a few moments he angrily
said, "Señor Fraser. Now you can show what we are fighting for.
Take pictures of those murdered men. Burned to death. My God
Eduardo, how could our own laborers resort to such vile acts?"

"I suspect it is Communist provocateurs, Don Cabrera,"
Hauptsturmführer Leitner said. "Much the same as we faced in
Germany in the early days. The Communists would incite the
impressionable rabble. Those with no sense of national culture."

Turning to Major Cabrera, Leitner said, "And how do you
plan on dealing with these crimes, Herr Major?"

Cabrera turned and motioned to a nearby junior Legionnaire
officer. "Lieutenant, spread the word to the other companies.
Sack this miserable place. Make an example. Execute an appropriate number of men in reprisal for these murders. The Moroccans have been without women for several weeks. Let them take
their pleasure. Quickly though. We move south on Morón in a
few hours."

The scene just witnessed was horrific enough but what ensued for the next two hours was something one did not envision possible in the twentieth century. It could only be conveyed in pictures. Words simply could not communicate the nature of such loathsome acts of bestiality. These Moroccan *Regulares* were like a pack of wild dogs. He now knew what Elizalde was trying to explain about the horrors inflicted during the suppression of the Asturias Miners' Strike.

After several rolls of film, Fraser thought he captured every scene of wanton murder and mutilation imaginable. Men lined up in small groups and shot. One group tortured first by gunshots to the legs then fatal shots to the lower abdomen for a prolonged agonizing death. Ears severed as trophies. Crude beheadings by machete. Several chopping swings required to finally severe the head. Mutilation of genitals.

After the gunfire quieted, a final abomination. Screams from obviously multiple women came from a large house. Fraser attempted to enter but a Legion officer physically barred his way.

"Let me pass. I am allowed anywhere," Fraser shouted at the officer. "Want to see my letter from General Franco?"

Before the confrontation escalated, Major Cabrera arrived.

"Señor Fraser. I would prefer you did not go in there. Such pictures would not be printable at any rate."

"What's happening to those women, Major?"

"I believe you can guess. It is sanctioned as a reprisal for the crimes of these people."

"Rape?"

"Señor Fraser, this is war. But a different kind of war. Terror has a purpose. Extra-judicial executions are necessary to purge the enemy of their leaders. Otherwise they will continue their armed resistance behind our lines. When my troops move on we must know that the enemy will not be at our backs."

The screams abruptly stopped. He assumed the victims had been put out of their misery. Moments later a dozen *Regulares* exited the building. Several brandished women's undergarments from their bloodied bayonets.

Fraser caught himself from exploding. This was only his first encounter. If he wished to continue covering the rebels he could not openly be a harsh critic. Must watch his step going forward. Find every opportunity to make sympathetic overtures to these murderers. What he witnessed sufficiently sickened him to provoke a determination to expose what was going on.

Witnessing such appalling cruelty, Fraser clearly saw the focus of his reporting. A holocaust inflicted upon whole groups of people. Civilians not soldiers. Stamp out opposing ideology through death and terror. Warfare conducted without consideration for possible reciprocity on one's own troops but simply medieval butchery. And it would be told by photographs. Words seemed inadequate.

The Republicans were also guilty of excesses but the Nationalists, at least the Army of Africa, murdered on a larger scale while making torture and rape a pervasive tactic. The world must see this. If he could gather military-value intelligence for the U.S., all the better. The objectionable task would be to construct his overt reporting. Without directly pandering to their propaganda he still had to maintain his reporting stature to pass Nationalist censoring.

Because he had privileged access he would be expected to deliver more than lukewarm treatment in support of the Nationalist cause to his reporting. To get around this Fraser would write his material as if reporting on a real war, photographs included, dominated by factual events of the conflict. Geography. Casualties. Success or failure of tactics. Strategic importance. Damage to the enemy. Conditions of the average soldier. Photographs otherwise condemning of the Nationalists would be creatively captioned. The same photos might be used in his secret materials with a more appropriate caption. He would avoid offering opinion commentary.

To add the patina of right-wing political correctness he would point out Republican atrocities if he could document them. No reason to give them a pass on human rights violations. He would simply avoid any political polemic against the Left.

When necessary he could resort to extraneous anti-Communist commentary of upheavals within the Soviet leadership. Wasn't difficult to magnify the monstrosity of Stalin's dictatorship.

Reports were seeping out of Moscow suggesting that Stalin was embarking on campaign to purge many within the leadership including the Red Army. It appeared not only a purge of potential political opponents but also a grassroots move against tens of thousands of peasants unhappy with the economic disaster of forced collectivization. Fraser had no love for Communism, particularly as practiced by Joseph Stalin's regime. By inference those criticisms might bolster his anti-Communist stance among these Spanish Fascists.

His covert materials would be shaped around the photographs. The pictures were the key to constructing a visceral impact on the reader. The accompanying text would explain the context of the photos. The U.S. military would get photos of weapons, aircraft, along with any information he might pick up by being in proximity to command officers. That was just to encourage Dulles' cooperation to act as a conduit for his published material. He was here to expose things not to act as a spy for U.S. military intelligence.

Commandeering a café, the elder Cabrera, Leitner, and Fraser enjoyed wine under an umbrella. The frightened owner served them as his wife cowered in the kitchen.

Cabrera was uncharacteristically subdued. Even though he had contempt for these people perhaps he was chastened by the ugly spectacle of witnessing murder. Like Fraser, might he also feel physically sickened? In contrast, Hauptsturmführer Leitner was almost ebullient.

Sipping wine and chain smoking his strong cigarettes, Leitner said to Fraser, "I understand you spent some time in Germany, Herr Fraser. What are your views on National Socialism?"

"As a journalist, I avoid taking political sides."

"Come now, there can be no such thing as impartial journalism. You must hold views therefore it must color your reporting."

"Of course I have views. But I find that I do not embrace any particular political ideology. Every ideology demands adherence to a wide range of different positions. Collectively those become dogma. I find that to be a problem since there is always something with which I disagree."

"So what is agreeable to you about National Socialism?"

Here was an opportunity to pander to this Nazi and solidify his sympathetic credentials to Don Cabrera. The objective was to continually reinforce his anti-Communist credentials. After all, that was the basis for Hearst's sympathies to the Fascists.

"Certainly they have resurrected the German economy. I agree that the Treaty of Versailles went too far in punishing Germany. They have eliminated the Communist threat. Especially international Communism directed by that monster in Moscow. Communism is a disease. The Nazis have also succeeded in restoring a pride in German nationalism. What Don Cabrera would like to achieve for Spain."

"And what do you find objectionable?"

"This obsession with Jews. I don't buy into German Jews being the cause of any of Germany's problems. They're an exceedingly small minority."

"You are wrong, Herr Fraser. The Jewish problem is just like the Communist problem. Both are internationally directed. Both reject nationalism."

Before the discussion continued much further, Major Cabrera walked up to his older brother.

"We are leaving in ten minutes, Carlos. Morón will suffer the same fate as this town. We shall dine at our home this evening."

Unlike this decimated village, Republican elements in Morón had created a Defense Committee upon hearing of the uprising in Morocco by dissident army officers. The invading Army of Africa had crossed to the continent advancing north to now occupy Seville. Stirred with political enthusiasm, they prepared to defend Morón against the Nationalist rebellion.

Seeking to inflict less property damage on the town near to his family's estate, Cabrera did not engage his artillery. Expecting no resistance like at Arahal his troops however came under fire as they advanced on Morón. While the defenders put up a fierce resistance, they were no match for the well trained soldiers. Old rifles against machine guns. Within thirty minutes the lopsided battle concluded.

Bodies of defenders littered the streets. Wounded were dispatched by bullets to the head. Some bayoneted. The invaders had their blood up. They had taken casualties this time. Now they set upon the inhabitants of Morón with a fiery. People were dragged into the street and shot. Young women were stripped and gang raped in the open. When the bloodletting subsided, the soldiers commenced looting anything of value.

For the unfortunate survivors of Morón, they would endure terror throughout the night. Cabrera let his soldiers drink, eat, loot, and continue to rape before moving north the next day.

Without interference Fraser took photographs of this continued barbarity. Surely he would not be permitted to send many of the more gruesome shots for publication. Yet he had not been advised who would act as censor for his materials.

Fraser spent the night at Don Cabrera's estate. It remained unoccupied by any Republican militias probably unwilling to challenge Cabrera's own heavily armed men guarding the property. Carlos Cabrera celebrated not only freeing his home from Republican control, but also seeing his younger brother in command of troops.

In the broader sense Carlos Cabrera celebrated the beginning of the end to the hated Republic that had ruined his Spain. He longed for an authoritarian government whether a monarchy or military dictatorship. He envied neighboring Portugal. They seemed to have achieved a government in firm control even with a parliamentary platform. Opposed to Communism, socialism, anarchism, liberalism, it was nationalistic and firmly Catholic.

Fraser would accompany Major Cabrera's troops as they returned to Seville to resupply before pushing north to link with Yagüe's larger command. Over drinks after dinner Eduardo Cabrera explained to his older brother the broad strategy.

"Colonel Yagüe is already moving north into Extremadura. My troops will join his main force. We will take Merida first then moving on Badajoz. General Mola's forces already are consolidating control of Castilla y Leon. Galicia is already ours. Once joined together we will then have control of all western Spain. Attention can then turn to Madrid."

They were surprisingly free in discussing military specifics including German and Italian support in detail. Eventually Fraser brought up the subject of how to file his material.

"Major, what is the process for vetting my reporting before I send it off to America? I assume you'll want to make sure I am not revealing military sensitive information."

"Yes. I had not considered that. Not used to having journalists around. None cared to venture into combat in Morocco. I will introduce you to General Queipo de Llano in Seville. He commands our forces in Andalusia. He can advise you as to the necessary protocols."

In the morning, the convoy of troop lorries moved back through the main street of Morón. Thinking nothing could be worse than what he had witnessed, Fraser fought to hold back the rising bile in his stomach at a new disgusting sight. Pigs had moved in to feed on bodies still lying in the street. It was difficult to concentrate on getting these shots. The pigs pulling open the bodies to get at the soft viscera within the abdomen. So gruesome, the shots could never be published in newspapers.

Returning to Seville, Major Cabrera reported into Queipo de Llano's headquarters. Fraser was introduced to the tall distinguished looking older general. The same maniac broadcasting incitement to terror. Fraser presented the general with the letter from General Franco.

"Excellent. There are only a couple of foreign journalists with us I understand. None under my command at the moment. We need to counter the Communist propaganda coming out of Madrid. Foreign journalists have flocked there. The Government has even set up a censorship office so the rest of the world will hear only what they want to let out.

"I shall not do that. As long as you publish the truth it will not be censored, Señor Fraser. No military information of course. Tell the story of how we are returning Spain to its traditions, to its glory. General Franco has called it the *Second Reconquista.*"

Another madman. Queipo de Llano's eyes reminded Fraser of Hitler's.

General de Llano summoned a young captain into his office. Introducing the captain to Fraser, the General instructed the captain in his responsibilities to review Fraser's material before it was approved for publication. His final instruction to the captain suggested he would have a fair amount of latitude at least in the photographs that would be allowed out. "Let the Communists and anarchists see in pictures what is in store if they do not capitulate."

Major Cabrera returned Fraser to the Hotel Alfonso. As a favor to his brother, he agreed to pick Fraser up the day after tomorrow if he wished to accompany his troops north to join with Yagüe's forces. That would give Fraser an entire day to write up his transcripts. Two sets of parallel activities with unusual demands.

Writing the copy intended for the censor would be troublesome. Forced to disguise his true opinions the result might be journalistic crap. Important to maintain at least basic integrity without pandering. For both the text and photographs of the secreted materials the task was to obscure himself as being the source. He would also have to develop the micro-negatives that night. Based upon trials back in Paris that would be a challenging endeavor using the bathroom as a makeshift darkroom.

Even with that task ahead of him he needed a couple of drinks to calm his agitated mood. But the hotel bar provided no escape. Over the radio he listened to General de Llano's nightly radio broadcast rant. This was even more extreme than the broadcast Fraser heard when first arriving back in Seville.

'An example has been made of Morón that I imagine will serve as a lesson to those who still foolishly maintain their faith in Marxism and the hope of being able to resist us. Just as in Arahal, in Morón there

were heedless men and women who committed unequalled acts of savagery, attacking individuals who had not provoked them. Some even burned alive. And I have heard that in various towns the Marxists have prisoners against whom they plan to commit similar barbarities. I remind them all that for every honorable person that dies, I will shoot at least ten, and there are already towns where we have gone beyond that figure. And the leaders should not hold out hope of saving themselves by flight, since I will drag them from out of the ground if necessary to implement the law.'

The rantings of a sociopath or psychopath thought Fraser. Not sure the distinction. And this from the person dictating the fate of so many Spaniards.

CHAPTER 24

The hotel bathroom proved a workable darkroom with a blanket over the window to exclude any light. A small plug-in red light bulb provided sufficient working illumination. Developing the 35mm film into standard negatives was a straightforward process. The major difficulty was lugging the necessary chemicals. If he was to stay in Spain very long, he would have to find opportunities to replenish along the way.

Knowing the subject of the photos still didn't prepare him for the sickening impact when seeing the images first revealed when removing the negatives from the developing tray.

The next step of creating the micro-reductions would be a laborious process. He had practiced it once back in Paris. The task involved first developing the standard 24x36mm negative taken with high contrast film. Then using a jerry-rigged setup to hold the camera, the convex lens, and the light source with reflectors, the negative is projected onto treated cellophane and rephotographed creating a reduction of 21:1. The two-step process results in a micro-negative image 1.1 x 1.2mm in size. Several could easily be concealed under a single postage stamp.

The arrangement was conceptually straightforward but rigging the components complicated. The process required precision to achieve good reduction quality. Repeated makeshift assembly of the setup would be difficult. The problem was solved by Fraser's filmmaker friend in Paris, Henri Marchand offering one of his studio handymen to construct an easily assembled simple contraption to hold all the equipment in place to perform the secondary photographic reduction.

The standard negative had to be held at a distance of one meter from the 35mm camera which was secured then the shutter activated by cable release to prevent any movement. The condenser lens then sat on top of the negative to project a reduced image. A high-wattage incandescent light bulb with a plug for an electrical outlet provided the right illumination using reflectors. The fixture consisted of screwed together parts that when disassembled weighed less than two pounds. Every component of the assembly was secure and properly aligned to expedite repeatability. A clever piece of work.

Drafting the text to pass the censor went faster than he thought. Just factual reporting of the locations and circumstances. Essentially no more than captions to the photographs which spoke more dramatically.

Selecting which photos to get out clandestinely was more difficult. Which ones would he dare to have published without pointing to him as being the source? Must be those that could be argued as taken by someone opposing the Nationalist rebels.

The photos portraying the atrocities spoke more dramatically than any words. The kneeling woman with her raised arm over a wounded man. The aborted rape at Coria del Rio. The execution of the mayor of Arahal. The beatings, the shootings, the display of the murdered rape victims' underwear hung from bayonets at Morón. The pigs feeding on the dead in the streets of Morón.

The photos selected for the overt submission would test the boundaries of the censorship. If this bizarre General de Llano broadcast calls for the rebels to commit the most horrific of atrocities then why not allow the photographic record? Fraser still selected somewhat less graphic photographs. As to the textual content, he could obscure the brutality with words like *combat expediencies, collateral damage, isolated excesses, and harsh measures of martial law.*

Fraser doubted there was much of value to pass along to Allen Dulles in the way of useful military intelligence but that was their problem. Best he could muster was an explanation of the alignment of support for the rebels, names of officers, presence of the Nazi SS, third-hand information about the German airlift of African forces from Morocco, and the type of artillery deployed at Arahal. After he was done it sounded like impressive spy-stuff even if he couldn't see the value.

Once he decided on the photographic negatives that would go out as the clandestine package, he had to prepare the accompanying transcript which must also be photographed and then reduced.

The re-photographing to achieve the size reduction went well but proved a laborious process. It was four o'clock in the morning before he finished. Looking at the negatives with a 30-power jeweler's loupe told him the photos came out clearly. The text was readable. Using fine tweezers, the trickiest part was not dropping the incredibly tiny negatives.

That left composing the transcript for the overt package later in the morning. Much tougher since it had to be a narrative worthy of publication yet pass the Army's censor. Not sure the latitude of reporting he would be allowed. He only had tomorrow to get the materials sent off before departing Seville with Major Cabrera's troops so no time to rewrite if rejected by the censor.

Deciding to charm his assigned censor he arrived at the military headquarters in Seville at noon. It was fortuitous timing. It was August 6th, the day General Francisco Franco arrived in Seville by plane from Morocco. Franco would take direct command of the rebel forces in the south to pursue the campaign to move on Madrid.

Fraser had just been ushered into the captain's office when Franco entered the headquarters building with the attendant jubilant commotion. Fraser found himself propelled into Queipo de Llano's office to capture the historic moment with the two generals posing for Fraser to capture in photographs.

The diminutive Franco was in sharp contrast to the tall Queipo de Llano. Where de Llano was bombastic, Franco was reserved. Introduced as the correspondent for the Hearst News-paper chain in America, Franco acknowledged Fraser with a slight nod and a limp handshake. Considering Franco's stature in this military coup, Fraser suspected a cunning intellect. While Queipo de Llano was an obvious psychopath, the reserved Fran-co might be far more dangerous.

Fraser suggested to the captain they might review his dis-patch materials over lunch. He suggested the captain call the Texaco representative's office and ask Roberto Sanchez to join them. That would expedite the dispatch of his materials to the United States. The captain jumped at the opportunity suitably impressed by Fraser's high-level personal associations with Gen-eral de Llano and General Franco.

Roberto Sanchez was happy to join them. Fraser let the cap-tain select an upscale restaurant. After a long lunch, the captain made some half-hearted attempts to alter some of the text but was troubled by some of the photographs. He relented when Sanchez sided with Fraser's arguments about certain photo-graphs.

"Captain, these photos only show what the General has been publically broadcasting," Sanchez said. "They will make their way eventually into newspapers in Spain to be seen by all those Republicans opposing you. It will serve to make new conquests easier. And look at these burned bodies. Clear evidence of atroci-ties committed by these Communists. Burned alive according to Mr. Fraser."

The captain eventually acceded to allowing everything. Two bottles of wine helped. Upon their return to the captain's office, the captain signed and sealed the package. Sanchez would post it to Lisbon to make its way via air mail service to South America then on to the United States. The materials for publication to the Los Angeles Examiner, the letter to Fraser's *sister in* New York, to Allen Dulles' address.

The next day, Fraser headed north accompanying Major Eduardo Cabrera and SS Hauptsturmführer Heinz Leitner in a staff car. From the front seat next to the driver, Fraser half turned and asked Cabrera in the back, "What is the strategy of this campaign to the north, Major?"

"We shall eventually link up with our northern forces under the command of General Mola. Once we take Badajoz, Republican controlled territory will be cut in two. We will then control the west and the north. Only a portion of the northern coast will remain in republican hands. Asturias and Basque Country. Isolated from Madrid. Their lines of supply severed."

"What about Madrid? Isn't that the ultimate target?" Fraser said.

"Of course," Cabrera said. "But we cannot leave an enemy in our rear. Badajoz must first be subdued before we can move east."

"I would think it important to also cleanse these pestholes of leftists," Leitner said. "The future of a strong nationalistic Spain will be founded on a purified population. General Franco speaks of a *Second Reconquesta*. A modern day cleansing just like the original *Reconquesta* that rid Spain of both the Moors and its Jews. We are completing that process in Germany."

"Hauptsturmführer Leitner is correct. Purification is the correct term," Cabrera said.

"So defeating the enemy, in this case forces loyal to the government, is not enough?" Fraser said. "The very existence of any opposing political view must be exterminated?"

Cabrera responded, "There can be no other way. This so-called Second Republic is no government. It is corrupt. It seeks to destroy Spain. It would give land and businesses over to the illiterate peasantry. Spain would become another Soviet Union. Hardly a workable model of anything."

"But aren't the working class necessary for any functioning economy? And must they not be able to feed their families? Have a life better than mere slavery?" Fraser said.

"That is all possible," Cabrera said. "It is not the working class that must be exterminated but those who organize and provoke these people to rebellion."

Leitner said, "It is the same everywhere. That is why the Führer and Mussolini have pledged their support. Military support. This is not simply a Spanish problem. The forces of nationalism are what define a people. Communists and Jews have no attachment to national cultures."

After some moments of silence, Leitner said, "It is obvious you do not share our views, Herr Fraser?"

"Well, let's say that I see certain things differently. As I told you, I'm here because Mr. Hearst is strongly opposed to Communism. I share that view. Nothing could be worse than Stalin's regime in the Soviet Union." Fraser was now questioning that assertion. Germany and Spain had descended into something just as perverted. Humanity in any of its forms was entirely suppressed. "However, this exercise in institutionalized brutality is disturbing."

"But necessary," Cabrera said. "Necessary to counter the brutality being inflicted by these leftists. In Madrid, priests are killed. Judges killed. Churches burned. The government allows armed mobs of Communists and anarchists free reign. Even common criminals have been released from prisons to prey on anyone that has property. We must counter with equal terror."

While the rebels were successful in the northwest and southwest, they had been defeated in the capital Madrid during the first days of the uprising. Armed citizens, police, and soldiers loyal to the government attacked the Montana Barracks held by rebels. The defending rebels fired machine guns and threw grenades into the attacking masses. Eventually overwhelmed, the rebels were then massacred in reprisal. A rallying cry now for the Nationalists. An excuse to justify their own brutality against anyone sympathetic to the Republican government.

Fraser would also report Republican atrocities if he could corroborate them first hand. He was not here to take sides. No cause could justify murder and torture. Both sides in this civil war were fouled by their self-righteous excesses. A plague on both your houses.

"Gentlemen. I am a reporter. By definition I chronicle events. You are personally involved in the worst of all kinds of wars. Civil wars always breed violence that transcends the battlefield. No one can escape its effects. I'm not here to paint any particular picture, certainly not to support any cause."

"I hope you appreciate the special circumstances you are being allowed, Señor Fraser," Cabrera said. "In Madrid, I understand that a government censor must approve every dispatch, every picture that goes out. Everything reduced to propaganda. I am not sure that I would allow you the freedom for reporting most everything. However my brother and General Franco are confident that you shall be *careful* in your reporting. After all this is a war. No army can permit the release of information damaging to its military operations."

"I am aware of the sensitivity of my dispatches, Major. I assume the officer on General de Llano's staff assigned as my censor shall continue to vet my work to insure there are no mistakes."

Two days later, Cabrera's forces reached the town of Almendralejo. Any thoughts that previous events Fraser witnessed might have been aberrations were quickly dispelled. Along the road leading north Cabrera's convoy passed through the towns of Monesterio, Fuente de Cantos, and Zafra. Colonel Yagüe's main force had moved through here a day earlier. Moroccan *Regulares* from Yagüe's rear guard carried all manner of looted household goods. Clothing, furniture, even sewing machines.

Entering Almendralejo, the scene worsened. Dead bodies lay randomly scattered. Some women. Several children. A group of six bodies lay crumpled in front of a building wall. Bullets had chipped scars into the stucco. Blood had dried into dark pools. Fraser snapped photos. Cabrera made no objection.

Cabrera stopped only long enough to allow his troops to stretch their legs from being cramped on the transport lorries benches. Fraser took the opportunity to quickly explore the scene of yet another bloodletting. Windows and doors of many buildings were blown out. Peering inside it was obvious grenades had been tossed through windows. Mangled bodies evident in some. Not one uniformed enemy among the dead.

Down a side street he came upon a house. The bodies of two men lay close by. A trail of women's undergarments led from the door to the street. Pushing open the door he called out for anyone inside. More clothing hung from the staircase railing. Suspecting what might lie upstairs still did not prepare Fraser. In one bedroom lay three female bodies. Naked. Their shredded clothing apparently ripped off. One a teenage girl. All were covered in blood from repeated stab wounds. Crisscrossed deep slashes across their breasts. Raped, tortured then bayoneted to die a slow death. Photos again too graphic for publication.

Would this nightmare of carnage just continue? Not only were words inadequate even a torrent of these horrific photographs might be beyond belief for someone in America. How could anyone possibly relate to these vicious forms of murder committed on such a mass scale? The American Civil War never experienced massacres of the civilian population. What was different about Spain?

The next objective for Cabrera's battalion was Mérida. Unlike the preceding towns, Mérida was prepared to mount a defense. A defense committee organized by a woman had assembled a collection of loyalist militias and peasants. But again they were poorly armed with no military training, no artillery. Collective bravery constituted their principle weapon. It was a mismatch attempting to counter Yagüe's thousands of battle-hardened Legionnaires and Moroccan mercenaries. The attacking rebels not only had artillery but aerial resources with German Junker Ju 52 and Italian Savoia-Marchetti SM 81 bombers at their disposal.

The lorry-born Nationalist forces moved swiftly. Just south of Mérida at a bridge over the River Guadiana they met fierce loyalist resistance. Unlimbering their 75mm artillery batteries, a sustained bombardment easily crushed any effective resistance.

Following attacks from multiple directions the loyalist militia soon retreated, abandoning Mérida's citizens to a terrible fate.

Fraser was at the side of Cabrera and Leitner as they entered the town. Another scene of massacre. Bodies everywhere. Sporadic gunfire continued. Fraser photographed the repeated shooting of people as they filed out from one building with their hands raised. This was clearly the avowed rules of engagement dictated by the Nationalist command. Exterminate loyalists. Invoke terror.

But Mérida was to also add another spectacle of revulsion for Fraser.

After being approached by a junior officer, Cabrera said to Leitner and Fraser, "Seems we have captured the defense committee that organized this resistance. They're being held in the mayor's office."

The mayor's large office was crowded. Behind the desk stood three men and a woman. Two Legion officers and several Moroccan *Regulares* guarded the prisoners.

"These are the town's defense committee, Sir. Given up by some others hoping to save themselves."

"Excellent, Lieutenant. Take them into the street and shoot them," Cabrera said.

"If I may suggest, Major," Leitner said. "They might be able to provide useful information before they die. Identify other loyalists. Perhaps those leading the militias that have retreated. With names you can eradicate their families, their associates. Part of the cleansing General Franco calls for."

"And what do you suggest?"

"You have spoken of the ferocity of your Moroccans. Do you have a soldier particularly talented in inflicting pain?"

Cabrera smiled. "Yes, of course. Good idea. Lieutenant, find me that sergeant named Toufali.

Turning to Fraser, Cabrera laughed, "I've seen him work on Rif prisoners. Not for the squeamish, Señor Fraser. This Moorish bastard likes to use a knife. Perhaps you should not take pictures."

Jesus Christ, no more! Fraser was not sure he could endure more of this. All to someday bear witness? Possibly he could sneak getting photos. Even so, would it matter?

Unless possessed of an aberrant sadistic psychology it is nearly unbearable watching someone being tortured. There can be no uglier expression of human depravity. Fraser's stomach tensed into a knot just anticipating whatever unknown spectacle was in store.

The four prisoners were marched down the street to a shop. A butcher shop appropriately. The back of the shop served as a slaughter house. Several carcasses, fully dressed out, hung from hooks.

"Hauptsturmführer Leitner, since this was your idea would you like to take charge?" Cabrera said. "Perhaps you have experience in this? I assure you the sergeant here can suggest his own methods if you prefer."

"I am sure he could, Major. But inflicting pain to extract information is more nuanced. A psychological exercise. The human mind can find ways to resist to the death. The trick is finding the key to unlock the tongue before that occurs."

Leitner ordered that the three men have their hands bound with butchers twine. The bindings were then strung over the meat hooks pulling their arms over their heads.

"We shall work on the woman first. Let the men see what we can do to a woman so there can be no doubt as to what torment they will face," Leitner said.

To the Moroccan soldiers, he ordered, "Tie her to that carcass. Face her into the cavity. Strip her to the waist."

As the soldiers prepared the woman, Leitner said, "Now for a suitable instrument. Let's see how we can improvise."

Looking about the shop Leitner turned to one of the Moroccan soldiers and said, "The fat one. Take his belt. Cut it into narrow strips the entire length. Tie a knot at the end of each. Something like a cat-of-nine-tails don't you think, Major?"

To the woman, Leitner said, "Before I begin, the Major will ask you some questions. Answer and you shall die cleanly with a bullet to the head. Resist and it shall be a long agonizing death. You will look like this raw carcass in the end. Your skin shredded."

Cabrera asked for names of anyone associated with the armed resistance of Mérida. It didn't matter. Whether no response or a flow of names, punishment would still be harshly inflicted on these four victims.

Anita López, the leader of the ill-fated defense of Mérida, remained silent. Leitner nodded for the Moroccan to begin the lashes.

The woman let out a load cry with the first strike. Ugly red welts shown on her bare back. Leitner nodded again. And again. The lash fell in a macabre rhythm. Fraser winced each time. Within minutes the woman's back was a mass of red. In some places repeated lashes over the same area broke the skin. Soon rivulets of blood ran down to her waist. Through all this she only uttered a grunt with each successive stroke.

Leitner was becoming exasperated.

"Enough. Turn her around. We will work on her fresh flesh."

The Moroccans turned her around with her wrists tied behind the hanging carcass. She remained alert.

"Again. Will you name those that helped you?"

Anita López said nothing. Her eyes flashed defiantly at Leitner.

"I warn you, this will not stop. Now the lash will ruin the soft flesh of your breasts. The agony will just go on with no end."

With no response the beating continued. Quickly, her breasts became lacerated. Blood flowed freely. The Moroccan wielding the lash was sweating profusely. The whole place stank of a terrible mixture of smells. Old meat and grease odors now mixed with human blood, sweat, and fear.

The torture was having its effect on the captured men. The woman's chin dropped to her chest. Her breathing was labored. With all eyes engrossed on the half-naked woman Fraser was able to take a sneak a series of exposures. For the record if not publication. Bearing witness.

Leitner walked to her and lifted her chin. Looking her in the eyes he said, "Shall we continue?"

Anita Lopez for some reason looked over Leitner's shoulder directly at Fraser. Her look of pure hatred was the most terrible thing he could imagine. Did she sense his unease? Why was he here? What was his part in this?

Turning her gaze back to Leitner she mustered enough saliva to spit it in his face.

Leitner retreated calmly wiping his face with a handkerchief. Nodding to the Moroccan, "Resume."

Fraser could bear this no longer. Even photos could not capture what it was like to witness this. Frustrated at being able to do nothing. My God, that woman thought he was part of this. He couldn't shake that thought. Outside he vomited. How could he reconcile just chronicling such evil? Like all involved he too was stained by this abomination. Every instinct screamed for retribution against these monsters.

Never had he witnessed torture. And what he just left inside the butcher shop would become even more hideous. They would turn next on the three men after the woman died. All would die terribly. He didn't want to contemplate what that fucking Moroccan would do with his knife.

Colonel Yagüe arrived that evening with thousands more troops to take command. Fraser was included at dinner that evening with Yagüe's senior officers at a commandeered restaurant. Introduced by Yagüe as a favored journalist authorized by General Franco.

"Gentlemen, in a couple of days I will take 3,000 *Regulares* west to attack Badajoz," Yagüe said. "It is more heavily defended than Mérida but these Republican militias are pieces of shit. No match for our Moroccans. Once we take Badajoz, we then move on Madrid."

"A small detachment shall remain here in Mérida in the event of a counterattack which is unlikely. Tomorrow I expect your troops to make an example of Mérida. Cleanse this place of republican sympathies. These loyalist forces are weak, badly organized. Expecting certain death will diminish their will to resist as we continue to conquer territory."

"We have already started, Sir," Cabrera said. "We executed the leaders that organized the defense of Mérida. But not before we extracted names of others that will eventually be eliminated."

Later in the evening Cabrera and Leitner confronted Fraser.

Leitner said, "I see you could not take the harsh measures we used to get information, Señor Fraser."

"Torture you mean? And what vital information did you get? Was it even reliable? I think you whipped that poor woman because you enjoyed the spectacle. You did enjoy it did you not, Hauptsturmführer?" Fraser said.

Leitner bristled. Before he could respond, Cabrera said, "It was effective, Señor Fraser. The woman said nothing but after Sergeant Toufali worked on one of the men, the others talked. But I am sure you would have found that even more distressing. The sergeant simply took a meat clever and began to chop off one finger at a time. After all the fingers of one hand of the first man were removed, all three men provided information.

"But the real value of dealing harsh treatment lays in future campaigns. Unless a diehard Republican, no one will want to give support knowing such a terrible fate might befall them. You heard Colonel Yagüe. Spain must be rid of them."

"Like the Jews in Germany, Hauptsturmführer Leitner?" Fraser said.

"Why are you here in Spain, Señor Fraser?" Leitner said. "You do not seem sympathetic to the Nationalist cause."

Shit. Fraser had forgotten himself. If Cabrera made a stink his letter from Franco might only go so far before he was denied continued access.

"It's not about your cause. It's your methods that I object to. I told you before, I'm opposed to Communism. I don't see torture as necessary to defeating Communism."

That night and the following night Fraser worked for hours to develop negatives both to send out with his dispatches as well as the micro-reductions to be secreted in his letters to his *sister*.

True to Yagüe's orders, the following day was another day of indiscriminate murders by Moroccan troops. Fraser had more atrocities to photograph. So many that this was becoming repetitious. Even if published the American reading public might soon become numbed to such horrors.

Cabrera assigned Leitner the task of acting as censor for Fraser's dispatches to be sent to Seville with the normal military courier. Unlike the captain in Seville, Leitner denied a number of photographs. The written transcript was acceptable. Fraser had painstakingly written favorable comments as to the rebels' military prowess. The atrocities were referred to as *harsh measures inflicted upon the conquered populace*, but no mention of torture. Murder was referred to as *extra-judicial executions under military tribunal*. Of course there were no such proceedings.

The clandestine material this time included military information. He still doubted that it had any useful value but derived some satisfaction from doing something to fight these barbarians. The officers talked freely of the details of German and Italian support. Weapons, aircraft, troop strength, unit designations. They seemed not to object to Fraser's presence but admonished him that no military information was for publication. He was somehow accepted into this circle even though critical of their methods.

Fraser followed Yagüe's forces to Badajoz. After shelling the town for a day the rebel forces attacked. Cabrera's battalion led a frontal assault on a well defended position. They were stopped by withering machine gun fire. An entire company of Cabrera's Legionnaires lost 76 of their 90 officers and men. Yet this spirted defense proved insufficient. Assaults against the town from other directions overwhelmed the numerically superior but inexperienced defending Republican militias. Fighting was hand to hand. Bayonets and knives by the better trained rebels proved decisive. No quarter was given to defenders after laying down their weapons. Wounded Republican militias were even executed in the hospital.

Extraordinary bravery on the part of the Republican defenders. Not the disorganized rabble portrayed by Colonel Yagüe.

One of Fraser's observations concerned the fate of the African Army, particularly the Spanish Foreign Legion. Effective as they were in the campaign to subdue Andalusia, they suffered heavy losses at Badajoz. To the senior rebel commanders casualties to their own forces mattered little if they could seize the objective. Attrition was acceptable. It was all about taking territory. Casualties seemed only a justification to commit subsequent wholesale slaughter. Strategically it was about destroying that segment of the population that posed a post-war political threat. Franco's *Second Reconquista* was a political cleansing of Spain.

Badajoz was just another such example. Yet even in this campaign of butchery it was to rise to a place of ignominy in history.

Staying close to Cabrera he sensed something even more foreboding might be happening. Cabrera seemed to be orchestrating the corralling of prisoners, herding them into the bull ring. Not just captured republican militia but civilians including many women. Gunfire was still prevalent as people were being indiscriminately shot throughout the town. What was to happen to those being pushed into the bull ring?

"What is going on, Major?" he asked Cabrera.

"Just suppressing any further resistance."

Several hours later, Cabrera was heard barking an order, "Is everything ready, Captain?"

With that, Fraser followed Cabrera to the box seats of the bullring. Machine guns had been strategically placed on their side of the stadium. Several thousand people stood in the sand of the bullring. A hot day with no shelter. Cabrera sat down and lit a cigarette.

"What is to be done with these people, Major?" Fraser asked.

Cabrera looked at Fraser but said nothing. He then turned toward a junior officer and nodded.

Understanding what this was about Fraser began taking pictures. More poignant perhaps capturing the prelude to what he knew was about to take place.

Seconds later the machine guns opened up.

The firing kept up for twenty minutes. Amazed that he was able to even function Fraser captured the massacre on two rolls of film. Even with thousands of machine gun rounds fired many victims remained alive. Moroccan troops then moved about the periphery of the mass of bodies shooting or bayoneting those still alive. As with a bullfight the sand soaked up the blood. In the summer heat the stench soon became overpowering.

Later that evening, Colonel Yagüe complimented Cabrera on his efficiency.

Looking for a quote, Fraser asked Yagüe, "Why was this massacre necessary, Colonel?"

Yagüe replied, "Of course we shot them, what do you expect? Was I supposed to take 4,000 reds with me as my column advanced racing against time? Was I expected to turn them loose in my rear and let them make Badajoz red again?"

It was increasingly difficult to write the material for publication. Avoiding propagandized writing suitable to the rebels after Badajoz was even more difficult. Only the photographs provided dramatic interest. For the most part he was able to report faithfully on their murderous excesses simply because they wanted to communicate terror. Although not able to explore rebel atrocities in depth, much less with any critical insight, at least his reporting maintained journalistic integrity.

He legitimately identified atrocities committed by Republican loyalists. There were some but the toll was far less than perpetrated by the Nationalists. The difference took the form of wholesale murder, rape, and torture committed as a directed policy from the highest leadership. Not only intended to promote terror but for the more pragmatic objective of cleansing the population of future opposition. Whereas Republican committed murders occurred in spasmodic outbursts often from internecine conflict between the various Republican political factions themselves. Fraser had no problem condemning any of these acts.

His ethical salvation was the clandestine material he produced, especially the secreted photographs. Here he could describe events in both a broader context as well as provide more detail. There was an obligation to communicate to the outside world that something uniquely grotesque was going on in Spain. The only constraint being the need to disguise himself as the source.

The answer to that had been the creation of a fictional anti-Nationalist reporter. The artifice provided a construct from which he could write from a credible perspective of how this secret reporter gained access to material similar to his own. Hopefully this material would see international publication under the byline *Odiseo*. The Spanish rendering of *Odysseus*.

But maybe it didn't matter anymore. Badajoz proved to be too much. Fraser needed to regain his equilibrium. He must leave Spain.

That night he again worked into the early morning hours preparing his micro-negatives. No need to secret these under a stamp. He would just take these with him wedged between a stack of razor blades. Enough of this horror. Witnessing atrocities was troubling enough, yet being unable to do anything was maddening. His feeble attempts to get out the truth might come to nothing. His fledgling spying activities could not amount to anything useful. Yagüe's forces would now move east to attack Madrid. The killings, the rapes, the torture would continue. Fraser was not going to follow that campaign of continued bloodletting.

Solidifying his decision was his growing antagonism with Leitner. Leitner even suggested openly to Cabrera that he questioned having Fraser allowed within their circle. Not sure how much influence Leitner carried with Cabrera. They certainly shared an appreciation of Fascism. Both were sadists. Getting crosswise with Cabrera could prove dangerous.

Before Fraser left to make his way back to Seville then to make his way back to Paris via Lisbon, Cabrera authorized Leitner to personally search his personal effects thoroughly. All film exposed or unused was to be confiscated. Many developed negatives Leitner again deemed inappropriate. Leitner's parting shot as Fraser was about to catch a ride with wounded troops being sent south, "I hope not to read anything negative from you if you ever intend to return to Spain."

In a pique of disgust, Fraser could not constrain himself. Not having revealed his fluency in German so far, he replied in German, "I have been to Germany, Leitner. I have seen your kind. Drunk on your own power. Treating your political opponents as less than human. An excuse to justify your sadism. You're something worse than Communists. You Nazis are a disease. So go fuck yourself, Leitner."

Leitner turned red. "I'll have you shot, Fraser."

"On whose orders? You're a visitor here like I am. Are you going to tell Major Cabrera that I was unkind to you? Think he cares about you Nazis all that much? I have a letter from General Franco. Think you're more important?"

Furious, Leitner turned and stalked off.

Not sure if he had gone too far, Fraser was glad to immediately leave in the front seat of a lorry transporting wounded to Seville.

CHAPTER 25

From Paris, Fraser could view what was happening in Spain from a clearer prospective. Mérida and Badajoz suggested General Franco's strategic plan. Neither represented important military objectives. Except for leaving a small pocket of loyalist troops in Badajoz in their rear, the rebels fight was to the east in the capital of the Republic, Madrid. Mérida and Badajoz served the dual propaganda purpose of symbolically uniting Nationalist control of the western half of Spain along with advertising the cost in blood of resisting their forces.

Fraser had come to realize the distinction between the atrocities committed by both sides in this civil war. Republican excesses tended to take the form of localized random murders. Nationalist terror was a matter of articulated policy. Murder on an industrial scale. Torture, rape, public humiliation. The avowed intent had the same objective as genocide. Kill enough of those of opposing political and social persuasion so as to prevent a future threat. Kill or imprison everyone of leadership or intellectual stature. Decimate the population sufficiently that those remaining were terrorized into a submissive underclass. Franco's tactics patterned after Hitler's in Germany.

This cold-blooded view was shared not only by Franco but his fellow senior conspirators, Generals Mola and Queipo de Llano, and his most effective field commander, Colonel Yagüe.

Total disregard for life while inflicting torture for no purpose other than terror came easy for those with unchecked power. Justified by declaring the victims as less than human. The Nazis in Germany. Stalin's regime in the Soviet Union. It starts as a pragmatic exercise to achieve political power but quickly degenerates into widespread brutality as darker human impulses are unleashed.

Fraser needed to explore this theme to develop his own rationalization of what circumstances allowed this to happen. Not psychological theory jargon but in terms that could be understood at least by its symptoms if not its origin. Perhaps in fiction where he could show rather than try to explain?

It took a good two months to decompress. Sleep came fitfully. But strolling about Paris with the onset of autumn proved a balm to his psyche. After meager field rations and rough Spanish wine, Parisian cuisine and good French wine did its part to promote recovery of his spirit. Beyond his landlady and his friend Henri Marchand, no one knew he had returned. He ignored correspondence from his editor. Let them think he maybe died in Spain. Not sure if he wished to continue reporting for Hearst anyway.

The stuff he secreted out did get published both in the United States and Europe. This was real journalism not the crap he passed through the Nationalist censors. This anonymous Spanish reporter *Odiseo* created a temporary furor. To his gratification, the reporting of *Odiseo* was critically appraised when compared to that of Hearst reporter Marc Fraser. Many of his photographs continued to be published to accompany commentary by others. But the impact was short-lived when the flow of material ceased.

Eventually he had to return to the troubling realities of the world. Paris might still seduce with its charms but it too faced the uncertainty of the political turmoil in Europe. France had just brought into power its own Popular Front government composed of Communists and socialists. From the onset it struggled to govern in the face of continued economic weakening.

Hitler continued to enlarge the German military. Persecution of German Jews had reduced them to non-citizens. Mussolini had invaded Ethiopia. While Spain had descended into a vicious civil war it was also proving a testing ground for German and Italian military operations. Stalin commenced a massive political repression in the Soviet Union. What would become known as the Great Purge decimated the political leadership and the Red Army. A restive peasantry was culled by sending tens of thousands to Siberian labor camps to quell dissatisfaction over privations caused by government dictated social dislocations.

In November Fraser resurfaced professionally. He agreed to continue reporting for Hearst from Paris. Perhaps to even journey across the Channel to Britain. Reporting from the perspective of life within the only two major European powers seemingly sided against what was becoming a Fascist dominated continent. Returning to Germany or Spain was out of the question. Surprisingly, his editor wired that Hearst agreed. Hearst apparently had a personal affection for him.

The political crisis of the time notwithstanding, Fraser spent the entire winter of 1936-37 in comparative comfort. Even the winter cold could be countered by the view from his apartment window, a good book, sipping wine by a fire. He was also making good progress on his second novel.

Female companionship of any permanence however remained lacking. Maybe he was too particular? Probably too self-centered. A marked difference from his lustful earlier years. Was it maturity or did he have a problem with relationships?

By the spring of 1937 he was feeling restive. Armchair reporting did not suit him. Why not return again to writing some real hard-hitting journalism? The Spanish experience still haunted him. Why not go on the attack and test the boundaries of what Hearst would allow to be published?

Since leaving, circumstances had changed in Spain. Republican government forces had mounted a successful resistance. Foreign fighters of the International Brigades were proving decisive against the Nationalist rebels. The Soviet Union equipped the Republicans with aircraft and tanks. Nationalist troops suffered massive losses throwing themselves again the defenses of Madrid. To the north of Madrid the Nationalists failed to take Guadalajara. Italian ground troops suffered heavy losses and retreated in a rout exposing their combat shortcomings. It had become a war that might continue for some time. Spain would bleed to death.

Fraser's next dispatch read, '*To accomplish this new vision of a sanitized Spain, General Franco is prepared to sacrifice great numbers of his own forces. Casualties among his own forces, especially colonial Moorish troops, were acceptable if it bled the enemy. Franco's strategic vision lay with a social landscape cleansed of any left-wing base. The working classes must be left leaderless. A repressive post-war bureaucracy would insure it would remain so.*

Franco's often unimaginative, plodding military tactics are the product of his post-war vision. Contrary to political wisdom, those tactics almost always result in the most costly loss of life on both sides. Franco is not interested in just simply winning the war or arriving at some sort of settlement in an armistice. His is on a crusade. He is retaking Spain in a Second Reconquista. This time to expel all vestiges of leftist political ideology. To remake Spain into a conservative nationalistic state directed by his vision of autocratic corporatism governance.

With a developing stalemate in the Nationalists campaign to overrun Madrid's defenses, General Franco has turned his attention to the remaining Republican held territory on the northern coast in the resource-rich Asturias and Basque regions. Asturias was of course the location of the failed Miners' Strike in 1934 and the Basque people have a long history of seeking independence from Spain. So Franco intends to not only conquer the entire western half of Spain but to further decimate the populations of these restive troublesome regions. Eventually Franco must turn again to Madrid. He is confident that political dissention among the Republican factions will eventually erode their military will. The thought of a mass attrition of casualties on both sides is acceptable to Franco. There can never be a negotiated peace. Franco intends to win all of Spain on his terms.

For those in America this civil war has been portrayed as between Communism-socialism versus Spanish nationalism and the Roman

Catholic Church. These are over-simplifications. Whatever political leanings one has, this does not mean that either side is right much less righteous. I have been there. I assure you, neither side is righteous. But I can also assure you that the Nationalist rebels have descended into barbarity. They commit murder, rape, and torture in the name of their cause. If they succeed, then it will be the same as an America ruled by Al Capone.'

Before receiving any response from his editor, Spain again moved to the front page around the world. That event was the bombing of a small market town in the Basque Country. A town of 7,000 with no military value but with the symbolic designation as the spiritual capital of the Basque people.

Guernica was also to be the testing ground for modern bombing tactics. On orders from General Franco, aircraft of the Condor Legion of the German Luftwaffe and the Italian Aviazione Legionaria bombed and strafed the town on the afternoon of April 26th. There was greater loss of life elsewhere in the civil war but this singular event of the bombing of an entirely civilian target for the purpose of terror grasped the world's attention.

It made obviously clear that the Non-Intervention Pact preventing military aid to Spain was a sham. The New York Times ran the story front page of Guernica every day for over a week after the attack. Yet Britain, France, and the United States still did not weigh in with military assistance to the beleaguered Spanish Republic.

Soon after the destruction of Guernica Fraser received a letter from Loretta Elizalde.

Dear Marc,
Having heard nothing of you for months, I wondered if you survived Spain. This letter assumes that you are now back in Paris. I call you now by your first name since you are more than a fellow journalist for all you have done. I know you to be the anonymous Odiseo. Those photographs are difficult to look at. They do not fuel terror as much

as hatred. How you secreted them out from under their noses is remarkable. Terribly dangerous. If someone else is reading this letter then they will know what happened to you.

As for Spain, things continue to deteriorate. Madrid is a place of chaos. Competing political factions are at each other's throats. Infighting. Tribunals. Secret police. Censorship that stifles reporting the truth. I have left Madrid to return to my homeland in Basque Country. Madrid is no longer about fighting the cause for social justice. Thousands of suspected rebel supporters have been killed by loyalists. How can we condemn the rebels for their atrocities? As with most everything it is a struggle for power. The Government will eventually lose to the rebels.

My home of San Sebastian fell last September cutting off supplies to Republican forces coming over the border from France. My fiancé fled to Bilbao. Now the Nationalists are pushing to crush this last pocket of resistance in western Spain. I'm reporting now from Bilbao. At least Rafael and I are together. I fear there is no hope. It is only a matter of time. The Basques are cut off. The world has abandoned us. Tell that story. Marc.

Loretta

He could only hope that Elizalde had a way out of Bilbao. As a hated journalist she would certainly be executed by the Nationalist rebels if captured.

Allen Dulles then called from New York. He told Fraser he wasn't sure he was still alive. Hadn't heard anything from him for the last six months until his piece was published in the United States.

"That was powerful material you smuggled out of Spain. Seems you have a real knack for spy craft. The military found your reports useful as well. Better intelligence than their military attaché in Madrid I was told. Being with the Nationalists you were obviously in a better position to report on German and Italian military support. What happened?"

"You saw the photographs, Allen. Just got sick of seeing the butchery. Got sick of being in proximity to these monsters. Besides, what I was doing had no impact."

"I wouldn't say that," Dulles said.

He ignored Dulles' comment. "When I returned to Paris I found that the photographs had been widely published. It was really good work. It produced some outcry. But only a ripple in the United States I understand. Americans simply can't imagine such things happen. Too alien for them to absorb. Too far away."

"But you're still reporting for Hearst aren't you? Are you returning to Spain?"

"No." Yet he wasn't that sure. Elizalde's letter struck a chord. As a journalist could he avoid the opportunity to be present in the midst of history in the making? If he was to write compelling fiction, was this not a unique opportunity for more first-hand material? There remained a dramatic story to pursue in the north of Spain.

Dulles said, "Here's what I think will happen in Spain. I read your piece on Franco's tactics. I agree. And in the end the Nationalists will win. The Republican government is too quarrelsome. If not for the International Brigades Madrid would have already fallen. The Republicans are now dominated militarily by Soviet leadership. Their only outside support is from the Soviets. The West cannot abide a Communist Spain, especially one under the control of Moscow, so they will do nothing. Certainly not partner with the Soviets.

"That is why there is no assistance to counter German and Italian involvement. It's all about Communism. Yet the more immediate threat to Europe is Fascism. Germany is the threat. You can see that in those dispatches you sent. Hitler is using this as a testing ground for weapons and tactics of his Luftwaffe. If you add a Fascist Spain in league with Germany and Italy then there is a staggering threat to republican Europe. It would be helpful to have somebody inside their camp again."

Already wavering about returning to Spain, Fraser rang off without committing to Dulles, saying only, "If things change you'll hear from me in the usual way."

Leaving Paris in springtime would be disheartening. But the atrocities committed in Spain as a matter of policy left him with a profound hatred for Franco's Nationalists. He couldn't let it go. Of all the horrors he witnessed he could not shake the haunting vision of Anita López's accusing stare as she was being tortured to death.

CHAPTER 26

Several weeks later he was headed back to Spain. For a finite period only he told himself. Only long enough to witness the fall of the Basque Country and Asturias. Stiff as the resistance might be, this now isolated territory of Spain on the Atlantic coast would eventually be defeated by the rebels. He would expose what he expected to be yet further instances of atrocities. Maybe find more effective means of provoking international outrage. Guernica showed the world was not entirely apathetic.

The conflict had moved into a more organized phase of warfare than those early months of 1936. Armies in the tens of thousands now staged pitched battles. Materiel included modern aircraft, tanks, and artillery provided by the Germans and Italians to the Nationalist rebels and by the Soviet Union to the Spanish Republican government. Italian army divisions fought alongside the Nationalist rebels. The German Condor Legion and the Italian Aviazione Legionaria provided superior airpower for the rebels. The International Brigades provided committed fighters to bolster the Spanish Republican forces.

Spain became a testing laboratory for the latest weapons technology and tactics.

Franco halted the long-running offensive against Madrid in March to turn attention to what was called the Biscay Campaign for the corner of the Atlantic comprising the northern Spanish and western French coastlines. Spanish Basque Country and Asturias provided valuable resources of iron ore, steelmaking, and coal. The Nationalists could leverage those resources to economically support their revolt while denying them to the Spanish Government. It would also divert attention from the protracted difficulties in taking Madrid and central Spain.

The rebel Army of the North under the command of General Emilio Mola was facing off against a determined Basque Army defending their homeland. However the attacking rebels had a substantial superiority in materiel. Five times more aircraft, more artillery, with heavy naval capital ships lying off the coast.

Republican forces also suffered from lack of unity. The Asturians and Santaderinos to the west would not support the Basque Army defending Bilbao. Therefore in practical terms, the rebels also enjoyed numerical superiority. The campaign intended to bleed this Republican stronghold that had long sought autonomy from Spain. Again Franco's application of controlling territory while decimating the opposition population.

Getting to the northern front was not easy for Fraser. There were no flights from France to rebel held areas. So it was two days from Paris to Toulouse to Lisbon just to get to rebel-held Seville in the south. Checking in at General Queipo de Llano's headquarters in Seville, he was able to catch a military flight to the northern front. Armed with his original letter from Franco, he was also able to secure an additional letter of introduction from Queipo de Llano to present to General Mola commanding in the north.

Along with Franco, Emilio Mola was one of the original senior leaders of the army revolt. All of them shared an approach to war that saw their mission in a fanatical sense, allowing for a total disregard of life for anyone opposing them. All were veterans of the Rif War in Morocco. Perhaps that accounted for their loss of humanity. Few correspondents had this kind of access. This would be his next series of articles once he left Spain after this current mission. Free then to unleash a vituperative series of pieces in condemnation of the Spanish Nationalists rebellion.

Fraser eventually reached Mola's headquarters in Vitoria-Gasteiz by hitching rides with rebel supply transports. He presented his letters of introduction from Franco and Queipo de Llano, his safe conduct pass, and Carlos Cabrera's letter to the tall, bespectacled General Mola.

Mola appeared impressed with Fraser's credentials. "Very good to have you. Few foreign correspondents reporting from our perspective. Fewer yet from America. These letters suggest that your newspaper is sympathetic to many of our views. Is that true?"

"Certainly anti-Communist," Fraser said.

"And you?"

"I have no love for the Communists. I have seen how things are in Moscow."

"But there is much more to our cause than just fighting Communists," Mola said.

"True, General. But those other things are Spanish nationalism issues. I'm not a Spaniard. I am therefore neutral. Just a reporter."

Mola nodded but now less congenial. "Then stay neutral. Do not become an enemy, Señor Fraser." Handing back the letters to Fraser he said, "I have a new commander within the Navarrese Division by the name of Cabrera. Lieutenant Colonel Eduardo Cabrera. Might he be related to this Señor Carlos Cabrera?"

Shit. Cabrera was now here in the north?

"Yes. I accompanied Major Cabrera in the campaign in Andalusia and Badajoz last year."

"Excellent. A fine officer. His bandera suffered heavy losses in the battle for Madrid. Losses reduced his command below fighting strength. His remaining troops were reassigned to other units. Cabrera was promoted and given a new command. I'm glad to have him. I'll put you with his command since you know each other."

Fraser was numbed by this turn of events. Unlike SS Hauptsturmführer Leitner, there seemed no obvious animosity from Cabrera but it was difficult to tell. Cabrera was more reserved than Leitner. Might Leitner's antagonism have tainted Cabrera's opinion of him? Especially Fraser's parting insults to Leitner? Cabrera at least knew he was not sympathetic to their murder and torture. Whatever the circumstances, Cabrera certainly elevated the risk of playing this dangerous game of espionage.

Cabrera's command was located in Durango. Hitching a ride in a supply convoy, Fraser arrived at Cabrera's field headquarters, a requisitioned large farm house.

It was evening. A tiring bone-jarring ride. He could use some food and a drink. Walking toward the house with his bags he was stopped by a shouted command in German. *"Nach rechts stoppen, Herr Fraser."*

His worse fear recognized. The voice of Hauptsturmführer Leitner.

Turning, Fraser said, *"Guten Abend, Hauptsturmführer."*

"I would have thought you had had enough of Spain, Herr Fraser. What brings you back?"

Deciding to tread lightly avoiding another confrontation, he said, "It's my job. I report on events for the American public. War is ugly. That is what I report. Soldiers kill opposing soldiers. It is the other violence that I find objectionable."

"But that is war, Herr Fraser. To defeat a political enemy requires harsh measures."

"You'll have to excuse me, Hauptsturmführer, I must report to Lieutenant Colonel Cabrera."

If not exactly gracious, Cabrera showed no particular hostility to Fraser. Reading General Mola's letter he smiled and said, "You do seem to know the right people, Señor Fraser."

The following day, Fraser was allowed to listen in at Cabrera's staff meeting. Cabrera outlined the current strategy for making the push on Bilbao, the last stronghold of the Basque Army.

"In a few more days, the Communists will be driven from the sky thanks to the Condor Legion," Cabrera said.

The Condor Legion of the German Luftwaffe had deployed their most advanced aircraft in Spain. The Messerschmitt Bf 109 fighter in particular was decimating the inferior Soviet-made and piloted aircraft supporting the Basques.

"Then we shall move on Bilbao with our ground forces."

"What about this *Iron Ring* around Bilbao, Colonel?" a captain asked.

"A Basque fiction. We know the layout. A Basque deserter has presented us with detailed plans of the fortifications. The Condor Legion continues to bomb selected targets along their defensive line. Our information suggests we have a three to two superiority in forces. Far more artillery. And we will soon control the air."

The *Iron Ring, el cinturón de hierro* was a hastily constructed system of fortifications consisting of bunkers and fortified trenches comprising several rings supported by insufficient artillery. An antiquated concept made even less effective by being severely undermanned. Nationalist forces easily breached the defensive ring by exploiting under-defended gaps. Bilbao fell in seven days. The Basque commanding general withdrew his forces to the west toward Santander to establish a defensive line against the attacking Nationalists supported by 25,000 Italian troops.

Bilbao was therefore saved from destruction. Fraser entered the city with the victorious rebels. It was a miserable scene of a starving population made worse by the influx of tens of thousands of refugees pushed ahead of the advancing rebels, too exhausted to flee further.

Fraser found more value in gathering information that might prove useful as military intelligence. German and Italian aircraft now numbering over two hundred, manned by trained foreign German and Italian pilots. Advanced artillery. Tactics. Command structure and commanders. Force effectivity such as the performance of the Italian troops confirming their prior poor showing against Madrid. Was this really of importance to U.S. military planners? At any rate, he had gathered significant material now converted to micro-negatives safely hidden until his next dispatch. Unfortunately the censor was again to be Leitner.

Within a month the superior rebel forces launched an assault against Santander. The defending Republican troops and the Basque Army were not only outgunned but demoralized. The final push into Santander on the coast lasted only a matter of days. The few surviving non-Basque Republican forces fled further west. The Basque Army however surrendered to the Italian forces expecting better treatment than from the Nationalist rebels. 60,000 were taken prisoner. Like Bilbao, Santander also escaped destruction.

Fraser could only hope that Loretta Elizalde had escaped. No telling what she may have run into once she returned to her homeland. Even before the rebels captured Bilbao and now Santander, violence was widespread. Here political persuasions ranged widely from separatists, monarchists, anarchists, socialists, to Communists. As in Madrid, outbreaks of indiscriminate violence increased as things begin to come apart. No place for an outspoken journalist.

Santander was probably a pleasant place in better times. On a peninsula defining a natural port, it was blessed with miles of beaches. Unlike Bilbao, it had little industry. A resort city on the sea.

Fraser found a room in a hotel commandeered by officers of the occupying rebels on the Paseo de Pereda running along the harbor. It offered a bath and clean sheets along with a fine ocean view after weeks in the field. Asleep for only a couple of hours, he was awakened by loud pounding on his hotel room door.

He opened the door to see a Spanish Legion lieutenant pointing a revolver at him.

"You will come with us, Señor Fraser," the officer ordered, pushing into the room followed by two soldiers. "Get dressed."

"What's this about?"

"Now!"

While Fraser dressed the soldiers began pulling out his belongings dumping everything on the bed.

"Careful with the photography gear," Fraser said indignantly. Yet his stomach was churning with fear. What the hell had happened?

He was taken downstairs and escorted into an office, probably the former hotel manager's office. There he was confronted with his worst fears. Loretta Elizalde was seated in a wooden chair, her wrists bound to the arms of the chair. Next to her stood Heinz Leitner. He was without his uniform jacket, just his undershirt. In his hand was what appeared to be a rubber hose about a foot long. Seeing Fraser, he slapped the hose into the palm of his other hand.

Elizalde's face was badly swollen. Vivid red welts marked her cheeks. Dark bruising began to show. Blood trickled from her nose. Her lip was split. Her hair was matted with perspiration. She was dressed in a white blouse and gray slacks now splattered with blood.

Cabrera stood in front of Elizalde. Two Moroccans stood in the back of the room.

"What did you find?" Cabrera said to the officer that brought Fraser down from his room.

From Fraser's bag one of soldiers dumped his photographic gear onto the floor.

"How is it you know this Communist bitch reporter, Fraser?" Cabrera said.

"I don't. Who is she?"

"I think you know. How is it she has these pictures? Your pictures."

Cabrera grabbed a stack of photographic prints from the desk thrusting them to Fraser.

Fraser took them and thumbed through them. Photographs taken of atrocities perpetrated by Cabrera's troops in Andalusia and Badajoz.

"Yes, these are mine. So what? They were sent out after going through the censor in Seville," Fraser said. "These were authorized for publication."

"That is ridiculous. The censor would never have allowed these to be published," Cabrera said.

These pictures were indeed not those the censor passed for dispatch to the U.S. But that would take some time before Cabrera could sort that out. They were 800 kilometers north of Seville in the middle of a war.

Fraser responded, "General de Llano encouraged these acts of rape and murder. He wanted them published for their terror value."

"But your material went to America. How did Elizalde get these?"

Fraser smiled condescendingly. "Colonel, I don't think you know how a news service works. You see I send these to the Hearst news service. They first publish them in the chain of Hearst newspapers. A day or two later they are released to any other newspapers for a fee. Newspapers across the world. That's how the news reporting business works. So why wouldn't whoever this reporter works for get hold of these pictures?"

"I would not be so sure that is all true, Colonel," Leitner said. "I never felt Fraser should be trusted."

Leitner was squatting down examining the photography equipment. He selected out several items. Lifting first the convex lens, he said, "And what might this be, Fraser?"

"For making enlargements," Fraser said.

"And this large light bulb?"

"That too."

"But aren't enlargements used for making prints like these?" Leitner said grabbing the photos from Fraser.

Shit. Fraser knew where this was leading. He was trapped.

"Yes."

"Yet I believe you send out your photographs as negatives which you develop. That's what you showed me. While I'm no photographer, the process for developing those negatives I believe requires a darkroom. No light. That's why you use this small red light bulb that won't ruin the exposed film. Am I correct?" Leitner said fingering the small red light bulb.

Fraser did not reply.

"And these other items. Can you explain their function?" Leitner said picking up first the expanding stand then the sheets of cellophane.

Fraser turned to Cabrera, "Colonel, I don't know what is going on here. I do not know this woman. I have authorizations to report from your lines by Generals Franco, Queipo de Llano, and Mola. I request I be taken to their headquarters."

Cabrera now smiled. "General Mola is dead, Fraser. Died in a plane crash two days ago. Colonel Yagüe is away at the front. General de Llano is in Seville. General Franco is too far away and much too busy to deal with spies. That he leaves to his local commanders. Therefore, I shall proceed with getting to the bottom of this."

"If I might suggest, Colonel," Leitner said. "We have several photographers assigned to the Condor Legion. Let me get one of them here to advise what these unusual items might be used for. Herr Fraser does not make enlargements. He has no photographic print paper. Yet he is carting around these items that he says are used for that purpose?"

Cabrera nodded. "Yes. Arrange for that immediately, Hauptsturmführer. Use the field telephone set up in the lobby. Then you can return to our questioning of Señorita Elizalde. And perhaps Señor Fraser as well."

Leitner returned in a few minutes.

"Within the hour my photographer will be here, Colonel," Leitner said. "We can proceed with the interrogations."

"I am afraid we have not told you everything Señor Fraser," Cabrera said. "We know your story about news services spreading photographs is not how Elizalde got these photographs. And I do not believe the censor would ever have authorized these. You know Elizalde. She has your address in Paris.

"It is the middle of the night, Fraser. I am in no mood for this charade to continue any longer. Tie Señor Fraser to a chair," Cabrera said motioning to the two Moroccans. "Perhaps if you experience some of the same treatment as Elizalde you will realize it is better to confess rather than suffer."

The soldiers grabbed Fraser and tied his arms to another chair set next to Elizalde.

Leitner approached to stand in front of Fraser. A broad grin on his face. With no warning he lashed the hose across Fraser's face.

The pain was searing. Moments later his cheek was still throbbing from the blow. For the next thirty minutes Leitner kept this up.

With Fraser barely conscious and bleeding profusely, Leitner turned back to Elizalde. "Let us try something else."

He held down Elizalde's right hand with one hand while taking hold of one finger with his other hand. Slowly he pulled her finger back until a loud pop signified its dislocation. Elizalde screamed. After an interval to allow for the full effects of the pain, Leitner repeated with another finger, then another, then another.

Elizalde's screams trailed off into a constant wail.

Fraser wanted to settle this with a confession if it would end this torture. Holding him back was doubting that it would end anything. This was not about getting information. This simply fed into Leitner's and Cabrera's sadism.

A German enlisted man entered the room. After addressing Leitner his face registered distress upon seeing the condition of the two victims tied to chairs.

"Come over here, Sergeant," Leitner said. Singling out the questionable items among Fraser's possessions he said, "What would these be used for?"

After a few moments examination the sergeant said, "I'm not sure, Sir. This is a lens. Looks like something from an enlarger. But this, I have no idea," he said examining the adjustable stand. "The cellophane I have no idea. The large light bulb might be used in making a print enlargement."

"But not for developing negatives?" Leitner said.

"No, Hauptsturmführer. Darkness is required to develop negatives. Enlargements come with printing the positive image from the negative requiring bright light."

"So it seems we still have a mystery, Herr Fraser. Why do you have these items? We must therefore continue our questioning. That will be all, Sergeant. You can return to your duties."

The German sergeant appeared in thought before saying to Leitner, "Perhaps it could be used for making reductions, Sir."

Leitner turned to him, "What do you mean, Sergeant?"

"At photography school the instructor explained a process whereby you could re-photograph a negative and reproduce another negative much reduced in size."

"And you would use these items?"

Appearing to regret volunteering the theory, the sergeant proceeded as guardedly as possible. "Well, Sir, as I recall, you could use an enlarger seemingly for reverse effect. The process involved re-photographing the negative using a convex lens from an enlarger. The cellophane could be used as part of that process but I don't recall the precise details."

"And this can produce a small negative?" Leitner asked.

"That's what the instructor said. A very small negative. But I never saw it done."

Leitner looked at the pile of photographic items on the floor. Among them were several envelopes. One was addressed to New York with postage affixed. Picking up the stamped envelope, Leitner saw immediately the only opportunity to smuggle out very small negatives. Turning to a soldier, he ordered him to go to the hotel kitchen and bring a kettle of boiling water.

Ten minutes later Leitner was steaming off the postage stamps from the envelope. Removing the stamps with the blade of a knife once the glue dissolved revealed tiny squares of film negatives a sixteenth of an inch square under the stamp of one addressed envelope.

"Ah, so this is how you smuggled out photographs, Herr Fraser. I wonder what is on this latest cache?"

Leitner retrieved Fraser's jeweler's 30X loupe from the scattered items on the floor.

"That is what this is for I believe, Colonel," Leitner said smiling at Fraser. "But we need more light."

Taking Fraser's large light bulb with connected cord, he and Cabrera left the room to find a suitable place to see what was on the discovered micro-negatives.

Fifteen minutes later, Cabrera and Leitner returned.

Cabrera, his face reddened with rage at Fraser's deception, grabbed Leitner's rubber hose from the desk and began a renewed assault on Fraser. Within minutes Fraser's lapsed into unconsciousness. Fresh blood streamed from his nose and one ear. A nasty laceration opened up on one cheekbone. One eye became swollen shut. His face already darkening with the deep bruising.

Not content, Cabrera continued blows to Fraser's upper body and shoulders. After spending his fury, Cabrera ordered one of the soldiers to bring water and revive the prisoner.

"You are a spy, Fraser. These negatives contain military information. Photographs of aircraft are sufficiently visible. We cannot yet read the detail of the typed pages with this small magnifying device but I suspect it to be military information.

"You deceived my brother. Somehow you deceived General Franco to put you among us. Once we understand what this information contains we will resume our interrogation. You will of course die for this, Fraser. You and this miserable bitch. How unpleasant a death will depend on you telling us who you are working for."

Turning to the Moroccan soldiers, Cabrera said, "Take them to the wine cellar."

Roughly handled then thrown down the stairs, Fraser and Elizalde were locked in the hotel wine cellar. Both were in terrible shape. Fraser couldn't stand. Dizziness probably from a concussion. Barely able to see with the swelling of his face.

Elizalde looked not much better. One hand was useless with all the fingers broken or dislocated. Fraser guessed that they would be killed after undergoing further torture once what was on the micro-negatives could be read. It would be a terrible ordeal for both of them even if he told them who he was working for. Maybe Cabrera also wanted higher approval since Fraser had a letter of authorization from Franco himself, therefore needing incontrovertible evidence? For that they would need a microscope to read the text.

Whatever the reason for the temporary reprieve, they only had a small window of opportunity to attempt escape. Only a couple of hours before dawn.

"Loretta, if we can get out of here is there some place to hide?"

"I shared a hotel room with Rafael, my fiancé. It's close to the hospital where he works. He's a doctor. The rebels don't know of him. Rafael forced me to leave the city knowing I would be targeted if captured. Unfortunately I didn't make it out. Rafael doesn't know I was captured so he should still be staying there."

"How far to his place?"

"Two or three kilometers I guess."

"Can we avoid patrols?"

"If we could get to the rail yard just south of the hospital, maybe. But getting there means walking many blocks of back alleys."

"Ok. But that's our best bet. Besides I don't know how much longer before sunrise. We have a chance only if it's dark. If we don't make it to your fiancé then we might be able to hide out in the rail yard until tomorrow night and make another try."

"It all sounds hopeless, Marc. Look at us. I only have one good hand. You can't even stand without help. How do we even get out of here?"

Fraser pulled up his pant leg. Extracting the switchblade from his ankle holster, he flicked it open.

"Listen, Loretta, I know this is desperate. Only a poor chance to escape. We'll probably get shot in the attempt. But that's what awaits us anyway. Most likely a worse death. We've got to get the guard in here. You game to try?"

She nodded.

"Good. Pound on the door. Tell him something is wrong with me. Looks like I'm having a heart attack. I'll lie here and look semi-conscious. Get him to come over and look at me. Do it now. We don't have much time."

Elizalde nodded and went to the door and began yelling for help.

The door opened. But two guards entered both armed with rifles with fixed bayonets. One guard put the bayonet to Elizalde's abdomen pushing her back against the rack of wine bottles. The other went to Fraser lying on his side on the dirt floor groaning with his back toward the soldier.

As the soldier reached down and attempted to turn Fraser unto his back, Fraser thrust the knife into his neck.

The other soldier holding Elizalde turned then stepped immediately toward Fraser who was struggling to his feet. The soldier thrust the bayonet toward Fraser's midsection. Fraser saw it coming and stepped back. But not in time. The bayonet pierced his left side.

Elizalde with her good hand grabbed a wine bottle bringing it around in a terrific blow to the back of the soldier's head sending him to the floor unconscious.

She rushed to Fraser now on his knees clutching his side. Blood seeped between his fingers. The pain intense.

Elizalde tore the hem from her slip to make a bandage. After a couple of moments she stemmed the flow of blood. Apparently no major blood vessel was obviously pierced. Hard to about tell internal damage. Nonetheless a debilitating wound rendering Fraser a real liability now in making an escape.

Yet they must leave immediately. As Elizalde helped him to his feet he said, "One more thing to do." With the switchblade still in his hand he bent down and thrust it into the other soldier's neck.

Elizalde gasped.

In a raspy garble with his damaged face Fraser said, "Need every minute if we're to escape."

Even though repulsed by what he had done he still wiped the blade on his trousers and folded it before slipping it into his pocket.

Elizalde helped Fraser navigate up the cellar stairs. Checking the darkened hotel kitchen through opening the door a crack, they exited the rear of the hotel. Fraser could only walk being supported by Elizalde and one soldier's rifle as a crutch.

Sunrise was imminent but the night was still totally dark due to a heavy overcast. With Fraser's condition they could never hope to make it to Rafael's hotel before daylight. Not even to the rail yard. The only place she could think of to hide was at the marina. Only a few hundred meters away. Pleasure boats were still moored there. Not likely to be much rebel activity there. Their only chance was to hide in one of the boats. Spend the day out of sight before she would try for Rafael's hotel the following night.

She looked for the closest and the largest boat possible. Something with a cabin. Fortunately no one was about on the docks. Situating Fraser out of sight she went off to locate a suitable boat. It turned out to be a small stubby sail boat built more for day-sailing comfort than speed.

After prying open the cabin door lock with the soldier's bayonet she was able to get Fraser into the sleeping berth. She bound his midsection wound with some towels found on the boat. No food but two containers of water. Closing the cabin door, they could not be seen unless someone actually boarded the boat.

Fraser eventually fell into a fitful sleep. Elizalde stood guard within the darkened cabin holding the rifle. Fraser told her to shoot if they were discovered. Hopefully they would have a quick death in a hail of return gunfire.

The prospects of surviving their desperate circumstances until the following night seemed exceedingly slim. Rebel troops were everywhere, undoubtedly now searching for them. Even if they got to Elizalde's fiancé, how could they conceivably escape Santander? The Nationalist rebels controlled the entire region except for a pocket of resistance in Asturias. Not an option. The only possible escape was to France to the east. Yet that was 200 kilometers through rebel controlled territory.

A horrible day. Both were in terrible pain. Fraser passed in and out of consciousness. At sunset, Elizalde said, "Here is what we do. I will go to find Rafael. You must stay here. It's too far in your condition."

Fraser wanted to argue but knew she was right. He was in seriously bad shape. The pain of the stab wound had only gotten worse. Hard to focus with his head throbbing. Walking was impossible.

"If I can make it to Rafael he can come to treat you. It's another dark night. I'll make it. We've been lucky today. You'll be safe for at least tonight."

Unspoken was how to get Fraser from the boat into some other hiding place given his condition. And where to hide under the occupation of the rebel forces? Elizalde had no answers. She just had to get to Rafael.

Once Elizalde left it was hard for him not to think this was the end. Sitting propped up in the dark poised with a rifle to shoot if discovered. Getting chills. The first effects of a fever? Even if Elizalde somehow found her fiancé, what then?

Three hours later a loud whisper woke Fraser. Elizalde? Was he hallucinating?

Elizalde persisted hoping Fraser would not shoot.

"This is Rafael Solano, Marc," she said as Solano squeezed into the confined space to examine Fraser's.

"For the pain, Señor Fraser," Solano said as he injected morphine into Fraser's arm. As he cleaned the wound and applied a proper dressing, he said, "Loretta has told me everything. We must leave immediately. I have brought what little food I had. Some bread and cheese."

"Leave? To where?" Fraser said, already feeling the effects of the morphine knowing it would further inhibit his mobility.

"To France of course. By boat. This boat," Solano said. "But we must leave now. We need every hour of darkness. Another moonless night which is good. But I can't use the auxiliary engine. We have to sneak quietly out of the harbor. I'll row us out using the dinghy with a tow line. Fortunately we're close to the harbor entrance at the breakwater. But it will still take some time before we're out into the Atlantic and can hoist the sails. If we're not spotted leaving the harbor we have a chance."

Elizalde said, "But then what, Rafael? There are lots of ships out there. Spanish naval ships under Nationalist command. The Italians too. Maybe even German. A few British and French I'm told. We won't be able to distinguish the flag until it's too late."

"That's why we need the cover of darkness as long as possible. I hope to sneak through the line of ships going due north. Once out far enough we'll turn east for the French coast. Probably about two hundred kilometers. Should make Biarritz the day after tomorrow if the wind is right and the swells remain modest. And if we're lucky."

An hour later Solano had rowed the sailboat almost to the breakwater and returned on board. Having just raised the mainsail and jib there came a shout from the shore. Even in the dark their white sail must still be visible. Another yelled command to stop. Solano kept the boat on course heading for the end of breakwater at the mouth of the harbor. Progress was agonizingly slow by having to tack into the prevailing onshore breeze.

No shots were fired. Then light suddenly played across the water. Two beams obviously from the headlamps of a vehicle. An uncertain rebel sentry improvising to confirm before sounding the alarm.

But the direction of the light fell well to the stern of the sailboat. Luck continued as the vehicle adjusted its headlamps to scan a wider area but still missed the sailboat now out of effective range of the light. In another few minutes they cleared the breakwater. Ocean swells however promised a difficult sail in the small craft.

"Best if you try to sleep, Marc. Rafael says we still have a couple more hours of darkness. Enough to clear the line of naval ships before morning light. He says he can see their navigation lights. Enough distance to steer between them as long as they do not hear us. Best not to talk."

Mustering his strength, Fraser said, "Loretta. We must not be captured. Tell Rafael that. If it comes to that he must use the rifle. Do you understand what I mean?"

She just nodded. Fraser fell into a fevered-sleep with the effects of another morphine shot.

CHAPTER 27

Fraser woke with sunlight streaming into the sailboat's cabin porthole. Elizalde was there to comfort him. Thirsty, she allowed him a measured amount of their limited water.

"Where are we?"

Elizalde said, "Out into the Atlantic. Well north of the naval ships. Out of sight with these gray skies. Rafael got us through. He just made the turn toward the east. Unfortunately he says that puts us some of the time almost parallel to large swells. You can feel them now. But Rafael is a good sailor. I've been out sailing with him many times when we lived in San Sebastian."

Fraser was a little unnerved as they rode high up on a swell to then plunge into the trough before the next. Rafael Solano however proved to be an accomplished sailor. Later in the afternoon he came down into the cabin with Elizalde taking the tiller.

"Time for another shot, Señor Fraser. Pain still bad?"

"Afraid so."

"Painful but you were lucky. The bayonet appears to have struck a rib. Still a nasty wound but no apparent organ damage. No major blood vessels punctured. Danger is infection. Need to get you to a hospital where we can properly treat the wound. Get some antibacterial drugs into you to contend with infection that's causing the fever. The bruising to your face is only superficial by the way. Same for Loretta. In her case, it's her damaged fingers. I reset them but she is still suffering a lot of pain."

Solano shuddered with the thought of her enduring the torture. "Bastards."

"Is she piloting the boat?" Fraser said a little concerned with these heavy seas.

"Yes. She knows what she is doing. Been out with me many times before. Knows how to keep the wind in the mainsail while staying on course using the compass. It's a straight heading to Biarritz. Weather is giving us some good sized swells but manageable. Wouldn't let me give her any morphine for her pain. Said I needed to get a couple of hours rest before nightfall. She needs to stay alert. Wants me back at the helm once it gets dark.

The afternoon of the following day Solano announced Biarritz was in sight. He was not going to risk trying to navigate the small harbor under sail in the strong wind. The auxiliary engine wasn't powerful enough for these seas. Piloting the sailboat onto the beach north of Biarritz was unceremonious but a safer bet.

Fraser and Elizalde were taken to the small local hospital. Solano tended to their care. Elizalde's fingers were splinted. Unfortunately, Fraser's fever became worse the following day. It took several more days to stem the infection.

They spent several days in a refugee camp. Not yet the hellholes these French internment camps would become in a couple of years with the hordes of escaping Spaniards, but it was still Spartan. Tents. Primitive latrines. Subsistence food.

Fraser was able to establish his identity as an American through badgering the French authorities to contact military attaché Colonel Waite at the U.S. Embassy in Paris. Waite in turn contacted Fraser's friend Henri Marchand as instructed.

The French were conflicted over Spain. The leftist French government sided with the Republican Spanish government yet for the most part observed the non-intervention pact. To the local French on the southern border refugees were an unwelcomed burden in these difficult economic times.

By the time Henri Marchand arrived in Biarritz to aid his friend, Fraser had recovered from his fever. Well enough to travel, he invited Elizalde and Solano to return with him to Paris. They could stay at his apartment as long as necessary until they could determine what to do.

The Spanish Republican government would eventually fall to the Nationalist rebellion. That meant permanent exile for Elizalde and Solano as enemies of a Fascist Spanish state.

PART FOUR

FRANCE

✝

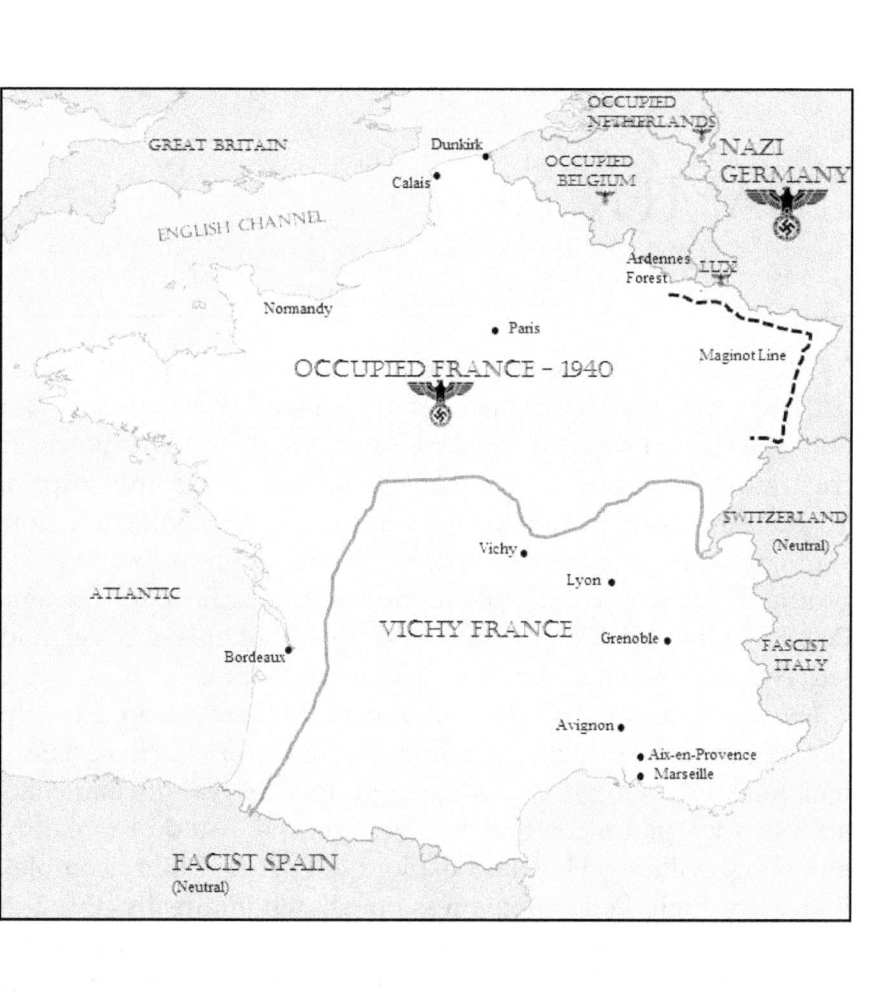

GREAT BRITAIN

OCCUPIED NETHERLANDS

OCCUPIED BELGIUM

NAZI GERMANY

Dunkirk

Calais

ENGLISH CHANNEL

Ardennes Forest

LUX

Normandy

Paris

Maginot Line

OCCUPIED FRANCE – 1940

SWITZERLAND
(Neutral)

Vichy

Lyon

ATLANTIC

VICHY FRANCE

Grenoble

FASCIST ITALY

Bordeaux

Avignon

Aix-en-Provence
Marseille

FACIST SPAIN
(Neutral)

CHAPTER 28

The thrill of the chase and the adventure of crusading against bad guys had worn off after the misfortune in Spain. Not only the danger of once again almost being killed but the shear frustration. His years working in Europe had made little impact. To the American readership just unintelligible conflicts in foreign countries. His earlier exposés of corruption in Los Angeles produced greater effect. More immediate concerns to his readers. People understood that type of crime. Wholesale murder and enslavement in distant lands was easier to ignore.

So once returned to Paris in late 1937, Marc Fraser gave up journalism to write fiction. Shape his own stories. He certainly had amassed enough material. A repertoire of real-life bad characters as templates for fictional antagonists. Couldn't make up any worse villains. He could explore deeper and more complex issues through fictional expression shown indirectly through character interaction rather than by reporting. Things that often defied understanding. Who would read another journalist reporting yet more world strife? More could be achieved by the reader experiencing circumstances through a story with vivid characters told as an engaging story.

He read his old acquaintance Ernest Hemingway's *The Sun Also Rises* and *A Farewell to Arms*. Having become famous as a novelist, Hemingway was now also reporting from Spain. But from the Republican side, the opposite of Fraser. Since Hemingway hadn't published any novels for many years maybe he needed more material? Maybe he was just trying to validate his macho reputation. Fraser felt no need to prove anything.

Spain left him emotionally scarred. Recurring nightmares reliving all the horrors witnessed. His killing of the two Moroccan soldiers was an ever present image.

Loretta Elizalde found work in Paris writing for the leftist newspaper *L'Humanite*. While closely linked with the French Communist Party, Elizalde professed not to be a Communist herself. She thought Joseph Stalin a villain equal to Franco. Her articles crusaded for the welfare of Spanish children refugees being sent to France in increasing numbers.

Rafael Solano found a position as a physician in a Paris hospital.

After a couple months staying at Fraser's apartment, Elizalde and Solano married. Marc Fraser served as best man hosting their wedding dinner.

By 1938, Fraser had reordered his life. Paris was now home. No desire to return to the United States. He applied for French citizenship while still retaining his American citizenship. Best of both worlds.

Settling into the writing life proved easier than he imagined. Working within his imagination proved consistently stimulating. Creating fiction was just as rewarding as rough and tumble journalism. The rewards of investigative journalism became easily replaced by immersing himself into creating art.

Life took on a fuller range of interests. Through his friend Henri Marchand he was commissioned to write a movie script based upon the Spanish Civil War. He developed a circle of friends, many within the French movie industry. Now part of their crowd, he also benefited with his former connection to Hollywood. The film industry was quickly becoming international. European stars, particularly beautiful actresses, frequently appeared in American movie productions.

He continued his artistic photography pursuits. Subjects varied as he explored new compositions of light, shadowing, exposure with his Leica always ready for an opportunity. The nude female form was replaced by the charms of Paris.

The lack of a steady female companion still eluded him. It had been a long time since he had photographed a woman. Longer yet since having any kind of relationship. Had he ever had a serious relationship? Perhaps Abigail Blumenthal? Recollections of the other women he had known were only a collection of abbreviated memories.

His friend Henri was determined to connect him with a suitable companion. Someone to connect with Fraser's difficult proclivities Henri said. That someone might be Fiona Marchand, his younger sister. But even Henri Marchand thought it a longshot. His sister had formidable defenses.

Fraser had met Fiona Marchand only once years before at a birthday party for her brother. He was intrigued when Henri told him she was an art historian. He remembered her. A striking woman. PhD from the Sorbonne in art history. Worked at the Louvre. Intrigued because she looked nothing like a stuffy intellectual. Dressed more like a lawyer or some other professional. But at the time, married with a hovering husband.

But at this year's birthday party Henri told Fraser she had been divorced for three years. Being unattached, nor currently involved, Henri endeavored to push them together. His two favorite people. According to Henri, both were interesting but equally difficult personalities.

Fraser made a more critical assessment of Fiona Marchand this time. Obviously very intelligent. Confident, self-assured. His type. Physically attractive. Tall, long legs. Good figure. Little makeup. Stylish hair but done imperfectly as if a bother to be too fastidious.

"Monsieur Fraser, so nice to see you again," Fiona Marchand said extending her hand, a glass of champagne in the other.

"It's been a long time, Madame Marchand."

"Yes it has been. However, you seem a familiar presence since Henri speaks of you often. He enthusiastically recounts your journalistic adventures."

"Well Henri is a movie producer always thinking in dramatic terms for the screen. I'm sure he exaggerates."

"Perhaps. But Henri likes you very much."

"Henri is a dear friend. Through him I now have a great circle of friends. And what do you think of your brother's latest movie?"

"I told him Shakespeare had done the story better in Hamlet than his screenplay. Good acting but I thought the writing somewhat flat for these conflicted characters. Perhaps Henri should have had you write the script. I read your novel by the way. Powerful dialogue. Henri said you are working on another novel?"

"Yes I am. Fiction is a whole different type of writing than journalism. What's your critique of my book?"

"Oh, I'm not a critic of literature, only the visual arts."

"I just meant what did you think of it as a reader?"

"Well it was certainly engaging. Fast paced adventure. A good read. Dangerous place your Los Angeles. Things like this actually happen there?"

"Unfortunately, yes. I based much of it on my own personal experiences as an investigative newspaper reporter."

"And the romantic theme?" Marchand smiled coyly.

"That is just fiction."

"Henri said you've been in Spain reporting for an American newspaper. He didn't tell me much about what happened except that you were badly injured."

Before Fraser could relate what happened, Fiona Marchand was pulled away by another woman. Not seeing her until again until seated together at the dining table for dinner, it seemed neither the time nor place to launch into the saga of horror he experienced in Spain. He responded as she raised her earlier question about what happened in Spain with the vague answer that, "It was a difficult assignment, a war zone, dangerous work,

fully recovered from a wound I sustained. Certainly an experience. Perhaps I could tell you about what happened over dinner
sometime?"

She looked at him with an expression that suggested she was
considering a difficult question. "That might be nice, Monsieur
Fraser. Perhaps when I return from Italy next month."

That was it. Off to Italy with no further elaboration. She
seemed decidedly underwhelmed.

The next day Fraser said to Henri when questioned about
how he had gotten on with his sister, "Intelligent woman your
sister, Henri. Very attractive. Somewhat self-absorbed though."

"Probably, but so are you, Marc. So what do think?"

Fraser sighed. Henri wanted so much to see them come together. "Henri, she didn't seem all that interested. Anyway, she's
away to Italy for a month."

"That's not unusual. She goes to Italy all the time. Consults
at the Uffizi in Florence regularly. It's her work not a holiday."

That brightened Fraser's outlook slightly.

"And another piece of information, my friend. Fiona did say
to me as she left last night, *your friend Marc is very interesting. Not
bad looking either. Perhaps I might take him up on dinner sometime.*
So you see she is also interested."

Fraser laughed at his friend's earnestness. "We'll see, Henri."

✝

Surprisingly, Fraser received a telephone call six weeks later
from Fiona Marchand.

"How good to hear from you, Madame Marchand. How was
Florence?"

"Hot. Summer of course in Italy. Knew it would be uncomfortable." There was a pause for several moments. "I was calling
to inquire if you might like to join me at a major art showing.
The gallery owner is a friend and has invited me to dinner with
his wife after the event. He wondered if I would like to bring
someone. It's this Saturday." The last words came out in kind of
a rush. Fraser sensed it was uncomfortable for her to be asking.
How quaint for someone so self-assured.

"I would be delighted. Thank you for thinking of me. Perhaps I could pick you up in a taxi?"

"No, that won't be necessary. The gallery is close to the Louvre. I'll just meet you there. The Galerie des Déchargeurs on the street of the same name. The galley owner's name is Émile Bernheim. About seven o'clock?"

"I shall look forward to it, Madame Marchand."

"Let's not be so formal. I hear Madame Marchand all day. Please call me Fiona, Marc."

Saturday in his best suit with a fresh haircut, Marc Fraser found himself anxiously anticipating seeing Fiona Marchand. He had thought a lot about her during the intervening weeks since Henri's birthday party. Actually couldn't get her out of his mind.

Arriving at the gallery, a matronly looking woman introducing herself as Phillipa Bernheim took him in tow, fetching him a glass of champagne from a passing waiter.

"Ah, so you are Fiona's escort this evening. I wondered who she might bring for dinner later. Fiona is a good friend but a little reclusive since her divorce. Have you known her long?"

"Not really. Her brother Henri is a close friend. I hadn't seen Fiona in some time. Just saw her again at Henri's birthday party."

"Knowing Fiona it seems you made an impression. And what do you do, Monsieur Fraser?"

"A writer. Novelist. Former journalist. A sometime photographer."

"Oh my. Would I be familiar with your work?"

"My first novel, *Provoke the Devil*, was published a couple of years ago in the United States. In English of course. I'm an American."

"I would never have guessed. You have no accent."

"My mother was French. Grew up speaking French as much as English. I studied at the Sorbonne."

"Well you are French then. And there's Fiona," she said grabbing Fraser by the elbow and guiding him to meet her."

Fraser couldn't help but to smile upon seeing her. A *most* attractive woman.

To Fraser's delight after Fiona Marchand greeted Phillipa Bernheim, she turned and embraced him giving him the formal light kiss on each cheek. She looked totally different from Henri's party. A stylish evening dress with fashionable heels. More makeup. A string of pearls. No hint that her day-job was a museum art curator. But it was her expressive eyes that drew attention. At Henri's party those eyes looked intimidating. Tonight they looked lively, maybe even inviting.

"So glad you came, Marc," she said giving him a genuine smile. Phillipa, where is Émile?"

They went off to locate their host. As they walked down a section of the gallery, Fraser stopped to look at some photographic art. Paris buildings, streets, average scenes not the iconic Paris images.

"These are remarkable," Fraser said.

"Yes they are," said a trim middle-aged elegantly dressed man. He kissed Fiona. "And this gentleman is?"

"Marc Fraser, Monsieur," Fraser said offering his hand.

"Why yes, of course. And I am Émile Bernheim. We shall have a marvelous dinner later this evening. But right now I will brave the critique of my latest acquisitions from the toughest art critic in Paris. Fiona spends all her time among so many of the greats in those musty museums that she is unduly harsh when it comes to the work of contemporary artists."

"That is not true, Émile. Good art is simply rare. Most works are just pretty pictures. Émile uses me to distinguish the difference so that he can price them accordingly. However, even his pretty pictures carry absurd prices."

"See what I mean, Monsieur Fraser? Now these photographic pieces you were looking at. What is your opinion?"

"I'm certainly no art critic, Monsieur, however I do appreciate photography. These are particularly impressive. It's the photographer's use of light. The way the shadowing works. His camera settings, his shot angle, the composition, all to capture his desired effect. Like a painter's use of brush strokes and color."

"Bravo. Now there is a critique to my liking. You know something of photography?"

"Yes. But I'm not as good as this photographer."

"There you have it, Fiona. From an expert. I shall immediately double the prices."

Fiona Marchand smiled. She obviously liked Bernheim.

The gallery showing was well attended. Fraser was impressed with how many luminaries of the art world Fiona knew personally. Dinner later was a particularly pleasant experience. The Bernheims were a lively socially engaging couple. Smart people. They brought out a different side to Fiona Marchand that he had not seen.

"I understand you were a newspaper correspondent, Monsieur Fraser." Émile Bernheim said. "Reported from Spain according to Fiona. Is the civil war there as terrible as we read in the newspapers?"

"Unfortunately much worse. Civil wars are always that way. Nothing is clear. No one can be neutral. Everyone is either friend or enemy. Murder, torture, and excuse me, Madame, but even rape are used as weapons of terror."

"And you witnessed such things, Monsieur Fraser?" Phillipa Bernheim said.

"Yes. Photographed some terrible scenes. I was reporting from the Nationalist rebel side. Atrocities are being committed by both sides in this war but overwhelmingly the Nationalists are the worse. Intended to terrorize. Directly encouraged by their military leadership. Remember this is a Fascist inspired rebellion. General Franco wants a political regime in Spain similar to Adolf Hitler and Benito Mussolini. Both Germany and Italy are even actively supporting the Nationalist rebels."

"How was it that the Nationalists allowed you to photograph these atrocities?" Émile Bernheim said.

"Some they wanted published knowing it would make its way into newspapers seen by the Republicans in order to terrorize. But the worst of the pictures I smuggled out. Scenes even the Nationalists didn't want exposed. I arranged for them to be published anonymously."

"Sounds dangerous," Phillipa Bernheim said.

Pausing for a moment, Fraser nodded, "Yes. I was discovered smuggling out contraband photographs so I had to escape Spain. Decided to pursue a new career rather than exposing bad characters."

Fiona Marchand's brother Henri told her only of traveling south to help Fraser after his escape from Spain but no details. Fraser had not elaborated as to how he was wounded only the escape by sailboat to France.

"Apparently you never told Henri many details about what happened in Spain. How were you wounded?" she said.

"I was imprisoned by the Nationalists along with another Spanish journalist. Things became ugly. Of course it's a terribly ugly war. That's what I was trying to expose.

"Getting out of Spain proved to be a desperately violent affair. I was wounded overpowering a guard. With the help of my journalist friend's fiancé we stole a sailboat and made it to France. Some other time I will relate the disturbing circumstances. Good material for a novel. But let's not spoil this pleasant evening with distressing talk."

Apparently Fiona Marchand found something to her liking in Marc Fraser. Before parting that evening as he dropped her off by taxi at her apartment on the right bank not far from the Louvre and the Opera House she said, "I had a most enjoyable evening, Marc. I believe the Bernheims also enjoyed your company. Phillipa was even flirting with you." Smiling, she embraced him and kissed him on both cheeks. Perhaps he imagined it, but was there more to it than just French familiarity?

"I too had a wonderful time. I like your friends the Bernheims. But it was your company that made for an exceptional evening, Fiona. Might I ask you to dinner another time?"

Her smile widened. "But of course. What about Friday?"

After that next dinner it was twice the following week, including a long lunch after which she personally escorted him on a tour of the back workrooms of the Louvre. He was fascinated by the specialized work in restoring priceless treasures.

He yearned to make love to Fiona. She had totally infected him over the last several weeks. Yet as close as they had seemingly become, he was concerned about potentially ruining things by a premature display of passion. They connected, enjoying each other's' company, yet he couldn't claim to know her mind.

After dinner one Friday night with the weekend ahead of them he worked up the courage. Over coffees and liqueurs he laid his hand on hers on the table and said, "You are achingly attractive, Fiona. I want to make love to you. Tonight."

Anticipating any number of responses, he was stunned when she laid her other hand over his and said, "About time you asked. I thought maybe you weren't interested in ….. well you know. I'm not very good at seduction apparently."

He grinned broadly. "Quite the opposite. Surmounting your defenses just seemed daunting. I didn't want to risk ruining anything. I'm more than just fond of you, Fiona."

"Then pay the check, Marc and let's leave."

†

Marc Fraser felt like he was maturing into the next chapter of his life. Finding his calling in investigative journalism had been rewarding. The danger adding the element of adventure. But he no longer felt driven to crusade against the evils in the world. Spain burned that out of him. He had even come to question the effectivity of the press. Pursuing a continuum of never ending terrible things with nothing ever changing. Writing fiction became his new calling. Maybe he could accomplish more that way.

Gone also was the succession of transient romantic affairs. Fiona Marchand changed that. She was everything he instinctively sought out in a woman. He wanted it to last.

The relationship flourished. For several months they both maintained their separate apartments, sleeping over at one or the other's depending mostly on Fiona's schedule. Eventually Fiona announced they should move in together. She liked his larger apartment with its better view, quieter street, yet still close enough to the Louvre across the Seine.

Neither discussed marriage. Nor was having children discussed. Mutually there was an unspoken understanding that children would alter their lives in ways neither wanted.

Fraser became fully accepted into the Marchand family. His good friend Henri was delighted. Told Fraser that he knew he and his sister were meant for each other. Even better, Fraser fell in love with Fiona's parents living in Aix-en-Provence. Her father was a University of Provence professor of history in Aix-en-Provence. Her mother had an art degree and was an accomplished painter. An older brother, a theoretical physicist also living in Paris only a short distance away in the 5th Arrondissement, provided an extended domestic balance with his two young girls. Both were especially fond of their Aunt Fiona and their new Uncle Marc with his stories of Hollywood.

Henri Marchand convinced Fraser that he should adapt his first novel, *Provoke the Devil*, by writing a screenplay. Fraser was intrigued. Screen writing was an entirely different format than the novel. But so was journalism. Together they decided to take the novel's setting of late 1920s Los Angeles and place it in equally corrupt Marseille, France.

Life was good for Marc Fraser. Finding Fiona made things complete. He was living in Paris, had new friends, and was able to pursue a new writing career.

Unfortunately for much of Europe, life was anything but good.

CHAPTER 29

Although not in the thick of the turmoil swirling in Europe, Fraser was acutely aware of worsening circumstances. France itself was struggling economically with the late onset of the effects of the world wide Depression. Now feeling increasingly threatened by a belligerent Adolf Hitler, the weak French government sought partnership with Britain.

In March, 1938, Germany annexed its ethnic Germanic sister country of Austria in the bloodless *Anschluss*. The German Wehrmacht simply marched across the border uncontested. The rest of the world only mildly protested. Emboldened, Hitler then made demands for absorbing the ethnically German populated Sudetenland region of Czechoslovakia into Germany. Acceding to Hitler's professed declaration that he had no further territorial claims in Europe, the weak leadership of Britain and France signed the *Munich Agreement*. Not only an act of appeasement to a madman but an act of self-serving arrogance to buy off a criminal using another country as currency.

An event in November, 1938 should have dispelled any illusions about the true nature of Adolf Hitler and his Nazi regime. A teenaged German-born Polish Jew living in Paris walked into the German Embassy in Paris and asked to see an official. He then shot an unfortunate young diplomat five times. The assassin stated he was distraught about his family in Germany being deported back to Poland. His act was to avenge the Jewish people.

With the assassination as an excuse, a Nazi sanctioned pogrom erupted across Germany and Austria. It became known as *Kristallnacht,* or *Crystal Night* for all the broken glass from damaged Jewish businesses. Hundreds of Jews were killed. 30,000 were arrested and imprisoned in concentration camps. 7,000 Jewish businesses were destroyed. 1,000 synagogues were burned. Hitler's venomous anti-Semitic rhetoric penned in 1925 in *Mein Kompf* took on physical form.

1938 closed as the fateful year of 1939 dawned. In March Hitler invaded the remaining portion of Czechoslovakia not previously ceded as part of the Sudetenland. His bold gamble paid off. Britain and France again did nothing. Josef Stalin understandably became more anxious by Germany's threatening aggression eastward.

The following month, the Spanish Civil War ended with the defeat of the Republican government. Fearing mass reprisals by the victorious Nationalists, there began a mass exodus across the border north into France. France was overwhelmed with the humanitarian crisis and not politically sympathetic toward the fleeing Republican refugees. To contain the hordes, the French set up their own concentration camps. Of a different motivation than the German camps, Spanish internees in these French camps nonetheless suffered terrible privations. Inadequate shelter and hygiene, starvation rations, little medical care. While suffering physically, inmates feared deportation back to Spain with even worse consequences.

Loretta Elizalde and Rafael Solano become outspoken critics of French treatment of the refugees. Leaving the comfort of Paris, both went south to work in Perpignan with the refugees. Elizalde continued to write for the newspaper. Solano treated the refugees under distressing shortages of medical supplies.

In a surprise move to the world as well as Communists internationally, Josef Stalin signed a non-aggression pact between the Soviet Union and Nazi Germany in August, 1939. The two extremes of the political spectrum had obviously come to a settlement for purely pragmatic reasons. Both Germany and the Soviet Union eyed Poland separating the two countries. Poland had land and access to the Baltic for the Germans. Russians historically coveted Poland. Now it served as a buffer to an aggressive Germany.

For the last couple of years Stalin had embarked upon a psychotic spasm to purge all Soviet leadership of any possible opposition to his absolute authority. Forced collectivization of agricultural production along with increased industrial output demands displaced millions. It created a climate that fostered opposition to his dictatorial power.

These preemptive purges also included the murder or imprisonment of half the senior leadership of the Red Army. Although vast in numbers, the Red Army became ill-equipped to defend against the better led, better armed German forces. The non-aggression agreement would provide Stalin needed time to prepare to counter the German threat.

To Britain, France, and the Low Countries, this alliance of convenience meant that Hitler could now focus westward with his eastern flank secured.

One week after signing the pact with the Soviets, Hitler launched an invasion into Poland. Perhaps thinking he could once again steal territory without the Western powers intervening. But Poland would be no bloodless walk-over. The badly out-classed Polish forces put up a fierce resistance. For Britain and France, Hitler had gone too far. France along with Britain and its Commonwealth partners of Canada, Australia, New Zealand, and South Africa, declared war on Germany the following week.

To secure itself from its own potential two-front conflict, the Soviets signed a non-aggression pact with an equally aggressive Japan. Japan could now pursue its territorial ambitions in China without fear of provoking a Soviet response.

As a consequence of the pact with Germany the Soviet Union launched an attack against Poland from the east two weeks later.

By the end of September, 1939, Europe had quickly become a very different place.

CHAPTER 30

Although France was now officially at war with Germany nothing happened for months. This period known as the 'phony war' was thought to be a result of the massive defensive posture on France's eastern borders. While still apprehensive of war, the French were lulled into a period of false expectations.

At the enormous expense of seven billion francs, France had constructed an impressive line of fortifications tied together with an underground rail system to move men and material. Massive concrete bunkers with heavy artillery emplacements stretched hundreds of miles along the northeast border with Germany. The Maginot Line was considered impregnable. It was constructed with a number of objectives in mind not the least of which was to protect the industrial rich Alsace and Lorraine regions returned to France in 1918.

The Maginot Line also allowed the French to concentrate their mobile forces in a shorter front along the Belgian border. This was the route of the German attack on France in the Great War twenty-five years earlier. Arrayed along this front north of the Maginot Line was the bulk of the formidable French Army. They were further bolstered with 300,000 soldiers of the British Expeditionary Forces. Britain saw this as its best line of defense to a German invasion of England.

The phony war erupted into the real thing in 1940. The Germans first successfully invaded Norway in April. This secured control of access to the Baltic, vital to the German Navy. In May they attacked with a massive ground offensive against the Netherlands and Belgium.

At the onset the two sides were numerically almost equal at over 3,300,000 troops each. But the German strategy did not develop as the French and British expected. With the initial German attack coming against Belgium and Holland, the French high command remained confident. The Germans appeared to be pursuing the same strategy as in 1914. Germany was not however about to repeat that failed attempt that led to years of stalemate attrition in defensive trench warfare.

The plodding infantry movements supported by horse-drawn artillery and supply of 1914 were a thing of the past. German *Blitzkrieg* or *lightning war* would now employ massed tank armor with mechanized infantry and close air support. The commanders of the Allied forces ignored the German tactics clearly evident in the crushing invasion of Poland the prior year.

As the Dutch and Belgians were swept aside in a matter of days by the onslaught of the German Wehrmacht, weaknesses in the French and British defenses soon became evident once they engaged the enemy. Perhaps equal in number to the invading Germans, the French and British were however under-equipped and poorly commanded. The German Luftwaffe dominated the battlefield airspace. German tank armor was deployed in separate divisions whereas the French clung to the outdated tactics of using tanks to support infantry. As a result, the Germans exploited their new tactics to devastating advantage.

The Germans had something further in their attack plan. Building upon their devotion to *Blitzkrieg* they identified the major weakness in France's eastern border defenses. Between the Maginot Line extending from Switzerland the length of the common border with Germany, and the largest concentration of French forces along the Belgian border, lay the rugged terrain of the Ardennes Forest in Luxembourg and the southernmost tip of

Belgium. The hilly, heavily wooded terrain was considered too difficult by the French and British to quickly move invading mechanized forces west. Limited routes through the area would expose invading forces to attack.

While engaging with the French, Belgium, and British forces in the north, the Germans proved that thinking flawed. They had mastered the use of mechanized warfare creating an entirely new tactical innovation. Simply ignoring the *invincible* defenses of the Maginot Line to the south, the Germans plunged through the Ardennes. Facing only light French defenses they tore through with their tanks penetrating deeply into France.

French forces were outmaneuvered. The German thrust through the Ardennes cut off the bulk of French and British forces in the northeast, severing their lines of supply. The poorly commanded French, with poor radio communications, inferior heavy weapons, no air support, suffered swift defeat. Only two weeks after the beginning of the invasion the Germans had isolated the decimated French and British forces to the seaport city of Dunkirk. Only with an ill-conceived German halt to the attack did the British accomplish a desperate rescue by sea of over 350,000 British and French soldiers.

But France was lost.

On 14 June, 1940, German troops marched into Paris. Only six weeks after the German attack began France capitulated. Under a new government with the French war hero Marshal Philippe Pétain installed as prime minister, France surrendered. The ceremony was attended by Adolf Hitler in Compiègne, France using the same railway car in which Germany had signed the armistice ending the Great War in 1918. In all but name only it was a German surrender as evidenced by the terms of the Treaty of Versailles the following year. Hitler had now exacted his revenge.

Paris was saved from destruction when the French government declared it an *open city* meaning there would be no military resistance. But the Paris encountered by the victorious Germans was a shadow of its former self. Three quarters of the population had fled the city for the countryside. A foolish desperation in the hope some French territory might remain unoccupied.

Fraser and Marchand decided not to leave the city. At the onset of the German incursion into the Netherlands and Belgium, Marchand became consumed with selecting artworks at the Louvre for removal and hiding to protect them against anticipated Nazi looting if the Germans were to reach Paris. Art was at the soul of Paris. Its great collections would not be carted off to Germany. Fraser volunteered to chronicle each piece of art before being wrapped and boxed for transport to safe locations in the countryside. Such treasures as the *Mona Lisa* and the *Winged Victory of Samothrace* would survive the rapacious German looting by hiding in private homes, attics, and barns.

Those first months of the occupation became a wrenching upheaval for all Parisians. German bureaucratic efficiency quickly co-opted French institutions. Public order was duly discharged by a cooperative French police. Curfews imposed. While the Germans endeavored to show their benevolence toward the conquered French, Parisians were not seduced. The *Boche* were still despised.

The Germans had long been fascinated with the idea of Paris. As occupiers, duty assignments in the City of Light became treated as a holiday. Yet no matter their individual attempts to interact in congenial terms with the citizenry, most Parisians remained if not outright disdainful then at least aloof. As the years of occupation progressed with increased hardships, particularly food shortages, collaboration in various forms would become more widespread. But not in those early months.

On the surface, France had seemingly salvaged some sense of sovereignty. Having signed an armistice with Germany the new French government under Pétain controlled the central and southern areas of France. The north and the entire western coastline however remained under direct German occupation. The unoccupied territory was headquartered in the central spa-town of Vichy. While there were decided differences living in the two different zones, it was obvious that Vichy was nothing more than a puppet government to the Germans. It retained nominal civil authority throughout both zones. The Germans found it convenient to administer civil governmental functions through the French themselves. Vichy France became in every way a German colony.

Germany immediately started to bleed France dry. Thousands of trainloads of food and industrial goods began flowing east to support the German populace and the war effort. Punitive reparations were imposed on France much the same as those imposed on Germany in 1919. Over 300,000 French soldiers fell as casualties in the brief war. 1.8 million French soldiers remained prisoners of war. Ten percent of the entire male population.

For those in the Vichy unoccupied zone it soon became evident that this was not France as it was before 1940. Vichy was naturally going to be a right-wing creation. Any anti-German sentiments were immediately subjugated. While daily French life was initially less changed within Vichy controlled territory much of the population was repulsed by the collaboration with the German invader. Latent French anti-Semitism soon became pronounced.

Early stages of French resistance began in both the occupied as well as the unoccupied zones. From the onset, resistance was more hazardous in the German occupied zone. Not only a collaborating French police force, but the Nazi Gestapo along with German military intelligence, the *Abwehr* made for a true police state. No judicial processes. Everything subordinate to Nazi authority. Resistance was punishable by summary execution or deportation east to concentration camps.

Even though Fiona and Henri Marchand had family in southern France within the unoccupied zone, neither had any inclination to leave Paris. As a film producer, Henri's work was in Paris. Fiona had her work at the Louvre. As for Marc Fraser he would not leave his beloved Paris, nor Fiona. But all three soon realized that passive resistance to the *Boche* was not enough for them. Like so many other French, they sought a means of more active resistance.

Finding meaningful ways of subverting the occupying Germans was not that easy. Within six months of the occupation even moving around Paris was difficult. Gasoline was severely rationed to the extent that private auto traffic was almost nonexistent. Paris often seemed a ghost city. Nighttime was particularly barren after curfew. Blacked-out windows in case of Allied air raids rendered the city dormant at night.

All French life suffered extreme dislocation. Food shortages, radically transformed industries, restrictions on movements, and a pervasive depression of victimization. The makings for a restive colony.

The French film industry had been important before the war. It became even more so now to the collective psyche of the French as an outlet of escape. The Germans recognized this therefore allowed French filmmaking to continue, albeit within the bounds of censorship. A placated populous was more easily controlled. As with the Roman gladiatorial spectacles, moviegoing served much the same purpose.

With active German encouragement, the Vichy government created *comités d'organisation*, or CO's to govern various industries. One of the first created was the *Comité d'Organisation de l'Industrie Cinématograhique*, COIC. Technically a Vichy institution although headquartered in Paris. Henri Marchand immediately joined since he intended to continue his filmmaking.

☦

Together for a not very festive Christmas at Fraser's and Fiona's apartment, Henri Marchand said, "We must do something. Other people are. I know someone who knows someone. He says there's a group forming to do something more than just snubbing the *Boche* when we meet them on the street. They're talking about taking real action."

Fraser said, "Stay away from that, Henri. It's dangerous and cannot achieve anything. What can random acts of violence accomplish against hundreds of thousands of German soldiers?"

"But we must do something, Marc. Who is going to save France? Shall we always be an occupied territory of Germany? I for one would rather die resisting."

"Henri, we need to be cleverer. Marc?" Fiona said.

Fraser knew what she meant. "Ok, Henri. I understand how you feel. Fiona and I feel the same. But let's do something less foolhardy. I never told you about certain associations I had before I ventured into Spain. People in the spy business. One such person was an American diplomat. The other was an officer in the United States Army. A military attaché here at the U.S. Embassy in Paris. I told you that I secreted photos out of Spain clandestinely. I was shown how to reduce photographs so small they can easily be hidden. Arrangements were made to get it to the right people under the guise of innocent correspondence.

"What I didn't tell you was this military attaché officer contacted me before he left Paris for London ahead of the German occupation."

"What was that about?" Henri said.

"It was about spying, Henri. I intended to stay on in Paris. I'm also an American. Both the diplomat and the army officer think that the United States will eventually enter the war. Even if it doesn't the United States will never side with Nazi Germany. So they were setting up a means of communication that might be exploited at some future time. Others besides me I'm sure."

"Yes, I see. But communicating what, Marc? We know nothing of value that could help the British or the Americans. And for what good? The Germans will soon invade Britain. America is not even in the war."

The *Battle of Britain* was another source of despair for the French. The last bastion against Nazi Germany was itself now suffering continual bombing raids across the channel by Hermann Göring's Luftwaffe. Once Hitler seized control of the Continent, he turned his attention on Britain in July, 1940.

"True, but I'm suggesting maybe we should consider developing our resistance along those lines. Intelligence could be more damaging to the Germans than random acts of violence.

And I'm not sure Germany will invade Britain. But even if they do, the United States will then clearly become Germany's enemy. Anyway, it's far better than what you're contemplating, Henri."

"Henri. We have a more specific idea how to go about this," Fiona said. "You could be an important part of that plan, Henri. Marc, please explain."

"Henri I've also been contacted by my old friends from Spain. You recall my story of the harrowing escape I made with Loretta Elizalde and Rafael Solano. They saved my life. Unfortunately they now need my help."

"Ok. What is it you need me to do?"

"Get me accredited with COIC. I have the draft of the screenplay for *Provoke the Devil*. I'm a published novelist. Make up some lies of my past involvement with scripts, production, or whatever with movies in Hollywood. My father was an executive with MGM in Hollywood. With COIC credentials I can get a travel visa to go to Marseille under the pretext of scouting locations for filming *Provoke the Devil*."

"Ok. That should be easy enough. But what about your friends? What's their problem?"

"Their work with Spanish refugees. Loretta Elizalde works with a private organization. She's a troublemaker for Vichy. She wrote for a newspaper critical of the camps. Called them concentration camps just like in Germany. Newspaper was shut down when Vichy came to power. Dr. Solano treats the Spanish interned at these camps. Both are now in hiding wanted by the Gendarmerie. They've joined with one of these resistance groups you speak of, Henri. Call themselves *Libération-sud*."

"So how can you help, Marc?"

"That's where the idea struck me, Henri. Elizalde and Solano need new identification papers under false names. I know a fellow that can help. Same guy who taught me how to create micro-negatives to smuggle out material under the noses of the Nationalist rebels in Spain. Runs a sleazy photography shop in Montmartre. Sex stuff. The military attaché said he did other work. Forgeries. According to the military officer the guy does good work."

"A common criminal, Marc? Is that wise?"

"A risk to be sure. But anything we do carries a risk. Anyway, I went to see him yesterday. The attaché had forewarned him and of course he remembered me. So I arranged for new identities for my friends. French identifications, but he put born in Portugal so they could account for their Spanish-sounding accents. Clever fellow. Now I need the means to travel to the unoccupied zone. Working with COIC authorization should do that."

"I see. I'll get to work on it right away, Marc. It's good to be able to help out your old friends."

"But that's not the idea I meant, Henri. Think about it. If we can travel about France somewhat freely then we can gather intelligence of military value. Intelligence even provided by others. Those others are everyone from committed resistance operatives to the normal Frenchman. People willing to offer something to feel they too are resisting the invader.

"And of course I have the means to secret this information out. My attaché friend gave me even more. Seems the Americans had developed their own intelligence network in Paris. There is a certain diplomat of a neutral country. Married to a Jew. He is a committed enemy of the Nazis for their persecution of the Jews. He will transmit my information through diplomatic channels. It will even appear innocuous while concealing the secret material on the micro-negatives."

Henri beamed. "Why yes! That is wonderful. Count me in on your scheme, Marc. You agree I assume, Fiona?"

"Totally. To think our very soul, our art has to be hidden in God knows where. Obscure, unsafe places. No proper environment for priceless treasures. The *Boche* do not appreciate art, they just covet it. Thugs from a brutish culture. Germany produces no art. It's a land of crude appetites. War and bad cuisine. Load music. Ugly architecture. Led by a raving madman. Paris occupied by these pink-faced farm boys in hobnailed boots is like something from Dante's *Inferno*. We must resist. France cannot survive ruled by Nazi Germany."

Henri Marchand had never seen this impassioned side of his sister. What they were embarking upon was risky. Yet all three felt less frustrated with a purposeful course of action.

CHAPTER 31

The British created what was called the Special Operations Executive in July, 1940. The SOE was a highly secret organization created for the express purpose of infiltrating enemy occupied countries. Their mission was espionage, sabotage, and reconnaissance in occupied Europe. By 1941, the SOE was parachuting operatives into France to liaison with French resistance groups. Their principle means of communicating intelligence was by short-wave radio. This increasingly became a dangerous undertaking as the Germans developed countermeasures to locate clandestine transmitters.

Transmitting photographs obviously required other means of getting the intelligence to London. Fraser's method of reducing the photos to exceedingly small negatives hidden under postage stamps, conveyed out of France to neutral Portugal through diplomatic channels then forwarded to London became a valuable conduit for the SOE. A phony letter from Fraser's sister, actually from Allen Dulles in New York, acknowledged in code his participation of the arrangements set in place by Colonel Waite. No doubt Waite was working with the British.

Fraser was back in the espionage business.

Soon, packages of exposed film began arriving at Henri Marchand's office. They came by personal couriers hand delivered with no identified source. Fraser then worked with the photographer Ladislav Kovač to prepare the micro-negatives. With the help of Fiona, Fraser then drafted letters to his *sister* at Allen Dulles' address in New York.

The last leg of the espionage process was the hand-off to the Portuguese consular official. An affable man in his thirties with a pleasant wife. His wife was French and also Jewish. Fraser assumed this to be the basis for diplomat's support against the Nazis.

The cover of a personal friendship provided the excuse to meet socially where Fraser would give him the letters. The diplomat's wife knew only that the American writer and his companion were an interesting couple. The American appreciated the help in communicating with his family in the United States.

Fraser often worked late into the night with Kovač developing the espionage materials into the photographic reductions. He would have to stay the night in Kovač's apartment over the studio until the curfew lapsed the following morning. Typically they would relax together over a couple of drinks before trying to get a couple of hours sleep. Kovač had acquired a taste for Fraser's Scotch. A costly luxury item on the black market.

After several Scotches, one night, Kovač said, "You have never asked about me, Marc. Are you not curious?"

"You came highly recommended by Colonel Waite. That was enough. All I know is you're Hungarian. A first-rate forger. A photographer with the eye of an artist."

Kovač showed a rare smile. Maybe the alcohol. "Yes, I am Hungarian. I am also a Jew." Fraser looked startled. "Does that bother you?"

Fraser said, "Certainly not, Ladislav. But you know of course you are at risk."

"But of course. If you are a Jew that is always the case." Kovač paused. He was a private man. "My wife and I left Hungary in 1925 for Germany. Sounds like a ridiculous move in retrospect but at the time anti-Semitism was more virulent in Hungary. I was a photographer, my wife a teacher. We both spoke some German. So we had transportable skills.

"Germany seemed a better prospect. For years it was better. We settled in Nuremburg in the south. Unfortunately my wife died within a year. During childbirth. The child also stillborn.

"A difficult adjustment. I never remarried. But I had become modestly successful. My portraits sold well. A reputation for artistically expressing the subject someone once commented. But with the rise of Hitler's National Socialists I could see a dark future. Adolf Hitler left little speculation as to the fate of Jews if he ever came to power. So I sold my business in Nuremberg and came to France in 1933.

"Wish my business was higher class, but as I told you when we first met, sex pays better. Better than ever right now. German soldiers pay top price. They tell their colleagues about the photographer that speaks German and has the best naughty photographs for sale. No problem getting willing woman to pose during these difficult times. We're at the center of Paris' prostitution quarter. Business is all about location."

"Are you known to be Jewish by the police? They're already rounding up foreign Jews."

"I don't believe so. Just in case I have created a phony birth certificate. Roman Catholic. Signed by father-somebody I made up. Of course that's why I have that cross on the wall over there. Somewhere in my belongings is my *mother's* rosary as another prop."

"Hope that's good enough," Fraser said.

"We shall see. Maybe not. Perhaps if it was just the Germans to fool. But the French police are fully cooperating. Latent French anti-Semitism is coming out. Many are only too willing to collaborate with the German occupiers. In times of great stress the Jews always come under attack."

In addition to making micro-reductions of photographs, Kovač was also a master forger. A fine hand at duplicating any signature. Stolen or forged official seal stamps. A small hand-operated printing press. After supplying Elizalde and Solano with new papers, he kept busy with supplying Fraser with fake identifications for those active in the Resistance. Kovač had a confederate in the police department that supplied blank identity forms for a price.

If Kovač were to be arrested the authorities would also confiscate the business. The most effective source of false documents to the Resistance would be lost.

"What if I buy your business, Ladislav? We'll set up a darkroom somewhere. I can get you to the unoccupied zone. You'll have money. A new identity of your own making. You can continue to provide forged papers under safer circumstances. I'll see you get paid accordingly. You can still help the Resistance."

Kovač shook his head. "No. I shall not run anymore. If my fake ancestry doesn't work here than a new identity will eventually prove no better. Besides, the situation in the unoccupied zone is no better for Jews. Vichy is not only collaborating but has embraced German persecution of the Jews wholeheartedly. No, my friend, we shall play this game with the cards we have."

Fraser nodded his understanding. He poured another Scotch into Kovač's glass.

Kovač said, "If they should come at night I will hide in the secret space I showed you where I keep my forgery materials. I discovered the narrow room when I first rented this place. Not unusual in Paris I understand. Secret rooms and secret passages between apartment buildings. If I'm lucky, they'll leave without finding me. So if you come looking for me and I'm not in the shop or apartment, knock and announce yourself."

✝

Toward the end of the year, photographs, maps, and all manner of reconnaissance information was pouring into Fraser's operation. Henri Marchand managed the clearing house operation from Paris. Fraser travelled by train, frequently using the ploy of scouting potential filming locations using his COIC travel authorization. The script for *Provoke the Devil* set in Marseille served for two trips to Provence. Both times Fraser was able take Fiona to visit her parents in Aix.

The flow of intelligence increased after Germany invaded the Soviet Union in June, 1941. The first of Adolf Hitler's many strategic mistakes. This one was born of his arrogant megalomania. No surprise to Fraser. Fifteen years earlier in *Mein Kampf,* Hitler outlined Germany's destiny to conquer Russia. The French Resistance benefited with a massive influx of French Communists into the Resistance ranks now that Germany was a declared enemy of Moscow.

Fiona herself was active in their Resistance operation. When not preparing the innocuous correspondence to secret out the microfilm she was preparing sham reports on movie production locations. She also proved talented at altering other screenplays to adapt to locales targeted for Fraser to visit throughout France.

As intense as their dangerous game was, Fraser and Fiona Marchand became unreservedly in love. Not only a perfect intellectual match but their lovemaking was frequent and mutually satisfying. As with anything else Fiona Marchand attempted, she excelled at making Marc Fraser happy in bed. She equally adored Fraser's complete devotion to pleasing her own sexual desires. Whenever possible she wanted to accompany him on his trips. Each time left alone in Paris she suffered terribly wondering if he would safely return.

Fraser soon established contacts with leaders of various Resistance groups. Most were located in the Vichy governed unoccupied zone. His ability to travel from the German occupied zone into Vichy France provided a certain security similar to crossing any border even though Vichy was just a puppet state. Resistance groups based in Vichy France could operate with much greater freedom than the far more restrictive German occupied zone. Areas along the northern and western coastlines of France were rigorously controlled by the German Wehrmacht and forbidden to non-residents without a special pass. Intelligence from these areas was fed to Fraser by indirect means since even for him it was off limits.

Yet for military value the material coming out of the forbidden zone proved the most valuable. Whoever took these photos did so at great personal risk. Hardened artillery installations on the northern coast all the way from Calais to Normandy. Troop strengths. Unit designations. Airfields. Annotated maps. Photographed lists of German rail manifests.

Real resistance to German occupation carried dire consequences. Arrest and deportation to a German concentration camp meant an agonizing slow death. Only a very few participated in gathering real espionage while maintaining a normal life cover. Most French could only muster gestures of passive resistance. Overt armed resistance was futile unless one abandoned everything and took to rural areas to operate with guerrilla units.

Apart from the personal risks of conducting sabotage or assassination operations, those involved had to consider the cost of their actions. Resistance attacks within the occupied zone were followed with German reprisal executions. In Nantes, forty-eight were executed for the killing of the local German military commander. Fifty were shot in Bordeaux. In the final three months of 1941, a total of 193 hostages were executed in France. Before the end of the year, a seventeen year old was executed in Paris for giving out Communist leaflets.

At a holiday dinner late in 1941. Fiona's older brother Claude made a surprising announcement. "Henri has told me what you are doing. He thinks I have information that might prove useful."

Both Fraser and Fiona looked at each other. Neither was pleased that Henri had spoken to Claude about their espionage activities.

"You see Henri has some idea of what I do. Do you know of Frédéric Joliot-Curie?"

Both Fraser and Fiona shook their heads no.

"Nobel laureate in chemistry. Professor at the Collège de France. I work with him. We both work in the area of nuclear energy research. Before the occupation we shipped all of our working documents to England. They couldn't be allowed to fall in the hands of the Germans."

"What is the concern over this nuclear energy research?" Fraser asked.

Claude Marchand said, "Nuclear energy might be able to be used to create a super bomb. Something inconceivably devastating. An atomic bomb."

Fraser did not understand the implications. "Good that you got it out of France then."

"Well that's where I need your help. We discovered more documents. Let's say they are very sensitive. They must not fall into the hands of the Germans. They need to get to London or the United States. Henri says you can reduce them in size photographically. He says you have a means of smuggling such materials out of France?"

Fraser was aghast that Henri had divulged this kind of detail to his brother. "How many documents do you have?"

"Maybe a couple of hundred."

CHAPTER 32

The year 1941 concluded with a slight glimmer of future hope for a Europe suffering under the thumb of Nazi Germany. That ray of hope came in the form of a cataclysmic event. The attack on Pearl Harbor by the Japanese on the 7th of December brought the United States into the war. But only against Japan. Even though Germany and Japan had signed a military alliance pact, the United States declared war only on Japan. In another colossal blunder, Adolf Hitler chose to declare war on the United States on the 11th of December. For the German occupied European continent and beleaguered Britain it provided hope. Although helping with massive material aide to Britain before Pearl Harbor, the American public still held divided opinions on entering the European conflict. Hitler changed that.

The vast industrial might of the United States would now come to bear on the Axis powers. Some comfort to Fraser and Marchand that their efforts might be contributing to something larger. Perhaps well into the future, but one day the Germans would be driven out of France. Possible only with the United States directly weighing into the conflict.

Over lunch with his Portuguese diplomatic friend just before Christmas, Fraser received the rare reverse communication from Allen Dulles. Under the ruse as being from his sister it read,

Hope you can listen to some cheerful holiday music on the BBC on Christmas Eve. Think of it as a loving message from us in New York.

Huddled around a radio on this second Christmas Eve of the German occupation, Fraser, Fiona, and Henri Marchand listened for the personal messages broadcast nightly by the BBC. *Radio Londres* operated by the Free French over the BBC broadcast nightly in French. Before starting the actual broadcast, the announcer began with *personal messages.* These were a continuous string of meaningless short messages coded for SOE and Resistance operatives in France with meaning only known to the recipient. Eventually came, *Odysseus should return to Penelope's home on New Year's Day to receive visitors.*

All three understood the instruction. Fraser's code name was *Odysseus.* Reference to Odysseus' wife *Penelope* referred to Fiona. Fiona's home was Aix. *Fraser was to go to the Marchand family home in Aix on New Year's Day to meet someone.*

☦

The elder Marchands were elated at the unexpected visit of their pseudo son-in-law. They would like Fiona to marry Marc Fraser soon but they knew their daughter. At least she had finally found the right someone. They were also aware Henri, Fiona, and Marc were involved in resisting the Germans. So Marc's visit to Aix was probably not social.

Living in the unoccupied south left them little means of personally contributing to whatever their children were doing. Best they could do was to provide bundles of food to take back to Paris upon their rare visits. Rural France had a better food situation. Easier to hide food from the Vichy authorities tasked with shipping massive quantities of agricultural products to Germany.

Fraser celebrated a second Christmas with his adopted *mère et père* in their apartment on the grand boulevard Cours Mirabeau in Aix-en-Provence. Fiona remained in Paris. Difficult to fully relax wondering what he was about to get into.

On New Year's Day mid-morning the bell rang at the apart-ment building entrance. Madame Marchand answered the inter-com. "*Oui?*"

"Is this the residence of Monsieur Odysseus?"

"*Qui?*"

"*Maman,* it is for me. Let him in," Fraser said coming to the apartment door.

By the sound of the foot-falls it was one man ascending the stairs. Fraser opened the door before the man knocked. A short man in an overcoat with a fedora and a scarf around his neck. Handsome, dark hair, perhaps forty.

"I am Max. You are Odysseus?"

"Yes."

"May we leave now?" the man said.

Fraser was already packed assuming he might have to leave immediately. The man merely nodded to the Marchands stand-ing behind Fraser.

"*Soyez prudent mon fils,*" Madame Marchand said after kiss-ing Fraser. A tear ran down her cheek as her husband then em-braced him.

Outside Fraser and Max walked to the end of the wide tree-lined boulevard then took a narrow side street. The street was lined with tiny garages running behind apartment buildings. No people about. Few parked cars on the street with the severe gas-oline rationing.

Fraser would learn only much later that Max was Jean Mou-lin. A former lawyer and government administrator at the re-gional level. Imprisoned by the Germans after the invasion for refusing to sign a false statement of French colonial troop atroci-ties. Tortured, he failed in a suicide attempt to slit his throat with a piece of broken glass. Eventually released he was soon dis-missed from his post as the Prefect of Chartres by the Vichy gov-ernment because of his left-wing political background.

"I will tell you briefly why I am here," Moulin said. "For security reasons please do not talk in the car. The two armed *résistants* accompanying me know nothing of my mission.

"You know of General de Gaulle I assume?"

"Of course. From his BBC broadcasts."

"Yes. He has sent me back into France to organize the military activities of the various independent Resistance groups. One day we shall take back France. That means an invasion. An organized partisan Resistance within France will be invaluable. Until then the real damage to the Germans comes from intelligence gathering. Both efforts require a centralized control."

"And my role?" Fraser asked. How much did Moulin know of his work?

"Continue what you have been doing but on a larger scale. You already have contacts with several Resistance groups. They have passed along important information to you. Photographs that cannot be transmitted by wireless. Information you have cleverly secreted to London. You have access to false papers. You also have the ability to travel about more freely than most operatives because of your filmmaking credentials. I was impressed when told of your accomplishments."

Fraser did not like the idea of someone knowing that level of personal detail. Someone vulnerable in France. If captured, someone that would put Fraser at risk.

"What makes de Gaulle think that these groups will work together? They all have different politics."

"Ideally we hope that patriotism will rise above ideological differences. But pragmatically I am to convey the more tangible inducement of arms, explosives, radios, and most of all money. Money to operate, to buy food on the black market, to pay bribes."

"And how will that work?"

"Payment in kind for useful information. Payment for building an effective clandestine operating force. Payment for following the directives of a central authority by not engaging in reckless unauthorized action. That's where you can help."

"I'm not an organizer. Nor am I qualified to help manage a military effort."

"None of us are qualified. But this is war. However, it is not in that role that we seek your help. Simply put, you have become a first rate spy, Monsieur Odysseus. You will simply continue what you have already begun only now more formally organized rather than just conveying random intelligence that comes to you."

✝

A short distance ahead on a quiet street a black sedan stood idling evident by its exhaust. A waste of precious fuel but a precaution for a quick escape if needed. Beside the car stood two men smoking cigarettes. As Fraser and Moulin approached both men could be seen holding British Sten 9mm submachine guns partially concealed against their thighs. Such openness was possible only in Vichy France in a city with relaxed French police patrols.

Their destination was Marseille. Fraser sat in on what would become an historic meeting. Through Henri Marchand's contacts he had received intelligence from several groups operating in German occupied France. His only familiarity in the unoccupied Vichy south was with the group known as *Libération-sud*. It was one of the first to be created following the German occupation.

Fraser was familiar with *Libération-sud* through Loretta Elizalde. With the false identifications provided by Kovač, she and Rafael Solano had disappeared into the *Libération-sud* group. Elizalde wrote for the group's widely circulated underground newspaper *Libération*. Solano joined the private practice of another doctor involved with the Resistance.

Fraser said little at the meeting. Moulin simply explained Fraser's role as an important conduit to secret out photos, maps, and the like. The code name Odysseus was previously known to only one leader, Emmanuel d'Astier of *Libération-sud*, the former head of French naval intelligence.

Shaking Fraser's hand d'Astier said, "I have some associates that I believe your network assisted. I understand you have a history of intelligence work going back to Spain. Ingenious was how a certain woman phrased your secret work."

Moulin was persuasive but this audience was a hard sell. Apart from their political differences they had differing views on methods of fighting the Germans. Gathering intelligence for use by some future invading armies was too abstract. Beyond that, they were being asked to take orders from an obscure French general who had escaped to Britain. De Gaulle was virtually unknown until he became the voice of France on the nightly BBC broadcasts. A colonel only two weeks before France capitulated. Who put him in charge?

The session lasted into the early morning hours. Bleary eyed, Fraser and an exhausted Jean Moulin had coffee at a Marseille café. Not far away the black sedan idled at the curb.

"And how do you think that went, Monsieur Odysseus?"

"Poorly I'd say. These fellows don't think much of taking orders from London even if it's from a French general. Someone not risking their own life like they are. A leader they don't even know."

"Perhaps. But they will consider the larger picture. These are tough men. Committed men. Patriots with a common love of France. General de Gaulle would like to control things as a military organization. Separate operations from the politics. I told him it would not be that easy. I've been in government all my professional life. In government it's all about negotiation. But negotiation is not really about finding common ground. It is finding the point where both sides will give no further. In short, leverage is the coinage. I think we have the leverage. You can only wage war with weapons and money. These men know that."

Both the weapons and the money came from the U.S. and Britain. The money flowed through the Free French government in Britain, headed by default by General de Gaulle. Moulin was the conduit in France through which those limited funds were dispersed. His leverage on all Resistance activities country-wide was therefore significant.

"Hope you're right. But why was it necessary to bring me along?" Fraser said.

"To help bring these leaders here in the unoccupied zone together to establish a coordinated effort for all French Resistance groups. Introduce you as the conduit for passing information that cannot be transmitted by SOE wireless. Our next meeting will be in Paris where your activities are more familiar. Same message there for centralizing military action. We especially want more photographs of Channel coastal defenses."

Fraser liked none of this. The more people that knew his face the more dangerous. And of course the reverse. Up to now he was the recipient of intelligence information third or fourth hand. Now he would know the Resistance leaders.

"More dangerous in Paris. In Vichy France it is only French authorities. There it will be the Gestapo. Dangerous for both of us."

Moulin replied, "Neither of us should therefore be captured."

Less than a month after their Paris meeting with the Resistance leaders, Fraser received what even he knew was a bit of highly valuable military intelligence; detailed plans of the immense dry dock and submarine pens at Saint-Nazaire on the Atlantic coast of France. A brilliant piece of espionage infiltration. In March the fruits of that intelligence became evident.

An obsolete British destroyer rammed through the dry dock gates in *Operation Chariot*. British commandos assaulted the strategically important safe haven for heavy German warships operating in the Atlantic. The sacrificial ship contained explosives that detonated rendering the facility inoperable for the remainder of the war. The loss forced the German navy to avoid operations of their largest capital warships in the Atlantic west of the British Isles for fear of being stranded and vulnerable if damaged. Large raiders like the great Bismarck-class battleship *Tirpitz* were thereby prohibited from operating in the Atlantic and decimating merchant convoys from North America with their great speed and heavy guns.

In June came news that greatly excited Henri Marchand. "Marc, did you hear? That Nazi Reinhard Heydrich was assassinated in Prague. Czech partisans. I wish we could do something like that."

The death of the operational architect of Hitler's *Final Solution* to the Jewish problem was a shot in the arm to all resistance groups throughout Nazi occupied Europe. But with a heavy cost in innocent lives. A week later came news of Hitler's reprisals for the death of one of his favorites. All the inhabitants of the Czech towns of Lidice and Ležáky were either executed or sent to Nazi extermination camps.

"See what I mean, Henri. Such a terrible price for an act that will change nothing. Heydrich will simply be replaced with another monster. What we're doing is laying the foundation for liberation one day. Stay the course, Henri."

Fraser and his small intelligence network consisting of Henri and Fiona Marchand and Ladislav Kovač settled into a busy routine. All had day jobs with the rest of their waking hours consumed with Resistance activities. The sense of doing meaningful work damaging to the Germans lightened the weight of danger. If arrested in Paris for these activities their fate was summary execution.

While Germany still controlled Western Europe the strategic situation became much different by the summer of 1942. During the prior winter the Soviets had stopped the German advance on the doorstep of Moscow. The United States had entered the war on the side of the British and the Commonwealth nations. By extension that now included the Soviet Union. Reluctantly for the Allies, the *enemy of my enemy* now became an ally.

U.S. industrial war output ratcheted upward to unimaginable levels. Vast quantities of military goods poured into Britain and the Soviet Union. For Germany stretched in all directions the situation was becoming untenable. Occupation of France, The Netherlands, Belgium, and Norway, the massive offensive against the Soviet Union faltering, while militarily supporting their unreliable Italian partner in North Africa, combined to define the limits of Nazi Germany's resources. With the failed air campaign, any invasion plans for Britain were long since abandoned.

Nazi Germany was no longer on the offensive.

CHAPTER 33

But this was still a war with no end in sight. An insidious war with an occupier that imposed deranged racial and social policies on their conquered civilian populations. Accused of spying meant immediate execution. But under Adolf Hitler's Nazi psychotic policies a host of other circumstances could also lead to a quick death, or a slow death of imprisonment under barbaric conditions.

Fraser's family on his mother's side had fled Paris in May of 1940 soon after Germany attacked France. After the first few weeks it was obvious that the French and British forces might suffer defeat.

Phillipa and Émile Bernheim did not however heed Fraser's warning to leave France.

Arrests of Jews in France started in 1941. Mostly foreign Jews in the beginning. These early detainees were held in the Drancy internment camp outside Paris run by collaborative French authorities. It soon became a hellish place of over-crowding, starvation rations, and terrible hygienic conditions. Yet the plight of the detainees became even worse when in March of 1942 the first deportations began to the German concentration camp Auschwitz, Nazi Germany. Auschwitz was actually a network of concentration labor camps along with an extermination facility.

Drancy and other French camps then became the marshalling sites for this conduit of death.

Before long the Bernheims had all their art confiscated. Evicted from their elegant apartment in the 1ˢᵗ Arrondissement they temporarily resided in a small apartment on the Left Bank secured by Fraser. Forced to wear the yellow Star of David on their clothing it was only a matter of time before they too would be arrested.

Only their money allowed them to avoid arrest and deportation to a German concentration camp through bribery. But not indefinitely. With the help of Ladislav Kovač's forged documents the Bernheims narrowly escaped to unoccupied Vichy France with papers as non-Jews with forged Vichy visas. Wealthy Parisians visiting their daughter in Lyon. Loretta Elizalde looked after them upon their arrival in Lyon before continuing escape to Switzerland just before that border was closed.

Within weeks of the Bernheims' escape real disaster struck. Arriving back in Paris from a short trip, Fraser was greeted by a distraught Fiona.

"Thank god you're home, Marc. Henri's been arrested," Fiona said. She was composed but her reddened eyes suggested deep distress. She began crying again as they embraced.

Fraser immediately wondered if they were all now in imminent danger. Should he invoke their escape plan? They had a full set of false papers, plenty of cash, pre-packed suitcases.

"What happened, Fiona? Do we need to leave?"

Knowing what Fraser was thinking, she quickly said, "No, Marc. It's not about what we've been doing. It's what Henri's been doing. All his life."

"You mean because he's homosexual? That's why he was arrested?"

While homophobia was institutionalized in Nazi Germany, in occupied France it had not yet translated into a campaign of eradication as was the case with Jews.

"Not that simple perhaps. I learned about it from a friend of his who came to the Louvre to tell me what happened. Henri was at a well-known gay café in Montmartre. More than a café. The rooms upstairs served for sexual encounters.

"Yesterday, the French police began a massive sweep to arrest Jews. It's still going on. Did you not notice the flurry of lorries and police cars on the streets when you walked from the train station?"

"Not really. I came into Gare Montparnasse. Walked the back streets."

"Well they're arresting every Jew they can identify."

"But what's that have to do with Henri?"

"Because he was caught in a compromising situation with a Jew. Seems there were many Jews there at the time. So Henri was swept up with the others. Maybe they think he is a Jew. But being a homosexual caught in the act might be enough to get him deported to a German concentration camp. What can we do, Marc?"

"I'll see if I can find out anything."

Fraser left the apartment catching the metro north to the Montmartre district. He'd first contact the photographer Ladislav Kovač. Since his shop was in Montmartre he might have an idea where Henri Marchand might have been taken.

As he walked up to the shop his heart sank. Across the door in white paint was written *"Juif"*, Jew in French. The door was open. Inside were two gendarmes. They were ogling Kovač's provocative photos.

"Who are you?" one asked Fraser.

"A customer. What happened here? I know the proprietor. He's no Jew."

"Papers."

After examining Frasers identity card one gendarme said, "He was a Jew in hiding. A foreign Jew. A filthy Slav Jew with that name. He did not wear the yellow Star of David as required. Tried to pass as Catholic."

"And how do you know he was not a Catholic?" Fraser said in a sharp tone.

"Perhaps you are a Jew too," the other gendarme said with a tone of menace.

Disgust at French collaboration with the Germans, Fraser was not intimidated by these French cops.

The first gendarme said, "Others on the street all knew him to be a Jew. He showed us this birth certificate. Fake of course. How can it be checked? Some impossible place to pronounce in Hungary. Besides, he looked like a Jew."

"Where would he have been taken?" Fraser said.

"The Vélodrome d'Hiver."

The massive roundup of the July 16-17, 1942 became known as the Vel' d'Hiv Roundup. The Vélodrome d'Hiver was a bicycle racing venue stadium where most of the arrestees were temporarily confined. Over 13,000 people sealed inside in the summer heat. Little food and water. Only five lavatories. As bad as the physical conditions were at the Vélodrome it was only the beginning of a worse ordeal for those imprisoned.

Five days later they were transported to French internment camps outside of Paris. From those camps followed the horror of being sealed for days in rail cars without food or water as the trains made their way east to concentration camps in Germany.

There had been previous roundups in Paris but nothing approaching this scale. More dispiriting, it was being conducted by French authorities. Even if acting on German orders this level of collaboration went far beyond just getting along with the occupier. A disturbing realization to most French that some of their countrymen would sink to such debasing servitude. This was the reality of living under German occupation.

A devastating personal blow to Fraser. Henri Marchand was his best friend. Equivalent to a brother-in-law, more like a brother. Now he was lost into the Nazi bureaucratic web of institutionalized depravity. Where to go for help? The French gendarmerie? Not likely since they conducted the arrests.

As for Ladislav Kovač there could be little hope for his rescue. There was also no way to know if Kovač's secret room was discovered. Doubtful from the way gendarmes reacted. Fraser realized he could have walked into a trap. Eventually Kovač's secrets would be discovered by someone after taking over the shop. If it was, Kovač was then certainly doomed. Probably was anyway. Gone was Fraser's ability to produce incontestable false identity papers.

It was a fruitless endeavor all afternoon after visiting several police stations. The Vélodrome d'Hiver was sealed like a prison. No published list of detainees. No place to even make an inquiry. He returned to the apartment just before curfew dreading having to face Fiona.

Fraser tried seeking help from the COIC, the official film industry organization. Henri Marchand was a respected film producer and Fraser thought well liked in the tight-knit movie industry. But prejudice can overshadow all else.

One member of the governing board of the COIC told Fraser, "Of course you know Henri was a homosexual. Indiscrete. Engaged in his perverted sex in some seedy backroom with a Jew no less. Perhaps tolerated before the occupation but he should have known German views on degeneracy."

Fraser wanted to kick the shit out of the guy. German views? It was the French who arrested Henri. French collaboration just like this asshole working for Vichy bureaucracy. But he needed his connection with the COIC to facilitate his travels so he said nothing.

Fraser and Fiona exhausted all possibilities. But they were unable even to find evidence of Henri's arrest much less where he was being held. Fraser assumed the Drancy internment camp, a northeastern suburb of Paris since the Vélodrome d'Hiver was just the initial collection point. At Drancy, without any official status, Fraser was rudely refused any information. Unfortunately he knew that Drancy was itself just another transit point to a final destination far to the east in Germany.

Fraser and Fiona Marchand eventually reconciled to the terrible knowledge that his friend and her brother had disappeared forever into the depths of the German concentration camp system. The fate of Henri Marchand and Ladislav Kovač was likely death. An unpleasant death.

✝

In November, 1942 there came the first evidence that Hitler's domination of Europe was under threat. A joint American and British force landed in French controlled Morocco and Algeria in North Africa. It was not unopposed as hoped. 125,000 defending French forces under Vichy government control attempted a defense. Overwhelmed by the Allied forces, fighting lasted only a few days before the Allied high command made a deal with Vichy to cease hostilities. Effectively the Vichy French forces removed themselves from the war. The deal allowed Allied forces to move eastward toward Tunisia without having to first subdue the French forces in their rear.

For French citizens it was an incomprehensible tangle of circumstances. Where did Vichy France stand? Who was the enemy? The picture became clearer when Hitler immediately ordered German forces into the Vichy controlled zone within days of the Allied North African landings. The Germans had little choice since they were now exposed from the south of France. Vichy was allowed to remain in existence but was reduced to administration functions. France was now entirely occupied by German forces with Italian forces occupying a small area along the southeastern border.

For those in former unoccupied Vichy France the less oppressive circumstances compared with the German occupied north came to an end. The better access to food came under increased threat with more shipments going to Germany. More crippling were requirements for conscripted labor for German industry.

To enforce all this along with German anti-Semitic racial policies of genocide against Jews, and to combat growing armed guerrilla resistance, a vicious Vichy right-wing paramilitary organization was created in January, 1943. The hated *Malice française* cooperated closely with the Nazi Gestapo.

Ranks of the Resistance increased with young Frenchmen fleeing German conscription. These armed *résistants* took the name of the *Maquis* from the mountainous Corsican scrubland since they hid in the rugged highlands of central and southern France.

German domination of Europe continued to erode. Not only were they defending on multiple fronts, Hitler's risky venture against the Soviet Union had utterly failed. Entrapped around Stalingrad, the beleaguered German Sixth Army surrendered. The Eastern Front was collapsing in a forced German retreat. Allied forces were pressing German and Italian forces in North Africa. From England the American 8th Air Force began daylight bombing raids on German cities to augment nighttime bombing by the British. German cities were suffered unrelenting terror round the clock. German civilian casualties mounted.

For those like Fraser and Fiona Marchand such news gave their own efforts renewed meaning. Eventually the Allies would take back France by military force. Intelligence would prove essential.

Henri Marchand's unknown fate however dampened that year's Christmas. Fortunately Fraser and Fiona were able to spend the holidays in Aix with Fiona's parents. But her brother Claude was not allowed to travel out of Paris. Identified as an important scientist he was required to periodically report his whereabouts to Paris police. Even the joy of seeing Claude's children was denied.

Fraser and Fiona kept busy processing intelligence gathered by Resistance groups throughout France. The Portuguese diplomat remained a solid courier conduit. Fraser set up a darkroom in a spare room of the apartment. Along with the developing paraphernalia he had constructed a fixed set-up for making his micro-negatives patterned after Ladislav Kovač's Paris studio backroom. Fiona became a skilled assistant.

After introductions through the meetings with Jean Moulin the flow of intelligence to Fraser increased. Remarkable how some of it must have been acquired. Hundreds of French men and woman risked certain death if discovered. Fraser knew that the French Resistance never did unite under control from de Gaulle's Free French government in Britain. However all the groups apparently understood that feeding intelligence was the means of sustaining their resistance through reciprocation in money and weapons.

Would any of this make a difference? Regardless, it was the best means of fighting the hated *Boche*.

Life under German occupation could never be said to have any sense of normality. Food shortages worsened. Everyone was always hungry. Even for someone with money like Fraser, the black market offered only meager relief if you lived in Paris. Fraser purchased scarce food items in his travels to rural areas where things were somewhat better.

Committing acts of espionage made for a life continually obsessed with lies to maintain one's *legend* in tradecraft-speak. The constant anxiety only served to bind Marc Fraser and Fiona Marchand closer in their love.

Lovemaking was the one pleasure the Germans couldn't steal. Fiona Marchand was an uninhibited lover. Having discovered the love of her life she relished their lovemaking with abandon. With Fiona, sexual fulfilment for Marc Fraser went beyond anything ever experienced with another woman. Perhaps their lovemaking was the singular thing that allowed them to emotionally survive this climate of unrelenting fear.

CHAPTER 34

In 1943, Nikolaus "Klaus" Barbie was only thirty years old. The short handsome young man was dashing in his SS uniform. With the German occupation of Vichy France, SS-Hauptsturm-führer Barbie had come to Lyon, France from assignment in Amsterdam. He was a trained investigator and interrogator. Interrogation was a SS euphemism for torture. Barbie learned well.

In Amsterdam Barbie rounded up Jews for deportation to German extermination camps. Tricking the leaders of the Jewish Council in Amsterdam to provide names of 300 young men, Barbie arrested all of them. He then paraded the leaders past the young men before supervising their execution. All 300 hundred were deported to Mauthausen concentration camp. All died before the end of the year.

Barbie was with the security service of the SS, the *Sicherheitsdienst*, or SD. Because of his zeal in Amsterdam, he became the newly appointed head of the Secret State Police section of the SD, the *Geheime Staatspolizei, or* Gestapo for Lyon in late 1942. The regimented Germans had a never ending list of interlocking security organizational units. Within occupied France the most feared organization was the Gestapo.

German occupation of the former Vichy France sent shock waves through the Resistance. Along with the creation of a new French paramilitary Fascist police force the Malice, there was

now the additional threat of the Nazi Gestapo. With their unchecked powers, no one was safe.

The ranks of the Gestapo contained SS officers as well as detective ranks and lower level operatives. Often dressed in civilian clothes they had unrestrained police powers. The Gestapo
could commit murder, torture, or condemn its victims to concentration or extermination camps. They were not police but rather
an instrument of terror. Terror directed at any threat to Nazi
authority.

Adolf Eichmann headed the Gestapo Office of Jewish Affairs
responsible for the extermination of Europe's Jews. As a field-
level Gestapo official Klaus Barbie was charged with not only
rounding up Jews but actively looking to arrest members of the
French Resistance. Where Eichmann was a desk-bound bureau-
crat, Barbie was a field operative. Cunning and clever, he was
fond of getting his hands dirty in his work.

As with most sadists it is rarely clear what may have con-
tributed to a human being descending into depravity. Whether
from a flaw of genetics or a combination of factors, war provides
endless opportunities for sadism to flourish. All the more so
within the perverse ideology of the ranks of the Nazi SS.

As head of the Gestapo in Lyon, Barbie reported to the regional head of the SD. His superior had served on the Eastern
Front in the Ukraine where he was responsible for countless
murders of Jews, gypsies, and Communists. Equally without any
regard for human life, he gave Barbie free rein to exercise his
sadistic tendencies.

Barbie's background was unremarkable. No different than
thousands of other German men coming to adulthood in the
turbulent 1930s. Yet later accounts from survivors and witnesses
of Barbie personally inflicting torture on prisoners defy comprehension.

A thirteen year old Holocaust survivor recalled a man
dressed in a gray suit holding a kitten. *"He was caressing the cat.
And me a kid of thirteen years old could not imagine he could be evil
because he loved animals. I was tortured by him for eight days."* She

was then sent to a German concentration camp along with her family.

A woman arrested while carrying a letter addressed to a low ranking Resistance operative was brought before Barbie. Asked to reveal the identity of the code name of the addressee the woman pretended not to understand. Four guards hung her from by her wrists from the ceiling using hand cuffs with spikes inside. She was beaten with a rubber truncheon. The following day she was stripped naked and forced into a tub of freezing water. With her legs tied to a bar placed across the tub, Barbie pulled a chain hoisting her legs and pulling her head under water. Barbie experimented with combining various forms of inflicting torment, in this case, humiliation, hypothermia, and simulated drowning. This went on for nineteen days.

On the final day of her ordeal, the woman was tied stomach-down across a chair. A guard beat on her back with a spiked ball breaking several vertebrae. Returned to consciousness the woman heard piano strains of Chopin being played by a young girl. Barbie stroked the victim's hand.

Another survivor recalled, "*Klaus Barbie had the eyes of a monster. He was savage. My God he was savage! It was unimaginable. He broke my teeth, he pulled my hair back. He put a bottle in my mouth and pushed it until the lips split from the pressure.*"

The daughter of a French Resistance leader based in Lyon recounted her father's torture by Barbie. After severely being beaten, skin was flayed from parts of his body and his head put in a bucket of ammonia. The man died soon after.

Although particularly creative in his methods of inflicting pain, Klaus Barbie was only one of thousands of such depraved sadists unleashed by Nazism. Central to Nazi institutionalized cruelty was a view that their victims were less than human. Nazi policies placing the Aryan ideal at the top of the racial hierarchy rendered anyone below irrelevant. Wherever sadism lurked within the species it was given unrestricted opportunity to flourish under Hitler's National Socialism regime.

All of France was now dangerous for anyone actively engaged in Resistance activities. None more dangerous however than in France's second largest city Lyon with Klaus Barbie as its Gestapo chief. He quickly earned the label of *the Butcher of Lyon*.

✝

Loretta Elizalde and Rafael Solano had made a life for themselves in Lyon under new false identities. Elizalde was the more active with her writing for the underground newspaper *Liberation*. She was also active in a good deal of daily Resistance activities such as procuring food, passing information, and sheltering operatives. But her principle role was active involvement in the *Bureau d'Information et de Presse,* the Press and Information Service of the Resistance.

Rafael Solano and his physician partner treated members of the Resistance but mostly cared for a suffering population. Food shortages led to increased medical problems such as tuberculosis. With everything in short supply including drugs, practicing medicine was a constant challenge of ingenuity. He supported Elizalde's efforts but remained primarily devoted to his medicine as his best means of contribution.

The *Bureau d'Information et de Presse* was Moulin's creation to act as a clearing house for intelligence materials from the various Resistance groups. Elizalde's job was to arrange materials for transport out of France by various routing methods. One such method was to courier materials to a contact in Paris known by the code name *Odysseus*. After being told *Odysseus* was able to smuggle out material cleverly reduced photographically to an exceedingly small size, she knew *Odysseus, or Odiseo* in Spanish, was her friend and benefactor Marc Fraser.

A telephone call was placed to a film production office using a prearranged code to signal the method of delivering the materials. Loretta Elizalde typically made the call. The cover was elaborate. Using the disguise of the call originating from a film stock distributor in Lyon she would call Henri Marchand personally at his production company in Paris. Film stock was hard to obtain during the occupation so a call directly to the film studio would not raise suspicions to any police monitoring telephone calls.

For security, Fraser knew nothing of the networking arrangements that funneled intelligence to him. He would simply get a note passed to him. Innocuous looking numbers written on a newspaper or a check at a café. The code indicated the time and location for one of two dead-drops in Paris. It also included a security code to authenticate the message. Not perfect if the courier had been coerced by the Gestapo but it added some security. Both drop locations were churches on the Left Bank; Saint-Germain-des-Pres and Saint-Sulpice. The drop consisted of a concealed cylinder fixed with a strong magnet that adhered to a metal support bracket underneath a designated pew.

Unknown to Fraser, the conduit was severed with the disappearance of Henri Marchand. Against security protocol Elizalde placed a telephone call directly to her old friend Marc Fraser using her false name. She was hoping that Fraser might be involved with the photographic reductions to smuggle materials out of the country.

"My name is Madame Romão with Produits Cinématographiques in Lyon. I have been trying to reach Monsieur Marchand unsuccessfully. I believe you are an associate of Monsieur Marchand?"

Fraser knew Romão was the false identity of Loretta Elizalde. What the hell was she doing calling him? This was dangerous. Had her organization not gotten the word that Henri Marchand had been arrested? She should not even know about Fraser's involvement in Resistance activities.

"Actually a personal friend. Unfortunately Henri Marchand has disappeared. I fear something must have happened to him. It has been over a week now."

"I see. Monsieur Marchand was most concerned about an important order placed with us. Might you suggest another person at his office that I might communicate with?"

"I shall contact someone at the studio's office right away. How should they contact you?"

She gave him a telephone number. "Thank you, Monsieur. That is most kind."

Fraser related the call from Elizalde to Fiona Marchand.

"Seems Henri was deeper into this than we thought," Fiona said. "He never let on that he was the one directly receiving the intelligence that routed to you."

Fraser smiled. "He was observing security. Of course I never divulged my part or how I received the stuff. To think Henri may have even architected the protocol to maintain the cut-out to protect me. Good for Henri."

Both Fraser and Fiona teared up at the thought of his friend and her brother. Whatever happened to him? Both knew Henri was not coming back.

Fiona said, "We need to reestablish what Henri had constructed. I will take his place."

"What are you talking about? I don't want you involved. It's too dangerous. You don't know Henri's network."

She just looked at him sternly with those piercing eyes. "Don't act like the typical male protector, my love. I can take care of myself. If you take these risks why should I not be right at your side doing my part?"

"We know nothing of Henri's network," Fraser said.

"We at least know Loretta Elizalde is involved," Marchand said.

"But you're not even involved with the studio, Fiona. That is essential to maintaining the legend that the communications with Lyon are legitimate business involving film stock purchases. The studio actually does business with Produits Cinématographiques. I know the name from talking with Henri about the problem of getting film stock. Elizalde's group must have someone inside the company to take any inbound calls as a cover. But I know nothing of the operation. I'm only the final leg of the pipeline."

"Then we'll construct our own network. It's easy, Marc. I shall make my presence known at the studio as Henri's sister. After all he is still the principle stockholder of the studio. I shall announce that I am overseeing my brother's affairs until he returns."

Both knew that Henri was never returning. Fraser also knew that nobody at the studio would probably challenge Fiona's authority.

"Therefore, I shall become the new point of contact starting with your friend Loretta Elizalde."

"But we don't know who was working with Henri. How did the materials get to the dead-drops? In fact who actually received the materials? Henri himself?"

"Well we certainly cannot go about inquiring. Perhaps someone might approach me if I am seen to be involved in my brother's affairs. If possible, I will replace Henri. At least I can start with Elizalde's organization."

"Fiona, please. Bad enough that you're involved by just being with me. It's too dangerous to attempt what you're suggesting. How will you know you're not getting involved with a collaborator?"

"Isn't that what you risk every time you pick up something from those church pews? Listen, Marc, we all must take risks. The alternative is to do nothing? Wait till we might be rescued by the Americans? When might that be? Perhaps never. But even then what do we say that we did to help ourselves?"

"I don't like it, Fiona."

"Neither do I but it's necessary. We may be the only way to secret out certain important information."

Fraser thought the matter dropped with Fiona investing her available time with integrating herself into the workings of Henri's film studio. They agreed to wait and see if Fiona was approached to replace Henri then decide what to do next. But two weeks later she announced, "We can't wait for something to just happen, Marc. So I've given a lot of thought for establishing a new connection at least for the Lyon source. The materials will come directly to me at the Louvre."

"What? You can't do that, Fiona. At least Henri used cut-outs to get the materials to me. My guess is he also didn't take direct delivery of the materials. "

Marchand said, "Listen to me. The materials come from Lyon in unmarked envelopes. They will be hand delivered to an older man I know in the receiving department. I got to know him when we moved out the artwork into hiding before the occupation. He likes me and he virulently hates the Germans."

"That's a terrible plan, Fiona."

"No it isn't. Listen to the rest." She was not to be put off. "The old man will receive the material in an unmarked sealed envelope. He will address it to me and add a different return address each time. Those addresses are of actual people known in the art world, known to me."

"Why bother with all that if it always comes to your guy?"

"I don't want him repeatedly delivering envelopes to me personally. And I certainly don't trust everyone at the museum. The deliveries need to appear as normal museum business.

"Even frequent deliveries to my friend at the museum might become suspicious. So the deliveries will happen away from the museum. To a specific café in the Marais district. My friend always takes a glass of wine there after work each day. Your friend in Lyon sends a courier. They find my friend who is easily described. They ask, *So hard to get a good glass of wine these days. Is this a good place?* My friend's response, *Passible. The proprietor is an old friend. Please join me.*

"The courier sits down with my friend and orders wine. The envelope is passed under the table."

Fraser shook his head displaying a sardonic grin.

"Don't be patronizing," she says. "Here's the best touch. My guy also adds postage along with the post's cancellation stamp. The package on my desk looks legitimate. Even has the German censor's stamp."

"How does he accomplish that?"

"It was his idea. His son works at the post office. Stole a cancelled-postage stamp along with one of the Gestapo censor stamps. The Germans have an office at the main post office.

"Once the envelope comes to my office everything looks like ordinary posted correspondence."

"So you've already discussed this with your guy?"

"Not everything of course. Certainly not what's in the envelopes. I told him it concerns our hiding of the Louvre's artwork. The continual moving to new hiding places, preservation, that sort of thing. And by the way his name is Louis. A darling old man that wants to do his part. His son was in the army, killed in 1940, if you're wondering about his motivation."

Creative, but Fraser still didn't like it. Fiona was now terribly exposed. At least it was always to be the same courier at this end. But lying in open sight on a desk? If the envelope were to be opened for any reason it would instantly be recognized as espionage material.

Concerned about Fiona's direct involvement, Fraser reluctantly journeyed to Lyon to set up the procedure. At least it was a chance to meet his old friends Loretta Elizalde and Rafael Solano for the first time since providing them with new identities. He was brightened by their mutual devotion and their shared determination to resist. The three of them celebrated an emotional reunion.

✝

For all those in Resistance movements throughout German occupied Europe, spirits were buoyed as Germany continued to suffer military setbacks. The war had clearly reached a turning point.

The German and Italian Afrika Axis Korps surrendered in North Africa in May, 1943. The Allies captured over 250,000 prisoners. The Allied invasion of Sicily commenced in July. By August, German forces had suffered defeat in the six-week long gigantic tank Battle of Kursk in Russia against numerically superior Soviet forces. Mussolini was removed from power in Italy. To shore up their southern flank, Germany was then forced to commit large numbers of German forces into Italy. In September, U.S. forces landed on the Italian mainland south of Naples at Salerno while the British landed at Taranto in the Italian boot heel.

The end of the war was not yet near but one could now conceive of an end. Even eventual defeat of Nazi Germany.

✝

The new arrangement constructed by Fiona worked well for several months. With Elizalde's apparent connection with someone high up in the newly former *Conseil National de la Résistance,* intelligence flowed through Lyon from all over southern France. Loretta Elizalde and Fiona Marchand became friendly with their periodic telephone conversations even though they talked in coded language.

"I like Loretta Elizalde. Is she pretty?" Fiona asked Fraser.

He looked at her and smiled, "I guess."

"You *guess*? That sounds evasive. Were you lovers?"

Fraser shook his head no. "No, certainly not lovers. Actually just met her twice while in Spain. The first time I arrived and when we escaped together. But I never told you everything.

"I did escape Spain with Loretta and her fiancé, now her husband, Dr. Rafael Solano as I told you. We were all in danger from the Nationalist rebel forces that had just captured Santander on the northern coast of Spain. What I left out were the uglier details. Both Loretta and Rafael saved my life.

"I was engaged in spying even back then. Smuggling out photographs that the Nationalists didn't want published. Loretta had been arrested as a radical loyalist journalist just before I arrived with the rebels. Photos only I could have taken were found in her possession. She was tortured but didn't give me away. However, micro-negatives were eventually discovered in my possession."

Marchand looked on with a stricken expression. "Were you tortured too, Marc?"

"Yes. Tied to a chair and severely beaten. So was Loretta. We would have been shot except I had a letter from Generalissimo

Franco personally authorizing my being imbedded with the Nationalist forces. They couldn't read the text on the micro-negatives without a microscope. My guess is they probably wanted to clear my execution first with Franco's headquarters after they had clear evidence of my spying. Bought us a few hours.

"After being beaten, Loretta and I were dumped into a wine cellar. We knew we had little time before being subjected to further torture. Probably something far worse. Certain execution after that. Franco certainly had no reason to save me. Loretta was obviously a known enemy since the Nationalists were intent on cleansing Spain of all left-leaning elements."

"So get to how you escaped, Marc. This is like the stuff in your novel."

Fraser turned inward a moment before proceeding.

"The details I've never talked about. Disturbing things necessary for survival. Both us were in very bad shape from the beatings. Loretta's fingers on one hand had all been broken under torture. I could barely stand because of blows to head and my abdomen. Wasn't sure of the extent of my injuries. One eye was swollen closed. Both of us knew we were going to be executed. We had only one chance for escape. Let me show you something first."

He went to the bedroom returning with his ankle sheath housing the switchblade. Handing it to her she took it warily.

"Take it out. Watch your hand then press the button to spring open the blade."

As the five-inch blade flicked open she jumped slightly. "Oh my God! What is this thing?"

"It's called a switchblade. Sharp enough to shave by. Took it off a thug back in Los Angeles that wanted to stick it into me. Broke the bastard's nose. Took his knife."

"That was in your novel. So that really happened?"

"Yes."

"I fear you're going to tell me something terrible happened with this."

She handed the knife back to him. He folded it and slipped it into his pocket.

"More than terrible. That's why I never told you. When you're about to die you'll do anything. Even stick a knife into a man's neck and watch him bleed to death."

Fiona put her hand to her mouth. "Oh, no."

"Loretta called to the guards. Two of them entered both holding rifles with mounted bayonets. Lying on the floor I faked distress as if maybe dying. As the soldier bent down I rammed the knife into his neck. The other soldier then lunged the bayonet toward me. I jumped backward but the bayonet still caught me. Loretta smashed a wine bottle over the head of the guard."

"You were stabbed? That's the scar on your abdomen?"

"Yes. Painful as all hell. Found out later the bayonet hit a rib. That prevented worse damage but I was still severely wounded. Bleeding badly. Now I really couldn't stand without Loretta's help."

"But obviously you escaped."

He nodded. "But I'll tell you the worst. I still get occasional nightmares replaying the scene. You see we could not leave the unconscious guard to sound the alarm if he recovered too soon. So I had to make sure he didn't recover. I stuck the knife into his neck as well."

Fiona was frozen with the mental image. She swallowed hard. He had scared the hell out of her. Never could she image this kind of violence.

"Loretta struggled to get me out of the cellar. She hid me in a sailboat since we were close to the marina. She somehow made her way through darkened alleys to the apartment of her fiancé, Rafael Solano. Remember, she was also badly beaten and in terrific pain.

"Rafael Solano was responsible for our escape. He's a skilled doctor and fortunately an accomplished sailor. Snuck us out of Santander harbor on a sailboat in the dark. Two days later we arrived on the French coast. Loretta Elizalde and Rafael Solano risked their lives to rescue me."

✝

Toward the end of June, 1943, Fiona Marchand received a cryptic call from Loretta Elizalde. *We have experienced some major production problems. We cannot fulfill your outstanding orders for some time. Unfortunately the matter is serious. The delays may be indefinite. So sorry.* That was the last communication they received from Lyon until September.

✝

"Monsieur Fraser, perhaps you recall me? This is Dr. Solano in Lyon. I treated that injury to your rib some years ago. Hope everything is well with you," Rafael Solano said using his real identity but still using guarded language.

Finally something. From indirect sources Fraser and Fiona heard about a major Gestapo raid in Lyon. No details were known but it might mean that Elizalde's and Solano's Resistance operations had been compromised.

Rafael Solano would not be calling now except out of desperation because Loretta could not. And using his real identity? Had his new identity become compromised?

"Of course, Doctor. Yes I am in good health. How can I be of service?"

"Another patient of mine has been hospitalized. A Madame Elizalde. I assumed you might be acquainted? She listed you as someone to contact in case of emergency. Regrettably she is in critical condition."

Loretta? What did he mean hospitalized. He fumbled as to what to say to participate in the charade in case the conversation was being monitored. "That is terrible. What is the nature of her illness?"

"I cannot be sure yet. She is undergoing intensive testing I'm afraid. Certain specialists have been put in charge of the patient."

Good God! Since he was being vague about medical specifics, was Solano saying Loretta had been arrested? By his tone, Fraser could tell that Solano was distraught.

"Is she expected to recover?"

Solano sounded like he might be weeping.

"That is difficult to say. The situation is in the hands of others."

Obviously Loretta had been arrested. Another of those close to him taken? "I see. Perhaps I should come right away."

"That would be recommended, Monsieur. As soon as possible I would say. I am afraid her condition might be terminal."

"And should I meet you at your office?"

Fraser knew the address of Solano's practice.

"No. I have moved. That professional partnership dissolved. The office closed. Best if I meet you. Perhaps the day after tomorrow? I believe there is a train that arrives here in Lyon in the afternoon. I would suggest the Hotel Victor Hugo only a short walk north from the Gare Perrache. Close to Place Ampère on Rue Victor Hugo just north of the rail station."

Fraser assumed that Solano must have gone to ground after his Loretta's arrest. Was he also being sought? By the Malice or the Gestapo? Giving the name of the hotel over the phone was not good security practice but he suspected Solano might not be thinking clearly.

"Very well, Doctor. I shall be there."

Shit. Everything had apparently come undone for his old friends. After years of flirting with danger of arrest or deportation back to Spain their luck had run out. If Loretta was arrested for Resistance activities there was little that could be done to save her. She might already be dead. But Fraser had to do what he could. He might at least be able to help Rafael Solano escape.

CHAPTER 35

Fiona Marchand insisted on accompanying Fraser to Lyon. With her new involvement at her brother's film production company she also obtained credentials from the COIC to travel about France on business. Her brother's partners agreed to appoint her to the position of Production Designer as a way to appease her involvement. She could no longer wait anxiously in Paris for Fraser's return knowing the danger involved. He was too much a part of her life.

After arriving in Lyon they walked the short distance from the train station to the hotel. Located in 2nd Arrondissement, this was the heart of Lyon situated between the parallel Rhone and Saône Rivers cutting through the city. Also the center of Lyon's famed gastronomic reputation now a mere shadow of pre-war days. Food was too scarce, wine even more so. Few goods of any type were for sale. Little money in circulation. The Germans continued to bleed France of anything of value.

The war on the Eastern Front continued badly for the Germans. Stalingrad had fallen. Surrounded, the German Sixth Army had surrendered in mass to the Soviets in February. Depleted Wehrmacht forces stretched on a long front effectively going into defensive retreat against a massive Soviet offensive. In the south the Germans were desperately defending against U.S. and British offensives moving northward in Italy. German civilians were suffering severe food shortages. French goods became vital to the German war effort.

Fraser and Marchand entered the small hotel. No one other than the clerk was in the small lobby. After checking-in they took a small lift to the second floor. As they exited the lift Fraser recognized Rafael Solano at the other end of the hallway near the stairway. Solano put a finger to his lips.

Without any greeting Fraser unlocked the door and all three slipped into the room.

Fraser immediately embraced Solano. The poor man looked in a terrible state. After Fraser introduced Marchand, Solano launched into his story. He spoke in a hushed whisper as they sat close together with Solano on a chair and Fraser and Marchand on the bed.

"Four months ago there was a high level meeting of eight Resistance leaders. Someone betrayed them. Looks like the Gestapo was after a top leader. General de Gaulle's personal representative. Code named *Max*. His real name is Jean Moulin according to Loretta. They were meeting at the surgery of a doctor in the suburb of Caluire to the north in the 4th. That's where I worked along with Dr. Dugoujon. Unfortunately he was also arrested."

"*Max* you say? Short, dark hair, wears a scarf much of the time?"

"Only saw him once myself but that's a good description. You know him, Marc?"

"Yes. Over a year ago I accompanied him after he parachuted into Provence. Only knew him by his code name *Max*. He introduced me to other Resistance leaders. I was to be a principle conduit to secret military-value intelligence to the British and Free French in London.

"And Loretta?"

"Arrested," Solano said lowering his head. "But that was only just a week ago. Bad luck.

"Loretta and I went underground after the raid in June. Loretta was to act as secretary to the meeting but arrived late.

From a distance she saw the Gestapo agents and the German military police *Feldgendarmerie* marching out the arrestees from my surgery. She escaped across the river and hid in the large Parc de la Tête d'Or. She knew better than to return to our apartment.

"Within hours of the raid in Caluire a wide net was cast for those involved with the Resistance. Of course I knew nothing of what had taken place since I was doing rounds at the hospital at the time. When a Gestapo officer accompanied by several gendarmes came looking for me at the hospital, I was warned by other staff. I snuck out the rear. The problem was where to go? No one involved in the Resistance in Lyon could now be considered safe.

"Loretta and I had a prearranged location to rendezvous in the event of just such an eventuality. My heart leapt when I saw her walking to the designated café where I was sitting outside."

Fraser wished his old friend would get to explaining what happened that led to Loretta being arrested but realized he was emotionally devastated. He had to get the whole story out.

"Once Loretta told me of the raid on the meeting we had to assume that everyone in our group might be compromised. Fortunately it is summer. We spent that first night in the old Roman ruins on the hill above Vieux Lyon. Desperate, the next afternoon I suggested we go to the home of Lucie and Raymond Aubrac.

"But Loretta said that was not a good idea. Raymond was to be at the meeting that was raided by the Gestapo. He must have been arrested. Lucie maybe by now also although Raymond went by another name so maybe Lucie had not been identified.

"We did not dare go to Lucie's door in case it was a trap. Besides, we might also be endangering Lucie. So we waited concealed across the street. I was armed with a pistol just in case. Take some of the bastards with me if it came to that.

"Loretta and I spent the second night outside keeping watch. If Lucie Aubrac had not been arrested, she would eventually have to leave the house for food.

"The following morning she appeared and we approached. Lucie's an amazing woman. Her husband had just been arrested by the Gestapo. She's a working teacher with a young child and she's six months pregnant. With all those burdens she still takes us in. That's where we stayed these last couple of months. Since we couldn't contribute ration coupons getting enough food has been a constant struggle."

Appearing finished with his background story of events, Fraser finally said, "What happened to Loretta, Rafael?"

Solano broke down weeping. Once composed, he resumed.

"Sorry. It was over a week ago. Loretta was moving about contacting selected Resistance operatives. Lucie is working on a plan to free Raymond. But I'll get to that in a moment. Loretta felt obligated to help Lucie. Working out of the house only writing articles for underground publication made her feel like a prisoner. I didn't want her exposing herself but you know how determined she can be.

"With our false identities compromised we reverted to our real identities. However that identified us as Spanish nationals. That alone had become dangerous. Spaniards in France were assumed to be Communists or at least leftists. Many joined the Resistance. Right-wing Vichy along with their German masters view any Spaniard as suspect. Those not already in the French internment camps could easily find themselves subject to conscription into forced labor for the Germans under *service du travail obligatoire* just like any Frenchman. Political undesirables could be subject to deportation back to Spain.

"Anyway, Loretta was caught. Even worse, it was by the Gestapo. After meeting a contact in the Parc de la Tête d'Or she was arrested along with the contact. Another betrayal Lucie thinks. That was how Raymond was arrested along with Moulin and the others.

"Lucie believed she knew who betrayed her husband and Moulin. One of those at the meeting that inexplicably managed to escape arrest. It has affected all levels of the Resistance in the

Lyon area. No one knows who has been compromised if the turncoat was the person Lucie suspected."

"Is there something that can be done, Rafael?"

"Possibly. That's why I asked for your help. Our friend Lucie is putting together a plan to attempt to rescue her husband Raymond. It might also rescue Loretta."

"Where is Loretta being held?"

"At the Ecole de Sante Militaire on Avenue Berholet."

Solano paused and took a deep breath before continuing. "Unfortunately she is now being held by the Gestapo. The head of the Lyon Gestapo is an SS officer named Barbie. There are terrible rumors about him. Likes to personally torture his prisoners in the basement of this former military medical school. Unbelievable stories about what he does to prisoners.

"Lucie heard that a visitor to a low-level prisoner at the Ecole de Sante Militaire learned that Barbie had personally tortured Jean Moulin. According to the accounts Moulin suffered hot needles under the fingernails, knuckles crushed in the space between a door and door jam, screw-levered handcuffs that broke his wrists. Unrecognizable after being beaten about the face. Moulin was in a coma when he was apparently displayed to other resistance leaders in Barbie's office.

"The idea that Loretta is in the hands of this Barbie is ....."

Fraser got up and laid a hand on Solano's shoulder.

"Is there a real chance of rescuing Loretta?" Fraser said.

"I'm not sure. Lucie is determined however to rescue her husband."

"Is he being held at the same place as Loretta?"

"No. He's in Montluc Prison. A former army prison in the 3rd on Rue Jeanne Haghette. That's where all prisoners are kept. They get moved to Gestapo headquarters for interrogation. That's where Moulin was until someone revealed his identity while undergoing torture at the Gestapo headquarters. So important prisoners might get moved back and forth.

"That's Lucie's plan. Raymond has been sentenced to death but they still think he might be made to reveal information.

Can't image what kind of treatment he has endured for these months."

Fraser said, "So Lucie's plan must be to hijack the prison transport when her husband is being moved between the two locations? How will she know when that will happen? Someone on the inside?"

This sounded desperate if not suicidal.

"Yes, there is someone on the inside. But only a cleaning woman. And yes that's the plan. Lucie has tried all sorts of things to get him removed from Montluc Prison. I even helped with trying to cause him some sort of medical condition by secreting in drugs concealed in allowed food packages. Something to cause serious enough symptoms to force them to move Raymond to a hospital. But it didn't work. So Lucie conceived this bizarre plan to request she be allowed to marry Raymond. Remember he's still being held under a false name so Lucie is not known to the Gestapo."

"Why would the Gestapo allow them to marry? And how does that even help?" Marchand said. Listening to these tales of unimaginable dangers was driving her mad. What were she and Marc getting into?

"If the Gestapo agrees to it she thinks Raymond would be transported from Montluc to Gestapo headquarters for the ceremony. There is a provision in French law called marriage in extremis – a person condemned to death may marry civilly before execution. Her excuse is to avoid her child being born illegitimate."

"That is truly bizarre. Might it work?" Marchand said.

Solano shook his head. "Who knows? But she must try."

"And Loretta?"

"That is only an outside hope. There are many others undergoing interrogation at Gestapo headquarters. Loretta is probably among them. We can only hope that Raymond and some of the others might be transported back to Montluc in a group. Maybe Loretta."

Fraser couldn't see how Solano could expect that Loretta might just happen to be part of Raymond Aubrac's return to Montluc. Of course he must hold onto any shred of hope. Perhaps this Klaus Barbie would not be finished *interrogating* her. Fraser would not raise that point to his friend.

"So how can we help?" Fraser said.

"Help us escape Lyon if we're successful in freeing Loretta. Madame Marchand has relatives in Provence. Might they help?"

"Certainly," Fraser said. "We'll do everything we can, Rafael. But first we must free Loretta. Can we meet your friend Lucie?"

CHAPTER 36

Fiona Marchand was appalled that Fraser was considering getting involved in what sounded to be an armed attack on the Gestapo.

"You can't do this Marc."

"I have to. I owe them. I need to help Rafael. I can't just stand by and watch others act."

"You know nothing about firearms."

"True. Most in the Resistance didn't either before they had to learn. But I certainly understand violence."

After meeting with Lucie Aubrac he was inspired. A truly exceptional woman. Amazingly keeping a positive and even cheerful demeanor in the face of crushing obstacles. Lucie herself was active in the Resistance. Being a pregnant mother did not instill any noticeable caution. She was not foolhardy but she was audacious and incredibly brave.

Lucie had approached Klaus Barbie himself to request the right to marry Raymond. Turned down, she approached a more junior Gestapo officer. A modest bribe convinced him. Furthermore, she was allowed to visit Raymond at Montluc Prison. Left alone for a few moments, she hurriedly told him of the rescue plan. When he was being returned to the prison from the Gestapo headquarters after the *wedding vows* the Resistance would attack the transport.

It was only a three-kilometer trip so events would happen quickly.

Accepted to participate, Fraser and the others in the strike force met in a repair garage. Most were armed with British Sten submachine guns. Everyone carried a backup revolver. Fraser was given a heavy .455 caliber Webley. The resourceful Lucie Aubrac presented the group with silencers for the Stens courtesy of British SOE clandestine air drops. Several of the men tried out the effect within the garage. The discharge sounded no louder than a wine cork being removed. With the resultant diminished muzzle velocity the weapons effectivity also diminished. They would need to shoot from close range.

Over the next several days Fraser trained with the attack force in the countryside well outside Lyon. They practiced shooting at a moving target while moving as well. Not too much shooting though since ammunition was in short supply. With no experience with a submachine gun Fraser volunteered as a driver. The others laughed after he told them he drove in Los Angeles, California which therefore made him an expert with automobiles.

Three days before the raid a mishap almost derailed the hijacking plan. One of Lucie's colleagues narrowly escaped capture after German gendarmes raided a house where he was meeting with others *résistants* outside of Lyon. Staying at Lucie's house at the time, Solano related to Fraser and Marchand what happened.

"One of our group, a guy named Serge appears outside Lucie's house last night calling to us in a whisper. We let him in. He's dirty, disheveled, and wounded. Cuts on his face and a bullet wound to his bicep. The stupid Germans did not search him thoroughly. He hid a second gun in his pants next to his genitals.

"He told us he pulled out the gun and smashed the German guard in the head. Then he jumped out a second story window and landed on a glass roof. The frightful noise aroused the other

Germans. A bullet caught him in the bicep. Walked all the way into Lyon. I've fixed him up but he can't participate in the raid."

"Is the raid still on then?" Fraser said.

"According to Lucie, yes. Some of the others thought it was a bad omen but she can be persuasive. We have enough men. And now you have joined us replacing the loss of Serge."

Fiona Marchand bit her lip. She dreaded Marc participating in this thing. It seemed so desperate. Everyone involved with the Resistance in Lyon seemed at heightened risk. Marc wasn't practiced in this sort of escapade. She surely wasn't.

✝

On the morning of October 21, 1943, everyone prepared for their assignments. Fraser and Solano joined the others in the attack party at the garage. Lucie Aubrac prepared for her mock wedding at Gestapo headquarters in the Ecole de Sante. Marchand would look after Lucie's two-year old son at the garage until his mother returned. Successful or not, Lucie Aubrac knew she would have to flee to the countryside after the raid.

Three cars and a van would participate in the raid. They would wait at strategic points for the lorry transporting the prisoners to Montluc Prison. Lucie Aubrac would be in the lead Citroën after leaving the sham marriage ceremony. In the front passenger seat was a man named Daniel. He was reputed to be the best shot. To insure a clear field of fire the side window of the Citroën had been removed since it did not roll down totally within the door.

Fraser drove a second Citroën with Solano in the back seat. Two gunmen rode with them in the back seat. The third car and the van were manned with two men each. They had no idea how many prisoners might be transported. All they knew was at least Raymond Aubrac *should* be transported back to Montluc. Everyone hoped others including Loretta Elizalde might also be rescued.

Late in the afternoon two German SS walked into the Avenue Berthelot to halt what little traffic there was. The gate to the Ecole de Sante opened. An Opal three-ton lorry with a canvas covered bed pulled out onto the street. Lucie Aubrac's Citroën pulled up behind. Fraser followed a hundred meters further behind. They soon passed the other two Resistance vehicles parked along the route.

With the short distance to Montluc Prison events unfolded rapidly. As the lorry slowed to turn left onto the Boulevard des Hirondelles, Lucie's Citroën accelerated. Pulling alongside, Daniel fired a short burst from his silenced Sten at the lorry driver.

The silenced rounds made only a muted report. Fraser heard nothing inside his vehicle.

Within moments the lorry drifted to the curb and came to a gentle stop.

Lucie's Citroën stopped slightly ahead of the lorry at an angle. All the gunmen exited. Fraser stopped his car behind the lorry. Everyone jumped out to take positions behind the car.

The German guards in the rear of the lorry with the prisoners jumped down not knowing why the driver stopped. Firing erupted immediately from both sides. In the course of the two-minute firefight the Resistance attackers emptied their submachine gun clips. All five German guards and the lorry driver lay dead. Only one *résistant* was wounded.

A surreal sight. Bodies everywhere. Blood pooling. Yet such a beautiful autumn day with the sun shining. A woman showing her six months' pregnancy hugging her husband, both shedding tears of relief. A frantic group of gunmen with submachine guns and rescued prisoners hurrying to escape the scene. Everyone giddy with delight having pulled off such a daring feat. Fraser wished he had his camera. The whole event could have been staged as a Hollywood movie action scene.

There were fourteen rescued prisoners including Lucie's husband Raymond. But Fraser saw the distress reflected in Rafael Solano's eyes when he realized that Loretta was not among them.

No other cars appeared on the boulevard. The scene remained quiet as everyone quickly got into the vehicles to escape the area. Bolt cutters removed the handcuffs joining every two prisoners together. Solano attended to the wounded man. Simultaneous with attending his patient he questioned the other prisoners in the van about Loretta.

Was she even there at Gestapo headquarters?

After returning to the same garage from which they embarked, all the freed prisoners and their rescuers dispersed according to prearranged plans. They had kicked over an anthill. Blackened the eye of the feared Gestapo. Drew blood. There would be serious repercussions. Lyon would not be safe for anyone associated with the Resistance.

After returning to the garage, Fraser embraced a frightened Fiona Marchand. Before she could ask, Fraser said, "Loretta was not among the prisoners. Lucie's husband was rescued and thirteen others. Everything went according to plan except no Loretta."

Fraser, Marchand, and Solano returned to the Hotel Victor Hugo by a metro trolley. Solano looked a broken man. He had not yet related to Fraser what he learned from the other escapees he spoke to in the van until they returned to the hotel.

Once in the room Solano said, "I learned from those rescued that a woman is being held at Gestapo headquarters. One of them described Loretta. Worse yet, Barbie has taken a particular interest in her. That means torture. Even during my brief conversations with these men while I was asking about their medical conditions, they related accounts of this Barbie's savage methods. Over the last couple of days they've heard a woman's screams."

Solano paused to compose himself. "I also learned something else. They learned the woman being held was a Spaniard. Somebody reportedly important enough for the Spanish to be interested in. They believe she is to be deported back to Spain. You know what that means? Loretta has a death sentence over her head under Franco's regime."

Fraser looked toward Marchand. She bit her lip reconciled to Solano's tragedy. They all must leave Lyon right away. At least save Rafael since he is actively being sought by the Gestapo. She and Marc could be in danger as well. With this bold attack by Lucie Aubrac it was not safe to remain in Lyon.

"Rafael, there might still be some hope," Fraser said.

"What do you mean?"

"Rescue Loretta when she is to be transported to Spain."

"What are you talking about? The Gestapo won't allow another such attack to free a prisoner."

"This will be different. It will be just one prisoner. And we can assume it will be by train."

Marchand said, "Marc, what can we possibly do?" What was he suggesting? "There is no one to help. All those that Lucie assembled for the attack have now fled to the countryside. It's just us. And Rafael is wanted so he must remain hidden."

Fraser nodded. "I will do it."

"That's ridiculous, Marc. By yourself? How's that possible?" Marchand said.

"Listen. It's just one prisoner. A woman." He did not add that she might also be in poor physical shape if she had undergone torture. Many of the prisoners rescued, including Lucie's husband, were in bad shape. "She will not be heavily guarded. I have a gun."

Solano brightened at the prospect no matter how desperate. "But even if you overpower them, what then?"

"I haven't thought through the details yet, Rafael. The most difficult part is getting Loretta away after dealing with her guards."

The three of them argued back and forth for hours. Eventually Marchand quit her attempts at dissuading Fraser from such a rash idea. All this violence was beyond her. Apparently not for Marc as she was coming to realize. Los Angeles, Germany, Spain, now Lyon.

The more Fraser constructed his plan on the fly the more possible it seemed to him. Nevertheless it was fraught with all sorts of pitfalls and dangers. It relied upon improvisation at every turn. Anything could alter what would dictate the next step.

Marchand was able to purchase some food and wine through the hotel clerk. Black market goods at black market prices. Solano would spend the night in their room. He had nowhere to hide now that the Aubracs had fled the city. The poor man was so despondent that she wondered if he could function in any capacity. Perhaps Marc's plan would at least provide the poor man with something to cling to. As for her, the idea that Marc would attempt something this brazen terrified her.

The following day all three gathered at a café. Terrified as she was, Fiona Marchand told Fraser that in no uncertain terms would she let him go about this alone. She intended to be at his side. She would do whatever necessary but he was to factor her into the plan.

Gathering his thoughts after several minutes, Fraser said, "Ok. Here's what we do. It's simple. My guess is there'll probably be no more than two or three guards escorting Loretta. Probably two Germans and whoever they send from Spain.

"Once on the train I'll wait until one of the guards goes toward the toilet. I'll be waiting nearby. I'll force him into the toilet under gunpoint. I'll incapacitate him then change into his uniform."

"Incapacitate? How?" Marchand asked.

"Permanently, but quietly, Fiona. I won't go into detail. It's necessary."

The plan to kill someone just added to her dread.

"Why change into the uniform?" Solano said.

"In order to get off the train without raising suspicion I need to look part of the official entourage. Doesn't matter if it's one of the Germans or the Spaniard. I can pass for either.

"Since you insist on being there Fiona, you will take a seat as close as possible to Loretta's guards across the aisle. Once I return from the toilet you will discretely show your gun for the guards to see."

"Gun? I don't know how to use a gun, Marc."

"I'll show you. Nothing much to learn. At pointblank range there's not much to do except point and pull the trigger. It's to scare them but you need to be prepared to shoot if necessary. Can you do that?"

She nodded hoping she meant it.

"Rafael, Fiona will need a gun. Do you have one you can spare?"

"Yes. Here. I have another."

He handed over his own Webley to Fiona. She took the heavy revolver, surprised by its weight. Could she even conceive of shooting somebody with this? Close up?

"I'll come up behind the remaining guards seated with Loretta."

"But what happens when you get off the train?" Solano said.

Fraser smiled. "That's where you come in, Rafael. Can you find a car?"

Solano nodded yes.

"And enough petrol? An extra can or two in the trunk would also be a good idea."

"I should be able to get my hands on the same Citroën we used in the raid."

"I checked the train routings. Only one obvious route to Spain. Lyon to Avignon, Nimes, Montpellier, Perpignan, then over the border into Spain. Avignon is about three hours. That's our target. I will make my play sometime before arriving in Avignon. We'll all exit the train claiming the need to seek medical attention for Loretta before continuing to Spain."

Solano grimaced at what that probably meant. Undoubtedly nothing would need to be exaggerated after being subjected to torture by Klaus Barbie.

"Here's the dangerous part for you, Rafael. You need to get to Avignon. By automobile. We'll need a car in Avignon and you can't travel by train anyway. Far too many identification checks in route. But driving might be just as dangerous if you are stopped.

"Best if you are already in Avignon ahead of us. You may have to use a less than direct route rather than the main north-south highway. Have your gun ready at all times."

Solano shook his head with an expression of disbelief.

Fraser said, "So what's wrong?"

"Everything, my friend. What if there are more than three guards? What if no one goes to the toilet? What if someone reports something suspicious to the conductor? What if Fiona has to shoot? If I'm captured or killed you'll have nowhere to go even if you even make it to Avignon."

"And how do we know when Loretta is going to be transferred?" Marchand said.

"You and I will stake out Gare Perrache. Our cover is scouting location scenes for a new film. The same cover I've been travelling under. Before we left to come here to Lyon I brought along my script set in Marseille. Restaurants and a train station play prominent parts in the script. Lyon can easily sit in for Marseille the way it is written.

"Gare Perrache is a photogenic place. We approach the station master and the French gendarmes for assistance. You and I both have COIC papers. Both of us are connected with Productions Artistiques Cinématographiques. I'll take pictures. Annotate the script with notes. You sketch scenes and diagram filming angles. We hang around until Loretta shows. Each day we bring our packed bags. Put them in lockers. Ready to leave immediately on the same train as Loretta.

"That's why I checked us out of the Hotel Victor Hugo this morning. We need to stay close to the rail station. I've made arrangements for a room at the Hotel Terminus literally right next to the station."

"Good God!" Solano said.

"What?"

Solano grunted. "The Hotel Terminus was the former Gestapo headquarters until they relocated to the Ecole de Sante just months ago."

"And when might Loretta show, Marc?" Marchand said. "It might be a week, maybe longer." Maybe never she thought.

"I don't know, Fiona. If she doesn't show we'll have to deal with that when the time comes. The one given we must work with is her transport to Spain has to be by train. No reason why she would be driven all the way to Spain."

But all three knew it was just one more variable that could wreck the rescue attempt before it ever materialized.

"Ok. Rafael, you'll have the toughest job. You can sneak into our room to sleep tonight. Get a wash and some food to take before you leave for Avignon tomorrow. Once you're there you'll have to look for us while making sure you're not asked to show your papers. You know the Germans. Efficient bastards. Your false name must be on lists everywhere. Under your real name your papers are not up to date."

Solano nodded. "If this all works, what happens in Avignon?"

"Hard to say. We can't know what kind of escort Loretta has until she arrives here at the train station. The Avignon station is just outside the ancient walls surrounding the old part of the city. I've been there. Busy place so be careful. You'll have to watch for us somewhere out in front of the station. Remember I will be in uniform holding a gun behind the guards so look for Loretta. At that point the deed is done but we're very exposed."

Fraser avoided discussing what was to be done with the remaining guards if they got this far. "We'll then head for Aix. Friends in the countryside will help hide you and Loretta."

Solano lowered his head. No reason for optimism. Marchand felt the same.

"Listen both of you. This is far simpler than Lucie Aubrac's spectacular raid. Fourteen prisoners rescued. We can do this. The plan is simple. Just focus on the key tasks since we must adapt the tactics to the variables we can't plan for."

Both nodded but remained unconvinced.

CHAPTER 37

The following morning Fiona went downstairs to purchase some food for Solano to take on his journey south. She and Fraser had a little time before walking to the rail station to begin their surveillance. Fraser had checked the southbound train schedule. The first train south did not depart Lyon until 9:15.

Solano looked none too rested after sleeping on the floor in their room. The nightmare images of Loretta enduring torture by Barbie made rest impossible. That and the anxiety over what lay ahead.

About to leave, Solano said, "I expect to be in Avignon by at least late afternoon. I will make it as fast as possible. But what if Loretta is on that first train this morning? I will not be there in time."

Fraser put a hand on Solano's shoulder.

"In that case Fiona and I shall improvise. That's just another variable that we cannot foresee."

"And if I am caught? What will you do then? You'll be trapped with no means of escape when you leave the train," Solano said.

Fraser gave a weak smile.

"We will manage. Now if for some reason we do not connect, make your way to Aix, Rafael. It's southeast of Avignon less than a hundred kilometers. If we made it there, I'll walk around the large Fountaine de la Rotonde at the end of the wide Boule-vard Cours Mirabeau close to noon each day. The fountain is a big elaborate thing with statues forming a hub for various streets. Stay out of sight and look for me."

As Solano left, Fiona embraced him and kissed his cheek.

Fraser embraced also him and said, "We'll get Loretta. Don't get captured, Rafael. And carry your doctor's bag at all times. If stopped, say you have just come from visiting a dying patient at his home."

Solano nodded. He might die but he would not be captured.

✝

The first day staking out Gare Perrache yielded nothing. Fra-ser and Fiona had their packed bags secured in lockers ready to board Elizalde's train. It was only necessary to stay vigilant for the southbound departing trains. Fraser hoped he was right about this being the only route that might be used to return Elizalde to Spain. Was the information about her return to Spain even correct?

As they arrived at the station they checked in with the sta-tion master to explain their mission. Told him they might be a couple of days working out shooting scenes at the station. Need-ed to make script changes to accommodate the new location for the shooting. His station was a magnificent architectural work. That's why it was chosen over locating these scenes in Marseille which is the other location for the film.

The station master fell all over himself to offer every assis-tance. Of course they could take pictures.

"Ah, you are most kind, Monsieur. And I believe there is a small part that might be ideal for you. Ideal with you in your uniform," Fraser said solidifying the man's cooperation. Every-one loved motion pictures.

The station master proceeded to explain to the gendarmes on duty. They were to assist the filmmakers in anything they need-ed.

Just as well that Elizalde did not show this soon. Solano should be in Avignon by now. Assuming he had not been waylaid by the Malice. Fraser had no idea how the poor man might survive in hiding since even his old identity papers might still list him as a wanted individual somewhere in the Vichy bureaucracy.

The routine repeated on the second day. He and Marchand were greeted warmly. Cleverly Marchand brought along a sketch pad. Ostensibly she was blocking out scenes in rough storyboards while he took photographs. It looked like real filmmaking work to a layman. The stationmaster and the gendarme sergeant were willing participants. He even had them read some trumped up lines. Yes, they might be engaged for these small speaking parts. Of course they would at least be needed as background extras. Ultimately that would be up to the director but he would recommend them as perfect for the parts.

On the third day, Fraser became concerned. Even if he was right about Elizalde being transported by train, when might that be? That was always the weakness of the plan. They could not keep this charade going much longer. Rafael Solano must be going through hell wondering what was happening.

Fraser and Marchand arrived at 8:30 on the fourth day to prepare for the 9:15 southbound departure. He had guessed right. Two black sedans pulled up in front of Gare Perrache. Fraser and Marchand were inside the station in the general waiting area seated off to the side.

"There, Fiona. That's her!" Fraser said.

Two men supported Loretta Elizalde. She was obviously in great physical distress. One man was a young Spanish army officer, the other wore a black leather overcoat. Gestapo Fraser assumed.

As Elizalde and her escorts approached, Fraser glimpsed three other men in uniform following close behind.

"Holy shit!" Fraser exclaimed in a hushed tone.

"What, Marc?"

"That Spanish officer is Colonel Eduardo Cabrera. One of the Nazi SS officers is Sturmbannführer Heinz Leitner. The other I don't recognize."

Fraser turned away and pulled his fedora down slightly to hide his face. "Let's go. This is it. Get us tickets. First class to Marseille. Mention we'll return in two days if the stationmaster should see you. I'll get our bags. Follow them out and stand by the train car they're seated if you can tell. They will recognize me so this complicates things."

"Is this about Spain, Marc?"

"Yes. Now get going."

With the bags, Fraser walked cautiously to the track platform making sure Elizalde and her guards were already boarded. He assumed that was the case as Leitner and the other SS officer walked back in the opposite direction presumably leaving the platform. That meant Cabrera had boarded with Elizalde.

Keeping a safe distance, Fraser shielded his face with his hat pulled low while looking away from the two Germans as he passed.

Approaching Marchand while shielding his face from anyone looking out the train car window, he said, "Walk to the next car and climb aboard."

The conductor announced, *all aboard.*

As they were about to step up into the car, Marchand turned to him and said, "Marc, the shorter SS officer was Klaus Barbie. I heard the other one address him as Hauptsturmführer Barbie."

†

After the train pulled out of the station, Fraser sent Marchand to reconnoiter. Where were Elizalde and her escorts seated? How many other passengers? Where was the nearest toilet?

Reporting back she said, "We're in luck. The toilet is at this end of the next car. Well behind where they are seated in the front seats. Only a few other passengers."

"How are they seated?"

"Elizalde is seated next to the window on the left side. The very front seat. Next to her is the younger Spanish soldier. Behind them is the man in the trench coat. Next to him the Spanish officer you recognized."

Fraser nodded. Taking a few moments to absorb the details he said to Marchand, "Ok. Here's what we do. You go and find a seat toward the back of their car. When one of the Spanish officers gets up to go to the toilet at the rear of the car I'll be waiting here on the platform between the two cars. I'll see him coming through the window in the door."

"And if it's the guy in the leather overcoat?"

"Ignore him. I need the uniform of one of the Spaniards."

"What are you going to do, Marc?"

"Disable him. Knock him unconscious. Then change into his uniform."

Marchand looked pained. She knew what Fraser had said before. "Then what? How do you hide him?"

"I don't. I'll dump him off the train. Then I'll take his place. A perfect disguise. I have a gun and so do you.

"Once one of the Spaniards passes by you walking back toward the toilet, watch for me after probably ten minutes. When you see me approaching in the Spaniard's uniform, move ahead of me and take a seat across from them. Once I reach the seat point your gun toward them without anyone else seeing."

"Marc, this won't work. What if you're seen dumping this man off the train? What if the other two pull their weapons? They must be armed."

Marchand was terrified at the prospects of every imaginable uncertainty.

"Fiona, listen to me. We will succeed. I've been in worse situations. If everything goes wrong then we shoot all of them and get off the train with Loretta. The officer's name is Cabrera. He and the German Leitner are sadistic butchers. Torturers like this Klaus Barbie. Cabrera and Leitner tortured Loretta and me in Spain. They all need to die."

Of course Fraser knew that was no alternative. Should it come to that they wouldn't get a mile away before being captured or killed themselves.

"If you have to can you shoot them, Fiona?"

She nodded yes but knew she had no idea if that would be possible.

"Let's hope it doesn't come to that. Loretta looks to be in bad shape."

"What if neither of the Spaniards goes to the toilet?" Marchand said.

"It's three hours to Avignon. Hopefully they had their morning coffee. But if we are getting close then we'll take matters into our own hands. Just follow my lead, Fiona."

The minutes ticked by either too slowly in anticipation or too quickly knowing they had only a limited window of opportunity. But chance favored them.

Two hours out of Lyon Fraser saw his target approach. As he had hoped it was Eduardo Cabrera. As Cabrera started to open the toilet door Fraser opened the rail car connecting door and confronted him. Cabrera's face registered shock upon recognizing Fraser who then jammed the Webley revolver under his chin.

"You!"

"That's right. Into the toilet!" Fraser said in a whisper forcing Cabrera inside the toilet.

No more than a couple of seconds had passed. Only Fiona Marchand saw what happened.

Not meant for two occupants, they could barely move once inside. Fraser took no chance on Cabrera resisting. "Like I heard you say in Spain, no prisoners."

Facing Cabrera's back, Fraser smashed the butt of the revolver into Cabrera's temple as hard as he could.

Cabrera slumped to the floor but remained conscious. A second harder blow completed the task. Fortunately the wound did not bleed profusely. Fraser needed the uniform.

Even if it was Eduardo Cabrera, his torturer, what he must do next was still repugnant.

Fraser undid his own tie and wrapped it around Cabrera's neck. He pulled tightly holding the garrote in place for a full two minutes. Mercifully Cabrera remained unconscious from the blows to his head so there was no struggle as he was strangled.

Breathing heavily, Fraser released the tie from Cabrera's throat and checked his neck for a pulse. Nothing.

It was an awkward task to remove Cabrera's uniform in the cramped confinement. Mindful of the elapsed time so as not to raise suspicion among the other two, he quickly changed into Cabrera's uniform. Both were similar in physical size so the fit was acceptable.

By now fifteen minutes had passed. Fiona must be suffering terrible anxiety. But maybe the worst was over. They would arrive in Avignon shortly therefore limiting the time they needed to contain Elizalde's two guards. That also helped to prevent Cabrera's body being discovered until they left the train.

Fraser never had any intention of dumping Cabrera off the train. Far too risky being seen wrestling the body out of the toilet. From the moment he set eyes on Cabrera he also had no intention of letting him live.

The task now was to somehow disable the toilet door and affix an *out of order* sign. He had previously prepared a hand written sign on note paper but disabling the door lock presented a problem. He was sweating as he looked at the locking mechanism trying to figure out how to jam it closed from the outside. He needed to examine the door from the outside.

With his clothing and shoes in a bundle he exited the toilet. The clothes he put into his valise sitting on the connecting platform between the two cars.

A male passenger suddenly appeared from the other car intent on entering the toilet.

Fraser quickly said in French, "I'm afraid the toilet is out of order. Something awful is backing up. A real mess all over the floor. Wouldn't go in there if I were you. I was about to place this note on the door."

The man nodded, "*Merci, monsieur,*" then headed back to look for a toilet in another car.

Fraser pulled the sliding door closed, sticking the note in place. Taking a moment to look at his options he noticed the clearance of the opening for the door as it retracted into the wall. The solution became immediately obvious.

Taking out the switchblade he flicked it open. Inserting the blade deeply into the wall-to-door clearance until it jammed hard biting into the wood, he then kicking the heel of the knife for added measure. Applying a hard sideways pressure broke off the blade wedging the door closed. But once the jammed door was discovered by the conductor they may have only minutes to make their escape after arriving in Avignon.

Holding the Webley revolver at his side, Fraser strode purposefully down the aisle. Marchand saw him, relief evident in her expression. He nodded meaning she should take her position and ready her revolver.

Fraser sat down in the seat next to the man in the overcoat. The man looked at him with a split second of confusion before Fraser jammed the revolver into his side.

Assuming the man was Gestapo Fraser said in German, "Don't move."

The Spanish officer sitting next to Elizalde turned around. Fraser said in Spanish, "Don't move or you all die. Look to your right."

The Spanish officer turned to see Marchand in the opposite seat pointing a large revolver resting on her lap.

"Gestapo?" Fraser said to the trench coat guy.

The man nodded.

"You have orders?"

The man nodded and reached into his inside pocket.

Fraser pushed the barrel of the Webley into the small man's chest hard enough to cause a grunt of pain.

"Weapon?"

The man nodded again.

"Remove it with your left hand."

"Listen carefully. At Avignon we all get off the train together," Fraser said to the Gestapo agent in German. "Follow along and you may survive. If there is trouble I'll shoot you first."

Repeating this in Spanish for the young officer, Elizalde now slowly turned her head. Fraser winced when he saw the massive bruising of her swollen face. She looked awful. Her eyes were vacant, almost unresponsive. Looked far worse than the torture she endured in Spain.

A broken raspy whisper escaped her mouth, "Marc, oh my god how ....." Her words trailed off as she struggled to remain alert, her breathing labored.

"Not much longer, Loretta. Hang on. Can you walk?"

"Yes," came her weak reply. But Fraser doubted she could even stand the way she looked.

In Spanish to the officer, "When the train stops you get up immediately and help her off the train. Make any sort of move or call out and you will die. Keep your hand away from your holstered sidearm."

The officer's holster had a cover over the handle and a clasp. Not easily withdrawn quickly. Fraser would disarm him later.

As a precaution, Fraser said something to the officer first in French then in German. It did not appear he understood either. At least it would be more difficult for him to raise an alarm speaking only Spanish.

Fraser agonized about Elizalde's condition. Twenty minutes later the train began slowing. The conductor walked through the car announcing Avignon as the next stop.

Once the train jerked to a final stop Fraser said in German and Spanish, "Everyone up. Help the woman."

To the Gestapo agent, "Talk to the first gendarme you see on the platform. Act like the arrogant shit that you are. Tell them we must get this prisoner to a doctor. She is being deported but is too ill to go on. Tell them we have already telephoned ahead from the last stop for a doctor to meet us here in Avignon. Don't fuck it up."

Fiona Marchand exited the train first. The Spaniard followed lifting Elizalde's full weight to get her down the steps onto the platform. Fraser followed from behind with the Gestapo agent.

Immediately a gendarme approached.

"Do as I told you, Herr Gestapo. I'll be right at your side. You hold my valise. I'll hold your newspaper hiding my gun.

Now came the moment of truth. Had Rafael made it to Avignon?

The Gestapo agent spoke to the French gendarme in badly accented French flashing his credentials. Fraser handed him the orders signed by Lyon Gestapo SS-Hauptsturmführer Klaus Barbie.

The French gendarme scanned the document then saluted smartly offering his assistance. After looking at Fraser, the Gestapo agent said that was not necessary. There should already be a car out front waiting to transport them.

Fraser added in French, purposely accented with mixed Spanish pronunciation, "She is wanted for treason against Spain. Generalissimo Franco has personally signed her sentence of death as a spy. But you see we must deliver her alive."

Fraser smiled menacingly. The Spanish officer was now fully supporting Elizalde's weight. The poor gendarme looked compassionately at the poor woman, the obvious victim of torture. He quickly turned away from the tragic spectacle. Not his affair.

"Get her inside and sit her down," Fraser said.

Once inside the station waiting room the Spaniard settled Elizalde onto a bench.

"Get those goddamn handcuffs off," Fraser ordered.

Looking around, Fraser saw a man seated on a bench on the other side of the waiting area, hat pulled low. As the man tilted his head up, Fraser was buoyed with an immediate sense of relief. It was Rafael Solano. This might work out.

CHAPTER 38

"Rafael made it," Fraser said to Marchand inclining his head toward Solano. But the sense of deliverance promised by Solano's arrival lasted only a moment. The shrill sound of a whistle being blown incessantly from the track platform area signaled immediate danger.

Fraser instinctively turned at the sound. Had Cabrera's body been discovered already?

Seeing an opportunity, the Gestapo agent bolted in the direction of the track platform and the sounding alarm.

Fraser shot him in the back.

Marchand froze with the blaring whistle then the loud report of Fraser's revolver. The Spaniard took advantage of the confusion by swinging his elbow around catching Marchand on the side of her head. The blow dropped her to the floor, her gun falling from her hand then sliding out of reach across the tile floor.

The Spaniard removed his sidearm. As Fraser turned back to gather everyone to make a run for it the Spaniard got off a hurried shot. It missed.

Fraser dropped to one knee. He knew to take enough time to steady himself rather than wildly returning fire.

The Spaniard fired a second time but again missed. Fraser steadied the large caliber Webley with his left elbow resting on his knee. The round struck the Spaniard square in the chest. A second shot by Fraser assured the kill.

Fraser helped Marchand up. She was more dazed than injured.

"You and Rafael get Loretta. Get to the car. I'll cover us from behind. Hurry!"

He retrieved Marchand's revolver.

By now Solano was already lifting Loretta. With Marchand's assistance all three exited the rail station.

Fraser stayed back needing to give them a minute to get to wherever Solano had parked the car.

Unsure of the uniform, two French gendarmes with guns drawn approached Fraser cautiously who was holding two revolvers.

Fraser yelled to them in French, "The Resistance. An ambush!. Shot my lieutenant and the German. Took my prisoner. I am Colonel Cabrera of the Spanish Army. They ran that way. Four attackers. Move quickly!"

The two gendarmes were a little bewildered. First a whistle alarm by an incoherent conductor. Then gunfire. Two men down. Now this officer in an unfamiliar uniform brandishing a gun. Spanish? But at least one gendarme accepted the explanation. Both jumped down from the track platform and headed on the run along the tracks in the direction indicated by Fraser.

✝

"I'll drive. See to Loretta, Rafael," Fraser said.

They situated Elizalde in the back seat of the Citroën with Solano.

"A map?" Fraser asked Solano.

"In the compartment."

Marchand sitting in the passenger seat retrieved the map as Fraser pulled away from the Avignon rail station as quickly as possible. The station was just outside the great wall surrounding old Avignon and on the south side allowing for the quickest escape route southeast toward Aix.

After consulting the map, Marchand said, "Marc, take the next highway to the left. We'll head east toward the Luberon, the high country. Very remote. I grew up here in Provence. Look for signs to Cavallion. From there we can travel back roads on the south side of the mountain range working our way into Aix. I'll navigate, you drive."

Solano was examining Elizalde while speaking softly to her.

With labored difficulty, Elizalde said, "I worried they caught you too, Rafael. Thank God you escaped. Now you're here."

She groaned loudly with an acute spasm of pain.

"Something inside is wrong, Rafael. The pain gets worse. I urinate blood."

Solano undid her blouse then untucked it from her skirt.

Fraser heard a slight gasp emit from Solano. Even though he was a doctor this was his wife. The bruising covered her entire abdomen. The ink-dark coloration suggested extensive internal hemorrhaging.

In the rear mirror, Fraser saw the tears running down Solano's cheeks. He wanted to ask Solano his professional opinion as to her condition but knew Loretta should not hear. The prognosis could not be encouraging.

They proceeded for an hour before Marchand directed Fraser onto a dirt road. The bouncing of the car in the ruts even at reduced speeds increased Elizalde's agony. Up to now, Solano had withheld injecting her with his limited supply of morphine.

"Marc, we need to stop for a short while," Solano said. "Loretta needs some relief. And I want to make a thorough examination before I give her a shot of morphine that will put her out. Then we can go on."

Well into the high back country of the Luberon southeast of Cavallion, Fraser pulled off the back road. He and Marchand exited the car to stand watch. It was a good vantage point. They could see back down the road some distance. Fraser said he was walking a short distance ahead to watch from the other direction.

Had they not just come through a traumatic ordeal they might enjoy the day. A cool sunny autumn day. Leaves were starting to turn colors. War seemed far away but for the fact that a friend was suffering terrible injury in the back seat of the car. Once again a victim of torture. Plus they were now all fugitives. He probably killed the Gestapo agent. Certainly killed Cabrera and the other Spaniard. Execution for all of them if captured.

Fraser took the down-time to reflect on their situation. The involvement of Cabrera and Leitner changed everything. Fraser's name certainly would have come up in connection with Elizalde's escape from Spain. Would the Gestapo have his name on a list throughout France? No way to know but they could not risk returning to Paris. That meant looking for an escape route out of France.

Returning to the car, Marchand approached him.

"Marc, Loretta's condition is very serious. We helped her out of the car to relieve herself. It was awful. She urinated blood. A lot of blood. You could tell it worried Rafael. Any movement causes her terrible pain."

Outside of Elizalde's hearing, Fraser said, "How is Loretta's condition, Rafael?"

Solano shook his head. "Not good. As bad as she looks externally those injuries will eventually heal. But she clearly has internal organ damage. At least the kidneys as evidenced by consistent blood in her urine. According to her that has been apparent for the last several days. Can't tell what other damage yet. Without access to a hospital there's not much to be done except get her to some place comfortable. I gave her some morphine for some relief. How much longer?"

After consulting with Marchand and reviewing the route to Aix, Fraser said, "Should be no more than two hours. Unfortunately we can't take the most direct route for fear of being stopped. No telling what kind of alert has been spread outward from Avignon."

✝

Fraser parked on the tree-lined wide boulevard Cours Mirabeau in the heart of Aix-en-Provence. Marchand pressed the buzzer to her parents' apartment.

Surprised but glad to see their daughter and Fraser they were immediately bombarded with a secession of unsettling shocks. Their daughter now on the run for freeing a prisoner from the Gestapo. This injured woman with the terrible bruising. Needing to hide them all until the woman is able to travel.

Fiona did not however tell her parents of the violence and those Marc had killed.

For all this being outside the realm of their experience, the elder Marchands took matters in stride. They were French. They had lost a son. They hated the *Boche.*

While Rafael made Loretta comfortable in the spare bedroom, Fiona and her mother prepared something to eat. Professor Marchand opened a bottle of wine while Fraser shared a sanitized version of the events that brought them here. For the first time Fraser shared what their son Henri had been doing in the Resistance movement. Tears of pride welded up in the older man's eyes.

This respite from the horrors of the last days lasted only until the following morning.

Over what served as wartime ersatz coffee, Rafael entered the dining room. His face was drawn with lack of sleep. "Loretta is dead."

Madame Marchand gasped. Fiona put her arm around her. Fraser sat numbly.

Solano took a seat. His eyes were red but no tears came. "My guess is renal failure. If any consolation her end came gently while sleeping under sedation."

They all sat in silence for some time. Fraser now thought about the practical matter of disposing of Elizalde's body. Rafael Solano resolved that delicate dilemma.

"Marc, it is necessary to bury Loretta. Will you help me?"

Fiona insisted on helping since she knew the countryside. Driving into the hills north of Aix, Loretta Elizalde was buried under a large tree in a picturesque remote location.

As they were about to return to Aix, Solano made a declaration that jarred Fraser and Marchand.

"I cannot thank you enough my friends. But I cannot return with you to Paris. I must finish this."

"What's that mean, Rafael?" Fraser said.

"You won't understand, Marc but I must return to Lyon."

"Lyon? You can't do that. There's nothing there for you, Rafael. You've no place to hide. You're a fugitive wanted by both the Gestapo and the Malice. The war can't last that much longer."

"I must kill this Barbie. For what he did to Loretta. For what he will do to others."

"Revenge will not eliminate your pain, Rafael. Besides, it's suicide. You can't get close to Barbie."

"Why not? Someone got close enough to Heydrich in Prague."

"And they were killed. A lot more were then killed in SS reprisals. Besides, you can't even identify Barbie by sight."

"Marc, I intend to do this nonetheless."

Fraser sighed but did not respond for several moments. "Ok, Rafael. Then I'll help. At least I can *finger* this Barbie as they say in the gangster movies."

"No, Marc," Marchand said. She couldn't go through anymore of this.

"I won't actively participate, Fiona. I'll just point Rafael to his target. I owe him that. We must return through Lyon to get back to Paris anyway. We'll be away from Lyon when Rafael does whatever he thinks he must. He's certainly right, Klaus Barbie should die."

Horrified, Fiona Marchand however made no further protest. She was resigned to seeing this never ending saga of violence to whatever end was in store. Paris seemed so far away.

Fraser harbored another reason to delay returning to Paris. Someone else that needed to die; Sturmbannführer Leitner. Might he still be in Lyon? Perhaps kill both Leitner and Barbie?

There was a bittersweet hurried departure from Fiona's parents after they returned from burying Loretta. Stoically the elder Marchands kissed them wishing them well. Stoically they encouraged them to also keep up the fight to free France from the *Boche*.

Fraser and Marchand bought tickets from the Aix train station back to Lyon. Perhaps a risk if his name came up in connection with Elizalde's past. But he was an American at the time. He now carried French identity papers. Their names should not be on a Gestapo watch list. At least yet.

Solano however was known as a wanted member of the Resistance especially in Lyon. He would have to make the reverse automobile trip back north, this time with perhaps heightened German patrols. It was a long journey requiring Solano to steal petrol along the way. Fraser said they could only give him two days to get to Lyon. Having exhausted their film production cover story their presence in Lyon would appear too suspicious.

†

Fraser briefed Marchand on their cover story. They were returning to complete their work on setting production filming scenes in Lyon after canvasing Marseille, the other locale featured in the film. Changing trains in Avignon invoked disturbing memories of the violence only days before as they walked past where the shootings took place.

Marchand remained quiet while reflecting on what seemed another fanatically desperate Resistance mission. The intellectual Marc Fraser had an unknown darker physical side. What exactly had he done to Colonel Cabrera on the train? He never said. She hadn't asked fearing the answer. Was it like what happened in Spain with that knife? Then his shooting of the Gestapo man and the Spanish soldier in Avignon. It didn't rattle Marc like it did her.

She still loved him madly. If only they lived long enough to see this war end.

Disembarking at Lyon's Gare Perrache, Fraser visibly tensed. There was nothing about this venture that he liked although he said nothing to Fiona. It was all about helping his old friend, a debt of honor. Yet they all knew it was clearly suicide for Solano.

He and Fiona were also at risk. But she would not leave his side. While the rescue of Elizalde had been a desperate act, Fraser had a bad feeling about this. He had no plan.

From the train station they walked to the Hotel Terminus. Entering the lobby, Fraser abruptly stopped.

Marchand said, "What?"

At the desk stood Sturmbannführer Heinz Leitner. Fraser recognized first the voice then confirmed as Leitner turned in profile to take the lift upstairs.

"Nothing. I'll tell you later."

Fraser checked in telling the desk clerk they would be staying three days. Their room key was for the floor above Leitner's room 209. Fraser overheard the clerk call out the room number when he handed Leitner the key.

Be careful what you wish for Fraser thought. Leitner was still in Lyon. Now what would he do? Did his hatred extend enough to try to kill Leitner along with Barbie? The thought struck Fraser that he had by now killed quite a number of men. Why not Leitner too?

After telling Fiona about Leitner she said, "So it was both this Cabrera and Leitner that tortured you and Loretta. What did you do to Cabrera on the train, Marc?"

He wasn't about to lie to her. "I killed him in the toilet. Jammed the door closed."

Assuming all along that was what happened, she just nodded. "And this German, Leitner? You want to kill him too?"

"Yes. But we're not here for that. Rescuing Loretta was worth the risk. Killing Leitner is not. We'll help Rafael than be on our way to Paris. We'll have to stay here in the same hotel as Leitner since Rafael only knows to look for us here. I also want to be close to the train station."

Fraser and Marchand dined at a café that evening some distance away from the hotel mindful not to be seen by Leitner. The following day they spent the day wasting time mostly in the quaint Vieux Lyon neighborhood. The same cover about working on locations for a film if they were stopped and questioned. That evening they were surprised as they were about to enter their room after returning to the hotel.

In a whispered tone sounding out of breath from the stairwell came, "Marc." Solano had waited for them to return then saw the floor they selected at the lift while he raced up the stairs.

What might have been celebratory was dispelled by Solano's face. Exhausted by what must have been a stressful journey, his look was vacant. The look of a man no longer alive.

Solano refused Marchand's offer to go get some food for him. A glass of wine would suffice.

Marchand nearly dropped the glass of wine she was pouring for Solano when Fraser said, "An idea occurred to me today, Rafael. Perhaps a way for you to fulfill your mission. And perhaps even get away."

Marchand handed the glass to Solano. Will this ever be over? What new foolhardy act was Marc contemplating?

"Leitner is still here in Lyon. And staying at this very hotel. The floor below. I know the room number. Here's the plan. We confront Leitner and force him to call Barbie to join him for dinner. Close by at the Brasserie Georges next to the train station. Fiona and I go to the restaurant. Once Barbie enters we leave. You'll be waiting outside. Hidden of course. I tell you which table Barbie is sitting at. What he looks like. Enough so you'll easily recognize him.

"Is your car close by?"

Solano nodded.

"Do not allow yourself to be captured, Rafael."

He nodded again.

"Ok. Fiona and I will return to the hotel. It will be chaos after you shoot Barbie. Germans swarming all over. Maybe worse than when we freed Lucie's husband and the others. But our papers are in good order. The stationmaster knows us. The gendarmes at the station know us.

"But you my friend have a poorer chance. Know anyone in the Resistance that can hide you?"

"Yes I think so," Solano said. But he sounded unconvincing, even unconcerned. "When do we do this?"

"Right now. No telling if Leitner will be here tomorrow. Besides, it's too dangerous for you here in Lyon. But there's just one more thing, Rafael. If we do it this way there is no turning back."

"What do you mean?"

"I mean that once we deal with Leitner the clock is ticking. If Barbie cannot be contacted, or for whatever reason he cannot come to the restaurant, then we all must leave."

Solano absorbed Fraser's words. "Then perhaps I should take a different approach."

"Like what, Rafael? You're wanted by the Gestapo. You don't know what Barbie looks like. Lots of Germans officers in uniform. And I assume Barbie is holed up most every day in Gestapo headquarters. Hardly a place where you can get close to him. This is not only your best shot, Rafael but your only shot. Yet it might not work. Can you live with that?"

Solano nodded.

"If this fails, Rafael, get to somewhere safe and try for Barbie another time if you must. Maybe mount an attack with others in the Resistance. Or come to Paris and wait out the war."

Marchand had been listening to all this with growing anxiety. Using the SS officer Leitner to lure Barbie would only make their escape more dangerous. Unless ......

"Marc, do you intend killing Leitner after he makes the call to Barbie?"

Fraser nodded yes.

"Not only did I witness his repeated acts of sadism, he personally tortured Loretta and me along with Cabrera. A wartime expediency. Maybe provides a way for Rafael to kill Barbie. An extra-judicial execution just like Cabrera."

Marchand acknowledged only with a slight nod. She got up coming over to Fraser. Holding his face with both hands she kissed him. "Come back to me."

"Are you ready, Rafael?" Fraser said.

Solano nodded and got up from his chair picking up his doctor's satchel.

Fraser said to Marchand. "Be ready when we return."

Fraser and Solano left the room. They took the stairs down a level. Solano stayed back as Fraser approached Leitner's room.

Fear accompanied by a flood of hatred flowed through Fraser the moment before knocking on Leitner's door.

"*Ja?*" Leitner replied at the knock.

"*Eine meldung zum Sturmbannführer Leitner,*" Fraser said in German.

Leitner opened the door. Fraser jammed the Webley into Leitner's cheek forcing him back into the room.

Leitner's eyes grew wide with the recognition of his assailant. But his arrogance quickly returned. "*Ah, die amerikanische.*"

"That's right, the American. Now sit down on the bed. Hands behind your head. Yell out and you get a bullet to the head."

Solano entered behind Fraser and closed the door.

Leitner did as ordered. He was partly dressed but without his uniform jacket. Suspenders hung from his waist. On the bureau were a glass and a bottle of brandy.

The room was actually a suite. With a telephone.

"Here is what happens, Leitner. You will make a call to your colleague, Hauptsturmführer Barbie. You will request he join you for an early dinner. One hour from now. The Brasserie Georges nearby."

"You mean to kill Barbie don't you?" Leitner said. "And me?"

"That's right. It's Barbie we're after. But if you cooperate you'll survive, Leitner. The doctor here will give you a strong sedative. You'll not awake until the morning. We'll be long away from here by then."

"If I don't cooperate?"

"Then the doctor gives you something else. Something more permanent."

"And if I do as you say what's to prevent the doctor from killing me anyway?"

"Nothing." Fraser said. "But you have no choice but to take that gamble."

"No, I could yell out, force you to shoot me. That would mean you do not escape."

Fraser smiled menacingly. "If you yell out the first thing I do is hit you across the face with this gun. Probably break your jaw. Certainly will stop you from raising any alarm. After that more unpleasantness. Can you image what I'll do since I was one of your victims, Leitner?"

Fraser motioned to Solano to bring over the telephone.

"Hold it to his ear," Fraser said to Solano. Then to Leitner, "Now once you get Barbie on the line, if you give any warning then I will shoot you. But understand this, *arschloch*, I'll make sure you die in agony. First I'll shoot you in the balls. Then a bullet to the stomach. A very bad way to go. A long time dying. Keep that vision in mind, Leitner. You or Barbie."

Leitner returned a defiant expression but his eyes reflected real terror. He knew he probably wouldn't survive this even if he cooperated. But he also knew had no choice.

After the hotel desk put the call through someone answered at Gestapo headquarters. Eventually Klaus Barbie came on the line. Fraser listened in on the receiver while Solano held his own gun pressed into Leitner's crotch for effect.

Barbie being junior in rank to Leitner readily accepted to join him for dinner. In one hour at the Brasserie Georges.

"Now what?" Leitner said.

"Well you should make yourself comfortable. You'll be asleep for a good long while. Take your boots off and lay down on the bed. The doctor will inject you with the anesthesia."

"What is it?" Leitner said his eyes wide in terror that it was something lethal.

Solano said, "Sodium thiopental, a standard general anesthetic. You'll be asleep in moments."

Leitner was breathing rapidly with fear but allowed Solano to inject him without a struggle.

In less than a minute Leitner was unconscious.

Fraser said, "Will that kill him?"

"Sodium thiopental is a short-acting barbiturate, not intended for long-term anesthesia. It's usually a precursor to an inhaled anesthesia like chloroform. I could have given him a lethal dose but I have a better idea. Something to make it appear as a natural cause of death. A heart attack. I'm going to inject air into an artery. A *lot* of air. The result will surely be an arterial embolism. If it reaches his heart, a heart attack. If the brain, a stroke. Just watch. It will happen quickly."

Fraser wanted Leitner dead but hadn't counted on this grotesque spectacle. Solano stood passive. He had gone into his own dark place emotionally.

Within a matter of minutes Leitner's rhythmic' breathing was interrupted. First a large exhale followed by some movement of the torso. In seconds that movement became more violent.

Solano calmly said, "I'd guess a massive heart attack."

They both watched as the body eventually settled back into repose. Minutes later a final exhale of breath.

Solano reached into his bag and took out a stethoscope.

"He's dead. Now only Barbie remains." Turning to Fraser he said, "You and Fiona have helped enough. You must leave. It shouldn't be difficult for me to identify Barbie. How many SS officers would be entering the Brasserie at precisely that time? And you have described him."

"We'll see this through, Rafael. We won't be at any more risk than we are already. Still wish I could talk you out of this. You know there's little chance you'll be able to escape."

Solano shook his head in the negative. "What he did to Loretta. The awful torment she suffered. Not simple murder but delight in inflicting pain. He is not human. Others will suffer at his hands. But for me it is simple. There is no way that I could live knowing that he also lives. Nothing more complicated than that."

Fraser acknowledged his understanding with a slight nod.

They both left Leitner's room, hanging the *do not disturb* sign on the doorknob.

†

Seated in the large dining area of the Brasserie Georges, Fraser and Marchand sat sipping wine. Ten minutes yet before the appointed time of Klaus Barbie's arrival.

Fraser said, "Remember, once Barbie is seated we leave. I'll lay money down for the bottle of wine and we'll walk out. Rafael will approach and I tell him where Barbie is sitting. We immediately return to the hotel. I'll check out telling the desk clerk we are returning to Paris on the 9:30 train. If we're stopped in the aftermath our papers are in order. We are known at the rail station. Our cover story is solid."

Marchand nodded although terrified. Time crawled.

†

Outside, a large black sedan pulled to the curb in front of the restaurant. The driver exited then proceeded to open the rear door. A uniformed SS officer stepped out then turned to look back inside the car.

From only few meters away, Rafael Solano rapidly approached the officer from the rear of the car. Solano fired three rounds from his revolver. One shot caught the officer in the back sending him down.

Behind the officer the SS driver reacted by drawing his own 9mm automatic pistol. With Solano now almost at point blank range the driver fired several times. More practiced with weapons, his three rounds all found their mark. Rafael Solano fell face down on the pavement. Blood began pooling beneath him.

From the other side of the car a second SS officer exited with his pistol drawn.

"Are you injured Hauptsturmführer?" the driver asked the more senior second officer.

"*Nein*. And Gerhardt? How is he?"

"Untersturmführer Gerhardt has been wounded, Sir.

Once satisfied there were no other assailants, Hauptsturmführer Klaus Barbie came around to where the two men lay. The driver was kneeling down to the wounded SS officer. After kicking Solano's gun away, Barbie nudged Solano's head with his boot.

"Turn him over, Mueller. Let's see who this is," Barbie said to the SS driver.

✝

Upon hearing the gunfire, Fraser said to Marchand, "We're leaving. Something's gone wrong."

As they exited the restaurant, Klaus Barbie entered passing by them in a hurry. Outside only a few meters to their right lay the lifeless body of Rafael Solano. Marchand let out a gasp. Fraser pulled her in the opposite direction toward the hotel. Gendarmes and SS soldiers began descending on the area.

Fraser told the hotel desk clerk they decided to leave this evening. The hotel could charge for the extra night. Finishing at the desk, Fraser heard commotion from behind as they walked toward the lift.

Barbie was approaching at a run across the lobby with two SS soldiers.

"Shit!" Fraser said.

"What?" Marchand said wondering how this could get any worse.

Under his breath Fraser said, "Leitner of course. Barbie didn't find him at the restaurant. Assumes he's still at the hotel."

"Oh my god!" She immediately understood. Barbie would find Leitner dead.

Fraser said, "Once they find Leitner they'll lock down Lyon. Doesn't matter now if it looks like a heart attack. Too much coincidence with the attempt on Barbie."

Barbie yelled at the desk clerk, "Sturmbannführer Leitner's room number! *Schnell! Schnell!* "

Not waiting to take the lift, Barbie joined two other SS soldiers taking the stairs.

Fraser said, "No time for the bags. We're leaving right now."

Grabbing Marchand's hand they left the hotel walking briskly to the train station.

"We've got a little time if we can get on a train quickly. Any train just leaving soon. Barbie may prevent anyone departing Lyon. That could be a problem. If Barbie digs deeper he may recognize my name on the hotel registry. Leitner must have related details to Barbie of events in Spain involving Elizalde."

Fraser, the former American journalist? A spy in Spain? Perhaps connected now to the French Resistance? In Lyon doing what? After torture he'd certainly be shot. And Fiona? If not shot then sent to die in a German extermination camp?

"But if they don't close the train station right away then we have a chance. We will not be captured, Fiona."

A *chance?* Marchand wondered how the situation could have collapsed so badly. And not being captured? Using their guns in a final death scene is what he means.

As they hurried out onto the track platform a conductor called out *all aboard.*

"Hurry, track two!" Fraser said to Fiona pulling her along as he saw the train starting to move.

They begin to run. Passing a luggage cart, Fraser grabbed a bag lying on top. The train was gathering speed.

"Fiona, jump on board!"

Marchand grabbed the closest hand rail and hoisted herself onto the step. Turning she looked with panic as Fraser didn't seem to be gaining ground on the accelerating train. What the hell was he doing with that suitcase obviously slowing him down?

"Get back!" he yelled to her making a last ditch sprint.

As she stepped back into the rail car, he swung the suitcase up to clear the stairs. Unfettered, he grabbed the railing and lifted one foot onto the bottom step. Close, but he made it.

"Why the suitcase?" Marchand said.

"Looks less out of place. Who travels without luggage?"

Within only moments they watched the track platform fill with a squad of gendarmes. The few waiting people on the platform were being corralled for questioning. Fortunately the train had by now picked up sufficient speed leaving the station. Would it be ordered to stop and reverse back into the station?

Fraser and Marchand stood for a full five minutes as the train continued to pick up speed. More likely it would be thoroughly searched at the next stop.

"Where is this train going, Marc?"

"I have no idea. I know the Paris departures but this is not one of them."

"Let's move to first class. I'll buy tickets from the conductor. Try to find out where we're headed without appearing suspicious."

Eventually a conductor came around to punch tickets.

"Monsieur, we barely just made the train. Change of plans at the last minute. No time to get our tickets at the station. Can I just pay you?"

"Yes, that is permitted."

"How much for the two of us, first class of course."

Fraser pulled out a hefty sheaf of bills. Might as well appear slightly arrogant.

"Where are you going?"

Fraser wasn't expecting that. Thinking quickly he said, "Not sure all the way to the end of the line tonight. Haven't eaten in some time. What's the next stop?"

"Grenoble. About one hour."

"How long all the way?"

"You mean to Marseille?"

"Of course."

"Three hours."

Turning to Marchand, Fraser said, "See I told you we should have stayed the night in Lyon. Best food in France. Now we either spend the night in this cold alpine backwater or get into Marseille in the middle of the goddamn night too late for dinner."

To the conductor, "Let's just do Grenoble for tonight. Should have stayed in Lyon. We'll press on to Marseille tomorrow."

The conductor looked at Fraser longer than comfortable before stating the fare.

After the conductor left, Marchand looked at Fraser, "We can't go back to Paris can we, Marc?"

"No."

"What about Provence?"

"Afraid it's too dangerous once our names become known from the hotel. Perhaps there'll be no immediate connection. But when our belongings are found in the room it will certainly provoke interest. Your name might not be remembered since I registered us as Monsieur and Madame Fraser, although the desk clerk did look at your passport. Doesn't matter though. Eventually it leads back to Paris. After Leitner and Cabrera we'll have to assume my name will become known to the Gestapo. Can't risk remaining in France."

Uttering that finality troubled Fraser as much as Marchand.

"So where do we go?"

Fraser took out Solano's map of France. He knew nothing of Grenoble other than it was in the Savoie region of France. The French Alps. Ski country in pre-war times. On the border with Switzerland. *Neutral Switzerland.* Also the new base of operations for Allen Dulles.

A message had been delivered to Fraser earlier that year in the form of a cheery letter from his *sister* in New York. The fake letter informed Fraser that his old lawyer-diplomat friend from Berlin had just been appointed as Special Assistant to the Minister of the American Legation in Bern, Switzerland. He had set up residence in the city's quaint old quarter at No. 23 Herrengasse.

He knew his old acquaintance was now with the OSS, the newly formed United States intelligence and espionage organization. Spying from a base in neutral Switzerland made sense being surrounded by Nazi Germany, occupied France, and Axis allied Italy.

"We try for Switzerland. Just have to figure how to get across the border."

Marchand assumed yet another hastily conceived dangerous undertaking. She was too emotionally exhausted to discuss what he had in mind. "Ok, Marc. If you think that's best."

"We get off the train in Grenoble. Find a hotel for the night. Get some rest and something to eat. In the morning we'll make a plan on how to get into Switzerland. At least this train took us eastward."

☦

Without warning the conductor walked up from behind them. There were only three other passengers seated well to the front of the rail car. Bending down he said in a low voice, "I watched you run to catch this train as we were already moving out of Lyon. Watched you steal a suitcase from the platform."

Fraser tensed and put his hand on the butt of the Webley stuck in his waist under his coat.

"Something must have happened back in Lyon. The police swarming the track platform as we departed. Obviously looking for someone. Someone maybe trying to escape Lyon on this train?"

As Fraser's eyes narrowed, the conductor raised his hand in a calming gesture. "Don't worry I'm not going to give you away. I'm here to warn you."

"Warn us about what?"

"Monsieur, if they're looking for somebody on this train then they surely have telephoned ahead to Grenoble the next stop. Are your papers in order?"

Fraser did not answer.

"Whatever the problem you will be questioned when we stop in Grenoble whether you disembark or stay on the train. Are your papers in order?"

Fraser was torn. Trust this stranger with their lives?

Marchand said, "Marc, we have to trust someone. We need his help."

"Yes," Fraser answered still uncertain.

"Good. Best I can do is provide some help when you are questioned by the police. If you want a reason, it's my son. Captured in the first weeks of the war. Sent off to a forced labor camp in Germany. The *Boche* are France's enemy, so are the collaborationists in Vichy. That is why."

"What do we do?" Fraser said.

"Where are you from?" the conductor asked.

His mind racing, Fraser wondered why the conductor was being so personal. But their papers indicated Paris addresses so no point in evading the question.

"We live in Paris. We're in the movie business. Scouting filming locations."

The conductor replied, "Good. At least the Paris part."

Before anymore was said the conductor reached into his shoulder satchel. Thumbing through tickets, he extracted two, punched them with his validation tool then handed them to Fraser.

"Two tickets. First class. Paris to Grenoble. You never got on this train in Lyon. Good luck."

✝

Looking around to make sure no one was close by, Fraser transferred the revolver to his waist in the small of his back. Potentially less conspicuous if standing eye ball to eye ball with a gendarme or Gestapo agent.

As soon as the train came to a stop, the conductor accompanied by a gendarme, walked quickly through the rail car announcing, "Everyone must disembark the train. A security check."

"Listen carefully, Fiona. Make sure the gun in your handbag can easily be retrieved. Don't do anything unless I do. Remember this. We must not be captured. You have seen what kind of an end that would lead to. Don't hesitate to shoot, Fiona."

She nodded. He was encouraged by an expression of resolve on her face.

"I love you. Let's go."

Fraser grabbed their stolen suitcase and proceeded toward the end of the car. Outside was an unsettling sight. A number of German soldiers seemed to have taken up positions along the platform as the train slowed to a stop. If there was a gun fight he and Fiona would never survive. And what if they were arrested immediately with no chance of drawing their weapons?

Stepping off the train, Fraser and Marchand along with the few other passengers disembarking were surrounded by the soldiers with rifles at the ready. Behind the soldiers were French gendarmes as the token civilian authority.

At least these were regular German Wehrmacht soldiers rather than SS or Gestapo. Less vigilant, less suspicious, less inclined to intimidate. But then again, having been hauled out into the cold of the night they might also be in a bad mood. However as they approached, Fraser saw the lightning bolt insignia on the collar of the officer in charge signified him as SS.

"Papers!" the officer said to Fraser and Marchand. The train conductor stood next to the SS officer.

Fraser handed over his *carte d'identité* first. He placed his right hand casually into his pants' pocket as a relaxed ploy to be prepared to reach for the gun at his back waist if necessary. He tensed as the officer looked at the ID for no more than a couple of seconds but it still felt too long.

After examining Marchand's identification card the SS officer said, "Did you arrive from Lyon?"

"No, Paris," Fraser said.

The SS officer looked at the conductor with a questioning look.

The conductor said, "Paris passengers. They were already on the train when we stopped in Lyon."

Fraser extracted the bogus Paris tickets the conductor had provided offering them to the SS officer.

"Your business in Grenoble?"

"We are with Productions Artistiques Cinématographiques, a movie production company. Scouting locations for a movie with an alpine background."

Fraser and Marchand both handed over business cards. The officer merely glanced at them then handed the cards back. Without another word he turned to question the next passenger.

Fraser and Marchand stood there not knowing what to do. Were they free to leave the train station? After a short time the SS officer had moved down the line of waiting passengers. Three unfortunate passengers were detained. Maybe for nothing more than having gotten on the train in Lyon.

The conductor having followed next to the SS officer glanced back at Fraser and Marchand. He smiled then tilted his head for them to leave. The flush of relief was overwhelming.

CHAPTER 39

The hotel room in Grenoble was drafty with a wind coming off the mountains. However it did possess a private bathroom with a bathtub. Seeing Fiona naked in the chipped porcelain tub proved too delightful to pass up no matter how exhausted he felt. He undressed and joined her in the tub. Their scrub lasted just long enough as necessary to accomplish a good cleaning. Fiona remarked on his state of arousal which only increased with the attention of her hand.

Even though spent with the stress of the ordeal over the last several days their lovemaking was intense. Both fell into an exhausted sleep while still entwined under the down comforter.

☦

Fraser was awakened by of all things Fiona laughing. Sunlight streamed through the window curtains. A beautiful day with laughter.

"What are you laughing at?"

"Look at these. What do you think?" she said still laughing as she held up a rather large pair of women's cotton underpants.

"Where'd you get those?" he said smiling at her infectious mood.

"The suitcase you stole. I just opened it. Hoped maybe to find something clean to wear. But it's old lady's clothing. Some poor old woman with a big butt is now wearing dirty drawers."

He could do with a shave but he had no razor. At least they were clean and rested. If they had time they would buy some clothes before attempting the final try for Switzerland.

Looking at a most desirable naked Fiona renewed his arousal. Unfortunately there was no time. They had to move quickly. They were still in occupied France. Still in serious danger. Germans everywhere. They would soon to be identified as fugitives with their names on lists. No time for complacency.

How to get across the border? Must be a better way than attempting to cross at some remote wooded area. Probably roving German patrols. It was also cold in November at these higher elevations. Nighttime was out of the question. He and Marchand weren't dressed for a trek in rugged terrain.

Consulting his map of France with only limited detail, what about Lake Geneva? What drew his attention was the line in the middle of the lake defining the French-Swiss border. Looked to be less than twenty kilometers across the lake. Maybe a boat for hire? Steal one if necessary? Certainly easier than the long ocean escape from Bilbao, Spain.

The map indicated a small French town on the southern shore off the lake, Thonon-les-Bains. No way to know if it was assessable by rail. If not, it might be hard to get to without raising suspicions.

Turning to Marchand he said, "Here," putting his finger on the map. "If we can cross the lake into Switzerland we'll be safe. I know someone in Switzerland who'll help us."

After the chance assistance by the train conductor their fortunes continued to improve. Returning to the train station in the morning there was only one French gendarme in sight. Fraser looked at the train schedules. There it was. Thonon-les-Bains. The route went north from Grenoble via a town called Bellgarde-sur-Valserine then skirting the Swiss border east to Thonon-les-Bains on the south shore of Lake Geneva. A four hour trip with a

departure at noon. Enough time to buy some clothes and warmer overcoats before setting out.

†

With fresh clothes, a shave for Fraser, and applied make-up
for Marchand, they felt human again. Don't let our guard down
Fraser admonished Marchand who was now almost cheerful.
Well dressed with first class tickets they looked the part of their
cover story. The ticket seller commented that Thonon-les-Bains
was nothing more than a remote spot on the map. He commented, *in winter an unusual destination for people like you.*

The movie business ploy again became a convenient cover
that explained everything.

"Need an ocean background scene. A boat on the water.
Wintertime. Can't very well film on the Atlantic coast or the
Channel with all the German military activity. Couldn't even get
a special permit to film there. So Lake Geneva is a stand-in. Big
enough expanse of water for what we need."

†

Arriving in Thonon-les-Bains in the late afternoon allowed
some time to reconnoiter. Not much of a town. Few people were
about on this blustery November afternoon. A cold breeze out of
the northwest blew across the lake. No German soldiers in sight.
No French gendarmes patrolling the small marina. An unguard-
ed border? Not likely. Probably just keeping warm somewhere.

Using their cover story they arranged for a charter immediately after setting eyes on the perfect boat. A spiffy mahogany
motor launch. Big enough, fast enough. Good charter boat for
the summer crowd in season. The captain was an older man with
a gray beard. Weathered complexion. Looked like a sailor.
Smoking a pipe.

They told the man they needed to scout the view using the
remaining daylight then into the twilight hours. After sunset
they needed some night shots looking back on the lights of the
town from out in the lake. Perhaps they could use him as an extra in the movie? They would pay well for the four hours work

but they had to push off right away. Fraser handed over enough money to counter any objections.

Once well out into the lake, Fraser asked, "Do the Germans run patrol boats out here?"

"Oh yes. Two fast patrol boats. They moor a short ways from here."

"That a problem?" the old man asked.

"Could be. Here's the situation. That was all lies about making a movie. You're going to take us over to the Swiss side of the lake. Is that a problem, old timer?"

The man remained silent, no expression readable. After sizing up Fraser and Marchand the man said, "It is if I get caught coming back. Germans are a little sensitive about people sneaking into their territory. The patrol boats are armed. Not worth the risk no matter what you're willing to pay."

"Not sure you understand, Monsieur. First of all, you have no choice." Fraser pulled out the Webley from his overcoat pocket. "Second, I'm going to pay you double. Or if you like, you can decide to escape occupied France along with us and stay in Switzerland. I'll even help you. You don't have to return."

Puffing on his pipe, "Since I have little choice, I'll take the offer of the money. Not much of that this time of year. Times are difficult. But I can't leave my wife all alone. Poor woman is not doing well with her arthritis. The winter cold gets harder each year. Harder yet with so little food.

"No need for that big gun, Monsieur. Can't see myself jumping a young fellow like you holding that thing. If you're running from the Germans that's not my affair."

Fraser smiled. "Then head to Switzerland. Can you get us all the way to Lausanne? Don't care to walk too far in the middle of a cold night."

"Guess so. It's a little further. Be close to three hours though. I'll be keeping the speed down to make less noise. No need to announce our presence out here at night," the man said. "Don't know if the Germans patrol at night. I suspect they must. Big lake though. We'll keep as quiet as possible. Just the engine noise. If there are any patrols boats out they shouldn't hear us above the noise of their own engine. But no lights. No smoking."

Looking toward Fiona the old man said, "Looks like you're a bit chilled out here, Madame. There's a bottle of cognac down below. Some shot glasses. Perhaps we should all take the chill off this damp night."

The shallow draft fast boat had only a narrow hold in the bow section. Marchand ducked her head and stepped down inside.

Just as she disappeared below there came the sound of a large engine coughing to life. A patrol boat? The bastards sitting idle just listening? Must be. The engine noise grew louder.

Seconds later a strong search light beam began traversed in an arc while approaching fast in their general direction. Only a couple of hundred meters away. Close enough to hear commands yelled in German.

"*Merde!* I'm cutting our engine," the old man said. "It's our only chance. We'll stay absolutely quiet and hope they don't spot us with their search light. No talking."

A much larger craft by the sound of the engine. Could they out run it? No way to know. If they ran for it and guessed wrong they'd be fired on. Probably by a machine gun. The old man was right not to attempt to make a run. Just hope they didn't see us and went past in the dark. If luck was with us we could then continue on at low speed. As long as they continued to hear the patrol boat engine then the Germans would not be able to hear the speedboat's engine.

The strategy to sit silent and hope the German patrol boat passed without sighting them proved only partly right. The Germans didn't see them. The search light never picked them out in the absolute blackness. The German boat's speed raised its bow causing the search light to play over the low-sitting speedboat as it closed the distance.

But Fraser looked on in horror as the patrol boat approached at high speed. Its position and proximity apparent by the source of the search light. *It was headed directly toward them!* He instinctively attempted to get to Fiona but he was too late.

The heavy patrol craft with its bow raised out of the water under speed came over the top of the bow of their motor launch. The impact not only smashed the wooden hull of the smaller boat but came down with its greater weight forcing it under the water. A terrible noise of splintering wood as the smaller boat's bow section broke away.

The German boat pushed through the wreckage of the smaller craft a short distance before coming to a stop.

The now severed wooded boat sank immediately. The old man was gone, presumably thrown overboard. Frantic shouts in German came from the patrol boat. The water immediately closed around Fraser in the sinking rear section of the motor launch as he desperately reached down hoping to grab hold of Marchand. But the severed bow section sank quickly into the black water underneath him.

His water laden overcoat and suit dragged him down. Sinking two meters below the surface with no further breath he thrust his way to the surface. Even then it was all he could do to tread water to keep his head up. Everything was black. Biting cold. No stars, no moon.

Something struck him in the head. Then a shout in German, "Take hold of the pole."

A German soldier hauled him on board the patrol boat using a Shepard's crook rescue pole. With difficulty the soldier hoisted Fraser out of the water dropping him face down on the deck.

The intense cold of the water was already beginning to inhibit Fraser's freezing fingers. His only thought, *Fiona was gone.* Drowned in this cold black water.

From the other side of the patrol boat two other soldiers were apparently searching for someone in the water. They were calling out for 'Fritz'. One soldier manned the search light now pointing toward the rear of the boat. A comrade obviously had gone overboard in the collision.

The soldier rescuing Fraser turned him over. Even while shaking with cold Fraser reached into his waistband and withdrew the Webley revolver. Would it still fire after having been soaked?

The young soldier pulled back in surprise raising his hands. Fraser then yelled at the other two in German, "Halt what you're doing. Make no move for your weapons or I'll shoot."

Both of the other soldiers turned in Fraser's direction. Immediately, the one holding the search light swung it around directly into Fraser's eyes. Turning away from the glare, Fraser saw the other soldier reaching down for a submachine gun lying on the deck. Fraser fired twice hitting the soldier and spinning him over the railing into the water. The younger soldier that had hauled him out of the water scurried away out of sight.

The search light beam now fell downward toward the deck. The soldier manning the light let it drop as he attempted to get to the mounted machine gun. A mistake that cost him his life as Fraser scrambled closer as the man reached the machine gun but too late. Two shots point blank from the reliable Webley killed him.

The remaining soldier had time to find a weapon. A rifle. At least not a submachine gun thought Fraser. But nonetheless, the soldier was now pointing the weapon at him. Fraser pointed his revolver at the soldier while stepping closer to him. The barrel of the rifle now only a meter away. A standoff.

"No closer! I'll shoot!" the soldier said. "Drop your gun!"

This close Fraser could see the soldier was probably no older than seventeen. The heavy Mauser rifle was shaking slightly. Fear or the weight of the weapon?

Continuing to point his own weapon, Fraser said, "Just us now. Your comrades are dead. You and I too if that's the way it must be. You shoot and I'll still get off a shot. Right into your face. I won't be taken so you'll have to kill me. Can you do that?"

Fraser had no idea how this would go. Didn't matter anymore. Seconds passed. Fraser's hand was also shaking as the effects of hypothermia became more acute.

"Help!" A faint cry from the other side of the boat. From the water? "Help me!"

A woman's voice? Fiona?

For a split second the soldier diverted his eyes toward the direction of the voice. It was long enough for Fraser to grab the barrel of the rifle while ramming the Webley into his throat.

The soldier released his grip on the rifle.

Fraser flung the rifle overboard then pushed the soldier toward the side of the boat. Fraser reached down and picked up the submachine gun and through it into the water.

"Find her you sonofabitch!" Fraser yelled in German. "The search light!" he said pushing the soldier toward the still illuminated search light.

Within seconds the light beam found her. Ten meters from the boat. Too far to grab her with the rescue pole.

Marchand was struggling frantically to keep her head above water. Fraser grabbed the soldier by the front of his tunic and pointed the Webley in his face. "Help her!"

As the soldier looked at Marchand somewhat bewildered as to what to do, Fraser pushed him into the water.

As the soldier's head bobbed up spitting water Fraser pointed the gun, "Save her or you'll die too."

The soldier was his best choice. Young and not soaked with this freezing water. Fraser was in no shape to rescue Fiona. He was dangerously cold having difficulty even focusing his thoughts. Besides, they must not be taken by the Germans. That was a death sentence.

Fortunately the soldier could swim. Wisely he shed his now water-soaked overcoat. But saving someone from drowning was a different skill. Especially now that Fiona Marchand's clothing was heavy with water and her muscles becoming unable to function with the effects of the cold. Once he got to her it was all he could do to just stay afloat. Slow progress back to the boat. His head went under repeatedly as he struggled to keep her head above water. But he was young and fit. And he wasn't about to die as well.

After several agonizing minutes he got her to the boat. All Fraser could do was keep her afloat with the rescue pole hooked onto her overcoat while the soldier hoisted himself onto the deck.

The soldier reached down and grabbed her coat while Fraser pulled her up with the pole. Eventually Fraser tucked the Webley into his waistband to use both hands.

Once on the deck she was only barely conscious. Fraser too was physically struggling. His hand now barely able to grip the revolver as he pulled it out of his waistband.

Shivering, the soldier said, "In the pilothouse. There's some heat below from the engine. Blankets too."

They dragged Marchand into the shelter of the patrol boat's pilothouse. Lifting a door, below was a storage hold.

Fraser said, "Get the blankets."

The soldier started to disappear below when Fraser said, "Bring a weapon from down there and I'll kill you."

Fraser began stripped off all of Fiona's wet clothing. Difficult using only one hand. He still had to hold the gun on the German and his fingers weren't working well.

The soldier brought out several blankets from below. Fraser ordered him to help undress Fiona. Under different circumstance the soldier would have been delighted by her naked body but right now he was also freezing. Nothing else mattered than getting warm. He knew he had to help the woman before being allowed to tend to his own needs.

They wrapped Fiona tightly in several blankets.

"We should move her below," the soldier said. "The engine's heat exchanger is rigged to provide some heat into the pilothouse. Comes up from the engine compartment. But it's warmer down there. Running the engine faster might produce more heat."

Fraser and the soldier moved Fiona below into the cramped hold. She was wrapped tightly in the blankets like a mummy. She appeared better but still didn't look good. Deathly pale. Her breathing was shallow and seemed at a reduced respiratory rate.

Fraser increased the engine rpm's. He could feel the blessed warmth coming from a vent in the hold. Hoped it would be enough to save Fiona.

Fraser was in trouble as well. Shaking uncontrollably he too had to quickly get warm. The soldier looked no better. They must get out of their water-soaked clothing. All they had were blankets. And the clothing of the one dead soldier on the deck.

Fraser left the shelter of the pilothouse. Dragging the dead soldier near, he said to the young soldier, "Strip his clothing off. Hurry!"

Once the dead man's coat and uniform had been removed Fraser said, "Give me the overcoat. You get the uniform."

The soldier nodded appreciatively. He expected Fraser might take all the clothing and let him freeze to death. Or perhaps shoot him now that the woman was rescued.

Fraser removed all his wet clothing including his underwear. Wrapping a blanket tightly around his body under his armpits, he draped the overcoat around his shoulders. The German's jackboots offered some warmth to his feet. Still cold, hypothermia was at least averted. Must present a bizarre appearance he thought.

The young soldier also stripped off his wet clothing replacing it with his comrade's socks, trousers, and badly blood-soaked tunic. A blanket wrapped over his shoulders. Both men then huddled in the pilothouse for the meager warmth coming up from the engine heat below.

Fraser sat holding the Webley in his lap. The soldier might attempt to overpower him, especially while he was preoccupied with Fiona. But the young soldier seemed to have no fight left in him. Seemed just glad to be alive. Probably his first combat situation. Miserably cold in the middle of this huge lake in absolute darkness with someone holding a gun on him. Someone that had just killed his comrades.

"Do you know how to get us to Lausanne on the Swiss side?" Fraser asked.

"No."

"Do you know how to operate this boat?"

"No."

"Neither do I but we'll learn. Now get below and see if we are taking on any water from the collision."

The navigation chart next to the wheel suggested a heading of north-northeast to Lausanne. But he was only guessing at their current position. At least they could proceed at full speed. The engine was operable. It had been idling ever since the pilot had put it into neutral after the collision.

The soldier returned from below saying he could see no unusual amount of water in the bilge.

Fraser checked the fuel gauge. Hoped it was enough to get them to the Swiss side of the lake. He pushed the throttle forward and increased speed. No need to be quiet. It was a German patrol boat.

Once a few lights became visible indicating they were nearing the Swiss shoreline Fraser turned parallel to the shore. Reducing speed, he was looking for a more populated spot indicated by more lights. Once on land they still needed to find help quickly. Fiona needed a warm shelter and medical attention. There remained the problem of finding that help once on shore. Fiona could not walk. Carry her? Send the German for help? Still hard to think clearly.

The dilemma was resolved quickly as a search light beam played across their boat.

From a loud speaker in German came, "Halt! Idle your engine. You are in Swiss waters. Put down your weapons." The Swiss clearly saw the German military markings. "Prepare to be boarded."

Fraser cut the engine. The Swiss patrol boat slowed as it eased closer.

"Drop your weapons. Show your hands."

Fraser yelled back, "We are French refugees escaping France. Commandeered this German patrol boat. Need medical help. Injured on board."

To the soldier he said, "Stand up. Raise your hands," punctuating the order with the Webley.

Fraser bent down to Fiona, "Hang on, Fiona. We made it. You'll be warm soon."

She managed a weak smile. She mouthed silently, "I love you."

As the Swiss boat came along side, the enormous relief Fraser felt gave him a sense of bonhomie to the German soldier. Why not? He looked like a kid. Every German wasn't part of the *Schutzstaffel*. And every SS wasn't a Heinz Leitner or a Klaus Barbie.

"You're a lucky young man. Germany is losing the war. The Führer eventually would have gotten you killed. Your war is over. You are young, you have a life. Now you can eat Swiss chocolates, drink beer, and make love to pretty *fräuleins*."

Lucie Bernard Aubrac, 1912-2007 (Age 94)

French history teacher and member of the Resistance during WWII. Born Catholic into a family of Burgundy winegrowers, she became active in left-wing politics where she met Raymond Samuel, a civil engineer and a Jew. They married in 1939 while Samuel was serving as an engineering officer in the French Army on the Maginot Line. Samuel was taken prison in 1940 by the German invasion of France. With Lucie's help he escaped the German internment camp and changed his name to Aubrac to obscure the Jewish origin. She joined the *Libération-sud* resistance group in Lyon formed by her husband. In 1941 they joined forces with another Resistance leader Emmanuel d'Astier to run the underground newspaper, *Libération*. That year saw the birth of their first child. In 1943, Raymond Aubrac was captured by the Gestapo in Lyon in June, 1943 along with several other Resistance leaders including General de Gaulle's personal representative to the Resistance, Jean Moulin. All were tortured by Lyon Gestapo chief, Klaus Barbie. In a daring raid architected by the six-month pregnant Lucie Aubrac, the Resistance rescued Raymond Aubrac and 13 other prisoners held by the Gestapo by attacking the transport truck returning the prisoners to the Montluc Prison from Lyon Gestapo headquarters. Lucie, Raymond, and their son escaped France to London in 1944.

Nikolaus "Klaus" Barbie, 1913-1991, (Age 77)

Known as the "Butcher of Lyon" for his torturing of French Resistance prisoners while chief of the Nazi Gestapo in Lyon, France. Responsible for the personal torture and death of the high ranking Resistance leader Jean Moulin. Born in the Alsace region on the border between Germany and France to an embittered, abusive WWI German veteran, he was an uninspired student but possessed a talent for languages speaking French and Spanish fluently with a strong grasp of other European languages. Barbie joined the *Sicherheitsdienst* (SD), the security service of the Nazi SS in 1935. Prior to being posted to Lyon he served in occupied Amsterdam arresting Jews for deportation to German concentration camps. He evaded capture after WWII as a war criminal by working for U.S. Army Counterintelligence and the West German foreign intelligence agency, the BND under an alias for 20 years. Under French pressure he ultimately was forced to emigrate from Germany to Bolivia where he served as an advisor to two dictators. Eventually pressure forced his extradition to France where he was tried and convicted of crimes against humanity in 1987. Barbie died of natural causes while in a French prison.

Marion Davies, 1897-1961 (Age 64)

Silent film era comedic actress best known as the mistress and life-companion of William Randolph Hearst, 34 years her senior. Hearst started Cosmopolitan Productions in 1918 principally to promote Davies film career. Unfortunately her career was often overshadowed by her relationship with Hearst and their social life at San Simeon and Santa Monica, CA. She continued acting in sound-movies into the 1930's but with little acclaim. When Cosmopolitan folded she retired to San Simeon in 1937 to remain Hearst's hostess and companion.

Allen Dulles, 1893-1969 (Age 75)

International affairs lawyer, U.S. foreign service official, OSS officer during WWII, and ultimately an early Director of Central Intelligence. A notorious serial philanderer that never derailed his career, Dulles nonetheless possessed a brilliant intellect with a charm that made him well suited for the complexities of foreign affairs. His early career started with the State Department in 1920. Acquiring a law degree in 1926, he joined the firm of Sullivan and Cromwell in New York where his brother was a partner. His legal duties were of an advisory nature to the firm's clients on international business dealings. In 1927 he became director of the private non-profit think-tank Council on Foreign Relations. Serving as legal adviser to the delegations on arms limitation at the League of Nations in the 20's and 30's afforded him the opportunity to meet Adolf Hitler, Benito Mussolini, and the leaders of Britain and France. After entry of the U.S. into WWII, Dulles became Swiss Director of the OSS working in Bern on intelligence targeting German plans and activities by establishing a network of German émigrés, resistance figures, and anti-Nazi intelligence officers. He was aware of the planned attempt to assassinate Hitler in July, 1944. In 1950 he became the Deputy Director for Plans for the CIA then promoted to Director in 1952 with the election of Dwight Eisenhower as President. Dulles oversaw the covert operation in Iran to overthrow the prime minister replacing him with Mohammad Reza Pahlavi as Shah of Iran in 1953. He oversaw the CIA-coup to replace the president of Guatemala in 1954. With the rise of Fidel Castro embracing Communism in Cuba, the CIA with Dulles as Director embarked on a number of unconventional failed attempts to assassinate the Cuban dictator culminating in the ill-conceived Bay of Pigs fiasco in 1961, following which President Kennedy forced Dulles' resignation. Dulles served on the Warren Commission to investigate the assassination of President John F. Kennedy.

Francisco Franco Bahamonde, 1892-1975 (Age 82)

Dictator of Spain from 1939 until his death in 1975. One of the principle Army conspirators to initiate the armed revolt against the Spanish government in 1936. Franco commanded the Nationalist rebel forces supported by military assistance from Germany and Italy fighting on Spanish soil. Following his father into the Spanish military, he graduated from the infantry academy in Toledo in 1910. His formative military years were spent in Morocco fighting in the Rif War. Eventually he rose to command the Spanish Foreign Legion based in Morocco. His meteoric rise culminated in promotion to brigadier general in 1926, perhaps the youngest general in any European army. A devoted Catholic, traditionalist, and conservative nationalist, he eventually joined other senior generals in fomenting a military revolt against the leftist Republican seated government. He was appointed commander of the Nationalist troops launching his opening attack with his Spanish Legion and native Moroccan troops transported to mainland Spain by German and Italian aircraft. His seemingly plodding tactical approach in prosecuting the war, often resulting in appalling casualties on both sides, was coldly strategic by design, intended to purge the population of all potential left-leaning political opponents after the war. The Republican government forces suffered factious discord in leadership and while receiving military aid from the Soviet Union and international volunteer brigades, the Nationalists supported militarily by Germany and Italy proved decisive. Upon cessation of hostilities in 1939, Franco assumed dictatorial powers ruling Spain for the next 36 years. He died of natural causes.

Hermann Wilhelm Göring, 1893-1946 (Age 53)
Vice Chancellor of Germany, Field Marshall, commanded Luftwaffe 1935-1945. A decorated WWI fighter pilot ace he became a colleague of Adolf Hitler in 1923, becoming head of the paramilitary SA. Wounded while participating in Hitler's Beer hall Putsch in 1923, recovering with morphine caused him to become a life-long addict. Arrogant, vain, with extravagant tastes, he was unpopular and figure of derision although Hitler remained loyal to his old comrade. He fell out of favor with Hitler in 1942 with the Luftwaffe's failure to subdue Britain as well as its shortcomings on the Eastern Front. In 1941, Göring ordered Reinhard Heydrich to prepare practical details to resolve the *Jewish Question*. Captured by U.S. forces at the end of WWII, he went on trial as a major war criminal at Nuremburg. Convicted and sentenced to death, he committed suicide using a secreted cyanide capsule the night before he was to be hanged.

William Randolph Hearst, 1863-1951 (Age 88)
American newspaper publisher who built the largest newspaper chain in the United States from his first newspaper in 1887. His approach to journalism profoundly influenced American news and editorial publishing. A self-proclaimed populist, his newspapers attacked government corruption and large corporations. In his later years he became a virulent anti-Communist even commissioning Adolf Hitler and Benito Mussolini for editorial pieces. Hearst built upon the wealth of his millionaire engineer father. He was particularly noted for his unrestrained spending on extraordinary residences and art. The most well-known being Hearst Castle in San Simeon, California, the Ocean House in Santa Monica, the Beverly House in Beverly Hills, and St. Donat's Castle in Wales. At the peak of his acquisition frenzy, Hearst owned nearly a quarter of the world's art. Even massive sell-offs after the Depression to satisfy debt allowed enough art to remain to fully furnish the 165-room San Simeon estate as a museum.

Reinhard Heydrich, 1904-1942 (Age 38)
Heydrich architected the means for Hitler's Final Solution of the Jewish question by which millions of European Jews were murdered on an industrial scale in what become known as the Holocaust. Born into a family of social standing and substantial means, the family suffered a financial crisis as a result of German hyperinflation after WWI. For a secure career he joined the German navy in 1922. In 1932, Heinrich Himmler appointed Heydrich to head the newly created counterintelligence division of the SS, the *Sicherheitsdienst* (SD). He was instrumental in crushing the *Sturmabteilung* (SA) and its leader Ernst Röhm in the purge known as the *Night of the Long Knives* in 1934. Sent to Prague to enforce German policies, his brutal methods earned him the name the "Butcher of Prague." Hitler described him as the man with the iron heart. Heydrich was assassinated by Czech partisans in Prague in 1942.

Adolf Hitler, 1889-1945 (Age 56)
Nazi Führer of the German Third Reich. Born in Austria. A WWI wounded veteran, he was unsuccessful in pursuing a career as an artist becoming an embittered near-vagrant during the financial collapse of Germany following the war. Unremarkable in intellect, he drifted into a political movement finding a talent in oratory. After co-opting the National Socialists German Workers' Party (commonly the Nazi Party) by 1921, he organized the movement into a potent political force along with creating a paramilitary wing, the *Sturmabteilung* (SA). Irrationally assuming the time was right for a political coup, he attempted to foment a wholesale revolt in 1923 in Munich with his failed *Beer Hall Putsch*. Tried and convicted of treason, he served only nine months in prison. During his incarceration, he drafted his intellectually incoherent political tract *Mein Kampf*. Seizing upon German disaffection, the National Socialists became the largest party in the Reichstag. Appointed Chancellor by the aging and senile President Paul Hindenburg, Hitler combined the two offices into one in 1934 upon Hindenburg's death, thereby assuming absolute executive powers. Hitler absorbed Austria and a portion of Czechoslovakia into a greater Germany in bloodless coups. After signing a non-aggression pact with Stalin of the Soviet Union, Hitler invaded Poland in 1939 resulting in Britain and France declaring war on Germany. Germany then invaded and occupied Norway, The Netherlands, Belgium, and France in 1940. Flushed with these early successes, Hitler singularly makes repeated irrational strategic blunders that eventually cost Germany to lose WWII to the Allies. Arguably he may have suffered from a mental disorder and quack pharmacology accounting for erratic behavior. During their 12 years in power, the Nazi regime was responsible for the killing of 11 million civilians, 6 million of which were Jews in what became known as the Holocaust. Rather than fleeing or being captured by Soviet forces, Hitler committed suicide in his bunker in Berlin in 1945.

Queipo de Llano y Sierra, 1875-1951 (Age 76)

Nationalist rebel general and a principle in the army-led revolt against the leftist Republican Spanish government in 1936 starting the Spanish Civil War. He was a career army officer having served in the Spanish-American War and the Rif War in Morocco with a history of rebellious behavior. In 1936, Queipo de Llano secured the capture of Seville then ordered mass killings to suppress the city. Subsequently, he was appointed the commander of the Nationalist Army of the South. Mentally erratic, he was noted for his bombastic radio broadcasts from Seville calling for the rape, torture, and murder of Republican loyalists. Toward the end of the Civil War his influence declined as Franco assumed the sole powers of state. To avoid Queipo de Llano's disruptive confrontational manner, Franco promoted him then sidelined him by appointing him head of the Spanish Mission to Italy. He died of natural causes in Seville.

Jean Moulin, 1899-1943 (Age 44)

After WWII Moulin became the martyred symbol of the French Resistance. Obtaining a law degree following WWI he pursued a successful career in public administration at the provincial as well as national level where he served socialist administrations of the Popular Front. It is commonly accepted that he used his position in the French aviation ministry to facilitate aircraft deliveries to Spanish Republican forces engaged in the Spanish Civil War. As *préfet* of the Eure-et-Loire department, he was arrested by the Germans after their successful defeat of France in 1940, for refusing to sign a declaration falsely accusing Senegalese French troops of civilian massacres. An unsuccessful suicide attempt with a piece of broken glass while imprisoned left a scar which he often hid by a scarf creating his iconic historic image. Removed from public office by the Vichy government, he joined the Resistance. Ultimately Moulin met General de Gaulle in London who gave him the assignment to unify the various Resistance groups in France under de Gaulle's control of their military operations. In January, 1942 he parachuted into Provence to meet with Resistance leaders. Moulin was largely successful in forming the *Mouvements Unis de la Résistance* (MUR) and subsequently the *Conseil national de la Résistance* (CNR) by acting as the principle conduit for allocating money and weapons provided by Britain and the U.S. through de Gaulle's Free French government in exile. Betrayed, he was arrested in June, 1943 in a Lyon suburb along with eight other Resistance leaders. Moulin suffered severe torture daily at the hands of Lyon Gestapo chief Klaus Barbie, subsequently dying of his wounds. In 1964 his ashes were interred at the Panthéon in Paris.

Leni Riefenstahl, 1902-2003 (Age 101)

German film director, producer, screenwriter, editor, photographer, actress, and dancer. Showcasing her beauty and athletic prowess, she made a number of successful movies in the 1920's and early 1930's with director Arnold Fanck, noteworthy for their spectacular alpine cinematography. Riefenstahl was best known for her two Nazi documentary propaganda films, *Triumph of the Will* (1934) and *Olympia* (1936). Both were considered technically innovative in their cinematography but the films forever hampered future acceptance of her professional work by their glorification of the Nazi Third Reich. Her later work included acclaimed photography of the native Nuba people in the Sudan and underwater photography which she pursued into her 90's.

Juan Yagüe y Blanco, 1891-1952 (Age 61)

One of the leadership group of senior Spanish Army officers that initiated the Spanish Civil War in 1936. He was a fellow cadet with Franco at the infantry school in Toledo. Along with Franco he commanded native Moroccan *Regulars* and Spanish Legionnaires in suppressing the workers uprising in Spanish Asturias in 1934. He was a strong supporter of the right-wing neo-Fascist *Falange Española*. At the outbreak of hostilities in 1936, Yagüe again commanded Spanish Legion and Moroccan *Regulars* forces ferried from Africa in the initial campaigns in the Spanish regions of Andalusia and Extremadura. During the campaign Yagüe became known as the "Butcher of Badajoz" after ordering thousands killed, including wounded prisoners, and authorizing indiscriminate torture, rape, and pillage by the forces under his command. Considered the most capable of all the Nationalist forces commanders for his confidence and battlefield adaptability, he participated in multiple campaigns throughout the civil war. After the war he was promoted to major-general and Minister of the Air Force by General Franco. He died of natural causes.

www.ingramcontent.com/pod-product-compliance
Lightning Source LLC
Chambersburg PA
CBHW051521050726
47503CB00014B/366